Rebeccah
and the
Highwayman

Barbara Davies

Bedazzled Ink Publishing Company * Fairfield, California

978-1-934452-01-1 paperback

First Published 2008

Cover art
C.A. Casey

Nuance Books
a division of
Bedazzled Ink Publishing Company
Fairfield, California
http://www.bedazzledink.com/nuance

Dedication

To Lucy and Reneé, with thanks for the inspiration.

Acknowledgements

The following "bibles" proved indispensable during the writing of this book:

1700: Scenes from London Life by Maureen Waller
Highwaymen and Outlaws by Michael Billett
The Favourite: Sarah, Duchess of Marlborough by Ophelia Field

The song "The Female Frollick," otherwise known as "An Account of a young Gentlewoman, who went upon the Road to rob in Man's Cloaths, well mounted on a Mare, &c.," dates from around 1690.

Chapter 1

"Turn around," said the Ordinary of Newgate, shouting to make himself heard above the mob's heckles and catcalls. Kate did so without reluctance—far better to look at those who had travelled miles to attend Tyburn's Hanging Fair than at the Triple Tree.

Hawkers were selling snacks and gin, and pretty girls in white were distributing flowers and oranges from baskets. That group of keen-eyed men must be surgeons seeking specimens for dissection. As for that old woman doing a brisk trade in flimsy pamphlets . . . Kate squinted and made out the title: *The Confessions of 'Blue-Eyed Nick', the female Highwayman.* No doubt a luridly exaggerated account of her exploits. She curled her lip.

"Here come your visitors." The guards around the cart parted to let through a group of four. She blinked down at the familiar faces of her parents and brothers. "Say your farewells and be quick about it." The Ordinary jumped down and went to talk to the hangman.

"Kate." Her father was gazing up at her, his expression sad. Beside him stood her mother, eyes bright with intelligence, the way they had been before grief and hardship fogged her wits.

"Thank you both for coming," managed Kate.

"What, no word of welcome for me?" Her younger brother was still wearing the uniform he'd died in at Blenheim.

"You are welcome indeed, Ralph." The ragged wound in his temple made her wince. "Does it hurt?"

He shook his head. "Not any more."

"And are you glad to see me too?" Eyes as blue as her own regarded her.

"When am I ever not, Ned?"

The ruggedly handsome face crinkled into a smile. "Bless you. Couldn't miss a good hanging, could I? Especially when it's my sister's."

Yet it's odd how I am the only one hanging today, thought Kate. *For this cart is wide enough for eight.*

"We've come to say our farewells," said her father, "haven't we, Mother?" His wife nodded.

"To give you a good send off," said Ralph.

"And provide a friendly face in the mob," added Ned.

Their kindness humbled Kate. "Thank you." She paused then said gruffly, "I'm sorry for . . . everything."

Her father sighed. "Too late for that, I fear."

Ashamed, she ducked her head, and when she looked up again, it was to see the Ordinary coming towards her, shouting, "Hurry along now. The time for farewells is over." He scrambled up onto the cart.

Kate watched with blurred vision as her family was escorted to the edge of the crowd, and scanned the people standing on either side of them. A familiar face stopped her in her tracks.

Philip Wildey!

"You may give your speech now," said the Ordinary in her ear.

Ignoring the prison chaplain, she glared at the handsome figure in the expensive clothes and brand new wig. He gave her a mocking smile and doffed his hat. Rage bubbled up inside Kate, and her hands balled into fists before she remembered—Wildey was dead. The shot from her own pistol had taken his life.

"Your speech," repeated the Ordinary, impatience seeping into his voice.

She glanced at him. "I have none."

His cheeks flushed with annoyance. "You had plenty of time! To the nub of things then." He jumped down and signalled.

The hangman secured the other end of the halter looped round her neck to the massive beam above her. He hopped up onto the cart and came towards her, a blindfold in his left hand.

"Take a last look," he advised.

She tried to fix her family's faces in her mind. Her father and brothers' eyes were glistening, and her mother was holding a handkerchief to her nose.

"Goodbye," mouthed Kate. Then the blindfold stole the view, leaving her feeling alone and vulnerable.

"Get on with it. We haven't got all day!" yelled someone in the crowd, triggering laughter. Nearby, the Ordinary had begun to pray loudly for "this wretched sinner," and above her a crow cawed.

The cart rocked, and she knew that the hangman had stepped out of it. She tried to still the trembling that had overtaken her. Then a whip cracked, and a horse whinnied, and a great yell went up from the crowd as the cart lurched forward.

Kate would have gone with it, but for the noose around her neck . . .

She woke with a gasp and sat up. Her heart was threatening to pound its way out of her chest. She took in the familiar surroundings with a sense of relief and wiped the sweat from her forehead with the back of one hand.

"Are you well?" asked the red-haired woman lying next to her.

"A bad dream, that's all." Already the nightmare of Tyburn was fading. "Remind me not to have oysters for supper again."

Alice wrinkled her nose and grinned. "It wasn't the oysters made you sleepy."

Kate laughed, leaned over, and pressed a kiss against a soft cheek. "No indeed," she said. "And very agreeable it was too. Thank you."

Before she had caught the widowed landlady's eye, Kate had rented a room on one of the lower floors of the four-storey tenement building in Covent Garden. The room was cheap; it was also cramped and dark (Alice's husband had bricked up one of the windows to save on tax). And as for "fully furnished," it boasted only a couple of benches, a table that wobbled, and a straw mattress placed directly on the floorboards. Sharing Alice's rooms on the top floor was a marked improvement, as was sharing her soft bed and even softer favours. And to cap it all, Kate still paid the same rent.

Her satisfied chuckle made Alice raise an eyebrow, then she rolled out of bed and crossed to the sash window raised to allow cool air into the August-hot room. Dusk was falling at last.

"Are you working tonight?" came Alice's voice as Kate assessed the hour and the weather.

She stretched then nodded. "It's a fine dry night for it." She returned to the bed, stooped, and pulled out the chamber pot.

While Kate relieved herself, Alice slipped into her robe and went through to the other room. She returned clutching some scraps of paper.

"For you." She put them on the table next to the basin. Kate grunted her thanks, finished wiping her armpits with a flannel, and dried her hands.

While Alice used the chamber pot, Kate sorted through the notes her hired informants had slipped under Alice's front door while she was otherwise engaged. Most of the almost illegible scrawls she discarded instantly.

The one from Edmund Speke at the Bull Inn posthouse on the London to Dover road was promising except that she had left it too late. She tapped it with her fingernail and pursed her lips.

"A likely prospect?" Alice covered the chamber pot with a cloth and shoved it back under the bed.

Kate reached for the shirt she had draped over a chair back. "Would have been. According to Speke, a passenger on the Canterbury stage had two bags of gold with him." She shrugged and finished buttoning then reached for her waistcoat, hose, and knee breeches. "Still, Shooter's Hill is not a bad idea. Haven't been there for a while."

Alice's brows drew together. "You will be careful, won't you? I'd hate to see that handsome neck of yours stretched."

"As would I," agreed Kate with a smile.

She tied her cravat and went hunting for her boots. One was under the bed where she had flung it earlier. With a grunt of effort she tugged them on. While she shrugged into her coat, slipped her baldric over her head, and settled the sword at her hip, her landlady set about dressing.

"Help me with these," ordered Alice, indicating her stays.

Kate complied, then watched appreciatively as the older woman stepped into her stockings and petticoats and pulled on the green silk mantua Kate had bought her last week. It complemented her red hair, and Kate told her so. Alice dimpled and blew her a kiss.

She glanced out the window once more. Night had fallen in earnest. She had better get going. After slinging her saddlebags over one shoulder, she grabbed the tricorne from its hook and settled it on her head. Alice followed her through to the other room without speaking.

As Kate reached for the front door knob, she was already preoccupied working out the route she must take to avoid the night watchmen that patrolled the streets of London. The Charleys were frequently old and decrepit, but why take any chances?

She was half way down the first flight of stairs when it occurred to her that she had forgotten something. Pausing, she peered back up to where Alice was standing silhouetted in the open doorway, watching her.

"Later, my dear," she called, raising a hand in farewell.

"Take care," came the soft reply.

✍

Clover flicked her ears forward, nudged Kate in the chest, and nickered a greeting.

"Miss me, did you?" Kate brushed away the oats the mare had deposited on her waistcoat and patted her neck. From the sleek look of her, she had been recently curried.

She glanced round and saw a stableboy in a dirty apron lurking close by, his attention split between Kate and his pitchfork.

"Tom," she called, digging her hand in her coat pocket and pulling out what felt like a crown. "Catch."

He dropped the pitchfork and snatched the spinning coin out of the air. A grin split his grubby face as he saw what it was worth.

"That's for taking such good care of my horse."

With a shy grin, he tucked the five shillings into his pocket, retrieved his pitchfork, and resumed tossing straw into an empty stall.

It was no wonder Clover was a favourite with the boy, thought Kate. She was a good-natured beast though she had her moments of mischief. The other stalls were occupied either with temperamental thoroughbreds or nags wearing themselves out pulling Hackney carriages.

"Let's get you tacked up," she told Clover, who nodded as if in agreement.

Kate fetched the heavy saddle from its place in the corner of the stall and settled it on the mare's back. As she tightened the girth, Clover tried to eat her cravat and then her cuff, and settled for lipping her ear.

"Not enough exercise, that's your problem," chided Kate, wiping slobber from her ear with a grimace. "We're going to remedy that."

She threw the saddlebags over Clover's neck, took out the brace of pistols, checked they were loaded, and put them back. Then she climbed into the saddle and with a light touch on the reins and soft press of the knee urged the mare into motion.

As they passed Tom, he raised a hand in farewell and called, "Good luck." Kate had never told him her occupation, but he had almost certainly guessed. His discretion was another reason why she paid him well. She returned his wave with a smile, then horse and rider emerged into the night air . . .

It took Kate a while to reach the outskirts of the city because of her circumspect route. It was a relief finally to join the London to Dover road, deserted after dark, and to let Clover break into a gallop.

As they sped through the night, dwellings became fewer, and cultivated fields changed to patches of heathland. Kate took off her hat, the better to feel the breeze in her hair, but redonned it when she reached Blackheath.

In daylight, the soil and vegetation of the heath were darker than that of its surroundings, hence the name. But at night everything was black, except to the north where the waters of the Thames reflected the gibbous moon.

Slowing Clover to a canter, then a trot, Kate urged the mare off the highway and towards a favourite copse near the base of Shooter's Hill. There, she dismounted and let Clover crop leaves and a clump of grass.

Kate pulled her mask and kerchief from her saddlebags and put them on, leaving the kerchief loose around her neck for now. She pulled out the brace of pistols and stuck them in the waistband of her breeches, then flipped open the lid of her pocket watch and squinted. Almost ten o'clock.

In her saddlebags were her clay pipe and a tobacco pouch filled with her favourite Mild Virginia. She found them and sat on a log, smoking contentedly, though the fragrant curl of sweet-scented smoke drew a nicker of protest from Clover. When the pipe was finished, she pondered whether to fill herself another one, but instead hummed folk songs and tried to identify the constellations.

She was beginning to think that everyone was abed and that this was a wasted journey when the hooting of an owl and bark of a fox were followed by a faint rumbling. Ironbound wheels on the highway? Kate squinted dark-adapted eyes and stood up. Surely that was the glimmer of carriage lights?

"Aha!"

She pulled the kerchief up over her nose and mouth, retrieved Clover, and mounted up. As the vehicle drew nearer, it became clear that it was a private carriage—a coach and four with a footman clinging precariously to the back.

"What do you say, Clover? Should Blue-Eyed Nick see what valuables they're carrying?" The mare pawed the ground, and Kate laughed and patted her neck. "You're as impatient as I am, aren't you? Very well. Let's go to work."

Chapter 2

Rebeccah tried not to belch pickled onion. Having something to eat at the last stop had been a mistake. At the time her grumbling stomach, without sustenance since breakfast, had seemed pathetically grateful for the ploughman's lunch and cup of small beer provided by the shabby coaching inn, but now . . .

She pressed her handkerchief to her lips and stifled a groan. It didn't help that she had a headache, and that Anne *would* keep prattling on about nothing in particular. Right now she was boasting of the admirers she had attracted while in Chatham, and speculating how jealous her two London suitors would be. Which led on to how much they must have missed Anne, and what they would be willing to do to prove themselves worthy of her hand.

Rebeccah ground her teeth. Since it was plain to anyone with the least ounce of sense that her sister cared neither for Rupert Filmer nor Frederick Ingrum (in fact she doubted if her sister *could* care for anyone except herself) she wished Anne would just toss a coin and get the decision over with. It wasn't as if either man were after her for her sweet nature, after all. Once Anne married, her husband would own her and all she brought with her—in this case their father's lucrative business and much of his fortune.

I will never marry except for love, resolved Rebeccah. *As if that is likely!* She gave an inward sigh. *You know very well most men ignore you when they learn how small your portion is*. A familiar stab of resentment flared, and she clamped down on it. *Papa said it was for the best*, she reminded herself. *In order to keep his business in one piece . . . Ah, but was it best for Mama, Anne, and I?*

The carriage jolted and lurched, and Rebeccah shifted in her seat. Carriages were fine for short trips around London, but the terrible state of the highways made long journeys an ordeal. Anne was too busy talking to notice her sister's discomfort, and their mother was staring out at the stars—it was a remarkably clear night and she had drawn back the curtain. But Rebeccah's maid threw her a sympathetic smile.

Mary had been the obvious choice to accompany them to Chatham. Though she was dumpy and rather plain looking, she was competent and reliable (though she did have a distressing tendency to speak her mind) and had been with the Dutton family the longest of all three maids. The choice of footman had been less straightforward. Rebeccah would have preferred Will to come with them, but they had a lot of luggage and his back had been plaguing him. So when Anne suggested the recently hired Titus, who was younger and stronger (and also, as Anne was fond of pointing out, more handsome), and their mother had voiced no objection, Rebeccah had reluctantly agreed.

Titus hadn't done anything to make Rebeccah dislike him. Indeed, he had done everything required of him and more while at Chatham. But though his sheep-eyed adoration of her sister might endear him to Anne, it made Rebeccah uneasy. At least he wasn't travelling inside the carriage with them. Armed with the flintlock pistol provided by his employers, he was keeping a sharp eye out for highwaymen and footpads.

That thought made her raise the curtain beside her and peer out into the darkness. They were crossing Blackheath she saw with some trepidation. Robert, the coachman, always carried a blunderbuss with him, but still . . .

"Not long now, Beccah," said her mother with a smile. "It was nice to stay with your Uncle Andrew and see your cousins, but it is nicer still to be going back to one's own home, don't you agree?"

"Yes, Mama."

Had it not been for the carriage's rear wheel, which a rock had splintered beyond mending, they should have been home three hours ago. But it had taken the coachman longer to locate and fit a replacement than he had bargained on. When Rebeccah realized they would not be home until well after dark she suggested stopping at a coaching inn for the night. But inns were not the most hygienic or comfortable of places, and both her mother and sister had voted for travelling on.

She let the curtain fall and willed the horses to go faster. To her astonishment, they did. "I beg your pardon!" The increased swaying and rocking motion had thrown her against her sister, who crossly shoved her aside.

"What's Robert playing at?" asked Anne, straightening her dress. It was hard to tell above the clattering of the carriage wheels and the clip-clopping of the horses' hooves, but Rebeccah could have sworn she heard a shot. Her heart began to pound. Distant shouts were followed by the sound of a horse whinnying. The coach slowed, then, from close by, came a loud *bang*.

Robert's blunderbuss?

So suddenly it almost threw Rebeccah to the floor, the carriage stopped. From outside came the sound of cursing and scuffling.

"Robbers!" Mary's eyes were as round as saucers. "They'll cut our throats."

Anne crossed herself with a shaking hand. "Why couldn't we have decided to stay at the coaching inn?"

Why indeed? thought Rebeccah. But now was not the time for recriminations.

"If only your father were here," murmured their mother, ashen-faced.

Had John Dutton been here he'd probably have been at as much of a loss as the rest of them, reflected Rebeccah wryly.

"We must stay calm," she said, though such a thing was easier to say than do. She had heard terrible tales of horses slaughtered, of victims robbed, beaten, and left for dead, but she kept that to herself. "Robert and Titus may yet succeed in driving them off. And if they do not, well . . . if we give them what they want, they should have no reason to harm us." She didn't dare pop her head out the window to see what was going on. A horse neighed, and the carriage lurched forward then stopped.

Silence descended. Rebeccah clasped her hands tightly and exchanged a frightened glance with her mother and Mary. Anne had closed her eyes and was muttering "The Lord Is My Shepherd" under her breath.

The carriage rocked. A series of thuds followed.

"Our luggage?" wondered Rebeccah aloud.

Anne looked outraged. "They'll smash that decanter Uncle Andrew gave Mama."

"It doesn't signify," said their mother. "Andrew can buy me a new one."

Then came a long pause that seemed to go on forever.

Anne's eyes blinked open and she looked round hopefully. "Perhaps they have taken what they want and gone—"

Footsteps crunched towards the carriage. The handle beside Rebeccah turned, and the door was wrenched open. Rebeccah put a hand to her mouth and shrank back in her seat.

A stranger peered into the carriage, one hand resting on the sword hilt at his left hip, the other brandishing a pistol. "Ladies." A kerchief over the bottom half of his face muffled his voice. Behind his mask his eyes were bright and startlingly pale, though it was hard to make out their colour in the moonlight.

Mary let out a gasp. "Blue-Eyed Nick!" Oddly, her terror seemed to ease at the sight of him.

"You have heard of me, Madam?" Amusement coloured the intruder's voice as he turned to regard the maid. "I'm flattered." He doffed his tricorne and bowed, and Rebeccah saw that, regardless of the fashion for wigs, his hair was his own, long, and black, and tied at the nape of his neck.

"My apologies for any inconvenience," continued the highwayman, straightening, "but I must ask you to hand me your valuables." He turned once more to Rebeccah and thrust his upturned hat at her. "Let's start with you, Madam. That pretty trinket around your even prettier neck."

Her hand rose to her pearl choker necklace, then stopped as a thought occurred to her. "Our coachman and footman," she managed. "Are they hurt?"

"Give him what he wants, Beccah," urged her mother, her voice fearful.

"They were well the last I saw." The man's tone was neutral. "If you would care to step outside and see for yourself, Madam?" He put his hat back on and held out a gloved hand.

"Stay where you are," hissed Anne. "Who knows what the blackguard will do to you once you are in his clutches."

The eyes behind the mask grew cold. "You have my word, she will not come to harm."

"The word of a murderer?"

The highwayman ignored Anne's question and turned his pale gaze on Rebeccah once more. Suddenly the cramped carriage that she had longed all day to escape had never seemed more desirable. *Robert and Titus.* She sucked in her breath, and with as dignified an air as she could manage, took the proffered hand, glad it was gloved since in the confines of the carriage she had removed hers.

Her fears that he might take liberties with her person proved unfounded as he handed her down to the hard ground and stood back. Only now that they were on the same level did she realize how tall the fellow was.

He gestured towards the rear of the carriage. She followed the direction of his pointing finger and saw two figures lying there, hands bound behind their backs. Beside them lay the Dutton luggage, which had been opened and rifled, and the servants' discharged weapons.

"Your pardon, Madam," called a dejected Robert. "He was too much for me."

Movement in the open doorway of the carriage proved to be her mother peering out. Rebeccah gestured reassurance and glanced round. A single black horse was cropping the grass by the side of the road. *One man managed to best two?*

"A lurching seat and a trembling hand can throw off a man's aim," said the highwayman, as though divining her thoughts. "Do not think too badly of them."

The comment brought a string of obscenities from Titus, and Rebeccah felt her cheeks heating in response. Pulling a kerchief from his pocket, the highwayman strode over, stooped, and stuffed it in the footman's mouth. Titus continued swearing, but now Rebeccah couldn't make out the words.

A highwayman defending my honour, she thought, with a sense of unreality. *Bless me!*

"Now we have settled the matter of whether I am a murderer," continued Blue-Eyed Nick, "perhaps we can get back to that trinket?" He took off his hat once more, upturned it, and held it out.

His effrontery triggered her temper. "Perhaps not a murderer, sir, but a common thief who preys on helpless women," she blurted, then wished she hadn't. But the eyes behind the mask crinkled with amusement not anger and she let out a breath in relief.

"Thief I may be, but common?" He chuckled. "As for you, Mistress . . . Rebeccah, wasn't it?" He seemed to relish saying her name. "'Helpless' is not the first word that comes to mind." Again he waggled the hat.

She remembered her instructions to the others. The highwayman was behaving pleasantly enough, if verging on the familiar, but who knew what turn his temper might take if she didn't give him what he wanted? Best not to try his patience. She reached up and undid the clasp, then dropped the pearl choker necklace into the hat.

"Thank you. Those too." He pointed at the matching peardrops in her ears. When they had thudded into the hat alongside the necklace, he picked one up, examined it, and said, "Exquisite."

"Your opinion, sir, is irrelevant." Was that a snort of amusement? To her annoyance, her cheeks grew hot.

"Are you well, Beccah?" It was Anne this time peering out of the carriage.

"I am," called Rebeccah. "And Robert and Titus are both safe, though bound."

Anne turned to relay the information to her companions.

"The ring too." The highwayman pointed to the signet ring.

"No!"

The pistol came up and he took a step towards her. "I did not give you a choice."

"Take it by force if you must." Hot tears spilled down her cheek. "But I will not give it willingly. For it was my father's and he is dead."

It had started out as any other Tuesday. Rebeccah's father was just finishing his dish of chocolate, his close-cropped head looking naked without its wig, when she descended to the dining room on the first floor.

George the butler bowed at Rebeccah's entrance and murmured, "Tea, Madam?" He knew she preferred it to chocolate. Receiving an affirmative, he hurried away.

"Morrow, Beccah." Her father gave her a fond smile. "You are the first down, as always."

"Good morrow, Papa." She kissed his cheek, pulled out a chair next to him, and sat down. "Are you well?"

"Indeed I am. Shan't be able to keep you company this morning though, my dear, for I have business to attend to. That ship from the West Indies has finally docked."

She helped herself to bread and butter and a couple of slices of cold mutton. The butler reappeared with a steaming pot of tea and poured Rebeccah a dish. She nodded her thanks and began to eat.

"And what are your plans for today?" Her father wiped his lips on a napkin.

Rebeccah finished chewing then swallowed. "I expect Anne and I shall go shopping." Father's birthday was fast approaching and she had yet to buy him a present. Some gloves, perhaps?

"You young women and your shopping." He gave her an indulgent smile and stood up. "Then I shall see you at dinner."

With that he left the dining room and she heard his shoes clattering down the stairs. Ten minutes later her mother and still bleary-eyed sister joined her and she forgot all about him.

After breakfast, Rebeccah and Anne drove to the Royal Exchange.

While downstairs was the noisy haunt of merchants like her father, its first floor boasted an array of nearly two hundred small shops, most specializing in apparel. Anne bought herself some silk stockings shot through with gold and silver thread, ribbons, and a fan. Rebeccah contented herself with finding a pair of snug-fitting gloves and the Jessamy butter her father liked to use to give the leather suppleness and fragrance.

Mission accomplished, they drank tea in an India House and returned home in time for roast beef and Yorkshire pudding. When her father didn't appear for his dinner as promised, Rebeccah wasn't unduly perturbed. Quite often business detained him. He was either at the Docks, supervising the unloading of cargo, or at the Exchange, or reading the papers and gossiping with his friends in Lloyd's coffeehouse.

When suppertime came and went, though, and it began to grow dark, and there was still no sign of her father, Rebeccah began to worry. From the constant glances towards the door, her mother was concerned too. When at last the senior footman came to announce a gentleman, "a Mr. Edgeworth," her heart gave a thump and her mother's face paled.

"Isn't he father's clerk?" asked Anne. "Whatever can he want at this hour?"

"Show him in, please, Will," ordered Mrs. Dutton, standing up. Her mother's hands were visibly trembling, and Rebeccah stood next to her and gave them a comforting squeeze.

"It may be nothing serious," she cautioned. Her mother didn't answer. Her gaze was fixed on the door, which opened to admit the slightly old-fashioned young man Rebeccah had met once at her father's place of business. He took off his hat, bowed, and regarded the three women gravely.

"Mr. Edgeworth," managed her mother. "To what do we owe this honour?"

"I am sorry to be the bearer of bad news, Mrs. Dutton."

Anne's eyes widened. "Why, what has happened?"

Her mother sank into her chair and Rebeccah threw her a concerned glance, before motioning Edgeworth to continue. If the news is as bad I fear it is, I must be strong for all of us, for certainly Anne and Mama will not take it well.

"This morning . . . at the Docks . . . Mr. Dutton complained of gripping pains in his chest and left arm, but the attack passed and he thought no more about it." Rebeccah wondered if Edgeworth's tricorne would survive the violent kneading he was giving it.

"Is he dead, sir?" Her blunt question drew shocked glances from everyone in the room.

"Uh . . ." Edgeworth grimaced. "Yes, Madam. I regret to have to inform you that at three o'clock this afternoon Mr. Dutton passed away."

Her mother's wail almost deafened Rebeccah, and she turned to comfort her. But Anne beat her to it. The two clasped one another as though it were all that stood between them and insanity. And perhaps they were right.

So. Papa has gone to join dear William. *A lump formed in Rebeccah's throat. No more would he stride along the London streets, avoiding sedan chairs, calling out greetings to friends and acquaintances, doffing his tricorne to the ladies, and always tap . . . tap . . . tapping that ivory-topped walking stick of his.*

He'll never see the gloves.

"I can assure you that everything that could be done was," continued Edgeworth, trying not to look at the weeping women and mangling his hat still further. "We sent for a physician, but by the time he arrived there was nothing he could do."

"I am sure you have nothing to reproach yourself for, sir," managed Rebeccah. She blew her nose and stood up straighter. Papa always said I was the strong one. Now is not the time to prove him wrong. There are preparations to make. *"May I enquire where . . . he . . . is now?"*

"I took the liberty, Madam, of conveying your father's . . . ah . . . mortal remains here. They are outside, in a carriage."

"I see." She gnawed her lower lip and considered. Her father had always said his clerk was a fount of knowledge. "May I ask . . . do you have any advice as to an undertaker?"

Edgeworth produced a small rectangle of card from the pocket of his coat. "I can vouch that this is a reputable firm, Madam."

She took it and glanced at the morbid picture of a shrouded figure. Eleazor Malory, Joiner. Coffins, Shrouds, Palls, and all things necessary to funerals. *"Thank you, Mr. Edgeworth. I can see why my father relied so heavily on you."*

He shuffled his feet at the compliment. "Shall I ask the footmen to bring Mr. Dutton into . . . um, the parlour?"

Rebeccah glanced at her sobbing mother and sister and saw no help would be forthcoming from that quarter. "If you would be so kind." She tapped the card. "And if you would also be so kind as to ask Mr. Malory to present himself at his earliest opportunity?"

"As you wish, Madam." He bowed then, and excused himself, and

Rebeccah set about comforting her mother and sister and getting them both to bed.

Much later, after the undertaker had been and gone, she went down to the parlour to gaze at her father's body, now laid out in his Sunday Best, and to give vent to her grief.

When the worst of the storm of weeping passed, she noticed the garnet signet ring glinting in the candlelight. Her father had known she admired it and promised she could have it when he died—so she removed it and put it on.

From that day to this, the ring had never left Rebeccah's finger.

"Have pity!" Her heart raced. "It can mean nothing like as much to you as it does to me."

For a long moment, the highwayman's eyes drilled into her. Then he gave a single curt nod and stepped back. "Very well. You may keep the ring."

There was a roaring in her ears, and she felt distinctly giddy. A hand under her elbow steadied her. "Are you well?" She waited for her heart to slow. "Mistress Rebeccah?" Since he seemed set on an answer, she nodded. After a moment more, the supporting hand withdrew.

She wiped away the tears, conscious that her nose must be red, and her cheeks unbecomingly flushed, and then annoyed with herself for being concerned with such matters.

"Let us return to the carriage," said the highwayman, gesturing. "I still have business with your companions."

He helped her up, and, while Rebeccah took her seat, proceeded to deprive her sister of a pearl necklace and bracelet (a gift from Mr. Ingrum), and her mother of her purse, her watch, and a diamond hairpin.

Mary had only sixpence in her pocket. The highwayman flipped the coin, caught it, and handed it back to the maid with a bow. "Your need appears to be greater than mine." Anne frowned at this show of favouritism, but said nothing.

By now the tricorne was full of Dutton jewellery and the highwayman whistled to the black horse, which trotted over and stood quietly while he emptied the contents into a saddlebag. He donned his hat, put one booted foot into the stirrup, and mounted up.

Rebeccah gaped, as he drew his sword and rode towards the rear of the carriage. *He cannot intend to hurt them now, can he?* She leaned out the door and peered towards the two servants.

"Stand up," she heard Blue-Eyed Nick order. Made awkward by their bound wrists, the coachman and footman struggled to their feet. "Turn around."

Moonlight flashed on honed steel, and Rebeccah put a hand to her mouth as the rapier snaked out and sliced cleanly through their ropes. Her gasp drew his head round towards her, then those pale eyes were holding hers once more. The kerchief hid his expression, but she thought he was smiling.

"Has the rogue gone yet?" hissed Anne behind her.

He touched his sword to his hat in a mock salute and rode away.

"Did you hear me, Beccah?" Her sister's voice was impatient. "Has that vermin gone?"

The highwayman increased his speed to a canter, then to a gallop, and disappeared into the darkness. Rebeccah stared after him, puzzled by the conflicting emotions he had stirred in her.

"Yes," she murmured. "That vermin has gone."

♋

Home at last, thought Rebeccah.

As the coach and four rumbled around the central garden in St. James's Square, she saw that while most of the houses were dark, their residents presumably snoring in their beds, one had all its lamps blazing. The carriage had barely pulled to a halt in front of it when the front door opened and servants wearing relieved smiles poured out to greet them.

They handed down the occupants and helped Robert and Titus to unload the luggage and carry it indoors.

"We feared something awful had happened to you!" exclaimed the butler, as Rebeccah followed her sister into the hall, the tension in her shoulders easing as familiar surroundings engulfed her.

"Something awful *did*," said Anne, allowing her maid Nancy to relieve her of her wrap and gloves. "A highwayman attacked us on Blackheath, and we are much the poorer for it."

Nancy's eyes widened.

"No one was badly hurt," added Rebeccah hastily. "Robert took a black eye and Titus has split his lip, but other than that we are safe and sound." She handed her gloves to Mary.

"Something to calm our nerves wouldn't go amiss," said Mrs. Dutton, joining her daughters in the hall. She discarded her outer garments and started up the stairs. "We'll take brandy, George," she called. "In the drawing room, if you please."

The butler nodded.

Rebeccah grimaced. "Sherry for me, please." She started up the stairs after her mother.

For all it was a warm night, a fire was burning in the drawing room hearth. Her mother stood rubbing her hands in front of it, as much for the comfort of routine, Rebeccah suspected, as to get warm. She crossed to one of the easy chairs and sank into its depths, easing off shoes that had grown tight and wiggling her toes.

The butler entered with a silver tray on which were several full glasses. Rebeccah accepted hers with a nod of thanks, took a sip—the lingering taste of pickled onions made the sherry taste rather strange—and stared into the flames.

"Bless me, what a day!" She pressed a hand to her aching temple.

"Indeed." Anne took an easy chair beside the fire. "A broken carriage wheel *and* a highwayman." She sipped her brandy and gave a ladylike shudder. "And to think that only this morning we were breakfasting in Chatham, with no thought of the ordeal ahead."

"Just as well," said their mother. She drained her brandy and reached for another. The butler's face remained impassive.

A knock at the door proved to be the senior footman. "Excuse me, but Mary has just told me what happened, Madam. Do you wish me to inform the sheriff of your losses? If so, we should lose no time."

Mrs. Dutton blinked at Will then looked to her two daughters for advice.

"Indeed we should, Mama," said Anne. "The sooner that rogue is brought to justice, the better."

"Yet we were robbed after dark," objected Rebeccah. "So recompense for 'daylight robbery' will not apply. Is that not correct, Will?"

"I fear so, Madam."

"Disgraceful!" said Anne. "But the sheriff can at least set the constables after the fellow. 'Blue-Eyed Nick,' indeed!" She gulped her brandy too quickly and spent the next minute coughing.

Rebeccah considered Mary's instant identification of the highwayman, presumably from the paleness of his eyes. "It will make little difference, for I suspect the constables know of him already." She turned to regard her mother who was still standing by the fire. "Tomorrow is surely soon enough for any notification." She took another sip of her sherry and thought longingly of her bed.

"We must also post a reward for the return of our property," added Anne.

Rebeccah opened her mouth then closed it again.

"You do not agree, Beccah?" asked her mother.

"In my opinion," she said, aware that all eyes were on her, "it would merely be throwing good money after bad. For even if our property should be found . . . which is unlikely . . . the finder's reward would swallow up half its value." She glanced down at her finger, where the garnet ring glinted red in the firelight. "Though I regret our losses, Mama, you must admit that nothing he took had any sentimental value."

"My necklace and bracelet were a gift from Mr. Ingrum!" protested Anne.

"Precisely." Rebeccah's murmur elicited an outraged stare.

Mrs. Dutton sighed. "There is some sense in what Beccah says, Anne." She put her empty glass on the mantelpiece and turned to the waiting footman. "A message tomorrow morning will be soon enough, Will. Thank you." He bowed and left the drawing room. "As for you, George, you may tell everyone below stairs that we shall be retiring shortly."

"Very good, Madam."

When the butler had collected the empty glasses and departed, Mrs. Dutton gave Rebeccah and Anne a rueful smile. "For we are all more than ready for our beds, aren't we, my dears? But if I don't dream of being robbed and ravished by some masked villain, it will be a wonder!"

Chapter 3

A sedan chair was hurtling along the pavement towards Kate.

"Make way," panted a red-faced bearer. "I said: make way, there."

She gestured rudely, checked no heap of horse droppings was lying in wait, and stepped into the road.

She had set aside today to take care of financial matters. First stop was the pawnbroker. Fencing cullies were best haggled with by members of their own sex, she'd learned from bitter experience. So as she remounted the pavement and strode along Drury Lane in the morning sunshine, she was wearing her working clothes, minus the mask and kerchief.

That someone might rumble her gender was a risk, especially in daylight, but male attire, her height and the deeper voice she adopted, along with the smudge of coal dust on her upper lip, would encourage people to take her at face value. And those few Londoners already familiar with the features of "Blue-Eyed Nick" were unlikely to turn "him" in.

She stopped at the sign of the three golden balls of Lombardy and peered through a grimy window bearing the lettering: "Wardrobes bought in Town and Country. By Henry Flude. Unredeemed Goods sold Wholesale and Retail."

The interior was empty, so she turned the door handle and went in.

"Won't keep you a minute," came a shout from the rear of the gloomy shop. Kate busied herself bolting the door and turning the "Open" sign to "Closed."

"And what can I do for . . . Ah, it's you." A little man with a crooked nose, his wig askew, beamed up at her in pleased recognition. He rubbed his hands together and zeroed in on the hessian sack lying at her feet. "What have you got for me, Nick?"

She heaved the sack up onto the counter, unknotted its neck, and reached inside. "These." She pulled out a silver snuffbox, placed it on the counter, then reached into the sack again.

By the time the sack was empty, the counter was covered with loot. Rings jostled hatpins, buckles, bracelets, and necklaces; brooches elbowed aside snuffboxes and lockets; a gold watch crowded a silver sword; silk pocket *mouchoirs* looked down their noses at ribbons; and bringing up the rear was a full-bottomed wig made of human hair.

Flude's eyebrows shot up. "Didn't think wool-snaffling was your lay!"

Kate grinned. "The fellow annoyed me. Once his head was bared to the breeze, he proved more amenable."

The pawnbroker chuckled and examined the wig. His gaze turned inwards, and she could see him doing mental calculations. "I can give you . . . thirty guineas for the lot."

"Hanged if you do! That wig alone is worth eight."

"Brand new, maybe, but . . ." He cocked his head and regarded her, like a robin viewing a worm.

"Forty-five," countered Kate. "That's fair and you know it."

Someone rattled the front door, then banged on the window and yelled, "Open up." Flude glanced round, saw it was only a blowsy young woman with a baby on her hip, and ignored her.

"You're forgetting the risk I'm running. Not to mention my overheads. Thirty-five."

"The risk *you're* running? Devil take it, Henry! Forty. And that's my lowest."

"Done." He shook her hand so heartily, she knew he had got the best of the deal. *Pox take him!*

While Flude went behind the counter to open his strongbox and retrieve Kate's money, she wandered around the shop, peering at the trays of jewellery and bric-a-brac, racks of used clothing, wigs draped over dummy heads. Outside, the woman had resigned herself to a long wait.

A delicate, painted fan took Kate's fancy. She fingered it, wondering if Alice would like it.

"She'll love it," said Flude. She turned to find him grinning at her. He winked. "I'll take the two shillings out of this, shall I?" He pointed at the coins stacked on the counter in front of him.

Kate sighed. "Very well." She put the fan in the pocket of her coat, pulled out the empty coin purse, and flung it at him. When he'd transferred the money, she pulled the purse's drawstring tight and stuffed it in the other pocket. "Until next time." She tipped her hat.

"Always a pleasure." He nipped ahead of her, turned the sign to "Open," and drew back the bolt.

"At those prices, I'm certain of it."

The woman with the baby brushed past Kate, digging an elbow in her side as she did so. Kate turned to give the hussy a piece of her mind, only to find the woman bent on giving Flude a royal flea in his ear. Chuckling, she left them to it.

✄

Kate's next stop was the Clerkenwell Road.

Unlike its grubby neighbours, the little house's windows gleamed in the sunlight, and its front step had been freshly scrubbed. She rapped the doorknocker and waited.

The rosy-cheeked young woman in the starched apron did a double take when she took in the "gentleman" standing on her doorstep, then she chuckled and stood back.

"Kate," said Eliza Wagstaff. "A welcome surprise. Come in."

She ducked her head under the low lintel and stepped inside, then waited for the other woman to close the door, before following her through to the kitchen. There, she placed her tricorne on a well-scrubbed dresser and flopped down in a vacant chair.

"How are you, Eliza? The last six months seem to have treated you well."

"I am well, thank you. And you?"

"As you see."

"I worry about you, you know." Eliza looked grave. "You take such risks . . ."

Kate shrugged. "I'm careful." The words "more careful than Ned" hung unspoken between them.

"But where are my manners? Would you like some refreshment? No tea, I'm afraid, but there's chocolate, and ratafia biscuits—"

"Nothing for me, thank you."

Eliza sat down. While the clock ticked and the fire in the hearth crackled the two women studied one another's faces, both apparently satisfied by what they found.

Kate smiled and sat back in her chair. "How's the boy?"

"Well." Eliza traced a circle on the table with a finger. "More man than boy now. Seventeen last month. You won't believe how fast he's growing. Looks more like his father every day." She sighed.

"Bunhill is still treating Adam well?" The old clockmaker would have Kate to deal with if he wasn't—it was her money that had paid the premium for the apprenticeship.

"Yes." A smile curved Eliza's lips. "He's of the opinion that Adam will make a fine clockmaker. Says he's strong and quick with his hands."

An image of her older brother groping every pretty young woman he met sprang into Kate's mind and she chuckled. "Just like his father."

Eliza's smile faded and she dropped her gaze. "Sometimes I wonder, if Ned hadn't got me with child . . ."

And if losing his apprenticeship as a consequence hadn't set him thieving, and the jail fever hadn't been rife in Newgate . . .

"Lord knows, I loved my brother, Eliza, but if it hadn't been that it would have been something else. He just wasn't cut out to be an apprentice shoemaker. Why my parents ever thought he was . . ." Kate rolled her eyes.

"You are probably right." Eliza's smile returned. "Adam has more application that his father, thank heavens!"

"Glad to hear it."

But it was time to get down to business, so Kate pulled the heavy purse from her coat pocket and plunked it on the table. "For you and the boy." She counted out twenty guineas, mostly in crowns, and pushed the coins across the table.

Eliza's eyes widened. "You are so good to us." Her voice was humble. "Thank you with all my heart."

"None of that," said Kate. "We both know Ned would have wanted me to look after you and his child." They also both knew that, without Kate's help, Eliza would be earning her living on her back, and her son, in all likelihood, would be a thief. "I've told you before," continued Kate, "when Adam is a fully-fledged clockmaker, he may support you both, but until then . . ." She pulled the drawstring tight and slipped the purse back into her pocket.

An awkward silence fell, then Eliza cleared her throat and changed the subject by enquiring, "And are you still sharing rooms with . . . Alice, wasn't that her name?"

Kate nodded. "Ay." Rather sheepishly she pulled the painted fan from her pocket. "I bought her this. Do you think she'll like it?"

Eliza regarded her with a smile. "Of course she will. It's from you."

"And you, Eliza," said Kate, more to change the subject than anything, "has no gentleman caught your eye yet?"

"As it happens . . . For the first time in years, there is someone. His name is George . . . George Parker." She blushed and threw Kate an anxious look. Ned wouldn't have expected Eliza to remain chaste, so she nodded encouragement. Eliza brightened. "He's six foot tall and has the most lively brown eyes, and he lives a few doors down. He's a tailor by trade."

With an inward sigh, Kate sat back and resigned herself to a long recital of the many accomplishments of Eliza's new beau.

⌀

Kate listened to a nearby clock tower striking three and frowned at the mustard spot she had just noticed on her cravat—a memento of the dinner she had bolted at a little cookshop in Aldgate Street. This was her last appointment. She hoped it would go as well as the others had.

The cottage door creaked open.

"Mistress Milledge." The big-breasted woman in the shabby gown didn't bat an eyelid at Kate's odd attire, just stepped back and beckoned her inside.

For the second time that day, Kate ducked her head to avoid a low lintel and followed a woman through to her kitchen. Whereas Eliza Wagstaff's kitchen had been the picture of order and well-scrubbed cleanliness, this room was chaotic, and in need of a clean. It was also warm, comforting, and smelled of tobacco and dog. Rather like its owner.

Beau the lurcher was sprawled on the rug by the hearth; he uttered a wheezy groan by way of greeting. Kate grinned at him, then took the rocking chair that didn't have a sewing box and square of red silk lying on it.

"How is she?" She took off her hat and placed it in her lap.

"Upstairs, resting." Jane Allen took the other chair and resumed edging the handkerchief as they talked. "Do you want me to bring her down?"

Kate shook her head and indicated herself. "Better not." Dressed like this, she looked like her brother, or so she'd been told. The last thing her mother needed was to be reminded of him. "One of her bad days?"

Martha had occasional moments of lucidity. When she did, the memory of what she had lost—a husband and six of her seven children—returned and made life almost unbearable. It was better when her wits were addled. Then she was like a child, happy and carefree. She also no longer recognized Kate as her daughter, but that was a small price to pay.

"Her memory is clear as crystal," confirmed Jane. "Fortunately, it won't last. It never does."

Kate fiddled with her hat. "I was thinking of taking Mama to Bartholomew Fair tomorrow. But if you think it will be too much . . ."

"Not at all." The other woman beamed approval. "It will be just the thing to cheer her mood."

When her mother had first lost her wits, well-meaning friends had suggested Martha belonged in Bedlam for her own safety. But Kate had rejected that notion out of hand and searched for an alternative. She found it in Jane Allen. *Thank God I did!*

Kate relaxed, leaned back in her chair, and began to rock. Beau huffed and flipped his tail out of harm's way. "That's settled then. If you could have her ready by ten . . . I'll buy her some dinner as well."

Jane nodded her agreement, bit off the thread, and set aside the handkerchief and sewing box.

"I've brought you this month's money," said Kate, pulling the purse from her coat pocket. Jane nodded her thanks and let Kate count the usual ten guineas into her palm. "Do you need anything more?"

The other woman thought for a moment, then shook her head. Kate opened her mouth, but Jane forestalled her. "Rest assured, Mistress Milledge, if there is ever anything your mother needs, I will send to let you know at once."

She thrust the now much lighter purse back in her pocket. "Thank you, Jane."

Beau yawned, got up, approached his mistress, and lay down again, his chin resting on her shoe. "You great lump!" Jane bent and scratched him behind one ear.

Kate smiled. "I must go." She put on her hat and rose, setting the chair rocking. Her hostess made to get up too. "No, stay and pet the brute. I know my way out by now."

She made her way towards the door, then stopped and looked back. "Ten tomorrow morning?"

Jane smiled up at Kate and nodded. "In her Sunday Best."

೫

Kate took the last flight of stairs at a run, turned the doorknob, and flung open the door. The room was empty. She closed the door behind her, slung her baldric and sword from the hook, and placed her hat on it too.

"Is that you, Kate?" called Alice.

She turned as the redheaded landlady appeared in the bedroom doorway. "No, it's Good Queen Anne come to ask you to be her lady in waiting."

Kate drew close to Alice and kissed her, losing herself in the pleasant activity for a moment before pulling back. "My day went well. How was yours?"

Alice grimaced. "The Wilsons have done a flit, and taken my furniture with them. Now I have to find new tenants for the ground floor *and* re-furnish the place too."

Why anyone would want to steal the worm-ridden stuff that Alice provided in her cheaper accommodation, Kate couldn't imagine, but she kept her thoughts to herself. "You'll manage. You always do . . . Here." She pulled out the painted fan. "I bought you this."

Alice's eyes went wide in delight and she took the fan, unfolded it, and regarded the design from several angles. "How pretty! Thank you."

"Maybe you could show your gratitude later . . . in more tangible form," suggested Kate, enjoying the blush that rose to the older woman's cheeks. The image of a younger, prettier face, cheeks suffused with a delicate blush, green eyes made brilliant by tears, rose unbidden.

I wonder where Rebeccah is now.

A rap on the nose brought her back to her surroundings. "Hey!" She pushed away the folded fan and the hand holding it.

"You hold yourself in high esteem indeed, my bold Highwayman, if you think you can buy my favours with a mere painted fan." But Alice's eyes were twinkling. "Now if you were to buy me a good supper at The Rose and Crown, and some decent wine to go with it . . ."

♌

Kate draped a lazy arm round Alice's shoulders and sucked the stem of her pipe.

The Rose and Crown served an excellent meal for a shilling, so they had dined on Mrs. Elborrow's oyster pies, and afterwards, Alice had downed a pint of best claret while Kate savoured her favourite ale.

"Let me clear these away for you." The buxom barmaid, whose name was Nan, began to clear away the plates, making sure that Kate got an eyeful of her ample charms. Alice stirred and muttered something indignant. Kate gave her shoulder a consoling pat and winked at Nan, then exhaled a puff of smoke.

The snug was full tonight, the chatter, laughter and fiddle music almost deafening. In the far corner, just visible through the blue tobacco fug, a rake and his whore were kissing and fondling. In another corner, two gamesters had shoved back their chairs and were standing glaring at one another across the card table. There were fights here most nights—Kate had started a few herself.

John Elborrow, his staff, and many of the regulars knew her identity, but since most were footpads, thieves, fences, or informants themselves, they turned a blind eye. Occasional sums of money also helped to quiet wagging tongues. Here Kate felt at ease, whether dressed as a man or a woman. The fact that several Mollies were also regulars and turned up from time to time in women's clothing didn't hurt.

The fiddler reached the end of his jig and called out, "Give us a song, Kate."

"Ay," called John Stephenson, a friend and fellow highwayman. "Give us 'The Female Frollick.'"

She sighed and looked at Alice, who grinned and mouthed, "Go on."

"Very well." Kate withdrew her arm and stood up, the action bringing a cheer from onlookers. She made a mock bow, took an open stance and a deep breath, and launched into the first verse.

You Gallants of every Station,
give ear to a Frollicksome Song;
The like was ne'er seen in the Nation,
'twas done by a Female so young.

She bought her a Mare and a Bridle,
a Saddle, and Pistols also,
She resolved she would not be idle,
for upon the Pad she did go.

Those who knew Kate's identity let out a shout of approval, and from behind the bar, Nan batted her eyelashes. What would it be like to have Rebeccah looking at her like that? Kate banished the stray thought and took another deep breath.

By the time she had finished the song, she needed something to wet her whistle. As she sat down, to roars of applause, and the fiddler struck up another jig, Alice pushed Kate's cup towards her and smiled, her gaze fond.

"You have a wonderful voice, Kate," she said. "You should sing more often."

She took a gulp of her ale and patted the landlady's hand. But even as she did so, she realized that Alice's praise meant little.

Why is love always beyond my reach? Now lust . . . I know what that's like. She glanced towards the corner of the snug, but the rake and his whore had vanished.

Feeling suddenly depressed, she signalled to Nan for a refill. The barmaid dimpled, nodded, and hurried round the bar with a jug of ale.

"Are you well, Kate?" Alice was frowning at her.

She forced a smile. "Fit as a flea, my dear."

Chapter 4

Rebeccah gazed out of the drawing room window. It was another sunny morning, and for the next fortnight Londoners of all classes would be flocking to Bartholomew Fair. Her family and friends considered themselves too genteel to attend such a disreputable event, though, and she couldn't possibly go on her own—cutpurses plagued the ground at West Smithfield, taking advantage of the crowds and noise. Not that it would match up to her fond childhood memories anyway, she consoled herself.

Papa had taken her to the Fair when she was eight, too young to notice the drunks and brawlers and the harlots plying their trade. To Anne's annoyance, the treat had been for Rebeccah alone, meant to soften the blow of imminent departure to Mrs. Priest's boarding school in Chelsea. Papa hadn't left her side as they walked through the chattering, laughing crowds, seeing everything there was to be seen.

Rebeccah had been almost sick with excitement at the colourful clowns, acrobatic tumblers, jugglers, ropewalkers, and a broadsword fighter challenging all comers. She hadn't liked the freak shows then and still wouldn't—the unfortunate grotesques on display might amuse some (those who drove to Bedlam for entertainment) but drew only pity tinged with revulsion from her. She would probably appreciate the strolling players' satire more now though. Then, she had preferred a squeaky-voiced puppet show called "Punchinello and the Devil."

Her father had bought her some pork crackling from a food stall, then wiped the grease from her fingers and presented her with a poppet in a fashionable striped silk dress—she still had the doll somewhere. She had refused to be parted from it even while on the flying coaches, whose swinging had made her giddy. The memory of that wonderful outing had seen her through those awkward first days at boarding school.

I wonder if Blue-Eyed Nick will be at the Fair.

It was hardly surprising that the highwayman was in her thoughts. Across the room, Anne was recounting to her two admirers the details of the robbery two nights ago.

It was odd how her sister's recollection of the encounter on Blackheath differed so markedly from Rebeccah's. The brief encounter with the highwayman had metamorphosed into a half-hour life or death tussle with the Devil himself, and he had made off with half the Dutton family heirlooms. Titus's attempts to defend his employers also seemed to grow with each telling . . . and there had been many such. Odd how Robert the Coachman had disappeared from the story. Odd also, how all mention of the highwayman letting Rebeccah keep her father's signet ring had vanished too. Anne believed Blue-Eyed Nick must have mistakenly believed it of no value. Rebeccah, however, was convinced the reason was different—quite simply, the highwayman had taken pity on her. She had given up trying to set the matter straight though, as it merely earned her a glare and an acid rebuke about defending vermin.

She sighed and watched the two men fawning on Anne. She knew from bitter experience that, when her sister was absent, they made sheep's eyes at other women. Papa had done Anne no favours by making her sole heiress to his business, though he thought he had.

He'd confided his reasons to Rebeccah one day not long before he died. Perhaps he was feeling guilty about the small marriage portion coming to his youngest daughter. "It's like this, Beccah." He sighed. "Sad truth of it is, your sister don't have your looks. You'll do well enough, but . . ." He scratched his nose. "Can't have her turning into an old maid, can we? Two birds with one stone, d'you see? Anne gets a husband. Dutton's stays in one piece."

"He should have known better," murmured Rebeccah. *Marriage for the wrong reasons is worse than no marriage at all.*

"Who should have, dear?" Her mother was sitting next to her, sewing.

"Papa. If it wasn't for him, those dolts wouldn't be after Anne."

"Are you referring to Mr. Filmer and Mr. Ingrum?" Mrs. Dutton plied her needle. "They are pleasant enough young men, Beccah." She threw her daughter a sideways glance. "You must not let envy get the better of you."

"Envy!" Her exclamation drew curious glances and she lowered her voice. "Why should I envy Anne the attentions of such shallow creatures?"

"If they are shallow, let us hope that is to the good. For with your father gone, Anne needs no one's approval but her own." She sighed. "If only your brother had lived."

"Beg pardon, Mama." Rebeccah squeezed her mother's hand. "I didn't mean to reopen old wounds." William had died five years ago, returning from the East Indies on one of his father's ships. They still missed him, especially Anne. Without his benevolent presence, she had become more self-absorbed than ever.

"Well, we must not expect the world for Anne," resumed Mrs. Dutton. "As long as her husband is kind, keeps her in funds, and gets her with child swiftly, so she has plenty to occupy her . . ."

"Mama, how can you say that?"

Mrs. Dutton bit off the thread and reached for a bobbin of a different colour. "Because it's true."

"What about love?"

The older woman glanced at Rebeccah and smiled. "You always did have overly romantic notions, Beccah. Where you got such foolishness from I have no idea."

"But you loved Papa, didn't you? I know he loved you."

"Not at first, dear. That came later." Mrs. Dutton glanced at Anne and exchanged a smile. "I'm sure your sister will find things just the same."

Rebeccah kept her scepticism to herself.

"What did you think of that nice young man in Chatham?"

She blinked at the change of subject. "I beg your pardon?"

"For heaven's sake, Beccah! It's time you stopped concerning yourself with your sister's marriage prospects and thought more about your own. What did you think of Mr. Dunlop?"

Rebeccah considered the dull young man who, while she had been staying at her Uncle's, had kept seeking her out when she would rather be alone. "Mr. Dunlop doesn't want a wife, he wants a brood mare. All he could talk of was horses and life in the country . . . And the fact that he wants a house full of children . . . That's when he wasn't talking about architecture of course. Apparently there are some particularly fine examples of Norman churches in his county."

"What's wrong with that?"

"Mama, I cannot marry him. I'd die in childbed, or if not there then of boredom. Besides, he's fat and has a double chin."

Her mother chuckled. "Not *that* fat. You are too particular, Beccah. You must lower your sights."

"Do men ever lower theirs?"

"You cannot blame them for being concerned about financial matters, dear. But there are other considerations. Your face and figure are acceptable, thank heavens, and you have other assets besides your marriage portion. I didn't agree with your father sending you to Mrs. Priest's—education only makes a woman dissatisfied with her lot—but I own that it instilled in you many of the accomplishments desirable to a husband."

Rebeccah doubted any gentleman would appreciate her calligraphy, but held her tongue. "Then why aren't gentlemen queuing to ask for my hand?" Her question was only half in jest.

"Be patient. Once Anne is married, it will be your turn. We will find you a man who is moderately wealthy, kind, well mannered . . ."

Rebeccah tuned out the rest of her mother's list. *I don't want "kind," I want passionate. Someone whose merest look can start butterflies in my stomach and make my palms damp.* A pair of pale eyes popped into her mind's eye. *Oh, go away!*

Silence brought her back to her surroundings. Her mother was looking at her. "Well?"

"Er . . ." She tried to remember what they had been talking about.

Mrs. Dutton rolled her eyes. "Really, Beccah. Sometimes I wonder where your wits are. I was asking you whether you wish to come with me to Hampstead, to take the waters this afternoon. Anne has agreed to come."

Bartholomew Fair would be much more to my taste. "Of course, Mama," she said aloud. "I'd love to."

Chapter 5

Kate ducked an overhanging branch and straightened in her saddle.

"What rich pickings will tonight bring us, eh, girl?" She guided Clover round an old oak tree then, as the wood opened up ahead, kneed her into a trot. "Enough for me to hang up my mask for good?"

The toss of the mare's head was probably just irritation at a horsefly, but Kate chose to interpret it otherwise.

"No," she agreed. "Then I will settle for refilling my purse." She hummed a few bars of "The Female Frollick," her thoughts rewinding the events of the day.

She had spent an agreeable if expensive morning and afternoon with her mother, who had once more forgotten Kate was her daughter. Fortunately Martha always recognized her as a familiar face, and trusted Kate enough to accompany her to Bartholomew Fair.

There, as Kate had expected, her smiling, vague mother had proved irresistible to pickpockets. Like wolves picking out the weakest member of the herd, they arrowed towards her, eager to cut the strings of her purse. They would have known better than to mess with Blue-Eyed Nick, but with her hair pinned up, and dressed in a mantua, she was unrecognizable to all except those who knew her well, and few of those were at the Fair.

The would-be predators soon learned that, for all her ladylike appearance and lack of a sword and pistols, Kate was more than able to defend her addled companion. By the time the second thief retired, nursing a black eye and broken wrist, a warning to give the tall woman a wide berth was spreading like ripples over a pond throughout West Smithfield. Her mother had been untroubled by thieves for the rest of the day.

Delighted by the childlike pleasure with which Martha greeted everything, Kate had let her watch every attraction, paid the entrance fee for every booth she desired to enter, fed her sweets from various food stalls (and hoped they wouldn't spoil her appetite). At last, though, the hustle and bustle and endless walking made Martha fretful, and they retired to a cookshop for dinner and ale.

It was nearly four o'clock when Kate delivered her tired-but-happy charge into the welcoming arms and paws of Jane Allen and Beau, and decided it was less exhausting robbing a stagecoach.

It had been a good day, she reflected. She hoped the night would turn out as well.

She reined in Clover at the edge of the heath, well away from the handsome houses that were springing up as well-to-do folk decided this was an agreeable spot to spend their summers. To the south lay London, looking beautiful in the moonlight and deceptively serene considering its stench and bustle.

Hampstead was a popular watering hole, and the gentry flocked here on Mondays, Thursdays, and Saturdays in search of diversion. After taking the medicinal spring waters, some would gather to gossip and smoke in the coffeehouse, while those with a passion for the English country dances that were all the rage could go to the adjacent Assembly Room. Most would have travelled back across the heath in daylight or, if after dark, in convoy, but with luck there might still be some foolhardy straggler making his way back to the city alone.

The mare tossed her head. "Easy, girl." Kate patted Clover's neck and peered through her mask's eye slits. "Can you hear something?" She cocked her ear, and after a moment heard what Clover must have—the clop of hooves and rumble of wheels.

She pulled the kerchief over her nose and mouth, drew her pistols and waited. When the carriage came into view, she blinked at it in astonishment. "Surely not!"

Kate stood up in her stirrups for a better look. The four horses were identical to those pulling Rebeccah's carriage, and the servants were undoubtedly the same.

She took off her hat and resettled it, to give herself time to think. Her heart was racing. Just because it was the same coach and four, it didn't mean that the young woman was aboard. *Someone else could have hired it.*

She sat back in the saddle. It would be rash to attack the same coach twice. This time they would be ready for her. *But if Rebeccah is aboard. . .*

A sudden urge to see those blushing cheeks and green eyes again overtook Kate, and before she could stop herself, she had dug in her heels and urged Clover forward, angling the mare to intercept the approaching carriage.

In the event, repetition worked in her favour. The coachman and footman were so startled to see the same highwayman attacking them, they fumbled (and in the footman's case dropped) their weapons. By the time the coachman had got his blunderbuss cocked and ready, Kate had brought the team of horses to a halt and was pointing her pistol straight at him.

"Drop it," she growled. He didn't need telling twice. "Get down and join your friend."

Ignoring the twitching of the curtains at the carriage windows, she followed the coachman round to where the footman was standing, looking with dismay back along the track to where his dropped pistol lay.

From her saddlebag, she drew out a short piece of rope and threw it to the coachman. "You know the drill. Tie his hands behind his back." By the time he had finished, she had dismounted and, with another piece of rope, proceeded to tie his hands too.

She walked back along the track, retrieved the dropped pistol, and brought it back. The coachman watched her remove the bullets from pistol and blunderbuss and drop the now harmless weapons at his feet, his expression bemused.

"You won't hurt my mistresses, will you, sir?"

"No," she assured him. "You have my word."

"What good is your bloody word, you godsbedamned—Ow!"

Kate's gloved fist had knocked the footman on his arse.

"Keep him quiet and out of my way," she ordered. The coachman blinked, then nodded, and she turned her back on him and strode towards the carriage.

Startled green eyes met hers as she wrenched the door open, and her heart skipped a beat. "We meet again."

"Good God! You!"

"I'll see you hang for persecuting us like this!"

Kate ignored the outbursts from Rebeccah's companions, who from their slight resemblance to the pretty young woman must be her sister and mother.

"Have you not yet learned, Mistress Rebeccah, that it's unwise to travel alone after dark across deserted heaths?"

For a moment there was silence, then Rebeccah gave her a rueful smile. "We did not plan this, sir. A horse threw a shoe and rather than risk laming him we had to seek out a blacksmith."

The young woman's hands were trembling, but otherwise, thought Kate with admiration, she appeared remarkably composed.

"An unfortunate occurrence indeed," she agreed, "though not for me."

"I suppose you mean to rob us again?" Rebeccah frowned. "After our last meeting, it hardly seems fair."

Kate remembered the garnet ring. *Her father's, wasn't it?*

"You may pass unharmed for a minor toll." She heard her own words with a sense of amazement. What was she doing? She needed money and this family obviously had more than sufficient. "A kiss."

The older woman lurched forward, and Kate's reflexes were so fine-honed she almost pulled the trigger.

"Mama!" hissed Rebeccah.

For a long moment no one moved, then Kate exhaled in relief. "For your own safety, please," she indicated the cocked pistol, "no sudden movements." Looking quite shaken, Rebeccah's mother resumed her seat. "Good. Now." Kate turned back to Rebeccah. "About that kiss . . ."

"You Devil!" shouted Rebeccah's sister. "Lay one finger on her and I'll . . . I'll . . ."

"What?" prompted Kate.

"Oh! If I had a pistol I would shoot you dead."

"I have no doubt of it." She turned back to find Rebeccah regarding her, her cheeks pink, but her gaze steady.

"I will pay your toll." Rebeccah ignored her sister's sharp intake of breath and her mother's shocked protest. "On one condition."

Kate was intrigued. "Name it."

"You may kiss only my hand."

Still holding her gaze, Rebeccah began to remove a glove, finger by finger. Kate wondered if she was aware how arousing that was.

She laughed and made a small bow. "As you wish, Madam. And then I shall escort you to safer territory."

"Safer from whom?" asked Rebeccah's sister.

Kate didn't reply. She was busy transferring her pistol to her other hand and tugging down the kerchief from her mouth.

Rebeccah's hand was smaller than her own. It was warm and trembled in her grasp as she raised it to her lips. When she made to turn it over, palm side up, the other woman resisted. Kate glanced at her, cocking one eyebrow in query before realizing it was hidden by her mask. Rebeccah swallowed then acquiesced.

"Beccah!" said her mother.

Kate planted a kiss in the centre of the small white palm and kept her lips there a long moment, before releasing the hand back into the custody of its owner. When she raised her head, Rebeccah was staring at her like a startled fawn.

"There," she murmured. "The toll is paid." She smiled, then remembered that the lower part of her face was visible and pulled up the kerchief once more.

"Villain!" hissed Rebeccah's sister. "I will not forget this insult to my sister's honour."

"Not insult, Madam, but rather homage to her beauty. And now, since our business is concluded . . ." Kate backed out of the carriage, gave her most extravagant bow, then closed the door and turned to where the bound servants waited.

"You two," she said, striding towards them and drawing her sword. The footman quailed as moonlight glinted off her naked blade. "Heed me or face the consequences. When I cut you free, you are to resume your posts. I'll escort your carriage to the edge of the heath, then you are on your own."

The coachman gaped at her. "*Escort* us?"

"Are you hard of hearing?"

He shook his head.

"Good." Kate described a circle with her forefinger, and he turned round so she could slice through the rope binding his hands. She repeated the action with the footman, who seemed less than grateful for his release. The threat of her raised fist shut him up.

A whistle brought Clover to her side, and she shoved her booted foot in the stirrup and mounted up. Rebeccah's servants exchanged a confused glance, bent to gather their weapons, and scrambled to their posts. Moments later, reins in hand, the coachman was urging his team forward.

As her mare fell into step beside the carriage, Kate saw that the curtains of one of the windows were drawn back and a pair of green eyes was staring out at her. She winked at Rebeccah, expecting her to blush and turn away, but the young woman continued to stare at her, brow creased.

What are you thinking? wondered Kate. *Did my kiss disgust you or give you pleasure? Would you like another? I would be more than happy to oblige, especially on those pretty lips.*

Then she sighed and chided herself. *Dolt! She's not in your league. What's more, she thinks you're a man, and you will probably never see her again. Besides, what about Alice?*

She rode on a few more paces, considering. *What* about *Alice?* A twinge of remorse made her bite her lip. *She deserves better.* But her gaze was drawn irresistibly back towards the charming face framed in the coach window and all thoughts of Alice deserted her.

They reached the edge of the heath too soon for Kate's liking. As she watched the carriage pull away, she doffed her hat and thought for a moment that she saw a small hand waving at her, then decided she must have imagined it.

Seeing their escort was no longer with them, the coachman whipped the team of horses to a full gallop. As she watched the coach rattle and sway into the distance, Kate cursed under her breath. Far from sating her appetite for Rebeccah, this latest rash encounter had served only to whet it further.

✄

Kate was halfway home, and just about to urge Clover over a hedge, when movement made her rein the mare in. She frowned and squinted at the hedge's margins. What was lurking in the shadows, an animal? If so, it walked on two legs. She drew her pistol.

"Don't shoot!"

She blinked at the familiar voice. "Stephenson?"

"Ay." The shadow split into two as her friend emerged. "I hoped it was you, Kate. Can you give me a ride back to town?"

"That depends." She stowed her pistol. "Where's Fury?" There was no sign of her fellow highwayman's stallion.

"It's a long story."

Kate grinned and rested her hands on the saddle pommel. "I could do with a good laugh."

"Have a heart."

"Or I could just ride on."

Her friend sighed, drew closer, and patted Clover's neck. "You're cruel, Kate. Very well. If you must know, I came across this rider. A woman."

"Some people have all the luck."

"Do you want to hear this story or not?"

She shrugged. "It's you who wants the ride back to town."

"Point taken. Well. At my 'Stand and deliver,' she threw her purse over this hedge and galloped off."

Kate pretended to consider. "If you bathed more frequently . . ."

He threw her an indignant glance. "I didn't want *her,* I wanted her purse. And when I dismounted to retrieve it . . ." He paused and hung his head, then the words came out in a rush. "Fury galloped off after her."

She gave a great shout of laughter. "Her mare was in season?"

Stephenson scratched his chin. "Must have been."

"That's what you get for riding a stallion. Clover never runs off after mares."

"She would if she shared her mistress's proclivities."

Kate pretended to take offence. "For that remark I should let you walk home, sir."

Panic spread over Stephenson's face. "You wouldn't." He paused and shook his finger at her. "Ah, Kate. That wasn't nice. For a moment you almost had me believing you. But you wouldn't leave an old friend stranded, would you? Come now. If the positions were reversed . . ."

She grinned. "Of course not. Especially since the contents of that purse are going to pay for your passage."

"What?" His look of outrage made Kate chuckle.

"All right, make it half. I'm sure you agree, given your current situation, it's only fair we split the purse."

"What choice do I have?"

"None." She moved forward in the saddle to make room.

The highwayman was still grumbling under his breath when he climbed up behind Kate. Clover shifted and nickered a protest at the extra weight, but a few soothing words and pats on the neck quieted her.

"Half my profits for the night, gone. And you call yourself a friend!" complained Stephenson, as she urged the mare into a trot.

"A friend who thanks you with all her heart, for until you came along, her own profits were paltry, not to say non-existent."

"Lean pickings, eh?" The thought seemed to console him somewhat.

"Indeed." A smile curved Kate's lips and she urged Clover into a canter. *But only if you discount the kiss.*

Chapter 6

Rebeccah linked arms with Caroline Stanhope and headed towards St. James's Park. It was another fine day, and from the looks of it, half of London's gentry were taking the air.

"You let him kiss you?" Her friend's brown eyes were round.

"On the hand." Rebeccah felt defensive. "What choice did I have? It was that or be robbed . . . again." Even as she spoke, she knew she wasn't being entirely truthful. Blue-Eyed Nick had wanted to kiss her, that much she had sensed, and a small part of her had been intrigued enough to let him.

She had thought the kiss would be of no consequence, but it had been . . . unexpected. How soft the highwayman's lips were! And how odd she had felt when they touched the skin of her palm . . . as though butterflies were dancing in her stomach.

"But wasn't that dangerous, Beccah?" pressed Caroline. "Suppose he had tried to, you know—"

"He wouldn't hurt me."

"Bless me, Beccah! How could you possibly know that?" Caroline's raised eyebrows took Rebeccah back to the early days of Mrs. Priest's boarding school, where the two had first met and everything Rebeccah did and said seemed to astonish the other girl.

"I know because of the ring. Remember, Caro. He could have taken Papa's ring, but when I told him what it meant to me, he declined."

Caroline stopped walking and turned to her with a frown. "Beccah, you haven't fallen for him, have you?"

Her cheeks grew hot. "Don't be foolish!"

"Because if you have, well, first of all he's not respectable. And second, the chances are high he's just amusing himself."

"He wouldn't—" Rebeccah stopped in some confusion. All this presumption based on two brief meetings. What was she thinking?

Caroline's hand flew to her mouth as a thought occurred to her, and she scanned the park. "Oh! You don't think he's following you, do you? How else could he be on hand to hold up your carriage twice on different roads?"

Rebeccah followed her friend's anxious gaze and shook her head. "I would have spotted him. He has his own hair, whereas most men of my acquaintance wear wigs. And then there's his height and bearing, and those striking eyes." She sighed. "In all likelihood I will never see him again."

"I've never heard you speak this way before, Beccah, and I confess it shocks me. Even the most civilized and chivalrous highwayman is hardly a realistic prospect for a husband."

"Do you think I don't know that?" asked Rebeccah, nettled. "Unfortunately, realistic matrimonial prospects are not in great supply. Unlike *some* I could mention, I have no handsome cousin of a suitable age waiting in the wings."

"Thomas and I were fortunate indeed," agreed Caroline, who had married her childhood sweetheart last year. "You just haven't been mixing in the right circles, Beccah. Take those suitors of your sister—"

Rebeccah gave a snort of disgust. "At least Blue-Eyed Nick is open about his intention to steal a woman's money."

Caroline chuckled. "As I was saying, they are not the type to win your heart. I have known you many years, Beccah, and the man who does that must first earn your respect." Her gaze turned inward and she gave a nod. "I shall ask Thomas if there is anyone of his acquaintance who might do."

"He has a hard task ahead of him, then, Caro, for my mother says I am too particular." She sighed. "Oh, why do we have to marry at all?" The other woman assumed she was joking and laughed, and Rebeccah didn't correct her.

By unspoken consent, the two friends continued their stroll in thoughtful silence, breathing in the fresh air with pleasure, and idly regarding the cows and red deer grazing on the far side of the park.

"Now I come to think of it," said Caroline after a while, "Thomas once told me a tale of your highwayman. At least I think his name was Blue-Eyed Nick, and there can't be two such, can there?" She shook her head in irritation. "I don't know why I didn't remember it sooner."

"My highwayman?"

Her friend smiled and pressed her hand. "It concerned the Fleet."

"The Debtors' Prison?"

"The same. Apparently, he turned up on the Keeper's doorstep last New Year's Eve. The fellow was in a drunken stupor, so Nick dunked his head in the basin to sober him."

"Bless me! It's a wonder the Keeper didn't lock him up."

"He was furious at the unexpected baptism," agreed Caroline, "but he calmed when Blue-Eyed Nick crammed a bag of guineas into his hands."

"What did Nick want for his money?"

"Are you aware that some of the Fleet's inmates find it impossible ever to pay off their debts? They can remain imprisoned for years, decades even."

Rebeccah nodded. "Such a system of punishment has always struck me as inefficient, not to mention callous."

Caroline gave her an approving glance. "The highwayman wanted to purchase the freedom of as many of those unfortunates as he could. Even after the Keeper had taken his share, there was still enough left to free five men and women."

"That was kind! Were they friends of his who benefited from his largesse?"

"I don't believe so."

"Then that was a handsome gesture indeed."

Caroline chuckled. "Of course, the money probably wasn't Blue-Eyed Nick's to dispense in the first place, but . . ." She fell silent.

"I have heard a tale of him too," said Rebeccah after a moment. "From my maid."

"Indeed!"

"It goes as follows. He was riding home one night when he came across twenty men, pressed and roped and looking very sorry for themselves. They were being taken to Portsmouth. Blue-Eyed Nick ambushed the convoy—"

"On his own?"

"So Mary says. He freed the men, tied up their escort with the ropes that had bound them, and robbed them of everything of value." She paused and gave her friend a glance. "What do you think of that?"

"Some might say," ventured Caroline, "that by his actions Blue-Eyed Nick upsets the natural order of things. For debtors must be imprisoned, and if ships cannot be crewed by volunteers, men must be pressed."

"Some might indeed," said Rebeccah. "But I am not among their number. Indeed, it has often occurred to me that those whom society deems 'civilized' are often more barbaric than those it deems 'rogues.'"

"It has occurred to me too," said Caroline. "Perhaps that is why we are friends."

They walked on a few paces. "But to revert to our original topic," continued Caroline, "that still doesn't mean you may marry Blue-Eyed Nick. Oh, isn't that Sophia Andrewes?" She waved at one of two young women walking arm in arm up ahead. "She's looking positively haggard. Whoever told her yellow suited her?" She grabbed Rebeccah's arm and tugged. "Come on. I want to ask her if she is going to the Assembly Room next Thursday."

With a sigh, Rebeccah let herself be hurried.

☙

Rebeccah was in the hall, giving her gloves and wrap into Mary's safe-keeping, when Anne pounced on her.

"Where have you been?"

"Caro and I went first for a walk, then to an India house for some tea and cinnamon water, and then—"

"Well," Anne interrupted, "it is immaterial since you are here now. Mama said I should tell you. I've engaged a thieftaker to apprehend that highwayman who robbed us and insulted you."

"What?" Rebeccah stared at her sister. *But I don't want to see Blue-Eyed Nick hang.*

"From your horrified expression I know what you are going to say, Beccah, for the thought crossed my mind also. But you need have no fear of it being an expense we can ill afford. Titus tells me it is the government who will pay the thieftaker £40 for apprehension of a highwayman, not us."

"Titus?"

"Our footman, of course! Apparently, should the thieftaker prove successful, our only debt to him will be half the value of any stolen property recovered and our profound gratitude. I checked with Mr. Edgeworth, and he confirmed it is the case." Her expression showed she was expecting Rebeccah to congratulate her on her thriftiness.

Rebeccah commanded her racing heart to slow. The incompetence of most thieftakers was well known. In fact some were unlikely to come across their quarry unless they tripped over him or he gave himself up. *Pray God she hired one of those.*

"And if the thieftaker should fail?"

"Then we owe him nothing. But he won't, Beccah, for with Titus to advise me, I have hired Samuel Josselin."

Josselin? Why was that name familiar? *Oh no! Didn't he succeed in tracking down the notorious Charles Meade when all others failed?*

"You may rest easier in the knowledge that the rogue will not be free to take liberties with your person for much longer. He is as good as hanged. And now I must go and pack." Anne turned and began to ascend the stairs.

"As I told you last week, Beccah, tomorrow I am going to the country to stay with Anne Locke." The "two Annes," as they had been known at school, were still fast friends, and her pleasure in the forthcoming trip was evident. "Mary." Anne glanced to where the dumpy maid was waiting. "When you have put away those things for my sister, will you send Nancy to help me?"

"As you wish, Madam." The maid curtseyed and hurried away, leaving Rebeccah staring up at her sister's retreating back with a mixture of anxiety and anger.

Chapter 7

The old man in the powdered wig eyed Kate's pistol and sniffed. "I'll make you a wager, sir." His travelling companion, a young clergyman by his clothes, rolled his eyes.

"Will you, by God?" Kate had encountered some strange reactions to being held up, but this was a new one.

"Ay. Consider yourself to be a good swordsman, do you?"

"Good enough."

The over-rouged ancient, who from his garb and the coat of arms on his carriage door could be none other than the Earl of Avebury himself, cocked his head. "Then I have twenty guineas that say you can't beat my chaplain in a fair fight."

"My lord!" protested the chaplain.

"Remember who pays your wages, Berrigan."

The clergyman sighed and examined his fingernails.

"Let me get this clear." Kate resisted the urge to scratch her head. "You want me to fight a man of the cloth?"

"That's the size of it. Rapiers. No daggers. First man disarmed is the loser."

A thought struck her. Maybe this was the Earl's way of stalling for time. She backed out of the carriage and satisfied herself that no men in the Earl's livery were rushing across the moonlit heath towards them, then ducked back inside.

"Well? What do you say, sir?" Avebury's eyes glinted. "Think my chaplain might be too much for you?"

This was madness. If the old man had twenty guineas on him, Kate should simply demand he hand it over. But the wager intrigued her. What could a chaplain know about swordplay? "What's to stop me from relieving you of the money even if I lose?"

The old man smiled, revealing stained, gapped teeth. "Your word."
Kate snorted. "The word of a highwayman?"
"Of a fellow gamester, sir."
She pursed her lips. The chaplain was wearing neither sword belt nor baldric. "Do you even own a sword, sir?" Berrigan nodded. "And you have no objection to this bout?" He glanced at his employer, opened his mouth, closed it again, and shook his head.
Avebury cackled. "That's the ticket."
Kate hesitated a moment longer then pulled a coin from her coat pocket. "Heads, we fight. Tails, I just take the money. Agreed?"
The Earl rolled his eyes. "Agreed. For heaven's sake, man, get on with it."
She tossed the sixpence. Three pairs of eyes followed its spinning progress before it clattered onto the carriage floor beside the chaplain's scuffed shoes.
Heads.
The Earl rubbed his hands together and turned to his employee. "It's up to you then, Berrigan. Lose and the money's coming out of your wages."
"My lord!"
Kate retrieved her sixpence and backed out of the carriage. The chaplain stepped down and walked past the bound figures of the footman and coachman to retrieve a rectangular case from among the Earl's luggage. Avebury's stubby legs dangled out of the door as he settled himself on the carriage floor for a ringside view.
She removed her hat, baldric, and coat, and drew her sword. The clergyman took an elaborately tooled scabbard from the case, unsheathed a swept-hilt rapier, and made a few practice passes with it. Kate's eyes widened as the finest Toledo steel glimmered in the moonlight. This was no novice.
The Earl chuckled and she threw him a filthy glance before returning her attention to the man in the black cassock. He lifted his rapier in salute, then assumed the on guard position. She did the same, muscles tensing in readiness.
For a long moment they eyed one another, then Berrigan engaged her blade. Kate found the going easy at first, but she didn't relax. He was merely gauging her reach, she knew, testing her mobility and defences. Once he had her measure, he would begin in earnest. And so it proved. Soon a flurry of controlled yet vicious strokes had put her on her back foot. Grimly, she parried, riposted, twisted, and lunged, evading a slash to

her masked cheekbone by the fraction of an inch, watching her opponent's eyes for clues as to his intentions and finding few. At last, with difficulty, she managed to regain the initiative and to force Berrigan back a few steps.

By mutual consent they broke off to regroup. Her forearm stung, and she saw that her sleeve now sported a bloody slash. The chaplain was unmarked and though his colour was heightened, his breathing sounded even. Kate's shirt, on the other hand, was soaked and her chest was heaving. She wished she could take off her disguise and wipe the sweat from her face.

"Better than you thought he'd be, ain't he?"

Kate ignored the Earl's taunt and kept her eyes on the chaplain.

"Ready?" Berrigan raised his blade once more. She nodded.

This time, when the chaplain's edge came cutting towards her, she was ready. *Parry. Riposte. Quick forward step. Upward cut. Ward. Duck and roll. Oof!* She scrambled back to her feet. *Slash. Lunge and thrust.* Determined to finish this quickly, she pressed her attack with all the energy she could muster.

Silvered blades flashed in the moonlight as the combatants swayed to and fro, the heath echoing to the sounds of feet stamping on turf, lungs gasping, and the clash of steel. Horses whinnied and rattled their traces as Kate pressed Berrigan backward towards the carriage, until he recovered himself and forced her in her turn to give way step by grudging step. This time it was Clover who nickered a protest and moved out of her mistress's way.

Kate lost all track of time and of the reason they were fighting. This was no longer about guineas but about which of them was the best. She slid out of Berrigan's body charge, turned, and engaged his blade again. Then, just for the barest moment, she found herself inside his guard. Quick as thought, out snaked her rapier.

"'S blood!" The oath revealed, if his expert swordsmanship hadn't already, that he hadn't always been a clergyman. He pulled back and examined his cut sleeve and bleeding forearm. His gaze when it returned to hers was edged with respect.

"Better than you thought I'd be?" He gave her a rueful nod. "Shall we finish this?" She resettled her grip, raised her rapier, and stepped forward.

Traverse. Lunge and thrust low. Almost got him then. Disengage. Slide. That was too close for comfort. Parry and riposte. Horizontal cut. Devil take him, but he's good! Ward. Reverse cut. Didn't like that, did you? Circle. Feint. Diagonal rising cut . . .

They were so well matched, the bout could have gone on forever, but suddenly Berrigan, straightening from a crouch, caught the heel of his shoe in the hem of his cassock, and for a crucial moment his balance went and his attention wavered. Kate brought the flat of her blade up hard, aiming for the knuckles, which at this angle weren't protected by the swept-hilt. He yelped and in spite of himself loosened his grip. With a deft flick, she disarmed him and watched, chest heaving, as the expensive sword sailed through the air and landed several yards away.

"Deuce take it! You let a common highwayman beat you, Berrigan. Shame on you." They ignored the Earl's indignant shout.

"My wager, I think." A relieved Kate held out a hand.

Still flexing his stinging fingers, the chaplain straightened. "Indeed, sir." He clasped her hand and shook it, then indicated the bloodied slashes on both their forearms. "We were evenly matched, you and I. May I ask where you learned to use a sword?"

Kate was silent, remembering long summer days spent with Ned and Ralph in the yard, using wooden swords to start with then progressing to the real thing. Her good-natured brothers had been overjoyed when at last she had succeeded in besting them, but she had found the victory oddly dissatisfying. "My brothers taught me."

"They taught you well." Berrigan bowed and she returned the gesture.

While the chaplain retrieved his weapon, wiped it clean of grass and dirt, and slid it into its scabbard, Kate put on her coat and hat and wished she had a change of shirt in her saddlebag. The bewigged old Earl had struggled to his feet by the time she returned to the coach. His expression was disgruntled.

"My winnings, my Lord." She held out a gloved hand.

He dug in the capacious pocket of his coat, pulled out a leather purse that clinked, and flung it at her. "Here, damn your eyes!"

Not very sporting. She plucked it out of the air, checked its contents, grinned, and bowed. "A pleasure doing business with you."

✠

The night air felt wonderful against Kate's face and she took off her tricorne to allow it to cool her hairline.

"Hardest twenty guineas I've ever earned," she grumbled, as she let Clover set her own pace across the springy turf and heather. For all Kate's complaining, a sense of wellbeing suffused her. Berrigan had been no mean swordsman, yet she had beaten him.

She had left Avebury's coach far behind, and the track she was following was barely discernible in the moonlight. But even by night she knew the heath like the back of her hand. As she rode past a copse of spindly trees, a barn owl took flight with a hiss and a flap of pale wings. She turned her head to watch it begin a long, slow glide, its unwinking gaze fixed on the ground below. Lord help any small rodents tonight.

Somewhere a dog fox barked. Had Kate been of a superstitious bent, the shrill, lonely call combined with the ghostly shape now sweeping low over the heath would have made her shiver. Instead she pictured herself in the snug of the Rose and Crown, ale in hand, telling of tonight's duel. Some of her friends would applaud her audacity. But Stephenson would most likely call her a fool for risking injury in pursuit of what was hers already. And he would be right.

Yet if I had to do it all again, I probably would. She chuckled and shook her head.

The southern edge of the heath came in sight, and more importantly, the highway alongside it. Though badly maintained, the surface would be easier going than the uneven thatch, occasional bog, and rabbit holes that posed a constant risk to both horse and rider. Kate urged Clover up the gentle incline, and seconds later hooves were clattering on stone.

Kate had been humming to herself as she rode, lulled by the rhythmic motion, thinking first of the duel with the Earl of Avebury's chaplain then of the kiss she had given Rebeccah. How else to account for her lapse of attention? Too late she registered the approaching clip-clop of hooves and jingle of harnesses.

A group of dragoons, their scarlet coats black in the moonlight, rounded the bend up ahead. Public discontent about the prevalence of footpads and highwayman in and around London had been growing more strident. Perhaps this armed patrol was the result. Whatever the reason, it was unfortunate. Though Kate was no longer wearing her mask and kerchief, the mere fact of her presence abroad at this hour would be enough to raise their suspicions. And should they discover her gender and the contents of her saddlebags . . .

"You there, halt!" bellowed the dragoon captain, using his tricorne to whip his horse into a gallop. With whoops and shouts, his men spurred their mounts and followed.

"That's all I need," muttered Kate, "to play the fox to their hounds."

Muttering an apology for bruising Clover's mouth, she hauled on the reins, and urged the mare off the highway. Close by was an area of dense woodland that Kate knew well but hoped her pursuers didn't.

As she arrowed towards it, a loud *crack* was followed by something whizzing over her right shoulder. She ducked in reflex, then glanced back and saw one of the soldiers was lowering his musket. Glancing forward once more, she found she had reached the edge of the wood and Clover was about to plough between two trees, speed unchecked.

"Whoops!" Kate ducked a low branch intent on removing her hat and reined in Clover to a less suicidal pace.

As she made her way deeper into the wood, the tree trunks crowded closer, muffling the shouts of her pursuers. Whipping branches left sap and scratches on her cheeks, and the leaf litter churned up by Clover's hooves added an earthy note to the aroma of rotting wood, fungi, and foliage.

The track Kate was following led eventually to a clearing, and as Clover thundered through it, past a startled badgers' sett, a blackbird burst from the undergrowth with a loud chattering cry of alarm. Kate managed to keep her seat as the mare shied, but it was a near thing.

"Steady, girl!"

After a heart-pounding moment, she regained control of her mount. Somewhere close by, a twig snapped like a musket shot. With a muffled curse, Kate kneed Clover into motion once more.

She took a deer trail that led down a wooded, steeply descending slope. Twice Clover lost her footing, first on a stone, and then on a protruding tree root, each time sliding several feet. Kate soothed the snorting mare and made noises of encouragement, resisting the urge to look over her shoulder.

The sound of running water grew steadily louder. At the bottom of the incline, she paused to let Clover catch her breath, then guided her towards the line of trees marking the brook. Urging the mare past an over-hanging willow and into the shallow water, Kate turned her towards the north. Clover shook her mane in protest then resigned herself to placing her hooves carefully on the stony bottom. The brook burbled, and Clover's legs swished, and in the distance Kate could hear the dragoons shouting and calling to one another.

They went several hundred yards upstream before Kate was satisfied. With a squeeze of the knees and a light tap of the reins, Kate urged the mare up the bank. Once on dry land again, she turned onto a bearing that would, if her sense of direction was up to scratch, bring her back to the point where she had entered the wood. The dragoons would not expect that. At least, she hoped so.

And so it proved. Soon, to her relief, the shouts, curses, whistles, and sporadic *crack* of twigs under hoof had faded. The sounds of the night returned. Somewhere, an owl hooted. It was a peaceful sound.

She slowed Clover to a comfortable pace and patted her lathered neck. *This time, the fox outwitted the hounds.*

When at last she emerged into the open, there was no sign of pursuit. Somewhere deep in the dense woodland's heart, the dragoons were searching for her. Kate gave a satisfied grunt and headed Clover back towards the deserted highway. An hour later than she had planned, she turned the mare's head towards London.

♉

"Where have you *been*?" Alice put her hands on her hips.

Kate raised an eyebrow and finished closing the door. "Pardon me, my dear. I intended meeting you at the Rose and Crown, truly, but other . . . matters detained me." She gestured at herself, and the landlady's eyes widened as she took in Kate's scratched appearance.

Kate dumped her saddlebags on the floor and hung her hat and baldric from the door hook.

"It's just as well you were delayed." Alice stepped forward to help Kate out of her coat. "Or you'd be sharing a cell with John Stephenson."

"What the Devil?" Kate stopped unbuttoning her shirt and stared at the other woman. "What happened?"

"Josselin."

"Samuel Josselin?"

"Who else? We were enjoying a quiet drink in the snug, and in comes the thieftaker and a band of his bullyboys armed with sticks and truncheons. They were looking for you."

Kate frowned. "Me?" *This is an unwelcome development.*

"'Blue-eyed Nick' at least. Said they had reliable information you frequented the Rose and Crown."

"Did they, by God!"

Alice nodded. "I was never so frightened in all my life. They took their cudgels to any who refused to answer their questions or who so much as looked at them ill, especially the Mollies, poor wretches. I've never seen so many broken heads and bloodied noses. One of the fiddle players had his own instrument smashed over his head. And all the while, Josselin just looked on with this strange smile on his face." She shuddered. "That monster!"

Kate resumed her unbuttoning and took off her shirt. "And Elborrow stood by and did nothing?"

"Even if he hadn't been so badly outnumbered, he hadn't much choice, Kate. I was close enough to overhear their conversation. Elborrow was furious. Asked what did Josselin think he was doing, for he paid Bodenham Titt well to leave the tavern alone."

"The Beadle, eh? I knew Elborrow had someone in his pocket, just didn't know who." Kate scratched her chin. "What was Josselin's reply?"

"He couldn't give a fart what Elborrow's prior arrangements were. He'd just paid the Beadle a handsome sum for immunity, and if his men broke limbs or even killed some of the regulars in the course of tracking down a felon, it was no skin off his nose. Especially since they were most likely pickpockets and footpads who would be no loss to society."

"Christian of him!" Kate stepped out of her knee breeches, picked up the pile of discarded clothes and carried them into the bedroom where she dumped some in the laundry basket and flung the rest on a chair. Alice followed and watched her cross to the washstand and pour water into the basin.

"Go on," said Kate, wincing as soap found its way into the gash on her forearm and the scratches on her cheeks.

"When Josselin's men told him they'd found no trace of you," continued Alice, "he started looking for others to arrest. That's when Stephenson made a run for it."

"Fool!" She reached for a towel. "Chances are Josselin didn't know who he was."

"I know." Alice sighed. "And for a moment, I thought Stephenson had made it to safety. But the thieftaker had more of his bullyboys stationed outside the exits. Last I saw, Josselin had him trussed like a turkey and bound for Newgate."

"Poor devil!" Kate loosed her hair and tried to get the knots out with her fingers.

"Here, let me." Alice grabbed a hairbrush and pointed to a chair. Kate nodded her thanks and sat down. "When you didn't come home," heavy-handed brushstrokes betrayed the strength of Alice's feelings, "I thought you'd been taken too."

"Some dragoons chased me," admitted Kate, "but I gave them the slip."

"Dragoons?" The brushstrokes grew more violent.

Kate took Alice's hand and gentled her strokes. "I'm not a horse."

"It's getting too dangerous."

"That's half the fun."

Alice threw the brush across the room, stalked towards the window, and stood, arms folded, staring out into the night.

Kate rose and moved behind her, hesitating before wrapping her arms around the other woman and burying her nose in fragrant red hair. "I've never hidden either my occupation or the fact that it's dangerous, now have I?" she asked, her voice muffled.

"No."

"Then why so upset now? Thieftakers have tried to take me before and failed." *Not Josselin, admittedly.* "Nothing's changed."

"Yes it has." Alice's voice was thick with emotion. "I didn't . . . care for you then as much as I do now."

Ashamed she was unable to return the older woman's sentiment, Kate pulled her closer. "If it makes you feel any better," she murmured, "I'll avoid the Rose and Crown from now on, lie low for a few days . . . until Josselin has lost interest."

Alice gave a strangled laugh. "You wouldn't be welcome there anyway. Elborrow's barred you."

"What?" She blinked. "The ungrateful wretch! After all I've—"

"He had no choice, Kate." Alice turned within the circle of her arms and regarded her. "Josselin threatened to report him for receiving stolen goods. Said if he got off on *that* charge he'd tell the brewery Elborrow was running a disorderly house. Either way he'd lose his license."

"Ah." Kate scratched her nose. "Fair enough. I'll miss Mrs. Elborrow's oyster pies though."

Alice's eyes flashed, and she slapped Kate, hard. "Damn you!"

Kate rubbed her cheek. "What was that for?"

"For not taking anything seriously." The other woman stamped her foot. "Faith! If you had been at the Rose and Crown as arranged, Kate, Josselin would have earned himself a Tyburn Ticket for your capture."

"True." Kate brushed a lock of red hair behind Alice's ear. "But I wasn't." She leaned in to kiss a flushed cheek, the corner of a soft mouth. "I'm here with you. And much nicer surroundings these are," she indicated the bed, "than the condemned hold at Newgate." An earlobe loomed so she nibbled it. "Why don't we make the most of it, eh?" She caressed a corset-clad breast then glanced up and saw eyes glazed with desire. "Take off your clothes, my dear, and let's enjoy ourselves."

For a moment longer, Alice resisted her blandishments, then with a soft curse and a sigh, she allowed herself to be led towards the bed.

Chapter 8

Rebeccah peered out at the darkening sky and bit her lip. Instead of crossing Putney Heath while it was still light, in convoy with other concertgoers, they were alone and night was drawing in.

"It wasn't Robert's fault, Madam," repeated her maid. "Some urchins meddled with the traces."

"That's as may be, Mary, but they wouldn't have been *able* to meddle with the traces if he had stayed with the carriage instead of going off with you and Will."

Mary flushed and looked away, her manner stiff. "Beg pardon, Madam, I'm sure."

Rebeccah sighed. It wasn't the maid's fault, after all. "No, I beg yours, Mary. The truth is I would far rather have joined you three for a walk in the sunshine than been cooped up indoors, listening to that caterwauling. But please don't tell Mama I said so."

Mary's lips twitched. "I thought Mr. Abel was meant to be much admired."

"In moderation his voice may well be bearable. And I'm sure my mother, had she not been in bed with a sick headache, would have enjoyed him immensely—she is always eager to hear the latest songs from the Continent. But my preferred idea of entertainment," continued Rebeccah, glad that Mary was no longer upset with her, "would have been a trip to the New Theatre. Congreve's plays are always amusing, especially when Mrs. Barry and Mrs. Bracegirdle are on top form."

The concert at Richmond Wells had been Mrs. Dutton's idea. Anne was still visiting her friend in the country, so it had fallen to Rebeccah to keep her mother company. Five shillings each, the tickets had cost them, and at the last moment, a megrim had confined Mrs. Dutton to her bed. Worse still, she had insisted her indisposition should not prevent her daughter from attending the concert (in spite of Rebeccah's increasingly broad hints that she would not mind in the least).

So after the tedious drive, made longer by the carriage having to go via London Bridge, Rebeccah had found herself amongst an audience of inveterate fidgets, coughers, and sneezers, perched on a chair that grew harder by the minute, wishing herself outside listening to birdsong instead of to Mr. Abel, who seemed overly pleased with himself and his high-voiced performance.

When the concert ended at last, releasing her from purgatory, an eager Rebeccah sought the peace and quiet of her carriage, only to find that the horses had broken free of the traces and her red-faced maid, footman, and coachman were darting around trying to retrieve them, while the amused locals looked on.

In the end, a couple of onlookers took pity on them and came to the servants' rescue. Soon the four horses were recaptured and yoked to the traces. The delay had cost Rebeccah's party dear, though, and the other concertgoers' conveyances had departed an hour ago.

As the carriage swayed and rocked its way along the highway across Putney Heath, Rebeccah chewed her lip and wondered why the urchins had targeted her carriage. True, Robert had left it unattended, but Mary insisted that other coachmen had done the same. Was it just chance that had made the urchins release her horses, or had someone instructed them to do so? And had it been done out of a sense of mischief or to delay her?

A thought struck her then, making her heart race and her cheeks heat so that she was glad the dimness of the interior hid them from Mary's gaze. Suppose Blue-Eyed Nick was trying to contrive another meeting. It had been a week since the kiss. Would he demand another one? And this time, would he insist it be on the lips?

Distant shouts roused Rebeccah from her pleasant daydream. With a start she became aware that the coach's pace had increased to the point of recklessness. Then came a pistol shot, and the *boom* of a blunderbuss. The coach slowed, almost catapulting the maid into Rebeccah's lap.

They disentangled themselves. "It could be Blue-Eyed Nick," said Rebeccah, unsure whether she was trying to reassure Mary or herself.

But a moan from the footman's position at the rear of the coach turned her anticipation to dread, and she couldn't bring herself to peer out of the window for fear of what would meet her gaze.

The carriage door opened. "Well, well, what have we here?"

The man's bulk took up the width of the doorway. A mask hid the top part of his face, but the bottom half was bare. A badly healed scar at the corner of his mouth had left him with a permanent sneer.

He turned his head and called to someone out of sight, "Couple of birds ripe for the plucking, boys." Removing his tricorne to reveal a wig badly in need of refurbishment, he made a mock bow. "At your service, ladies." His laughter was cruel, and so was the glint in his steel-grey eyes, as he put on the hat and grabbed hold of the carriage door to help himself up.

The vehicle tilted under his weight as he stepped inside, lowering his head to avoid braining himself on the roof, bringing the stench of unwashed clothes, horseflesh, and fried onions with him. Both women shrank away until their backs were pressed against the far side of the carriage.

"Aw, don't be like that." The highwayman's grin revealed tobacco-stained teeth. "Just 'cause I ain't one of your fancy gents drenched in lavender water." He reached for Rebeccah's pearl necklace, and tugged, too hard. The string broke, scattering pearls everywhere. "Devil take it!" His grin became a scowl.

Another man, as small and skinny as his companion was bear-like, appeared in the doorway. Though masked, his sharp features reminded Rebeccah of a rat. "Only two?" said the newcomer with a frown. "How are we going to split 'em between three of us?"

"Jemmy'll have to make do with our leavings."

Rebeccah's signet ring glinted and the man with the scar reached out a meaty hand. "I'll take that pretty gewgaw." He winked. "And then I'll take you."

The threat galvanized Rebeccah out of the paralysis that had overtaken her. She kicked him between the legs, reached for the door handle, and tumbled out of the carriage to the hard ground.

"Ow!" She rubbed her stinging elbow and staggered to her feet.

A lanky highwayman (*Jemmy, presumably*) was using a willow switch to drive the unhitched team across to where three horses were cropping grass. He threw her a startled glance.

Rebeccah lifted her skirts, and ran, but had gone barely five steps when she heard, "Stop or I'll blow your friend's brains out." The bellow halted her in her tracks, and she turned, heart hammering.

The scarred man's sneer was more pronounced than ever. He had dragged Mary from the coach and now had the muzzle of a cocked pistol pressed to her temple. Every instinct was screaming at Rebeccah to keep running, but she couldn't leave her maid in such peril. Lifting her chin, she turned and walked back towards the carriage.

"Lookit that," laughed Ratface. "She's taken a shine to yer, Jack."

Rebeccah ignored the lewd exchange that followed and walked as slowly as she dared, her eyes darting from side to side.

A liveried figure lay motionless beside the highway. The coachman. *Is Robert shamming?* On the ground beside him lay his blunderbuss, but smoke curling from its muzzle revealed that she would have to look elsewhere for a weapon.

Remembering the moaning, she sought out Will. The footman was sitting on the road by the rear of the carriage, both hands clutching a bloodied thigh.

No help there.

She came to a halt a yard from Jack. The maid's gaze was full of terror and Rebeccah shot her an encouraging glance, which was difficult considering her knees were knocking and her mouth so dry she had to clear her throat to get the words out.

"Let her go, sir, I beg you."

The big highwayman cocked his head to one side. "Not so hoity-toity now, eh?" He shoved Mary aside with such force she fell over, and reached for Rebeccah, spinning her round and squashing her so tightly against his barrel chest she could barely draw breath.

"You're going to regret kicking me in the stones." His breath was hot in her ear and the scratch of bristles made her want to vomit.

Ratface, meanwhile, had decided to grab Mary and received a slap from the struggling woman, provoking guffaws from his colleagues.

"I'll make you pay for that, baggage!" He forced the maid's hands down by her sides and looked at Jack. "Can I take her now?"

Will tried to rise. "No! Take the horses and valuables, but let the women go."

Jemmy crossed to the footman and knocked him back down with a blow and a curt, "Shut up!"

"Please listen to him," urged Rebeccah. "If you release us unharmed, I'll give the constables a false description of you and say there were seven in your gang not three." But the arm around her tightened and she bit her lip against the pain.

"You shouldn't have kicked me," growled her captor, beginning to drag her backwards.

Oh God! His grip was unbreakable. She dug in her heels, but succeeded only in leaving drag marks. Then the scar-faced man let out an odd little *huf* and the arm imprisoning her went limp. Rebeccah gaped at it in incomprehension, then jerked herself free and turned round.

The eyes behind Jack's mask were sightless, and he had acquired a hole in the centre of his forehead. He dropped heavily to one knee, then to both, then toppled forward, teeth crunching on the surface of the highway.

Only then did Rebeccah register the drumming of hooves, which had been at the edge of her hearing for several minutes. She turned and blinked at the masked rider on a black horse thundering across the heath towards her, a smoking pistol in one gloved hand.

"Blue-Eyed Nick!" cried Mary, looking as startled as Rebeccah felt. He was a hundred yards away and closing fast. She found it hard to breathe.

"Devil take 'im!" Ratface drew his pistol and cocked it. "This is *our* snaffle. Look lively, Jemmy." He took careful aim.

"Mary!"

Rebeccah's warning came too late for the maid to do anything. The crack of the pistol was deafening. Fearful, Rebeccah peered through the acrid blue smoke that surrounded them and saw the rider still coming, his progress unchecked.

Thank the Lord!

Jemmy was rummaging in one of the horses' saddlebags. He emerged with a blunderbuss and took aim.

"No!" Rebeccah hurtled towards him, grabbing his arm just as the weapon went off.

"Damn you!"

The lanky highwayman tried to club her with his blunderbuss. Her ears were still ringing and bright afterimages flecked her vision, but she managed to dodge the blow. He raised the blunderbuss again then came the crack of a pistol shot and he grunted. For a moment he remained frozen, arm raised, then his eyes rolled up in his head, and he collapsed.

Rebeccah straightened cautiously. When the toe of her shoe in Jemmy's ribs didn't get a reaction, she stooped and rolled him over on his back. A dark stain was spreading from the hole drilled through his waistcoat.

The hoofbeats were louder now, and she looked up just as Blue-Eyed Nick reined his lathered horse to a halt five yards away. The pale eyes behind the mask were as icy as she had ever seen them. He discarded the smoking pistol and drew his sword.

"Let her go." The order was aimed at Ratface who now had a knife to Mary's throat.

"Damned if I will! We worked hard to set up this lay, and no jumped-up wool-snaffler is going to snatch the proceeds."

Blue-Eyed Nick dug in his heels and urged his mare forward. His rapier glinted in the moonlight, and Ratface's eyes widened as he backed a few steps, dragging his squirming captive with him.

"No need to take it nasty. We can come to some arrangement, can't we?" Sweat beaded the little man's upper lip as the horse continued to advance. "Now don't be unreasonable. She's my bargaining chip." Mary's mew of terror made Rebeccah's stomach lurch. "How about a third. That's fair, ain't it?" He licked his lips. "Come now, a third is a sizeable snack."

As the rider continued his silent advance, Ratface stepped back . . . and caught his heel in a tuft of grass. Blue-Eyed Nick struck, leaning so far out of his saddle Rebeccah was amazed he kept his seat. The rapier whisked the knife from the maid's throat, and she gasped, dropped to the ground, and curled herself up like a hedgehog. Ratface was still gaping down at Mary when the rapier skewered him through the eye.

It was like some macabre tableaux, thought Rebeccah, unable to tear her gaze from the horrific sight. With a dull sucking sound, the blade withdrew, sprinkling her with something warm and wet, and Ratface crumpled to the ground. Jolted out of her fugue, and clamping down on her revulsion, she hurried over to join her sobbing maid.

"There, there." She wrapped her arms around the other woman. "It's all right, Mary. We are safe." She caught sight of her blood-spattered skirts and grimaced. "Though our dresses are somewhat spoiled."

She glanced up and saw Blue-Eyed Nick was wiping his blade on a kerchief. He caught her gaze, his eyes warming perceptibly.

"We *are* safe, aren't we?"

"Indeed."

She turned back to the woman in her arms, whose trembling seemed to be subsiding. "Did you hear that, Mary?"

"Thank the Lord!" murmured the maid, uncurling.

Rebeccah looked up at their saviour once more and paused. Was it her imagination or was the highwayman swaying in his saddle? "Good heavens!" She released Mary, stood up, and took a pace towards him. "Are you hurt?"

He sheathed his sword, drew off a glove, and touched long fingers to his left shoulder. They came away coated with something dark and glistening. "I'll be hanged if that first shot didn't . . ." He turned to regard her. "A mere pinprick, Madam. Please, do not concern yourself." But the swaying was becoming more pronounced and his eyes widened. "Pox take it, I think I—" With boneless grace he toppled from his saddle.

The black mare's ears flicked forward, and she nosed the man lying at her feet, then tugged the cuff of one sleeve with her teeth. When he didn't stir, she nickered soft and low and tugged the cuff again.

Rebeccah bent to examine the fallen rider, but the mare startled her by squealing and butting her hand away with its nose.

"Hold, girl." She held out a hand, palm up. "I'm not going to harm him."

Nostrils flared as the horse scented her, and large brown eyes regarded her from close quarters. After a moment, to Rebeccah's relief, the mare nickered and backed a few paces.

She bent and examined Blue-Eyed Nick's left shoulder. The coat, waistcoat, and shirt beneath it were soaked with blood.

"Is he dead?" asked Mary, who had recovered enough to join her mistress.

"A swoon." Rebeccah bit her lip. "So much blood!"

"We must pack the wound." The dumpy maid scanned their surroundings and pursed her lips. "I need moss."

Rebeccah gave her a doubtful look. "Out here, in the middle of nowhere?"

"Ay, Madam. In fact we couldn't have picked a better spot."

Mary's mother had been a Cunning Woman, and she had learned country lore at her knee. The Duttons had quickly learned to entrust their health to their maid's care before paying out good money to an apothecary or physician, whose treatments were often ineffective and sometimes fatal.

But staunching Blue-Eyed Nick's wound was one thing, leaving him swooning and vulnerable on the Heath quite another.

"Help me get him into the carriage first," ordered Rebeccah, grabbing the unconscious highwayman under the arms. Mary hesitated then took his feet.

He was lighter than expected, but it still was hard work dragging him towards the carriage. The mare pawed the ground and followed them.

"May we assist you, Madam?"

The footman was limping towards them. Beside him staggered a dazed-looking coachman.

"Robert!" squealed Mary, setting her burden down. "You're alive."

The coachman grinned at her then winced and put a hand to the back of his head. "My head aches like Blazes. The whoreson clubbed me, Mary." He glanced at Rebeccah. "Begging your pardon, Madam."

"Granted." Rebeccah frowned at the footman's bloody thigh. "Should you be walking on that, Will?"

"It looks worse than it is, Madam. The bleeding's stopped though it stings a fair bit." He jerked his head at the figure slumped at her feet. "He looks in a bad way, though. Never thought I'd be so glad to see him!"

"Indeed, I believe he saved all our lives. And now it's our turn to repay that debt," said Rebeccah. "I'm taking him back to St. James's Square."

"As you wish, Madam. Though won't Mrs. Dutton object?"

"Only if she finds out." Rebeccah flushed under the servants' combined scrutiny. "She will be in bed with her megrim, so if we are careful, we should be able to carry him up to my room unobserved."

"Your room?" Mary looked shocked.

Rebeccah rolled her eyes. "He'll be too weak to make any attempt on my honour. Besides, where else can I put him so you may attend to his wound whenever you need to without raising suspicion?" She pre-empted Mary's next question. "By the time Anne has returned, he will either be dead or well enough to make good his departure." *Pray God, it's the latter.*

"Will you all give me your word not to betray his presence to anyone?" She held each of their gazes in turn.

The three exchanged glances, then shrugged and chorused, "Yes, Madam."

"Thank you." Rebeccah's shoulders sagged with relief.

They manoeuvred the highwayman into the carriage. Then the two men went off to get the team of horses back into harness. Mary, meanwhile, grabbed a carriage lantern and went looking for some moss.

Rebeccah gazed down at Blue-Eyed Nick, who was sprawled on his back on the seat, his knees drawn up so that his long legs would fit inside the carriage. A nicker from the doorway made her glance round.

"He's in good hands," she told the mare. "Be patient. Mary will be back soon with some moss." *I'd better prepare him for her.*

She stripped off the highwayman's mask and kerchief. *He'll be more comfortable without them. And besides, I want to see him.* It was a handsome face, she decided, reaching out a hand. Smooth to the touch too, not like that brute's bristly chin. Thoughts of what might have happened had this man not intervened made her heart race, and she took a few calming breaths before continuing.

With difficulty, she eased Blue-Eyed Nick's coat over his shoulders, followed by his waistcoat, then started unbuttoning his shirt. Beneath it, wrapped tightly around his chest several times, was a long narrow strip of coarse white cotton, now soaked with blood. She frowned and wondered if it were protection against the cold, though on a warm late summer night it seemed unlikely. With a shrug, she began to unwind it.

From outside came a jingle of harnesses and murmur of voices. The carriage jerked forward a yard then came to rest. Then it dipped as Mary climbed aboard, her arms full of moss.

"Found some."

The last of the cotton strip came free, and Rebeccah's startled intake of breath attracted Mary's attention.

"Bless me, now I've seen everything!" murmured the maid, peering round Rebeccah at the shapely breasts now revealed. After a moment she chuckled. "Well, well." She tried to ease past Rebeccah, who was frozen with shock. "Excuse me, Madam. But I'll need to get closer if I'm to treat her."

Her.

"I beg your pardon." A still disconcerted Rebeccah stood back so that Mary could examine the wound, tut that the shot had not passed cleanly through but was still lodged inside, and begin to pack it with moss.

The woman beneath Mary's capable fingers shifted and moaned, and Rebeccah winced and turned away, just in time to see Will's face in the doorway. Instinct made her block his view of the half-naked highwayman . . . *I mean highwaywoman.* She cleared her throat and hoped she didn't look flushed.

"How are you progressing?"

"The horses are hitched and ready when you are, Madam."

"Good. There's something else I need you to do." She remembered his wound and bit her lip. "But only if you think you are well enough."

Will asked gamely, "What is it, Madam?"

"Drape the bodies of the dead highwaymen over their horses' saddles and take them to Putney. I'm afraid you'll have to ride Blue-Eyed Nick's mount."

He looked askance at the black mare, who gave him a distrustful glance in return. "As you wish, Madam."

"Tell the Beadle we were attacked . . . but make sure not to mention Blue-Eyed Nick." Rebeccah pursed her lips and thought. "You and Robert killed the rogues while defending our lives and our honour. Your wound will reinforce your claim."

The footman nodded.

"While you're there, ask for directions to a reputable apothecary. Get him to treat your thigh and send the bill to me."

Will smiled. "Thank you, Madam."

"Then return home to St. James's Square. You can stable Nick's horse in the Mews with our coach horses. That's all, I think."

"Very good, Madam." Will limped off to gather the first of the bodies.

A groan from behind followed by Mary's protest made Rebeccah turn. The highwaywoman's eyes were open, and she had pushed herself up on one elbow and twisted to face Rebeccah. Her skin was ashen, and there was a glaze to the pale eyes that Rebeccah didn't like the look of.

"Lie still," ordered Mary. "Do you want to make the bleeding worse?"

"Your footman won't be able to . . . Clover." The injured woman slumped back, her eyes closing.

Mary and Rebeccah exchanged a puzzled glance, then Rebeccah had a flash of intuition. She leaned forward. "Is Clover your horse?"

Eyelids cracked open, then came a hoarse, "Yes."

"Are you saying my footman won't be able to ride her?"

"Unless . . . whistle."

"Pardon?"

At the second attempt, the highwaywoman managed a whistle—two notes at an oddly discordant interval. Rebeccah mimicked it. From outside came a nicker, and the mare's nose poked inside the carriage.

Rebeccah clapped her hands. The ghost of a smile curved the high-waywoman's lips then her eyelids fluttered closed, and a cross Mary pronounced her in a swoon once more.

"I beg your pardon, Mary," said a contrite Rebeccah. "But it was necessary if Will is to ride her horse."

Already, Will had got the highwaymen's bodies slung over their saddles, and tied the three mounts together so they could be led. She called him over and told him about the whistle, then demonstrated. The foot-man's dubious look changed to one of relief when, after using the whistle and calling her by name, he was able to mount Clover.

As Will led the train of three horses and their macabre burdens off towards Putney, Rebeccah took a last look at her surroundings and decided she had done all she could. She shut the carriage door and banged her fist twice on the roof.

"Take us home, Robert," she called. "As quick as you can."

Chapter 9

The ground felt springy beneath Kate's boot heels. She paused and frowned down at the turf. *Why am I on foot?* Turning full circle, she scanned the vaguely familiar surroundings for signs of Clover but found none.

Movement drew her attention to a clump of trees beside the highway. A rider had emerged and was heading towards her. Kate stared at the grey gelding with the white blaze on its forehead in confusion. *Newton?*

She lifted her gaze to the rider, a girl from her slender build. Shock coursed through her as she took in the pale eyes behind the mask, the black hair tied at the nape of the neck, the kerchief over mouth and nose.

Her world realigned itself. *How old was I then—fifteen, sixteen?*

Neither the girl nor the gelding had noticed Kate. She stepped back, but had the impression that if she hadn't they'd simply have ridden right through her without ill effect. Swivelling on one heel, she started after them.

A shabby coach and four, lacking a footman, had appeared. As it rumbled along the highway, the girl rode to intercept it. A feeling of déjà vu, so strong it gave Kate goose-pimples, overtook her. No wonder this place looked familiar.

Hounslow Heath. It's happening all over again!

"Stop." She sprinted after her younger self. "Don't go through with it. It's a trap." But the rider gave no sign of hearing her shout, and instead drew her pistol and cocked it. Even if her sixteen-year-old self had heard the warning, she probably would have ignored it. Right now, Kate knew, the blood was pumping through the girl's veins, and she was in a state of wild excitement. This was the first coach she had robbed alone.

They had planned the ambush together, Kate and her mentor, Philip Wildey. Then at the last moment he had sprung his surprise. It was time for Kate to show what she could do alone, he had said with a smile. She'd been eager to prove herself to him, hoping to use the proceeds to pay for the gelding and brace of pistols he had lent her.

"Little fool!" Kate balled her fists as the girl fired a warning shot then drew her second pistol.

The coach was slowing even before the bellowed "Stand and Deliver." That and the lack of a footman should have tipped her off that something wasn't right. But under the kerchief, the girl was smiling, congratulating herself on how smoothly everything was going. And all the time . . .

The carriage door opened and out spilled four dragoons, muskets at the ready.

Kate could remember her shock, dismay, and incomprehension at this turn of events, as though it were yesterday. It had stunned her so badly it robbed her of any chance of flight.

By the time her younger self recovered her wits, the soldiers had dragged her from her horse and thrown her to the ground. Musket butts rose and fell, and boots kicked. Though it made her sick to her stomach, Kate forced herself to watch.

When the beating stopped at last, the girl was like a rag doll. Two of the laughing soldiers tugged her to her feet, supporting her while another man, tall and handsome and from his dress not a dragoon, stepped down from the coach. He stopped directly in front of the girl and gave her a mocking smile.

"Whoreson," shouted Kate, but no one heard her.

Wildey untied the blue silk kerchief that had been his present to the girl and was now blood-spattered, and stuffed it in his pocket. Then he blew her a kiss and turned his back. She spat at him and screamed and cursed until one of the soldiers backhanded her across the face.

A dragoon handed Wildey the discharged pistols and Newton's reins. He nodded, tucked the weapons in a saddlebag, and mounted up. At a stroke the treacherous highwayman had earned himself the horse, its tack, the pistols, £40 reward, and a pardon for his own crimes. She had found out later she wasn't the first naive youngster he'd groomed then turned in.

As he rode off, the soldiers bound the lolling girl and bundled her inside the coach. Kate watched it trundle away, massaging her left shoulder, which had begun to throb. Hounslow Heath had taught her a severe lesson she had been lucky to survive, she mused. The throbbing intensified.

"It's nestling against the bone," said a woman's voice. Kate looked round in startlement but could see no one. "Tsk! I can't quite—"

Pain lanced through her, and she stumbled and fell to her knees, clutching her shoulder and wondering what on earth was happening to her.

"You're hurting her!" came a second voice that she was sure she had heard before somewhere.

"Almost there, Madam. Almost."

"Argh!" Kate curled around the white hot agony that was her shoulder, trying not to vomit. Her eyes watered, and it was hard to breathe.

"Almost . . . Got it. Would you look at that? Nasty—"

Then blackness overtook her.

ॐ

It was the smell that hit Kate first—the stink of unwashed bodies, damp straw, and corruption. She waited for her pupils to adjust to the gloom—the barred window on the far side of the vast room let in hardly any daylight—her heart sinking as the familiar surroundings became clear.

The Common Ward. She felt the beginnings of a headache. *Maybe I imagined finding that nail, and all these years have been a dream.*

Certainly the faces were familiar. That gangling boy pissing into a chamber pot in one corner was Dick Lemon, and wasn't that old man with a face like a walnut Ben Field?

". . . read it to her?"

The question was barely audible above the talk, laughter, obscenities, sobbing, and lunatic howling. In time Kate would be able to tune out the clamour, but for now . . .

"Pardon?" She turned to look at the questioner, a middle-aged woman in a stained green dress, a fading letter T branded on her left cheek. Her mind supplied a name. *Hannah Kneebone.*

"I said Lizzy Blake's had a letter. Will you read it to her?"

Memory returned. Life in Newgate, if you could call it that, was expensive. Blankets, candles, soap, cooked food, lighter fetters (or even none at all)—everything cost money. There was even a departure fee, if you were lucky enough to survive your stay. But little of the cash a prisoner arrived with escaped the Keeper's "garnish," so another source of income was vital. Since Kate was one of the few who could read and write . . .

"Has she a penny?" Hannah nodded. "Then I'll read it to her."

Kate stood up and made her way across the room towards the big-bellied young woman in the shabby dress, shuffling as fast as her ankle fetters would let her, stepping over chamber pots, elbowing ribs and kicking shins, returning greetings and ignoring obscene suggestions as she went.

One man glared before moving aside. She hadn't endeared herself to the male prisoners here. When her gender had first been revealed, some had offered to do Kate the "favour" they had done Lizzy Blake—until her baby was born, the girl would be safe from hanging. The offers were premature, to say the least. Kate had yet to be sentenced, and since it was her first offence, it was by no means certain she would hang. Had the "neck verse" not been restricted to males who could read, she might have opted for Benefit of Clergy. As it was, there was still the possibility the judge might sentence her to branding or transportation rather than the noose. But should it come to hanging, she would rather opt for a quick death than endure pregnancy and childbirth overshadowed by the gallows. Besides, what about the child? Was it fair to leave it motherless? Kate thought not, and said as much. It hadn't stopped her harassers from leering and pawing her though. In the end she had given one a black eye and kneed another in the stones so hard he was pissing blood for a week. After that they had left her alone.

Lizzy's face lit up as Kate settled on the straw next to her and held out a hand. Penny deposited safely in her breeches pocket, Kate accepted the crumpled letter and held a stub of candle close to the almost illegible scrawl.

It was from Lizzy's parents, full of reproaches and pious platitudes about atoning for her sins and making her peace with the Almighty. There was no mention of the baby. By the letter's end her pretty face was ugly with crying, nose dripping, eyes red.

Unfeeling brutes. Kate pulled out the penny. "Here." She pressed it into Lizzy's palm and folded her fingers round it.

"But—" The girl's gaze was confused.

"Just take it before I change my mind." Kate stood and made her way back. She felt drained and slightly nauseous, and ached all over.

"Why's Lizzy staring at you like that?" asked Hannah.

Kate gave a weary shrug and sat down on the hard wooden shelf that was her bed. "My head aches like the Devil." Her surroundings seemed to be wavering, like a heat haze rising off stone on a hot July day. She frowned.

"You look a bit flushed," commented Hannah.

Kate grunted, swung her legs up and onto the bed, then stretched out and pulled the threadbare blanket over herself.

The other woman reached over and pressed the back of her hand to Kate's forehead then drew it back like a scalded cat. Wiping her hand on her dress, she edged away. The words "Jail Fever" hung unspoken in the air between them, but Kate was too tired to panic.

"It's probably just a chill," she murmured. Then she remembered how Ned had said those same words to her on her last visit, here, in this very room. The next day her brother was dead. "I just need to rest." She closed her eyes.

But it was hard to sleep, what with the pounding headache, aching limbs—her throbbing shoulder was a particular trial—and the clamour of the Common Ward going on all about her.

At intervals, waves of heat drenched her with sweat, and she discarded the blanket and coat in an attempt to get cool. A little later, chills began running through her. Sure her hands and feet must be turning blue, she eased back into her coat and huddled into the blanket's barely adequate warmth. And so it went on, what seemed like hour after hour of fever alternating with shivering that left her drained, aching, and sore.

Thirst overtook her. Kate dug in her pocket and pulled out a threepenny bit, but it took all her energy just to raise her arm, and then the coin slipped from her fingers and rolled away across the floor.

"A drink, Hannah, for pity's sake!" she croaked.

"Here," came a woman's soft voice that was vaguely familiar. A hand slipped under her head and lifted it, then something cool was trickling between her lips, spilling down her chin, and pooling in the hollow of her neck.

"Not too much," warned another voice. The flow lessened but didn't stop. Like a dying man in the desert, Kate drank. "That's enough."

The source of the water dried up and Kate let out a wordless groan of protest. Then she felt her head being lowered, and something soft mopped her brow.

"More later," promised the soft voice. She tried to open her eyes, to see who it was. At first they wouldn't obey her, and when they did the light was too bright to make out much except that the eyes looking down at her were green and full of compassion. She tried to say "Thank you," but all that emerged was a croak. Against her will and to her frustration, her eyelids closed once more.

"Sleep now." A hand smoothed her hair.

So she did.

Chapter 10

Rebeccah's fingers were sore and her eyes burned from squinting at her embroidery. She set it aside and crossed to the sash window, then stared down at the activity in the sunlit square for a while before turning to find a pair of eyes regarding her.

"Oh!" Her hand flew to her mouth. It was the first time she had seen those striking blue eyes by daylight; the highwaywoman was well named. "You're awake."

"Am I?"

Rebeccah poured a cup of water and carried it over to the bed. "You must be thirsty. Drink this."

Blue-Eyed Nick tried to sit up, groaned, and flopped back against the pillow. "I'm as weak as a babe." Her mouth curled in self-disgust.

"You have been very ill. Here."

She took the cup from Rebeccah with her right hand—her left arm was in a sling—drained it in a single gulp, and handed it back. "Thank you."

Blue eyes scanned the bedchamber, lingering on the reclining easy chair that Mary had helped Rebeccah bring through from the dressing room. "Where am I? The last thing I remember is Putney Heath."

"Our house in St. James's Square."

Dark eyebrows shot up. "And how long have I been here?"

"Three days." Rebeccah tugged the bell pull that would summon Mary from below stairs, though it was Monday and the bustle of washday was in full progress.

"That long!" The other woman studied Rebeccah's face and frowned. "Are you well, Mistress Rebeccah? The shadows beneath your pretty eyes weren't there before." She glanced at the easy chair. "My fault, I fear, for I have taken your bed. Though *this* is not yours, I'd venture, or it would not fit me." She plucked at the nightdress that Mary had produced from somewhere.

Rebeccah tried not to blush. "Your condition caused us considerable disquiet."

"Us?"

"My maid has been supervising your care. Mary's mother was a Cunning Woman. She looks after all our ailments." She bit her lip, remembering her panic as she watched the highwaywoman fighting for her life. "We had some difficulty removing the bullet, then fever almost took you. Were it not for Mary . . ." She fell silent.

"So this rank-smelling item," the highwaywoman indicated the poultice peeping out of the left shoulder of her nightdress, "is Mary's handiwork?"

Rebeccah welcomed the attempt at humour. "Her own recipe." She had watched Mary preparing it in her pestle and mortar. There had been lard in it, and honey, opium for the pain, and myrrh—for which the apothecary had charged Rebeccah an outrageous sum—and lord knows what else besides.

A knock at the door made her jump, and sent her scurrying to answer it. She opened it a crack, saw Mary standing there, and opened it wider.

"Come in." She pulled the maid through and shut the door.

"You rang, Madam?"

"Your patient is awake." Rebeccah turned and led the way to the bed.

"I collect that I owe both of you my life," the highwaywoman told Mary, as the maid checked the whites of her eyes and condition of her tongue, examined her wound, gave a satisfied grunt, and replaced the poultice. "My deepest gratitude." The skin around her eyes crinkled.

"Consider it just recompense for your rescue of us," said Rebeccah. "Which brings me to something that has been nagging me . . . how was it that you were to hand when we needed you?"

Blue-Eyed Nick's gaze turned inwards for a moment, and she shivered.

Mary frowned and held the back of her hand to her patient's forehead. "Are you well? Your temperature feels normal."

"It must have been Chance or the Almighty Himself that guided me to you that day," said the highwaywoman. "For I had no idea it was your coach that had been targeted."

Rebeccah leaned forward. "Yet you knew there was to be an ambush?"

She nodded. "I was in a tavern I don't usually frequent, when I heard a whisper." She gave a rueful smile. "I had promised a friend I would lie low, but robbery is one thing, rape and murder quite another. I could not stand by and let it happen."

"Thank God!"

"And thank Blue-Eyed Nick," murmured Mary. She cocked her head to one side. "We can't go on calling you that. Do you have a name?"

"Mary!" protested Rebeccah.

The plump woman sniffed. "If she wants me to mind my own business, all she need do is say so, Madam. But Blue-Eyed Nick is a mouthful, there's no getting around it."

The corner of the highwaywoman's mouth twitched. "Call me Kate."

"Kate it is then," said Mary, "though it's probably no more your real name than the other was." Rebeccah rolled her eyes. "And while all this chattering is fine and dandy," continued the maid, "what you really need is peace and quiet and building up." Blue eyes tracked from Mary's face to Rebeccah's and back again. "We must put some colour back into your cheeks. Think you can manage some broth?"

Kate considered the question then nodded.

"You too, Madam." Mary turned a stern gaze on Rebeccah. "You've been eating barely enough to keep a sparrow alive."

She *was* feeling a bit peckish, she realized. "That would be welcome, Mary. Thank you."

The maid curtseyed, then hurried off.

"She's quite a character." The flash of Kate's strong white teeth made Rebeccah's heart race.

Realization that the undercurrent of attraction between them was as strong as ever made her feel off balance. "Were you mocking me?" she blurted.

"I beg your pardon?"

"When you kissed me . . . For you're a woman, are you not?"

Kate chuckled. "Whoever stripped me of my clothes . . ." She sobered as she saw Rebeccah's expression. "But I see you are in earnest. To answer you, my dear. Indeed I was not mocking you."

For some reason, that "my dear" soothed Rebeccah's agitation. "Then why did you kiss me?"

"For the simplest of reasons," said Kate gently. "Because the moment I saw you I wanted to." She paused. "Does that shock you?"

It should have, supposed Rebeccah. But instead all she felt was a warm inner glow. "I . . . I have read of such things," she admitted. "But . . ." She trailed off.

"God gave me an appreciation of the female form," said Kate, her tone unrepentant, "and I thank him for it." Her gaze became quizzical. "Forgive me, but I was under the impression that you did not find my attentions wholly repugnant. Was I mistaken?"

Rebeccah cheeks flamed. "I thought you were a man!"

"So you did." Blue eyes twinkled. "And now that you know otherwise?"

Fortunately for her composure—if she'd known how indelicate this particular Pandora's Box would turn out to be, she'd never have opened it—a knock at the door and Mary's reappearance with a laden tray prevented their conversation from continuing.

"Did Mama see you?" Rebeccah accepted a spoon and a bowl of broth that smelled of beef and vegetables.

"No, Madam. I was the soul of discretion." Mary eased Kate into a sitting position, propped the pillows behind her, and settled the tray on her lap. She handed Kate the spoon and nodded approval as she took her first mouthful. "Mrs. Dutton is supervising the laundering of the silks and lace as she always does."

"That's good." Rebeccah tasted the broth, which was delicious. "And so is this."

"Mmm," agreed Kate round her spoon.

Mary's smile was complacent. "Good food and plenty of rest and you'll be back on your feet in no time," she told Kate. "Just as well since Mistress Rebeccah's busybody of a sister—begging your pardon, Madam, but she *is* a busybody—is due home soon and you must be gone by then. Now, if that's all, I'd best get back below stairs, or the others will say I'm shirking my washday duties." She bobbed a curtsey and left the two women alone once more.

They finished their broth and set aside the bowls, then a slightly awkward silence fell.

"Is Clover well?" asked Kate eventually.

"Your horse?" Rebeccah thanked God for the neutral topic. "Yes. She is stabled with our mounts in the Mews around the corner."

"Thank you. She can sometimes be a handful but I would hate any harm to come to her." Kate tried to hide a yawn and Rebeccah remembered her recent ordeal and cursed herself for an insensitive fool.

"You are tired and should rest."

Kate scowled. "I have done nothing *but* rest for the last three days it seems."

"I would not call that rest. You were tossing and turning and calling out."

"What did I say?"

"It was confused. Perhaps you were dreaming of heaven, for you mentioned an angel."

Kate smiled. "A reference to you, I think."

Rebeccah blushed and hurried on. "Several time you mentioned Newgate and a man name Wild . . . no Wildey." A shadow passed over Kate's face. "A friend of yours?"

"No." The other woman's eyelids fluttered closed then opened again. "I beg your pardon." She blinked and licked her lips, but it was obvious she was fighting to stay awake.

"You must sleep if you are to regain your health and strength," chided Rebeccah.

Kate sighed. "If you insist."

The sun had shifted round and was threatening to shine straight in the highwaywoman's face. Rebeccah crossed to a window and drew the curtain, then removed the pillows propping Kate up and made her comfortable.

"Will you still be here when I wake?" There was something wistful in the eyes looking up at her.

She smiled and resisted an urge to brush back a stray lock of raven hair. "If I am not, Mary will come and fetch me."

"Then I shall sleep." Seconds later the highwaywoman was as good as her word.

♌

Caroline sipped her chocolate and regarded Rebeccah with a frown. "I see why your mother is concerned for your health. You look quite pale."

"I'm well enough," protested Rebeccah, glancing towards the other side of the parlour where her mother was reading a book. To her daughter's indignation, Mrs. Dutton had taken it upon herself to invite Caroline Stanhope round to the house in St. James's Square. Her aims had been laudable—to lift Rebeccah's spirits and restore her appetite—but unnecessary given that the woman upstairs was out of danger, though of course her mother wasn't to know that. "I have not been sleeping well, that's all."

Her friend put down the dish of chocolate. "The hold-up on Putney Heath still weighs on your mind?"

Rebeccah nodded. "I can't help wondering what might have happened had Blue-Eyed Nick not come to our aid."

"Your mother told me the bare bones of what occurred." Caroline leaned forward. "A horrific experience, to be sure, Beccah. But once again 'your' highwayman," her smile was arch, "was to hand."

"And I thank heaven for it! Never was I so glad to see anyone in my life."

"He must have looked dashing indeed, galloping to your aid, pistols firing. I wish I had been there to see it."

"Be glad you were not."

The parlour door swung open and the senior footman came in, bearing a silver salver on which sat a solitary visiting card. The warning glance Will shot Rebeccah's way as he limped towards her mother made her heart beat faster.

Mrs. Dutton read the legend on the rectangle of white card, looked thoughtful, then muttered a reply. When Will nodded, bowed, and left the room, she returned to perusing her book.

Unable to contain her curiosity, Rebeccah asked, "Who has called on us, Mama?"

Her mother looked up. "Oh, it is only that thieftaker Anne has employed."

Samuel Josselin? Here? And his injured quarry upstairs and vulnerable? Rebeccah clasped her hands together. Surely everyone in the room could hear the blood thundering through her veins.

"He wanted to make his report," continued Mrs. Dutton, unaware of her daughter's turmoil. "I told him to come back in two days."

Relief washed over Rebeccah, and she managed a nod.

Caroline looked puzzled and said in a low voice, "Does your sister not know of your sentiments towards Blue-Eyed Nick?"

She shook her head. "Alas, Caro, Anne cannot see beyond his profession . . . or the insult he did my person."

Her friend's eyebrows shot up. "Insult?"

"The kiss."

"Ah." Caroline looked thoughtful. "But surely his rescue of you and your servants now shows him in a much more favourable light?"

Rebeccah sighed. "Perhaps, when she learns of it, Anne will indeed look more kindly upon . . . him and dispense with Josselin's services. But—" She shrugged. *Anne is hasty in forming her opinions and slow to change them.*

"Let us hope so, for your sake, Beccah." Caroline sat back. "Now." She gave Rebeccah a playful smile. "Tell me the details you left out to spare your mother's blushes."

Rebeccah felt an overwhelming urge to tell her friend everything. *But she would be shocked indeed to know that at this very minute Blue-Eyed Nick is sleeping soundly in my bed, and what's more that he is a she.* So she clamped down on the impulse and asked instead, "What can you mean?"

Caroline rapped Rebeccah's knuckles with her fan. "Did he ask you for another kiss?"

She hoped her cheeks weren't as red as they felt. "He had far more pressing matters on his mind, Caro."

"What, no sweet talk at all?"

Her friend's obvious disappointment made Rebeccah laugh out loud. At the sound, her mother marked her place with her finger and gave her daughter a pleased glance.

"I knew company would cheer you, Rebeccah," she called. "That the incident shook you badly and jangled your nerves, I can allow, but remaining cooped up in your room was not the answer."

Rebeccah said only, "No, Mama."

Mrs. Dutton returned to her book and Caroline reclaimed her friend's attention. "Is it true that your highwayman killed all three of the rogues who attacked you yet took no harm himself?"

"Indeed." Rebeccah winced inwardly at having to repeat the lie, but what else could she do? The fewer who knew Kate was here and injured, the better. "Fortune must have smiled on him . . . and on us that night."

"No wonder they named him Nick." Caroline's eyes sparkled. "He has the luck of the Devil."

⚕

The afternoon passed pleasantly enough, but even while Rebeccah was talking to Caroline, playing cards, eating sweetmeats (her mother smiling at this sign of Rebeccah's returning appetite), and drinking a glass of wine she found herself fretting about Kate and wondering how she was faring. When her old friend had finally departed with a cheery smile and a wave, it wasn't long before Rebeccah made her excuses and darted upstairs.

The injured highwaywoman was still asleep. But it seemed a restless kind of sleep—her eyes were moving rapidly from side to side beneath closed eyelids, her brow was creased, and she was muttering under her breath. A concerned Rebeccah held the back of her hand to Kate's fore-head, and was relieved to find it cool to the touch.

Not fever but bad dreams?

She pulled a chair next to the bed and took Kate's larger hand in hers, pleased to find that, almost at once, the frown smoothed and the muttering ceased. She contemplated the other woman's handsome profile, trying to decide which of her features she found most appealing, deciding in the end that it was those striking eyes, currently hidden from view, that caused her heart to flutter the most.

Kate looked both younger and more innocent in sleep. How old was she? *Older than me, I'd wager. Not more than thirty though—the life of a highwayman is precarious and short.* That thought saddened her.

A hand on her shoulder brought her back to her surroundings with a start.

"You have the touch, Madam," whispered her maid, indicating the clasped hands and the contentedly sleeping woman.

Rebeccah sighed. "I wish I could do more, Mary. Every moment she remains here she is in danger. Did you know that Josselin came to see my sister this afternoon?"

"Will told me."

"Kate must regain her strength and quickly."

"Have no fear, Madam. This one's as strong as an ox, else the fever would have carried her off."

"I hope you're right."

Their conversation must have disturbed the woman in the bed, for she stirred and began to stretch, then winced and thought better of it. Dark eyelashes fluttered open and blue eyes stared up at the two women rather dazedly before comprehension returned.

Kate's mouth curved into a smile. "Am I the topic of your discussion?"

Strong fingers tightened around Rebeccah's hand, holding it fast as she tried to withdraw it. To struggle with Mary present was more than her dignity was worth, so Rebeccah didn't.

"You look better," said Mary.

"I am. And what's more I'm hungry." Kate sounded surprised.

"A promising sign. More broth, or could you manage something solid? With your permission, of course, Madam." She turned towards her mistress who was being distracted by the oddly pleasurable sensation of Kate's thumb stroking her skin.

"Granted," managed Rebeccah.

"Something solid," said the highwaywoman.

"I'll see what I can find." Mary curtseyed and hurried away.

The instant the door closed, Rebeccah freed herself of Kate's grip. "Have you no sense of propriety?"

"Apparently not." Blue eyes danced. "But it was you who held my hand rather than vice versa."

"Because it seemed to help you sleep better."

"Whatever the reason, I am glad of it."

Rebeccah didn't know whether to return the impudent grin or slap Kate's face. She contented herself with a grunt. "While you were sleeping," she said, to change the topic, "We had an unwelcome visitor."

"Oh?"

"Samuel Josselin."

"'S Death!" Kate frowned. "What the devil was he doing *here*?"

"My sister has hired him to take you."

Pale blue eyes regarded her with astonishment then became thoughtful. "That explains the Rose and Crown."

"Pardon?"

"No matter. But I am sorry your sister desires to see me hanged."

"As am I." Rebeccah sighed. "It did not help matters, Kate, that the necklace and bracelet you took from her were a gift from one of her suitors." She ignored Kate's snort. "But regarding Josselin, you need have no worry on that score. My mother sent him away until my sister's return."

"Which is to be when?"

"In two days."

"Then I will endeavour to be up and gone from here by then. Though it is a shame our time together must be so brief." She threw back the corner of the bedclothes and started to swing her bare legs out.

"Where are you going?" Rebeccah held up a hand to stop Kate from getting up.

"I need to use the chamber pot."

"When Mary returns she will help you."

"I fear that will be too late."

Kate stood up, but as she did so, her face paled and she began to sway. Rebeccah grabbed her round the waist, and felt an arm go round her shoulders. She glanced up anxiously, relieved to see the colour already returning to Kate's cheeks.

"You stood up too quickly!" She released her hold on Kate's waist but allowed the arm to remain round her shoulder. "I told you we should have waited for Mary."

"But then I would have had no excuse to put my arm around you."

"You are incorrigible!" Rebeccah helped the other woman towards her dressing room. It was difficult for both of them to get through the door at the same time, but by turning through ninety degrees they managed it.

The highwaywoman lifted the lid of Rebeccah's close-stool and regarded the padded seat with the hole in the centre with obvious amusement. "This is a superior chamber pot indeed!" She removed her arm from around Rebeccah's shoulders and began to lift her nightdress.

Rebeccah squeaked and turned her back.

"Forgive my rough manners," said Kate with a laugh. "You are fortunate my left shoulder was wounded and not my right, or I would be asking for more intimate assistance." A rustle of material preceded the sound of liquid splashing on porcelain and a sigh of heartfelt relief.

Rebeccah waited, fidgeting, until Kate pronounced herself decent, then turned, relieved to find that it was true. She helped the taller woman across to the washstand and poured some water into the basin so Kate could wash her hands—awkwardly because of the sling—then helped her back to bed.

A few minutes later, Mary appeared with a tray containing slices of beef, bread and butter, a lump of Cheshire cheese, some blanched almonds, a cup of beer, and a dish of tea.

"Tea?" Kate grimaced.

"For Mistress Rebeccah." Mary handed the steaming dish to her mistress. "The beer's for you." The dark-haired woman grumbled when she discovered it was only small beer. "Nothing stronger until you are better," chided the maid.

Rebeccah sipped her tea and watched Kate eat. If the speed at which she crammed food into her mouth was any indication, she was indeed hungry. At last, with a contented sigh, Kate leaned back against her pillow.

Mary collected up the crockery and departed, leaving the two women in companionable silence. Rebeccah opened her mouth then closed it again.

"Ask your questions," said Kate.

"They will not tire you?" When there was no reply, Rebeccah paused for a moment longer then plunged in. "How old are you?"

Kate blinked at the personal question but said amenably enough, "Nine-and-twenty. And you?"

Rebeccah blushed. "Three-and-twenty. Why did you become a highwayman?"

"A flaw in my nature? For it suits me well."

"Did no one teach you your Bible?"

"I only steal from those who can afford it."

Kate flicked her expressive gaze around the bedchamber with its wainscoted walls and expensive furnishings, and raised one eyebrow. Now was probably not a good time to mention that her mother was second cousin to the Duchess of Marlborough, thought Rebeccah.

"You are saying that because others have more than you, it is acceptable to steal from them?"

"I must earn my living somehow," said Kate. "People depend on me."

Rebeccah's heart skipped a beat. "You have a husband and children?" Somehow she had not considered that a possibility. Kate smiled and shook her head but didn't elaborate further. Rebeccah's heart resumed its normal rhythm. "But the risk," she pressed.

"At first that was a consideration, but now it doesn't deter me. Might as well be hanged for a sheep as a lamb, as the saying goes. Besides, risk is what gives life its spice."

"There must be other occupations you could pursue."

"Indeed." Kate grinned. "My mother paid the premium for me to be apprenticed to a mantua-maker."

The image of the highwaywoman as a seamstress was incongruous. "*Mantua-maker?*"

"That shocks you. But my stitches were neat and my work of good quality . . . or so Mistress Coggs told me."

"What happened?"

Kate's face darkened. "Mistress Coggs' husband. Though I was just turned thirteen and he five-and-sixty, the drunken sot took a fancy to me. One afternoon, when his wife was out, he tried to rape me." She shrugged then winced and clasped her injured shoulder. "I was able to defend my honour—my brothers had taught me how. I kneed him in the stones and fled."

"Where did you go?"

"The streets, of course. But I had no intention of selling my body, so I became a cutpurse."

"But surely . . . Your parents . . ."

Kate shook her head. "My father died when I was five. And I could not bring the constables down on my mother. She had been through enough already. That was the year my sister died," she explained. "Jane was only nine. Smallpox."

"I'm sorry." Rebeccah puzzled about that for a moment. "But I don't understand. Why would the constables be after you?"

"I had broken my contract of apprenticeship," said Kate, as though stating the obvious. "And assaulted my Mistress's husband." She shifted against her pillow. "Hard labour in a house of correction is not unusual for such a crime."

"But you were only thirteen and he tried to rape you!"

Kate's laugh was unamused. "Who would take my word against that of George Coggs?"

"That's not fair."

"Life isn't," agreed Kate.

That silenced Rebeccah for a while. Then she continued, hesitantly. "You talked of Newgate often in your delirium. You seemed to know it well. Did you visit it often?"

Kate smiled. "You give me more credit than I deserve. It is true I visited my brother Ned there, but later my acquaintance with Newgate became more . . . personal."

Rebeccah tried to make sense of that. "But you sport no brand." She indicated her cheek. "Were you pardoned, or did some benefactor pay to set you free?"

"Neither. You are the only benefactress I know."

Rebeccah blushed but would not be put off. "Then how did you get out of Newgate unscathed?"

"I escaped."

"Impossible!"

Kate raised an eyebrow. "I assure you it is not. I am living proof."

"But how—"

"Fortune smiled on me, in the shape of a nail."

"A *nail?*"

"You'd be surprised at the uses to which a nail can be put. In the right hands it can unlock fetters, chip mortar . . ." Kate's mouth quirked. "Your mother would be horrified to learn her daughter has smuggled such a desperate character into her home."

She would indeed!

Yet it was odd, mused Rebeccah, how safe she felt with this self-confessed thief and escaped prisoner. Maybe that was an indication of just how dangerous Kate really was. She charmed her way inside your defences and before you knew it she had stolen your money . . . and your heart.

But how is that possible? She is a woman!

"You are very quiet." Kate settled back against her pillows with a yawn. "No more questions? As I feared, the account of my fall from grace has stunned you with its tedium."

"It has done no such thing. Very well, then. To continue. Can you not still become a mantua-maker as you planned?"

"You are set on saving my soul as well as my body. That is kind. But I fear you are too late. For the Law is relentless and will not let me escape its grasp without paying for my misdeeds."

The answer depressed Rebeccah and she played with her father's signet ring before glancing up, in time to catch Kate hiding another yawn.

"I have tired you after all!" She rose and removed the pillows supporting Kate's back so she could rest more comfortably. "Sleep now."

"That is all I seem to do, eat and sleep," grumbled Kate. "I would much rather stay awake and talk to you. Or I could simply gaze at you while you read or sew, or otherwise occupy yourself."

"Hush. You are babbling."

"And what about those smudges beneath your own eyes, Rebeccah. Should you not rest too?" Kate patted the bed beside her. "Come, let us be cosy. It will be more comfortable than that chair, and you will be quite safe, I swear." She yawned again, so widely her jaw cracked, then her eyelids fluttered closed. Moments later a soft snore emerged.

Rebeccah shook her head, though whether it was at the sleeping woman's suggestion or at herself for being tempted by it, she was unsure. For a long moment she stood watching her, then she went downstairs to join her mother for supper.

Chapter 11

Cries of "Four for sixpence, mackerel," and "Cherries ripe-ripe-ripe" from outside woke Kate. She regarded the lofty ceiling for a moment, then propped herself up on one elbow and glanced at the reclining easy chair. The alert green eyes of its current occupant looked back at her.

"Good morrow."

"Good morrow, Kate." Rebeccah sat up, rather stiffly. "How is your shoulder?"

The fiery throbbing had eased to a dull ache. "Better, I think."

"Good." The young woman threw off her bedclothes, slipped a robe over her shoulders, then crossed to the bell pull and gave it a tug.

Rebeccah wandered over to a window and stared out. It was another fine day, and sunshine glinted off her fair hair. Kate took the opportunity to admire Rebeccah's profile—her pert nose was delight-ful—and to speculate about the figure beneath the nightdress.

A knock at the door drew Rebeccah's attention, and she hurried towards it. Mary entered, carrying a ewer.

"Good morrow, Madam." The maid curtseyed. "Am I to help you dress?" She nodded a greeting at Kate who nodded back.

"Thank you, Mary. If you please." Rebeccah led the way to the little dressing room that adjoined her bedchamber.

Kate leaned back against her pillows and studied her surroundings. Were the furnishings Rebeccah's doing or her mother's? The chintz curtains were the latest thing and matched the bed hangings and quilt. The sheets everyone had been so careless of during her illness were of the finest Holland. As for the feather mattress, it was deeper even than Alice's.

With a pang of guilt she realized that she hadn't given a thought to the red-haired landlady, who probably thought Kate was dead or lying injured in a ditch somewhere.

As soon as I regained my wits, I should have sent word to her. Why am I so thoughtless? But it was no good crying over spilt milk.

Kate pushed thoughts of Alice aside, and wondered how long Rebeccah and Mary would be. It must be strange indeed to have a maid to help you dress . . . not to mention to empty your chamber pot. But Rebeccah probably took such things for granted.

She felt twitchy and restless, and the sunshine seemed to beckon. On a day like today, she would normally go riding. (*I wonder if they are feeding Clover well.*) Undoubtedly her health and energy were returning; she wouldn't be able to answer for her temper if she was forced to stay cooped up in bed.

Kate threw back the blankets and stood, pleased to find there was no dizziness today. She crossed to the window and stared down at the bustle below her. The streethawkers were standing by the Square's central garden, looking daggers at one another and striking poses to display the wares in their wicker baskets to best advantage. She scratched her head and yawned, and pitied a little milkmaid going from house to house with her heavy pails.

The sling supporting her left arm was a nuisance. She regarded it with pursed lips and unpinned it. Her shoulder twinged as she flexed her arm, then settled to a dull ache.

It will serve.

She returned to the bed, perched on the edge of it, and waited. Five minutes passed, then ten—still no sign of Rebecca or her maid. The pressure on Kate's bladder increased, and she crossed her legs and reached for the deck of playing cards Mary had provided. She was setting out the cards for a game of Solitaire when a rustle of movement made her look up.

Rebeccah was emerging from her dressing room, immaculate in a gown of pale blue silk, her hair brushed and neatly pinned into place. Kate blinked at this vision of loveliness and was about to pay her a compliment when Mary fixed her with a glare.

"What are you doing out of bed? And who told you you could take off that sling?"

"But I feel much better," protested Kate, rising and heading past the amused Rebeccah towards the dressing room.

"Wait!" called Mary. "Where are you—?"

"I need to use the chamber pot." Kate hitched up her nightdress, sat on the close stool, and began to make water. *Ah!*

"Leave her, Mary," came Rebeccah's muffled voice from the other room. "She must be feeling better to walk without assistance." Then, in a louder voice, "Kate, I must go down to breakfast. Mary will bring you something on a tray. I will join you later."

"Thank you."

When Kate had finished her business, she crossed to the washstand, emptied the dirty water from the basin into the close stool and poured herself some fresh. She peeled off her nightdress, washed and dried herself, and frowned as she realized she had no idea where her clothes were, or even if they had survived her adventure on Putney Heath.

Racks of Rebeccah's gowns filled one wall of the small room. She selected one at random, held it against herself, and chuckled. It reached barely to her knees. She replaced the gown and pulled on her nightdress once more.

The little clock on the dresser was showing nine a.m. On closer inspection, it proved to be a precision piece by Daniel Quare. Kate hefted the candlesticks standing either side of the looking glass. They were solid silver, as were the brush and comb. She was glad to see that no patch box sat among the bowls of cosmetics arranged on a muslin cloth—she thought it an ugly fashion.

The writing desk revealed some letters, stained either with seawater or tears, and signed "Your loving brother, William." She perused them quickly. *He must be dead, for she hasn't mentioned him.* And that jovial-looking man in the pen-and-ink portrait, presumably sketched by Rebeccah herself. It bore a strong resemblance to Rebeccah, though her nose and jawline were much prettier. *Her father?*

Kate moved on to the little cabinet, with its display of blue-and-white Oriental porcelain, and began to examine the contents of the drawers—a jewelled buckle, several diamond-headed pins, a painted and perfumed fan, a beautiful amber necklace . . . She was studying a diamond pendant, whose stones were of superior quality, when Mary entered the dressing room.

"Breakfast is—What are you doing with that?" The maid's tone was sharp.

"Just looking." Kate put back the pendant and closed the drawer, then eased past the maid into the bedchamber.

A tray lay on the chair beside the bed, containing slices of cold ham, bread and butter, and a steaming dish of chocolate. Kate sat down and pulled the tray onto her lap.

"I hope that is the truth, Kate." Mary had followed her and was standing, arms folded, gaze hard. "For if I find you have taken advantage of my mistress's kindness, I will turn you in to Josselin myself."

The accusation stung. But a dog could not complain if he was suspected of barking, so Kate pushed aside her hurt. "Your loyalty does you credit, Mary." She took a slice of bread and butter and added some ham. "But you may rest easy. I would not treat your Mistress so shabbily." She began to eat.

"Humph!" But after a moment the set of the maid's jaw softened and she unfolded her arms.

"Were my own clothes too badly cut up to be saved?" asked Kate, round a mouthful of food. "A shame if so, for they cost me a pretty penny."

The maid crossed to the tallboy standing against one wall and crouched. As she pulled open the bottom drawer, the scent of dried lavender filled the room. "Mistress Rebeccah asked me to mend and launder them." She pointed. "Your boots and sword are here too. Will cleaned them." She paused and looked uncomfortable. "We mislaid your tricorne. It must still be on the Heath."

"No matter. That was kind. Thank you." She sipped her chocolate without enthusiasm. She had never really acquired the taste for it—just as well considering how expensive it was.

Mary shifted her weight from one foot to the other. "I have duties to attend to. Is there anything else?"

Kate smiled and shook her head.

The maid left her to eat her breakfast in peace.

∅

It felt good to be wearing her own clothes, thought Kate, as she pulled on her hose and breeches and stamped into her boots. She felt far less . . . vulnerable.

She pondered whether to bind her breasts, then thought it would be good practice. At first her shoulder objected and made the going awkward, but she persevered and was tying the final knot in the strip of cotton when the door opened and Rebeccah entered.

The young woman let out a muffled apology, halted, and averted her gaze—but not before taking a good look at the half-dressed highwaywoman, Kate saw with a smile.

She pulled on her shirt and began buttoning it. "You may look now."

Rebeccah did, her cheeks slightly pink. "You should have waited for Mary to help you," she chided. "You will break open your wound."

"I have been in the habit of dressing myself since I was a child."

Kate reached for her waistcoat. The colour had faded—the result of much soap and scrubbing, she presumed—but Mary's stitches were almost as tiny as Kate's own, and the darned hole was only visible if you looked for it. "Nice," she murmured, slipping her arms through the armholes and buttoning it up.

"Are you planning to leave today?" asked Rebeccah, trying and failing to hide her dismay.

"What, and forego the pleasure of your company sooner than I must?" Kate shook her head and was charmed to see the other woman's frown disappear. "But go soon I must. For every day deprives you of your bed and risks your reputation."

And I am coming to realize that it is one thing to take advantage of an older, married woman such as Alice, wise in the ways of the world, but quite another to trifle with the affections of an innocent whose future depends on her unsullied good name.

Green eyes blinked at her and soft lips pursed. Kate turned away before the urge to take Rebeccah in her arms and kiss her got the better of her.

The clip-clop of hooves and the rumble of carriage wheels drew her over to the window, and she stared down. A coach and four had stopped outside the Dutton residence. The footman jumping down and running round to open the nearside carriage door seemed familiar. She chewed her lip as she tried to place him.

Rebeccah joined her by the window in a rustle of long skirts. "Oh!" Her hand flew to her breast. "It can't be!"

Kate's heart sank as she recognized the woman emerging from the carriage. The resemblance between her and the man in Rebeccah's pen-and-ink sketch was obvious. "Your sister has returned."

Rebeccah nodded.

"Then I must leave at once." Kate glanced to where her baldric and sword lay. It was fortunate indeed that she had got dressed.

The door opened and Mary rushed in. "Mistress Rebeccah," she called, then stopped as she saw her mistress standing by the window. "Your sister . . ."

"Is returned a day early. I know."

The maid glanced towards Kate. "We must get you away from here at once."

Kate reached for her coat, which like her waistcoat was slightly faded and bore signs of darning. She began to ease it over her wounded shoulder. "Wait!" cried Rebeccah. Kate threw her an enquiring look. "Dressed like that you will attract too much attention."

"Then what do you suggest? For your gowns," Kate's eyes tracked from the diminutive gentlewoman to her even shorter maid, "will not fit me."

Rebeccah frowned then her brow cleared. "Will is of a size with Kate, isn't he, Mary? Does he have a spare set of livery?"

The maid's eyes lit up. "A coat and wig should be enough, Madam. I will fetch them at once." As she darted out of the bedroom, Kate turned to Rebeccah for an explanation.

"People rarely look twice at anyone wearing livery. They will assume you are a servant, going about Dutton business."

Kate's look of frank admiration made Rebeccah flush.

When Mary returned a few moments later, Kate allowed herself to be helped into a blue coat that was slightly too large around the shoulders but otherwise a good fit. She tied back her own hair and let the maid cram the footman's wig on her head.

"How do I look?"

"It's not level." Rebeccah adjusted the wig and stood back. "Something's still not right, Mary."

Kate thought she knew what it might be. She darted into the dressing room, mixed some of the kohl from Rebeccah's toilette with face powder, and rubbed a little of the concoction into her upper lip, chin and cheeks to darken them.

"Better," agreed Rebeccah, when Kate emerged.

The tramp of footsteps on the stairs and the sound of servants' voices made Mary turn to her mistress. "You must greet your sister, Madam, or your presence will be missed."

"I know." Rebeccah threw Kate a stricken glance. "Oh, this is too bad! Had I foreseen your departure would be so soon and such a hasty one . . . And your wound barely healed."

"I will do well enough, Rebeccah," interrupted Kate. "Look to your own safety. For you must not be seen in my company."

"But . . ."

"Fare well." Kate bowed, and if it lacked her customary panache, perhaps she could ascribe it to her wound rather than to dismay. *I may never see her again.*

Whatever Rebeccah was about to say in reply was cut short by her maid's frantic, "Hurry, Madam."

She bit her lip and curtseyed—a gesture that touched Kate's heart—then started towards the door. She had gone barely a step before she paused and looked back. "See her safely to the back door, Mary." Her voice cracked.

"I will, Madam."

Downstairs, a woman's voice was calling, "Beccah. Where are you? Come and welcome your sister."

"And make sure no one sees her."

"They are waiting for you, Madam."

"Oh!" With a stamp of her foot, a last glance at Kate, and a muttered "God keep you safe," Rebeccah disappeared out the door. Moments later came an excited squeal and the sound of the two sisters greeting one another.

Mary crossed to the door and pressed her ear against it. "We will wait for them to retire to the drawing room," she said, "then I will take you down."

Kate tucked under her arm the bundle she had made of her coat, baldric and sword, and waited. At last Mary opened the door a crack, peered round it, and threw it wide.

"The coast is clear." She slipped through.

With a last wistful look at Rebeccah's room, Kate followed, placing her feet where Mary did to avoid the creaking stairs and pressing herself against the wall when the butler came into view then fortunately went about his business. The door to the drawing room was closed as they scurried past, or she would have tried to catch another glimpse of Rebeccah.

In the basement, Robert the coachman looked up from shining a harness, did a double take at Kate's appearance, winked at her and went back to his polishing. Mary led Kate to the back door, which opened into a yard.

Kate stood, one booted foot on the first of the stone steps that led up to the square, while Mary rattled off directions to the Mews and Clover's stall in a low voice.

"My thanks," she whispered. "I will send back Will's coat and wig as soon as I am able."

Mary looked round anxiously, then made a shooing gesture.

"Tell your Mistress," said Kate, knowing that she was breaking a cardinal rule, but unable to resist, "that I am greatly in her debt. And should she ever require my assistance, she can reach me at . . ." She whispered Alice's address in Mary's ear. "Have you got that?"

The maid blinked, owl-like, at her then nodded.

"Or if I am not there, leave word with Mr. Elborrow, the landlord of the Rose and Crown, and it will reach me."

Men's voices wafted from the door leading to the kitchen "Titus is coming," hissed Mary. "You must go. Now!"

So with a last reluctant glance at the house in St. James's Square, Kate did.

Chapter 12

Clover greeted her stall and the inhabitants of those on either side of it with a contented nicker. Kate grinned at the mare. Conditions at the Dutton stable in St. James's Mews had been good, but there was nothing like familiar surroundings and smells, she supposed.

"Glad to be back, eh, girl?" She patted the smooth black neck, but Clover tossed her head and pulled away. She was either still annoyed with her owner or impatient to be untacked. *Probably both*, thought Kate.

"Get away from that horse!" came a trembling voice.

She turned to find herself face to face with the lethal end of a pitchfork. "And a good morrow to you too, Tom." She arched an eyebrow.

The stableboy blinked at the highwaywoman, then flushed beetroot red. "Beg pardon, Madam. I didn't recognize you." He lowered the pitchfork.

"Took me for someone's manservant, did you?" She gestured at her borrowed wig and blue coat. He nodded. "As you were meant to." She winked.

His eyes lit up with curiosity but he knew better than to try to satisfy it. He licked his lips and said instead, "Shall I untack and feed her?"

Clover returned Kate's enquiring glance with a dark one of her own. "That would be a kindness, Tom. For she hasn't forgiven me for letting someone else ride her and I have no hankering to have my feet stamped on."

She felt in her pocket for a coin before remembering the coat wasn't hers. Her own was sadly crumpled when she withdrew it from her saddlebags—she hoped the worst of the creases would shake out. Rummaging in a pocket produced a half-a-crown and she flipped it to the waiting stableboy, who tucked it in the pocket of his dirty apron with a murmur of thanks.

He put down his pitchfork and set to work untacking Clover. As though to emphasize the personal nature of her grudge, the annoyed mare was as good as gold.

Kate sighed, slung her saddlebags over her left shoulder, then winced and slung them over her right shoulder instead. At the livery stable exit, she paused and turned.

"I likely won't be needing her again until tomorrow night," she called.

Tom looked up from placing Kate's saddle in the corner of Clover's stall and gave her a nod. "Very good, Madam."

⚹

Kate stopped at the top of the last flight of stairs to catch her breath and reflect on how out of condition she had become. As she gazed at the door to her landlady's rooms she felt a strong inclination to turn round and go back the way she had come. She squashed it, squared her shoulders, and reached for the door handle.

Alice was sitting down, which was just as well. When she saw the tall figure standing in her doorway, she swooned and slumped forward across the table and open account books.

"Alice!" Kate rushed forward, took a cold, limp hand between hers, and tried to chafe some warmth back into it. "'S Death! Are you unwell? Alice!"

But already, red-tinged eyelashes were fluttering open and colour was returning to cheeks so pale the freckles stood out in stark relief. A thankful Kate helped the other woman sit up.

"You're alive!" Relief filled Alice's eyes, and a smile curved her mouth. Her obvious delight at Kate's return made Kate feel ashamed, as did the dark shadows beneath Alice's eyes. "Won't you kiss me?"

Alice raised her face invitingly, and Kate obliged, though her kiss was clearly more perfunctory than the older woman would have liked. Kate straightened, pulled off the borrowed wig, which itched abominably, and scratched her scalp.

"Why are you dressed like a footman?" asked Alice, registering Kate's apparel.

"It's a long and convoluted tale and I will tell you about it later." She eased herself out of the blue coat and hung it over the back of a chair, aware that Alice was watching her every movement.

"And why are you favouring your left shoulder?"

For answer, Kate loosened her cravat and unbuttoned the top buttons of her shirt to reveal the bandage beneath.

"Oh!" Alice's hand flew to her mouth. "I *knew* something was wrong. Why else would you not return to me? Why else would you send no word?"

The landlady's words piled guilt on top of shame, and Kate concentrated on rebuttoning her shirt. "Fellow was handier with his pistol than he had a right to be," she joked.

"Who shot you? Josselin? A dragoon?"

"Neither." Kate grimaced. "A fellow tobyman, would you believe? Whoever said there is honour among thieves was talking poppycock."

"You're lucky he didn't kill you, Kate."

"I know."

"I keep telling you it's too dangerous." Alice stood up and began to pace. "But do you ever listen?"

"Alice—"

"Night after night dashing 'Blue-Eyed Nick'—" her tone was mocking "—must risk her life, and for what? Danger? Excitement? Some inner compulsion to get your neck stretched? And what about me, Kate? Stuck here, waiting, worrying about what might happen to you. Do you ever, for one second, spare a thought for what I must be going—?"

"Alice!"

The landlady stopped mid-sentence and looked at Kate.

"I'm sorry for causing you any distress. Truly. 'Twas wrong not to let you know sooner that I was well, though the truth of it is, I was incapable of doing so for several days. But what's done is done, and there is no point continuing in this fashion. Come now, we are friends, are we not? Let us not fall out over this."

"Friends!" Alice's mouth twisted.

A sudden wave of weariness washed over Kate. She pulled a chair towards her and slumped onto it.

"Kate?" She looked up to find a concerned Alice bending over her. "What is it?"

"I have tried to do too much today, that is all." She managed a reassuring smile. "A little rest and I will be my old self once more."

"Your wound . . ."

"Nearly finished me," admitted Kate. "But do not fret. I am over the worst, and fast recovering."

She stood and made her way through to the bedchamber. She sank onto the edge of the bed and made a half-hearted attempt to take off her boots. Alice had followed her through, and she tutted, turned her back towards Kate, straddled each leg in turn, and eased off the boots.

"Thank you." Kate stretched out on the bed and closed her eyes against the daylight coming through the sash window. But her hopes for peace and quiet were shattered as Alice began to cluck around her like a mother hen.

"Aren't you going to take off your shirt and breeches?"

"No."

"Would you like me to make you some broth? This weakness could merely be hunger."

"I'm not hungry."

"Perhaps your wound . . . How is your shoulder?"

Kate suppressed the urge to hide her head under a pillow. "It aches a little."

"I could change the bandage."

"That is unnecessary."

"You look flushed. Shall I get you a cold compress for your brow?"

"No."

"Then let me brush your hair. You might find it soothing."

Kate opened bleary eyes. "Just let me rest, Alice. I am tired to the bone."

The other woman looked affronted. "I was only trying to help."

"I know."

That response mollified Alice a little. "Very well." She pushed a stray strand of red hair behind one ear then pulled up a chair beside the bed and sat down. "I shall sit here, as quiet as a mouse, and keep you company while you sleep."

"Thank you."

Silence fell, but even that seemed pregnant with Alice's desire to be of service. Kate wondered if her landlady would be even more offended if she asked her to leave the bedchamber. Fortunately, before it could come to that, there was the sound of knocking from the other room.

"Who can that be?" wondered Alice crossly. Kate didn't open her eyes but she could hear the flounce in the other woman's step as she rose and went to investigate the caller at her front door.

An indistinct murmur of voices drifted through. Whatever the conversation concerned, it ended with Alice shouting, "Oh *very well*, Mr. Wilson. I'll see what I can do. But really, I do think you could have made some effort to sort it out yourself before coming whining to me."

Quick footsteps approached. "I have to go out, Kate," said Alice. "To fetch the night soil man. I'll be as quick as I can."

She kept her eyes closed. "Is it the cesspit again?"

"Ay."

The two cellar rooms were the cheapest lodgings available in the four-storey tenement building that Alice had inherited from her late husband. They also had the quickest turnover of tenants. The reason for both wasn't hard to find. The rooms lacked light, were damp and low-ceilinged, and when the cesspit in the back yard got too full (which happened whenever the night soil collection man fell behind schedule) were prone to invasion by turds. Evidently, the Wilsons had just learned of this last drawback firsthand. Kate pursed her lips. That probably explained the pungent whiff she had detected as she came up the stairs.

"Will you be all right without me?" asked Alice.

"Of course. Go."

"If you're sure."

"I am. Fetch the night soil man."

"Very well. Try to get some rest while I'm gone, my dear." And with a last solicitous murmur, Alice departed.

Kate waited until she heard the front door slam before uttering a fervent "Thank God!" Then with a blissful smile she settled down to sleep.

⚉

She woke to find that night had fallen. As the wisps of a very pleasant dream involving Mistress Rebeccah Dutton fled, she heard movement in the other room and realized it was Alice's return that had woken her.

A face peered round the door. "Are you awake?" Kate yawned and nodded. "How do you feel?"

She took a quick mental inventory. "Better. I told you all I needed was to rest."

"Thank heavens!" Alice entered, bringing a faint whiff of night soil with her. She crossed to the ewer sitting on the dresser, poured some water into the basin, and washed her hands.

"Did you solve the Wilsons' problem?" asked Kate, remembering.

The landlady nodded. "Of course the night soil man claimed it wasn't his fault. It never is." She shook her head but she was smiling as she turned and rested her gaze on Kate. She tossed aside the towel, and came and sat beside her on the bed. "It is so good to have you here." She took Kate's hand in hers and held it to her cheek. "You gave me such a fright."

"I know, and I'm sorry for it."

"Promise me you won't do it ever again."

Kate looked up at Alice, perplexed. "You know I cannot. Such things are beyond my control."

The landlady dropped Kate's hand. "You mean you won't." Her tone was sulky. "The truth is, you love robbing coaches more than you love me."

Kate sighed but said nothing. And when the reassurance she had angled for wasn't forthcoming, Alice's gaze became reproachful then a little resentful. But Kate was growing tired of the older woman's need for their relationship to be more than it was. Perhaps this increasing clinginess was because Alice too could sense that their time together was drawing to a close.

She longed to get it out in the open, to say, "Let's not ruin things now, Alice. Let's make the most of the time we have left," but feared it would only make matters worse.

Perhaps I should just get up right now, collect my belongings, and leave.

But it was dark outside, and she had nowhere else to stay, and Alice, her mood as volatile as ever, was removing her skirts and underthings in a playful, seductive manner, revealing the voluptuous body beneath.

As the other woman clambered into bed and began to unbutton Kate's shirt, Kate hesitated. Alice sensed it and paused. "Are you too tired still?" The hurt in her eyes was obvious, and Kate knew that, even though her heart wasn't in it, she couldn't refuse Alice's offer.

I may not be able to love her, God help me, but at least I can do this for her.

"Of course not." She smiled, finished the unbuttoning Alice had begun, eased her shirt off over the bandaged shoulder, and threw the garment to one side. "Help me strip off my breeches, will you?"

"Gladly," giggled Alice.

♫

"That house there," said Kate, pointing. "See?"

The urchin glanced at the elegant town house on the far side of St. James's Square. He scratched his nose then nodded.

"Good." She handed him the parcel containing the livery and wig, then a sixpence that disappeared into the pocket of his breeches as if by magic.

"Now?" He cocked his head in query.

"Now."

As he touched his greasy forelock and darted off to do as she had asked, she ducked behind a tree and watched his progress. He paused at the top of the steps leading into the Duttons' back yard, then disappeared down them. A few minutes later he was back, minus the parcel. He glanced over to where he had left Kate, then jammed his hands in his pockets and strode off, whistling.

Errand completed, Kate could have gone about her business, but the impulse to see Rebeccah one more time held her in place. She blinked as a figure appeared at the top of the Duttons' back steps—a dumpy middle-aged woman in maid's uniform.

Mary.

Rebeccah's maid scanned the square, her gaze pausing at Kate's tree before continuing. Either she couldn't see the highwaywoman hiding behind it, slouching to disguise her height, or Kate's skirts and the plain white cap pinned over her upswept hair had made her unrecognizable to someone who had only ever seen her in men's clothing. Whatever the reason, Mary shook her head and disappeared down the steps, and Kate let out her breath.

Minutes passed, and still Kate lingered. When a coach and pair turned into the square and pulled up in front of the Dutton residence, her hopes rose that she might at last catch a glimpse of the fair-haired young gentle-woman with the enchanting green eyes. But a plump, self-important-looking young man in clothes a size too small stepped down from the carriage and made his way to the front door. After doffing his tricorne and speaking to the footman, he was given admittance and the door closed behind him. Kate wondered who he was.

Her loitering was beginning to attract curious glances from passers-by, she realized. It was time to move on. Reluctantly, she left her hiding place and headed in the direction of Pall Mall, with the idea of taking a stroll in St. James's Park as she had no wish yet to return to Alice's house in Covent Garden and some gentle exercise after her recent illness would do her good.

The fact that she was a woman alone, and her attire was neither of the best quality nor the latest cut, drew disdainful glances from the fashion-able couples walking along the tree-lined avenue, but Kate ignored them, preoccupied as she was with her memories. For her time in the sickroom had been a surprisingly agreeable one, especially when she had Rebeccah all to herself.

But I must put her out of my mind, she chided herself. *For there is no future in this.* So saying, she stopped, drew in a breath, and made a deliberate effort to take in every aspect of her surroundings. As if the Fates themselves were mocking Kate and the resolution she had just made, along the avenue, heading straight for her, came a familiar figure in a blue mantua.

Rebeccah!

It was a moment before Kate could collect her wits, unfreeze her limbs, and seek cover. A red deer grazing behind the flowering shrub she had chosen shied and scampered away. Kate wondered if her expression was as startled as the deer's. Her heart was pounding as she peered between the branches, trying not to sneeze as pollen drifted up her nose.

Rebeccah had not seen her, of that she was sure. The young woman was deep in conversation with her companion, a handsome man of about Kate's age or a little older. From his expensive, well cut clothes and assured demeanour, he was one of the gentry.

The pang that shot through Kate surprised her with its intensity, and her lips curved in a rueful smile. *Just reward for the way I have treated Alice.* The gusting breeze blew the man's words to her straining ears as he passed the bush.

"But my dear Rebeccah," he was saying. *He must be an intimate acquaintance to address her so familiarly.* "Your happiness is my first concern. You may rest assured that I will do everything within my power to—" But he passed out of earshot then and left a frustrated Kate wondering whether to follow or not.

For I doubt I shall hear much to my liking. He is at least a close friend if not a suitor. And by her manner she is not averse to his attentions, Devil take him!

Then she cursed herself for her selfishness. For did she not want every happiness for Rebeccah? And was the young woman's companion not exactly the kind of fellow who might be best expected to provide it?

But as Kate turned, shoulders slumped, in the direction of the Park's exit and headed back towards Covent Garden, she couldn't help feeling aggrieved that Rebeccah had given her no inkling there was a suitor on the scene. *For did I not kiss her, and did she not act as though she enjoyed it? And have we not only saved one another's lives but also exchanged intimacies about our pasts?*

The realization that she was behaving in a manner every bit as sulky and clingy as Alice made Kate stop and laugh out loud, attracting the wary glance of a woman selling brightly coloured ribbons. Determined not to lose control of her emotions again, Kate took a calming breath, gave the hawker a reassuring smile, and resumed her walk.

Face it, you fool. We move in different circles, and our paths are unlikely ever to cross again. Rebeccah must get on with her life, as I must get on with mine.

Talking of which. Her purse was sadly empty; she must set about remedying that tonight. And tomorrow, well tomorrow would be a much more sombre affair. For she must go and see her good friend, John Stephenson, hang.

Chapter 13

"But surely you have an *idea* of the man you'd like to marry." Thomas Stanhope tucked Rebeccah's arm more firmly in the crook of his elbow. "All young women dream of their ideal suitor. Come now, don't deny it, for I know it is so. Caro has admitted as much." He grinned. "Fortunately, her daydreams centred themselves on me. Or so she claims."

Rebeccah rolled her eyes. "I thought matrimony would cure you two of all that billing and cooing, but you are worse than ever."

He chuckled. "If you mean by that that I am a fortunate man, I know that already."

Thomas's young wife was confined to her room with her monthly flowers, but she had insisted he keep their rendezvous with Rebeccah. Caroline had not forgotten her promise to her old school friend—she had instructed Thomas to find Rebeccah a husband from among his acquaintance. And he was taking the job seriously.

It was touching, really, how concerned he was to take Rebeccah's feelings into account—being so happily married himself, he wanted the same for her. But it was also slightly awkward. She could not tell him, after all, that her daydreams involved a certain blue-eyed highwaywoman.

"Paint me a picture of your ideal husband, Rebeccah."

"I fear I cannot."

"Young or old? Fat or thin? Tall or short?" His eyes danced. "You must have some partiality. I cannot imagine a gout-stricken old gentleman of four-and-eighty would suit, for example."

They waited for a coach and four to trundle past, then crossed the road and continued along the avenue. "Then you are wrong for he sounds perfect. He would not live long beyond our wedding day and I would be a merry widow."

"Tsk!" Thomas pretended to be shocked. "How can you expect me to find you someone," he resumed, his tone plaintive, "if you will not give me any indication of your requirements? You cannot surely be intending to marry someone you dislike? That would be insupportable."

"Is that not a woman's lot?" asked Rebeccah.

"Indeed not!"

"Oh, very well." She relented. "The person I see in my daydream—"

"Aha!"

Rebeccah ignored his triumphant exclamation. "—is a little older than me, but not by much. More experienced in the ways of the world . . . but not to the point of dissolution."

Thomas smirked. "Very wise."

"He is tall, has dark hair, high cheekbones, and the most striking pale blue eyes. He rides and shoots well . . . indeed he is an excellent marksman."

"This is beginning to sound like that highwayman of yours Caro is always going on about. What's the fellow's name?" Thomas snapped gloved fingers. "I have it, 'Blue-Eyed Nick.'" Rebeccah hoped she wasn't blushing. "I can see that he would be attractive to a young lady, but he is hardly a suitable match, my dear."

"I never said he was. But may I not be allowed to use him even as the *model* for my ideal husband?" she asked, with some asperity.

"I beg your pardon. You may indeed. Pray, continue." They had reached a bench, and he indicated that she might like to sit for a moment. She nodded and made herself comfortable. He sat next to her.

"Very well then. My ideal husband is gallant and dashing, brave and considerate, witty, good-natured and fond, and on occasion a rogue. I am always the centre of his attention—or at least he makes me feel so. He respects my person, my feelings and my property, and does not abuse them or take them for granted, even when they are considered his by law."

Thomas nodded. "You have not mentioned wealth or connections."

She considered the point then said deadpan, "A hovel would suffice, Thomas, for I will be unaware of my surroundings while in his company." He snorted, and she continued with a smile, "I do not require that we move in court circles, nor that we live in a mansion in a fashionable part of town, or even in the height of luxury. I ask only that our life together be a happy and comfortable one." She looked at him and raised an eyebrow. "Well?"

"A modest requirement indeed." He sighed. "And yet I fear that at present I can think of no one amongst my acquaintance who remotely fits this description. Now if you had said your prime requirements were laziness, an over-fondness for wine and gambling, and a tendency to selfishness and vanity, well then the choices would have been too many to list, but as it is . . ."

She put her hands on her hips. "You asked me to specify my ideal husband's attributes and I have done so."

"And see what good it has done me." He shook his head in mock chagrin then pulled out his timepiece and glanced at it. "But we should be getting back, my dear. For I want to see if Caro is feeling any better."

She smiled at this display of husbandly concern. "Of course."

They stood up and resumed their stroll, and Rebeccah let her friend's husband tuck her arm through his once more.

"If you were not already taken, Thomas," she said, "I think we would have suited. For we are friends and comfortable with one another, are we not? And that is a great deal more than many couples can say." He made her a mock bow, and two women passing raised their eyebrows and tittered. "You may tell Caro that you have done your duty, but that my requirements are impossible to fulfil. And then we can all resign ourselves to the idea of my becoming an Old Maid. Indeed the prospect no longer daunts me but rather is becoming more enticing by the day."

Thomas looked shocked at the very idea. "Do not give up hope yet. For someone as sweet and good-natured as you, there is a suitable husband out there, I am certain of it. It is just a matter of finding him."

Her, corrected Rebeccah sadly, but she managed a smile for her companion. *For I have already found and lost her, I fear.*

⚕

"May I take those, Madam?"

"Thank you, Mary." Rebeccah removed her wrap and gloves and handed them to her maid. "Whose coach and pair is that outside?"

Before her maid could answer, the swish of skirts, clatter of shoes descending the stairs, and murmur of voices announced her sister and mother.

"Did you enjoy your walk, Beccah?" asked a smiling Mrs. Dutton, reaching the bottom of the stairs and coming across the hall towards her youngest daughter.

"It was very pleasant—"

"Never mind that," interrupted Anne. "I have some news." From her flushed cheeks and glittering eyes that much was evident.

"Oh?"

"I have accepted Mr. Ingrum's offer of marriage."

"Is that all?"

Anne's eyebrows shot up. "What do you mean 'Is that all'?"

"Indeed, your response to your sister's news does leave something to be desired, Beccah," chided her mother.

Rebeccah flushed. "I beg your pardon, Anne. That was unpardonably rude of me. I wish you and Mr. Ingrum every future happiness."

"Thank you," said her sister, mollified.

"Have you set a date?"

"Not yet. He is discussing the matter with his parents. But it will be soon, I wager, for he seems eager."

And why should he not be eager, when he will be getting his hands on Papa's business and fortune? wondered Rebeccah. But she kept that thought to herself.

"May I ask," she said instead, "what made you opt for him rather than your other suitor? Before your stay in the country with Anne Locke I would have said you favoured Mr. Filmer slightly."

"True. But a lengthy conversation with Anne persuaded me otherwise."

Rebeccah could imagine the two friends huddled in a corner, heads close, gossiping about her sister's suitors, itemizing their every plus and minus, then totting up and comparing the grand totals. What had swung it in the end? The smart Bond Street townhouse Ingrum's parents had recently purchased and that would in due course come to him?

But several of the servants were lingering within earshot, among them Titus, whose normally handsome countenance was this morning marred by a frown like a thundercloud. She took her sister's elbow and said, voice lowered, "Should we not adjourn to the parlour where it is more private?"

For a moment Anne looked baffled then she glanced at the lurking servants, becoming visibly smug at the sight of the disgruntled footman. "Oh, I have no secrets from them." Her tone was dismissive.

It dawned on Rebeccah that Titus was annoyed about her sister's forthcoming marriage, and what's more that Anne was flattered by his reaction. From the start Rebeccah had feared that Anne's encouragement of the handsome young footman, who had taken to following her around like a devoted hound, would mislead him, and it looked like she was right. How cruel on Anne's part to raise Titus's hopes. And how foolish on his to entertain such ambitions. She pursed her lips in disapproval.

"Besides, the parlour is occupied," added her sister as an afterthought. "Oh?" Rebeccah turned to her mother, who nodded. "You have a visitor," said Mrs. Dutton, meaningfully. "Come all the way from Chatham."

"From Chatham?" Rebeccah's hand flew to her breast. "Oh, you cannot mean . . ." Her heart sank. "Is that Mr. Dunlop's carriage outside? But I gave him no encouragement, Mama, I swear. Surely he cannot—"

But the other women were nodding, and Anne's expression was almost gleeful as she said, "Just think of it, Beccah, we could have a double wedding. Me and Frederick, and you and . . . what is Mr. Dunlop's Christian name?"

"I think it may be Edmund," said Rebeccah faintly. "How long has he been waiting?"

"A quarter hour," said Mrs. Dutton. "So you had better see him without further delay, my dear."

"You know I cannot accept him."

"I know nothing of the kind." With a shooing motion, Mrs. Dutton urged her daughter towards the parlour. Rebeccah refused to budge, but her mother's hand in the small of her back propelled her forward.

"But I don't love him," she hissed. "And did I not tell you he wants a brood mare rather than a wife?"

"Bless me, are we back to that old song? A woman must learn to count herself lucky if her marriage brings her security and good company." Rebeccah's mother glanced at her, saw the stubborn set of her jaw, and sighed. "But I collect that you will do as you think fit, as always. Keep in mind, though, I beg you, that at three-and-twenty you are not getting any younger, Beccah, and another marriage proposal may not come your way."

That thought didn't depress her as it once might have. Of more concern was her mother's obvious worry at her gloomy prospects. "Mr. Stanhope has promised to look for someone suitable amongst his acquaintance, Mama," she offered by way of a sop. Then she felt duty bound to add, "Though he does not hold out much hope of success."

"Mr. Dunlop is still waiting," reminded Anne.

With a tart "Thank you, I am well aware of that," Rebeccah took a deep breath, squared her shoulders, and reached for the handle to the parlour door.

"Mr. Dunlop. What a pleasant surprise," lied Rebeccah, as the young man with the fleshy jowls put down his sherry glass and rose from the sofa.

"I hope it is." His smile was jovial. "I sincerely hope it is." She blinked at him in puzzlement. "Pleasant, I mean."

"Ah." She found it difficult not to stare at his waistcoat, which was strained so tightly across his ample stomach she expected at any moment to hear the ping of buttons. "I am sorry to have kept you waiting. But I see that you have had some refreshment. Please." She took an easy chair opposite the sofa and gestured for him to resume his seat. "How may I help you, Mr. Dunlop?"

Her heart was thumping so hard she felt dizzy. Her Chatham suitor didn't look any more comfortable. Sweat beaded his temples and he eased a forefinger round the inside of his cravat. For a moment he was silent, then he cleared his throat and began.

"I won't beat about the bush, Rebeccah. I may call you that, may I not?" He gave her no time to demur. "I much enjoyed our talks in Chatham, and I fancy you felt the same." Rebeccah suppressed a snort. "Which leads me to believe that you and I would rub along together tolerably well." Dunlop's smile broadened. "So I have come to ask for your hand in marriage." When the expected response didn't come, his smile dimmed, then vanished.

Rebeccah looked down at her lap, examining a suddenly fascinating fingernail while she considered how best to answer him. Should she tell him he had totally mistaken her feelings, that he was in fact the most boring man alive? But she had too much consideration. The silence stretched.

"Well?" Dunlop sounded indignant. She looked up and saw that his expression matched his tone; he had gone quite red-faced—it didn't suit him. "May I not have your answer?"

"Mr. Dunlop, I hope you will believe me when I tell you I am aware of the very great honour you have done me in asking for my hand."

"Harrumph!" But her compliment seemed to lessen his irritation a little. "And?"

"But I must regretfully decline."

"What the devil?" If intemperate language in front of a lady weren't sufficient evidence of his inner turmoil, his getting up and pacing was. "I was invited in, given to understand by your mother . . ." He stopped pacing and stared at her. "Was I got here under false pretences? It won't wash, Madam. It won't wash."

"*Got here?*" Rebeccah suppressed an indignant retort and instead crossed her fingers. She could be excused a lie if she was trying to spare his feelings, couldn't she? "The truth is, Mr. Dunlop, my mother was not in possession of all the facts."

His gaze sharpened. "And what facts are those, pray?"

"That my feelings are already engaged elsewhere."

"Was this the case when we met at Chatham?"

"No, sir. Indeed we came to our agreement only this morning, while I was walking in the Park." She hoped her cheeks weren't as red as they felt. "It is unfortunate we had no notion of your intention to come today, Mr. Dunlop. For if we had we should certainly have dissuaded you."

"Good God!" He tugged his waistcoat straight, and a button pinged into the fireplace. Rebeccah bit the inside of her cheek to keep from bursting into hysterics. "Do you mean to tell me that I have travelled all this way, risking hours of discomfort, highwaymen and Lord knows what else, and *this* is to be my answer?"

"I fear so. I can only apologize once more for the gross inconvenience you have suffered."

"Well, 'tis of no matter." He sniffed. "There are plenty of other sensible young women," he eyed her meaningfully, "who will be only too eager to become Mistress Dunlop."

"I'm certain of it." She stood up to ring the bell for a footman, but Dunlop pre-empted her by crossing towards the door, evidently eager to put as much distance between himself and this ungrateful family as he could. It opened, revealing a flustered-looking Anne and Mrs. Dutton, who both pretended to have been passing by the parlour at that very moment.

"Oh, are you about to leave us, Mr. Dunlop?" Mrs. Dutton feigned surprise. She didn't ask him how his interview had gone—if she hadn't already heard everything through the door, one look at his face must have told her.

"Indeed I am, Madam. Good day to you."

He accepted his tricorne, gloves, and cane, which the senior footman had hurriedly retrieved, and strode out the house towards his waiting carriage.

"Well I never!" exclaimed Anne, as the front door blocked their departing visitor from sight. "He looked as though he'd like to horsewhip the lot of us." She turned to her sister. "I take it there is to be no double wedding?"

"No." Rebeccah sighed. "Just as well. For a man as blind as he is to a woman's true feelings could not make *anyone* a good husband."

∅

"Mistress Rebeccah?" called Mary, hurrying up the stairs after her.

Rebeccah paused while her mother and sister went on ahead to the drawing room on the first floor. "What is it?"

The maid checked to see they weren't overheard before lowering her voice. "While you were out walking, a parcel came."

Rebeccah blinked. "A parcel?"

"Yes, Madam. Containing Will's coat and wig." She held Rebeccah's gaze.

The implications made her pulse quicken. "Oh! Was she here?" Both women knew who she meant.

"A boy delivered it, Madam. Said he'd been paid to. I took a quick look round the Square, to see if there were any . . . loiterers. None that I could see." Rebeccah's disappointment must have shown in her face. "Just as well," consoled her maid at once. "With the thieftaker due to make his report to your sister this afternoon . . ." She trailed off.

It would be too dangerous. "Indeed. Was there a note? In the parcel, I mean?"

"No, Madam."

She bit her lip in frustration. "What? Nothing? No mention of how her wound is?"

Mary smiled and pressed Rebeccah's hand. "Don't fret about that, Madam. I know my wounds, and that one was healing well. She'll be right as rain in no time. You mark my words."

She sighed and felt an overwhelming longing to see the highwaywoman again, if only for a moment. "I hope so, Mary."

"Beccah, where are you?" came Anne's voice from upstairs.

"Oh pish! I must go." She paused and turned back. "You will let me know if you should hear any more from her?" she whispered.

Mary nodded. "Of course, Madam. At once."

Chapter 14

It was one o'clock when Kate set off for Tyburn. If she was honest, it was a relief to be able to leave her rooms at last. All morning Alice had indicated her disapproval of Kate's intentions with her constant black looks, silences, and flounces. And all morning the church bells of London had rung, muffled as befit the occasion, announcing that a "collar day" was in the offing.

As she made her way north through the bustling rookeries of St Giles, then turned west towards the Oxford road, she wondered how John Stephenson was faring. Would he choose to wear his Sunday Best as many of those condemned to die did?

Kate had known her fellow highwayman since she was seventeen. After her escape from Newgate, she had let Fortune's tide sweep her where it would, before ending up at a shabby coaching inn on the outskirts of London. There, to her surprise she found herself very much at home. The footpads and highwaymen who frequented the Old Magpie had been wary of her at first, but soon became friends. Among them was Stephenson, who knew a fast horse she could hire cheap, and who first coined the name Blue-Eyed Nick.

Stephenson had taught Kate everything he knew about the rattling lay: how to assess a likely cully by his clothes and the weight of his luggage (the Old Magpie's yard was always abustle with coaches and passengers); which routes certain drivers preferred; and the perfect ambush sites. He had even asked her to go into partnership with him. But after Wildey, she found it difficult to trust anyone, and so declined.

And now, she would have to watch her friend die.

That she could do nothing to help Stephenson escape his fate on the Triple Tree was galling. She hadn't even dared visit him in Newgate for fear of discovery—Samuel Josselin was sure to have set someone to scrutinize all the condemned highwayman's visitors. Stephenson wouldn't hold her absence against her, Kate knew, but still . . . It had made her even more determined to offer him moral support as he went to meet his Maker, which infuriated the red-haired landlady.

"How can you? He'll be waiting for you there."

"Ay. But if I wear skirts, Alice, the chances are good Josselin won't recognize me."

"You cannot be sure of that."

"Nothing in life is certain. But Stephenson is my friend, and I owe it to him to witness his end. You will not dissuade me, Alice, and there's an end to it."

Kate hitched up her skirts and stepped over a pile of horse dung. The man crowding her heels let out a curse and halted to scrape the mess off his shoes.

Ten minutes' brisk walking brought her to the Oxford road and she turned west onto it and started forcing her way through the people lining the route along which the hanging procession would come. Some were standing on carts or barrels brought specially for the purpose. Some hung out of the windows of the houses on either side of the road. The balconies were mostly full, Kate saw, peering up at them, and some sightseers were even climbing out onto the rooftops in search of a better view. There was a carnival air to the proceedings. The shouts and laughter of families bent on a good day out combined with that of the hawkers crying their pamphlets, rotten fruit, flowers, and gin. Kate grimaced at the racket and increased her pace.

Paper crunched under her shoe and she glanced down and saw it was one of the pamphlets the hawkers were selling. She picked it up, smoothed it, and squinted at the crabbed print, made even more illegible by the smudged impression of someone's boot heel.

"A full and true account of the discovery and apprehending of the notorious highwayman, Jack Stephenson, as told to the Ordinary of Newgate," she read.

Prison chaplains were known for embroidering prisoners' last words, sometimes even fabricating their story entirely—the more blood-curdling the tale, the better it sold. Sure enough, as she scanned the account, she saw that not only had her fellow highwayman apparently committed some of the robberies that should be laid at *her* door, the thieftaker's part in his capture had been inflated—after all, it was sheer fortune that had led to Stephenson's capture at the Rose and Crown. *And if Josselin hadn't been looking for me in the first place . . .*

"Devil take him!"

She crumpled the pamphlet into a ball and hurled it into the gutter. A roar from the crowd a hundred yards back down the road announced the arrival of the hanging procession. *I'd better hurry.*

"What d'ye lack, what d'ye lack?" sang out a bent old woman selling flowers.

Nothing you've got. Kate brushed past her, evaded a red-cheeked pedlar whose coat was lined with laces and coloured ribbons, eased past the stall of a plump ginger-cake seller, then sidestepped a family bent on enjoying the hanging fair. The sullen oldest boy was clutching an armful of rotten vegetables; his squint-eyed father had brought along a dead cat. At least such missiles would be softer than the cobblestones some onlookers had levered up. Fortunately, Stephenson should be safe from the crowd's fury—there was nothing the mob liked better than a glamorous highwayman.

Up ahead, she spied the fearsome silhouette that was her goal. Some called the massive triangular wooden gallows the Triple Tree and others the three-legged mare. Many of the sightseers gathered around it had arrived early to be sure of their place and had been drinking steadily—the gin hawkers were doing a roaring trade. Scuffles and brawls were inevitable as those the worse for drink jostled for the best places. Kate dodged a flying bottle, stumbled into a barrow, and nearly sent the man standing on it flying, then elbowed her way towards the gallows.

The jeers and catcalls were growing louder as the hanging procession drew closer. Kate found a suitable vantage point by a wall, from where she could see the scaffold and the horse-drawn cart waiting beneath it, but be reasonably hidden from view herself. With a growl and a forbidding glare she evicted its current occupant, then settled back to wait.

◊

Though the City Marshal dismounting from his horse and the Under-Sheriff accompanying him were magnificent in their uniforms, Kate had eyes only for the two carts that had halted a few yards behind them. Flanking them on all sides were peace officers, constables, and javelin men, trying to hold back the rabble with their staves.

Kate shaded her eyes and peered at the first cart. Four coffins were stacked at one end; at the other stood the Ordinary and four prisoners: a hard-eyed harlot, her face freshly rouged; a weeping boy who could be no more than twelve; a rat-faced little pickpocket who Kate had seen several times at the Rose and Crown; and John Stephenson.

Her fellow highwayman looked dashing in a new tricorne, his boots polished and his coat, waistcoat, and breeches freshly laundered. He smiled and nodded at the crowd, who began to cheer and chant his name. After a moment, his gaze found Kate's. His eyes flicked to one side, then moved on. She puzzled over that then followed the direction he had indicated. The stocky figure of Samuel Josselin was standing with a group of peace officers, his arms folded, his small eyes alert.

Devil take him! She looked away.

"Let them hang," chanted the impatient crowd, as the prisoners from both carts were transferred to the wide cart beneath the gallows and urged by the Ordinary to say one last prayer and a psalm. Then the cordon of constables parted, and the relatives were let through, to scramble up and say their farewells. The buxom young woman Stephenson had been bedding for the last two years was among their number. Moll's face was blotchy from crying, and she hugged her highwayman lover fiercely.

Kate couldn't bear to watch their embrace or the reunion of the weeping boy with his tearful mother and silent father. She looked away, and when she looked back, Moll and the other relatives were being herded back into the crowd.

The hangman began to hood the seven prisoners. While Stephenson waited his turn, he glanced at Kate again. She tried to will strength into him for the ordeal ahead and mouthed, "Fare well, old friend." He nodded, then his eyes sought the weeping Moll once more, until the white sack covered his head.

As the black-masked hangman checked each prisoner's halter before tying it round the huge beam above, Kate could almost feel a rope resting around her own neck. A hawker came within earshot, and she called him over, bought a jug of ale and took a swig to ease her dry throat. The crowd hushed, every breath held in anticipation. Then the hangman whipped the horse, and the wide cart surged forward, and to a collective cheer, seven halters snapped taut.

Kate balled her fists and stared at the dangling figures now writhing like marionettes from the massive beam. The constables stood back and the hangers-on lunged forward, trying to hasten their loved one's end by clinging onto their legs or banging their chests.

Moll was trying to do the same service for Stephenson, but it clearly wasn't enough. Kate didn't even think about it. She fought her way to the front, shoving aside anyone too slow to get out of her way. When she added her weight to Moll's, the girl looked round in surprise then nodded her thanks. But even with Kate's help, Stephenson's limbs continued to jerk.

"Christ's wounds, he's strangling! What shall we do?" cried Moll.

Kate thought quickly. "Lift him," she ordered. "I'll count to three, then you give one sharp tug. Understand?" The girl nodded.

Kate took a firmer grip on her friend's legs and heaved him up. "One," she said through gritted teeth, for Stephenson was not a lightweight. "Two . . ."

On "three" both women gave a tremendous tug. Kate couldn't hear the snap of Stephenson's neck, but she felt it. Then something warm and wet soaked his breeches and his legs stopped jerking.

She closed her eyes and murmured a brief prayer. "God speed, my friend." When she opened them again, she found Samuel Josselin staring straight at her.

Though fifty feet separated her from the thieftaker, Kate's heart pounded. *Perhaps it's a coincidence.* She dropped her gaze, hunched her shoulders to make herself appear shorter, then peeked at him again. He was still staring at her, but now his forehead was deeply furrowed.

Hellfire and damnation!

Kate grabbed the weeping Moll to get her attention. "I have to go." But even as she sought the cover of the crowd, Josselin was signalling his men to follow her.

Chapter 15

The clock on the landing struck six o'clock.

"I cannot apologize for my daughter enough, Mr. Ingrum." Mrs. Dutton's voice floated up from the hall. "It is very unlike her to miss an appointment."

"Indeed it bodes ill for our future," came the answering growl. "Please tell her I called and was disturbed to find her not at home as arranged."

"You can be assured I will, sir."

"Thank you. Good night, Madam."

"Good night to you, sir."

At the sound of the front door closing, Rebeccah left the second floor landing, where she was eavesdropping, and made her way back to Anne's bedchamber. Where in heaven's name was her sister? Anne had made no mention of going out, and indeed her favourite walking dress and shoes were still in her dressing room.

A shadow loomed and she turned to find her mother, still a little out of breath from climbing two flights of stairs, standing in the doorway. "He was not pleased," she said, entering.

"So I heard."

As Rebeccah had done before her, Mrs. Dutton surveyed Anne's room, her gaze troubled. "Are you *sure* you have no idea where she has gone, Beccah? Anne would not upbraid you for revealing her secret if she knew how worried I am."

Rebeccah threw her an exasperated glance. "Mama, as I have already told you half a dozen times, I have not the least idea." She chewed the inside of her lip. "Perhaps Nancy . . ."

Her mother's brow cleared. She crossed to the bell pull and tugged it. But it was a breathless Will rather than Anne's maid who appeared a few minutes later.

Of course, remembered Rebeccah. *It's washday and all the female servants are up to their elbows in soap suds.*

"Yes, Madam?"

"Will you fetch Nancy, please?"

While the footman hurried off to do her mother's bidding, Rebeccah prowled round the bedchamber and the adjacent dressing room once more, looking for clues to her sister's current whereabouts and feeling a growing sense of disquiet. Anne's velvet slippers were missing, which meant she must still be wearing them. And a drawer in the tallboy was half open. She knelt, pulled it fully open, and began to riffle through the neatly folded garments.

A sound of puffing and panting drew nearer, then a skinny young woman in an apron, her mousy hair coming adrift, hands red and chapped from much scrubbing, came into view.

She curtseyed and took a moment to catch her breath before saying, "You sent for me, Madam?"

"Yes, Nancy," said Mrs. Dutton. "Do you know where my daughter is?"

The maid's gaze slid to where Rebeccah was kneeling by the tallboy. "Um, isn't she there, Madam?"

Mrs. Dutton rolled her eyes. "I am referring to Anne."

Nancy flushed. "Beg pardon, Madam . . . In that case, no, Madam."

"When did you last see her?"

"At dinner, Madam," answered Nancy promptly. "She said she knew I would be busy helping out with washday, but that was all right because she would have no further need of me until nearer to her appointment with Mr. Ingrum. And then I was to come to help dress her and pin up her hair."

Rebeccah got to her feet. "And did you?"

Nancy looked at her. "Um, no, Mistress Rebeccah. Truth to tell, I got so caught up in all the scrubbing and rinsing, I lost track of the time . . . I knew Mistress Anne could send Will for me, you see," she added. Her brows drew together. "But she never did."

She gestured at their surroundings. "Do you see anything odd about this room, Nancy?"

The maid cocked her head to one side. "In what way, Mistress Rebeccah?"

She pointed at the open drawer. "If I don't miss my guess, there is a garment missing from that drawer. Do you know what it was?"

Nancy crossed to the drawer, knelt, and as Rebeccah had done moments before began to go through its now not-so-neatly folded contents. After a moment, she looked up.

"Her newest nightgown is missing."

Rebeccah's heart sank. "Nightgown," she repeated. "Are you certain?" Nancy nodded and got to her feet. "Is anything else missing?" Thoughts dark, she watched the maid inspect the adjacent dressing room.

"Her hairbrush," said Nancy at last. "And her slippers." She turned an expectant look on Rebeccah.

"My dear." Mrs. Dutton's voice was anxious. "What are you thinking?"

"That her departure was a hasty one," said Rebeccah. "For she is still wearing the clothes she wore at dinner. And that—" her voice cracked "—she planned to be away overnight, for she has taken her nightgown and hairbrush with her."

Her mother looked horrified. "Surely you are not suggesting an elopement!"

"It bears the hallmarks of something of the sort, Mama."

"But Mr. Ingrum . . ."

"Is not so accomplished an actor," mused Rebeccah. "No, I do not think it is Mr. Ingrum she has eloped with."

"Mr. Filmer then? Or another suitor? Nancy?" Mrs. Dutton confronted the maid, who would surely be the first to know if such were the case. But Nancy shook her head, and her consternation looked genuine.

"The mistress had her sights set on Mr. Ingrum, Madam. Weren't no other suitor." Her certainty was cast iron.

Rebeccah considered what she knew of her sister and the scant clues she had unearthed so far. "I am of the same mind. Which means," she continued heavily, "that her absence may not be a voluntary one."

"What?" At this, her mother turned so pale that Nancy took her by the elbow and helped her to a high-backed cane chair. "What can you mean, Beccah?"

"What I said." She turned to the maid. "Nancy, did any of the servants see my sister leaving the house? And if so, was anyone with her?"

"Not that I know of, Mistress Rebeccah. But then, we've been run off our feet with washday. And as if that weren't enough, some of the male servants went to see the hanging, so we've been short handed. What with that and Titus coming back drunk . . ." She trailed off, obviously chagrined at revealing this last snippet.

"Titus?" Rebeccah's ears pricked up at his name.

The skinny maid sighed. "I'm not normally one to go telling tales out of school, Mistress Rebeccah, but the past couple of days he's been like a bear with a sore head. Coming back drunk from Tyburn was the last straw as far as Mr. Danby was concerned."

"The butler disciplined him?"

"Ay. Told him to pull himself together sharpish or he could find himself a position elsewhere."

"George said that?" said Mrs. Dutton faintly.

Anne and Titus! Rebeccah didn't like the picture these puzzle pieces were forming. "And have you seen Titus since, Nancy?"

"No, Mistress Rebeccah."

Anne wouldn't willingly elope with her footman, would she? Which meant he must have coerced her somehow. But what about the slippers— her sister could not walk far in those. Perhaps he had hired a sedan chair to convey her. "Thank you, Nancy. That will be all. Please don't mention this conversation to the others."

The maid glanced at Mrs. Dutton, who nodded confirmation. "Very good, Madam." She curtseyed and left the room. Only when the receding footsteps on the stairs had faded did Rebeccah resume the conversation.

"Titus has her," she said flatly. "There is no other explanation."

"Bless me!" Her mother looked ill at the thought. "Is that what you really think has occurred?"

Rebeccah nodded. "An unlicensed marriage would transfer Anne's fortune to her husband, would it not?"

"He would force her to marry him?"

"Yes. In revenge for the humiliation and pain she has visited on him in recent weeks."

"What humiliation?"

"How can you not have noticed, Mama? At every turn, Anne treated Titus as her favourite, encouraged him to dote on her . . . Then, as if his feelings for her were of no account, she blithely announced she was to marry Mr. Ingrum."

"Even so." Mrs. Dutton wrung her hands. "We cannot let this happen, Beccah. We must tell the constables."

Rebeccah bit a fingernail. "And have it bandied about that Anne and her own footman . . . Mama, we cannot. Her reputation will be ruined, if it isn't already. Besides, what good will the constables do? By the time they run him to earth, a crooked clergyman will already have performed the ceremony and Titus will have . . ." She couldn't bring herself to finish the sentence.

"Consummated their wedding to make it legally binding," murmured her mother.

"Yes." Rebeccah began to pace. "We must act quickly if we are to save her." *It may already be too late.* "Oh, if only there were someone who knew where Titus might take Anne, or where clandestine marriages are enacted."

She stopped, remembering a pair of pale blue eyes and an offer of help should she ever need it. The address Kate had left with Mary had been somewhere in Covent Garden, hadn't it? Not a very salubrious area, especially at this time of night, but "needs must."

Rebeccah became aware her mother was looking at her in bewilderment and gave her a reassuring smile. "I know someone who can help us." She strode to the bell pull and tugged it.

"Oh? Who?"

"Blue-Eyed Nick."

Shock brought her mother to her feet. "The highwayman? Have you lost your wits, Beccah?"

"No, Mama, I think I may have found them."

A little while later a panting Will appeared in the doorway. "Tell Robert to bring the carriage round from the Mews at once," said Rebeccah. "And tell Mary that I will need her to accompany me."

"Very good, Madam."

"But where are you going?" asked her mother.

"To Covent Garden, of course."

ॐ

Rebeccah gave the peeling tenement a dubious glance then turned to her maid. "Are you certain this is the correct address?"

Mary nodded. "Ay, Madam. You're to ask for the landlady, Alice Cole."

"Very well." Rebeccah reached for the door handle, which turned as the coachman anticipated her need. "Thank you, Robert." She let him help her down from the carriage, watched by two wide-eyed children playing on the pavement—a smart coach and four must be a rarity in these parts. Mary made to follow, but Rebeccah held up a gloved hand. "No, Mary. Please wait for me."

"But—"

"I am sure I shall be quite safe." She smiled up at her indignant maid.

Muttering darkly, Mary sat back down. Robert closed the carriage door with a click and gave Rebeccah an enquiring glance. She shook her head.

While he went to settle the restless horses, she lifted her skirts and took the two steps up to the tenement's front door, which was slightly ajar. She pushed it open with a ginger forefinger, stepped into the gloom, then wrinkled her nose at the faint aroma of night soil.

A flight of stairs on the left beckoned. She grasped the wobbly banister and began to climb. It wasn't long before her gloves, clean on today, were as grubby as the children's faces had been.

Several doors opened off the first landing, but there was no indication who lived there. She was wondering whether to knock on each in turn when the nearest one opened, and a grey-haired old woman with a basket of washing on her hip came out, pulling the door closed behind her.

"Excuse me," said Rebeccah.

The woman paused. "Eh?" Rheumy eyes raked Rebeccah from head to toe and an eyebrow arched. "Bit out of your way, ain't you, dearie?"

"Can you tell me where I may find the landlady, Alice Cole?"

"Alice Red, more like." The woman cackled at her joke and shifted the basket to the other hip. "Not the next landing up but the one after that."

"Thank you." Rebeccah continued up the stairs.

This must be it.

There was only one door on this landing—the others had been boarded up—and the main stairs ended, becoming a steep flight of narrow steps leading up to the roof. Rebeccah took a moment to catch her breath, then rapped her knuckles on the door. She was just beginning to think there was no one home, when she heard the faint thump of footsteps and the door creaked open.

A middle-aged woman with a sulky expression and tousled red hair eyed her. "If it's lodgings you're after," she said, "we're full up. Come back in a fortnight."

"Wait!"

The closing door paused. "Well?"

"I don't want lodgings. I'm looking for Kate. Is she in?"

The landlady's gaze sharpened. "Who told you Kate lives here?"

"She did."

The woman folded her arms. "Did she now? And what does she look like."

Rebeccah blinked at this odd question. "Very tall. Raven black hair. Striking blue eyes. Please. There's no time to waste. Is she here or not? I need her help."

"She's out." The tone was one of grim satisfaction.

Rebeccah bit her lip. "When will she be back?"

"Couldn't say, I'm sure."

"Then may I come in and wait for her?"

"No."

The unreasonable refusal made Rebeccah blink. "But surely . . . I wouldn't be any trouble."

"So you say. But I don't know you from Adam." The door started to close once more.

Panic overtook Rebeccah as she saw her only means of helping Anne beginning to disappear. "No, wait. Please. Will you give her a message?" Surely even this unpleasant woman couldn't refuse to do that.

Alice Cole pursed her lips, then said grudgingly, "I suppose so."

"Oh, thank you, thank you. You don't know what this means to . . . Do you have a pencil and paper?"

"Sorry."

Rebeccah resisted an urge to shake Kate's landlady by the scruff of her neck. "Then will you tell her the following: Rebeccah Dutton needs her help, and there is no time to waste." The other woman's expression was unfathomable. "Have you got that?"

Alice Cole nodded.

But what if she forgets my name? What if. . .? "And please give Kate this." Rebeccah pulled off her glove, then tugged off the garnet signet ring that had been her father's. She held it out, and after a moment the other woman accepted it.

"No time to waste," repeated Rebeccah, at a loss as to what else to do.

"I heard you the first time," said the landlady. And this time, she did close the door.

Resisting the unladylike urge to swear, Rebeccah turned and stamped back down the stairs. What on earth did Kate see in that woman?

As she emerged onto the street, the children, who at their age should surely have been in bed, looked up from their battered spinning top. Robert jumped down and rushed to open the carriage door for her.

"Thank you." She let him help her up.

Mary's face fell when she saw her mistress was alone. "Wasn't she there, Madam?"

"No," said Rebeccah shortly. She banged on the carriage roof and called, "Home, Robert."

"Very good, Madam," came his muffled reply, and seconds later the coach lurched forward.

Inside the carriage, silence fell. Eventually a tentative Mary asked, "If she wasn't there, Madam, then may I ask what—"

"I left a message for her."

"Ah." Mary sat back in her seat. "For your sister's sake, let's hope she receives it in time."

Chapter 16

"What kept you so late?"

Kate looked at the bed. Alice, who had been sleeping when she tiptoed in, now lay propped up on one elbow. "Sorry. I didn't mean to wake you. And don't you mean early? For it is two in the morning." She threw her sopping skirts to one side. "I ran into that whoreson, Josselin." The expected comment didn't come, so she threw the widowed landlady a wry glance. "You may say 'I told you so.'"

Alice merely looked at her. "He recognized you?"

Kate nodded. "These damned blue eyes, I think." She removed shoes that would never be the same again and peeled off torn stockings. Her garters were nowhere to be found. "Took me a while to shake his men off." She removed her cap and let down her hair.

The chase back from Tyburn had exhausted her. Not wanting to lead her pursuers back to Alice's house, she had taken a roundabout route, along rubbish-strewn back streets and once even through a crowded snug bar. Under arches and over rooftops she ran, evading lecherous drunks and cursing harlots. With every step she wished she were in breeches and on horseback instead of wearing flapping skirts that sopped up puddles like a sponge and shoes that were a danger to her ankles.

In a Soho alleyway, two of Kate's pursuers trapped her, their staves coming close to braining her. But the commotion outside his premises attracted the attention of a Huguenot silk weaver working late. His "*Qui est la?*" changed to "Oof!" as Kate scrambled through the sash window he had opened and made her escape out the back way.

At Charing Cross, one of Josselin's men grappled with her, and they rolled to and fro on the pavement, until something hard in her back proved to be an empty gin bottle which made a useful cosh. She untangled herself from her limp assailant, staggered to her feet, then took off running once more. Another of her pursuers sought to come to grips on the banks of the Thames, but she toppled him head first into its stinking waters and didn't linger to see if he came up again. Not long after, she managed to give the last of her pursuers the slip, and turned her limping steps towards Covent Garden.

Kate poured cold water into the basin and began to soap away the dirt and sweat.

"So now Josselin knows you in skirts too," said Alice.

"Ay." She winced as the soap found every scratch and burst blister. "Perhaps it would pay me to leave London for a while." She yawned.

"Perhaps."

She towelled her feet dry, then snuffed out the candle and crossed to the bed. The feel of cool sheets against bare skin as she slid in beside Alice was wonderful, and she groaned with relief. The other woman looked at her, opened her mouth, then closed it again.

"What?" Kate arched an eyebrow—the only body part she had the energy to move.

"Nothing," said Alice. "You look exhausted."

"I could sleep for a week." She closed her eyes.

✂

In the event though, Kate was too wound up to manage more than a couple of hours of fitful sleep. She kept waking in a sweat from dreams in which she was a fox, her attempts to escape the dogs baying at her heels constantly thwarted by the huntsman's bugle. The fourth time she woke, her pounding heart slowing as she took in familiar surroundings, the sparrows were chirping in the eaves, so she gave up and simply lay, resting and thinking about alternatives.

Could she bear to be away from London, even for a week? Her friends and dependants were here, and so was her livelihood. *But who will look after Mama and Ned's family if you are in jail, eh?* And then there was Rebeccah. *How long before she marries her suitor and forgets all about you?*

That thought depressed her, and she pushed it away and rolled over. A chink in the calico curtains had allowed through a stray sunbeam, and on Alice's bedside table something was glittering a deep, rich red. Careful not to wake the snoring woman, Kate reached for it.

The object in her palm was a garnet signet ring, carved with the initials

JD. Kate could not have been more amazed if Queen Anne herself had burst into her bedchamber and told her that Kate was the rightful Queen of England. What was Rebeccah's ring doing *here*, of all places?

Anger replaced shock, and she turned and shook Alice none too gently. "Wake up." The snores stopped and dazed grey eyes looked at her. "Where in blazes did you get this?"

Kate thrust the ring into the landlady's face, and Alice's eyes crossed as she tried to focus on it, then widened. Her cheeks pinked. For Kate that was evidence enough.

"Rebeccah Dutton was here, wasn't she? She came to see me and you kept it from me."

Alice pushed away Kate's hand and sat up. "I was going to tell you about it last night." Her tone was petulant. "But you were exhausted."

"When did she come? What did she want?"

"Give me a moment, will you?" Alice rubbed the sleep from her eyes. "It was early evening. I forget exactly when. She didn't say much, only that she needed your help, and that there was no time to waste." Kate's expression made her add quickly, "But I set no store by that. These gentlefolk with their airs and graces. *Everything* is urgent with them, and if they can't have it this minute it's the end of the world."

Kate threw back the bedclothes and got out. "Devil take it, Alice!" She drew back the curtain to let in the light. "How could you not tell me of this last night? Rebeccah would not lightly ask for my help." She pulled out the chamber pot and used it.

"Well, how was I to know? It's not as if you've ever talked about her." The landlady's resentment was obvious.

"That I told her how to reach me should have showed you I trust her." Kate crossed to the chest of drawers, grabbed her breeches and hose, and began to dress. "I only pray I'm not too late."

"You can't go out in those," objected Alice. "Josselin—"

"Will recognize me no matter what I wear." Kate tied her hair at the nape, bound her breasts with a strip of cotton, then pulled on her shirt and waistcoat.

A mutinous silence fell while she continued dressing, then Alice muttered, "Why did you not tell me of her?"

Kate stamped her feet into her boots, tied her cravat, and reached for her coat. "There was nothing to tell."

"Liar! Your eyes light up at the merest mention of her. And it's obvious you can't wait to go to her."

Kate tucked the ring safely in her waistcoat pocket. "She needs my help." *What kind of trouble can Rebeccah be in that she needs to come to me?*

She strode through to the other room, took the baldric from its hook, and settled it over her shoulders, making sure the sword slid smoothly in its scabbard. *If she were ill she'd send for an apothecary, wouldn't she?*

A barefoot Alice appeared in the doorway. "After all I've done for you . . . given you the run of my rooms, not to mention my bed."

Kate glanced at the other woman in irritation. "I owe Rebeccah my life."

Alice blinked. "Your life! Yet you did not mention her once."

Because I knew you would be jealous, thought Kate guiltily. *And because I wanted to keep her to myself.* "Well, you know about her now."

Alice folded her arms. "Ay. But only because she came here in person. When were you planning to tell me about her, Kate? Or weren't you? Were you planning to sneak off to her bed one night and never come back?"

"Alice," warned Kate. She had no time for this now. She crammed on her tricorne, slung her saddlebags over her shoulder, and reached for the door handle.

"She may be younger and richer, her skin smoother, eyes brighter, her figure more shapely, but I warn you, Kate, she's not one of us. She can't possibly understand you the way I do. You're nothing but an exotic specimen to add to her collection. She'll tire of you, and *then* where will you be?"

Kate paused. All she had to do was lie to Alice, soothe her wounded feelings, but she couldn't bring herself to do it. The other woman's eyes widened and she pressed a hand to her breast.

"Oh! You never did love me, did you?"

Pox on it! What a time to have this conversation. "Alice . . ." Kate began.

"No." Alice's tone was bitter. "Your silence is eloquent enough. But if you go to her, don't expect me to take you back."

Kate pursed her lips then nodded. "Very well. I never meant things to end badly between us. But if that is what you wish . . . I shall send for the rest of my things as soon as I am able."

She pulled open the front door and started down the stairs two steps at a time. Halfway down, an anguished cry wafted down the stairwell to her.

"Kate," wailed Alice. "Come back. I didn't mean it. Don't leave me!"

But it was too late for that. The words that had passed between them could not be withdrawn or forgotten, even had Kate wanted to, and right now Rebeccah needed her help. Clenching her jaw against the increasingly frantic cries, she continued down the stairs.

☙

Fruit and vegetable traders were wheeling overflowing barrows or setting out their stalls when Kate rode through the marketplace. Curious glances followed her, and she resisted the urge to hunch her shoulders, though she did pull her tricorne lower over her forehead. Without her mask she felt vulnerable, but it would attract unwanted attention and Josselin knew what she looked like now anyway.

"After this, perhaps we'll head for York for a while," she murmured, patting Clover's neck. "Think you'd like that?" The mare ignored her and concentrated on keeping her footing on the cobblestones.

Kate headed left into St. Martin's Lane, then right, taking back streets to the Hay Market. She liked this time of the day. London was waking up, and yawning servants were flinging open shutters, slopping out chamber pots, dragging in the sea coal, queuing at the pump for buckets of water, or greeting the milkmaids with their heavy churns.

At the entrance to St. James's Square, she dismounted and walked the rest of the way, using Clover as a shield against prying eyes. At the top of the steps leading down to the Duttons' back yard, she looped the mare's reins through the railing. "Wait there," she ordered, and started down.

The back door was open, and from the kitchen she could hear the chatter and bustle of the servants. She was about to go in when a skinny young woman in an apron blocked her path. She was carrying a covered chamber pot.

The two gaped at one another, then the maid said tartly, "And what do *you* want?"

Kate used her gruffest voice. "Is Mary at home?"

The maid shifted her grip on the chamber pot and yelled to those indoors, "Mary. There's a . . . a gentleman to see you."

"Gentleman? At this hour? Pull the other one," came a familiar voice, growing louder as its owner approached. "If it's that rogue who sold cook those pies—more gristle than meat, they were!—I'll give him a piece of my—Oh, it's you!"

"Know 'im, do you, Mary?" The maid grinned at the dumpy woman who had appeared in the doorway.

"None of your business, Nancy. And are you going to stand there clutching that chamber pot like it's your own babe or empty the smelly thing?"

With a last curious look at Kate, Nancy flounced off, presumably to find the cesspit.

"Good morrow, Mary." Kate tipped her hat. "Your mistress sent for me."

"Indeed she did. But you took so long about it she has all but given you up." Before Kate could explain, Mary tugged her inside.

"My horse," she protested.

"Will," said Mary, as she led Kate through the kitchen and towards the servants' stairs, "keep an eye on the horse outside, will you?" The footman looked up from polishing the silver, blinked at Kate, then smiled and nodded.

"Oh, she'll be so glad you have come at last," said Mary, puffing as she climbed the narrow steps. "She hasn't slept a wink all night. She is at her wits' end." She hustled Kate into the parlour.

"What is it? What is wrong?" *And why has she come to me and not asked her suitor for help?* But Mary had already pulled the door closed and darted away to fetch her mistress.

Kate tried to still her impatience by examining her surroundings. The room was large and pleasantly airy, with a fine plaster ceiling and new-fangled wallpaper rather than wainscoting. She caught a glimpse of her reflection in the looking glass between the two sash windows, grimaced, and turned away, just as the rustle of skirts, murmur of voices, and sound of hurried footsteps alerted her that someone was coming.

The door swung open and Rebeccah entered. Kate's heart leapt in her chest at the sight of the young woman.

"You came!" Pale cheeks flushed with colour as Rebeccah gazed at Kate. "I should have known better than to doubt you. Forgive me." She held out both hands, and it seemed the most natural thing in the world for Kate to move forward and grasp them.

With a pang she noted the dullness of once sparkling eyes, and the presence of deep shadows beneath them. "What is it, my dear? What has brought such a frown to that pretty face?"

Rebeccah glanced at the watching Mary, who nodded and left them alone together. "It is my sister. She is missing." Green eyes glistened.

"Missing?" Kate led Rebeccah over to the sofa. "Since when?" She released Rebeccah's hands, until they were both sat down, then clasped them again.

"Since yesterday evening. Titus is missing too."

The name meant nothing to Kate. "Titus?"

"One of our footmen. Anne's favourite."

"Their coach has been delayed?"

"No." Rebeccah took a deep breath. "Titus went to see the hanging and came back the worse for drink. Indeed his inebriation may be the cause of this, for I cannot believe even *he* would have done something this outrageous otherwise."

A memory surfaced of a handsome young footman, his mouth stuffed with Kate's kerchief to stop his swearing. "Ah. I recollect the man. His teeth once bruised my knuckles, I think." Rebeccah nodded. "But your sister? Where was she last seen?"

"In her bedchamber. But when her fiancé, Mr. Ingrum, came to call, she could not be found."

"I see." Kate's mind was whirling. "And you think Anne and Titus . . ."

"Are together, yes. But not willingly."

"Not willingly!" repeated Kate.

"He must have taken her from here against her will, conveyed her somewhere in a sedan."

"Some of the chairmen are friends of mine," said Kate. "They could find out where she went." Then she grimaced. "But I fear that horse has already bolted."

Rebeccah gave her a stricken look. "I know. They have been alone together the whole night, Kate! Anne must surely be ruined by now." She searched Kate's face. "Tell me I am being foolish. That this is all but fantasy on my part."

"Alas, I cannot. For your sister is an heiress, is she not?" Rebeccah's groan was answer enough. "But all may not be lost," said Kate, thinking aloud. "For your footman was drunk when he took Anne from here."

"How does that help us?"

"When a man drinks too much he is incapable of," Kate searched for the word, "performing. In short, it is unlikely he was able to force himself on your sister." Rebeccah winced and Kate gave her hand an encouraging squeeze. "And that it was so late in the day when he took her may also count in your sister's favour."

"How so?"

"Fleet weddings are only legal between the hours of eight and noon." She glanced at the parlour clock and saw it was still only seven-thirty. *Thank the Lord I woke early!* "It is true that some marriage houses do not wind their clocks, so that for them it is always morning, but they are unlikely to have been still open when Titus reached them."

It was Rebeccah's turn to glance at the clock. "Then we have half an hour until they open for business."

Kate released Rebeccah's hands and stood up. "Ay. There is no time to lose. I must get to the Rules of the Fleet." *Her suitor would not be able to help her in such a place, but I can.*

"I'm coming with you." Rebeccah stood up too.

"The Rules are no place for you, Rebeccah. Why, the stench from the Fleet Ditch alone—"

"I am not so delicate a flower as you think." Green eyes flashed.

"But—"

"Kate, think. If you manage to rescue Anne from Titus, do you think she will willingly come with the very highwayman she has set Samuel Josselin to catch? Is not she more likely to scream and struggle and attract the attention of the constables?"

Kate scowled. Rebeccah had a point. "Very well. But we must take your carriage and I need a pistol from my saddlebags. Oh, and Clover must be stabled."

Rebeccah gave her a brilliant smile and tugged the bell to summon Will.

Kate tapped her booted foot as Rebeccah specified what she wanted. While the footman went to do his mistress's bidding, Rebeccah disappeared upstairs with Mary to change into more suitable attire.

When Will returned with her saddlebags, Kate thanked him and busied herself loading one of the brace of pistols. Then she tucked it in the waistband of her breeches. Shortly after, Rebeccah reappeared, clad in her wrap and walking shoes.

"Ready?" asked Kate.

Rebeccah nodded.

There was a soft knock at the door. It opened and the maid popped her head round. "Robert has brought the coach, Madam."

"Thank you, Mary." Rebeccah turned and gestured to Kate, who strode past her, and for the first time since she had been at the Dutton residence used the front door.

Robert was waiting by the carriage. After a perplexed moment he offered Kate his hand, but she declined his assistance and stepped up nimbly. Seconds later, Rebeccah was settling in next to her.

The door slammed closed, and Kate felt the coach sway as Robert climbed up into the driver's seat. "May I?" she asked.

Rebeccah nodded.

She rapped her knuckles on the coach roof. "The Rules of the Fleet, Robert. As quick as you can."

Chapter 17

The stench was appalling—a mixture of fish guts, offal, and Lord knows what else. Rebeccah clapped a gloved hand over her nose and mouth.

"Don't say it," she warned, seeing Kate's grin.

"Wouldn't dream of it." The highwaywoman looked up at the coach driver. "Robert, it would attract less attention if you were to drive around for a while. Can you contrive to return here every," she arched a dark eyebrow at Rebeccah, "twenty minutes or so?" Rebeccah nodded.

"Very good, Madam." The coachman flicked the reins and the horses started forward.

Rebeccah watched the carriage trundle up the Farringdon Road, taking with it all that was familiar and civilized, then sighed and squared her shoulders.

"Let's start there," said Kate.

Rebeccah followed the direction of the pointing finger to the buildings close by the Fleet Bridge. She frowned in puzzlement until she saw that next door to the China shop stood a tavern named the Hand and Pen, and in its window was a sign: a man's hand joined with a woman's, bearing the legend "Marriages Perform'd Within."

Kate started forward, and Rebeccah hurried to keep up with the taller woman, lifting her skirts to avoid the filth. They made their way past a clutter of stalls where traders were selling ripe cheeses, pigeon pies, and cages of raucous hens, then past a barrel full of splashing carp. Overhead, a gull mewed.

"Won't let you fuck her till you tie the knot, eh?" called a winkle-seller, noticing their destination. The corner of Kate's mouth twitched.

"Got yourself a fine strong fellow," said a woman selling carrots from a barrow. She winked at Rebeccah. "I'll wager you're looking forward to the wedding night." Rebeccah wondered if her cheeks were as red as they felt.

"Ignore them and keep walking," advised Kate.

It was a relief to finally enter the Hand and Pen, but only for a moment. A smelly fug of pipe smoke and alcohol replaced the stench of the Fleet Ditch. Then a blowsy landlady was coming towards them, asking, "You two wanting to get hitched?"

Kate took Rebeccah's hand without asking, adopted the gruff voice she used for Blue-Eyed Nick, and said as though agreeing, "Is the Parson free?"

The landlady's grin was gap-toothed. "Ay. Follow me."

Wolf-whistles and lewd comments followed them through the bar, as the landlady led them to a private room at the back. Rebeccah's cheeks flamed afresh but then Kate's hand squeezed hers, and for a pleasant moment she was distracted by how right it felt. Then thoughts of why they were here returned, and with it overpowering anxiety for her sister's wellbeing.

Pray God we find some trace of Anne before it's too late.

"Here we are." The landlady ushered them into a dingy "chapel," a small room, empty apart from a table on which lay a stub of candle and a copy of the Book of Common Prayer, some chairs, and a clock. She halted, folded her arms across her ample bosom, and looked at them.

"It'll be half-a-crown," she warned. "Seven-and-six if you want a certificate and entry in the Fleet register." Kate dropped Rebeccah's hand—Rebeccah felt the loss at once—and pulled some coins from her coat pocket. The landlady glanced at them. "Good." She pursed her lips. "But where are your witnesses?"

"They're late," lied Kate. Rebeccah glanced at the clock, whose hands seemed to have stopped at nine a.m.

"If they don't turn up," continued the landlady, "we can provide a couple, but it'll cost you."

Kate nodded.

"Right. I'll fetch the Parson." With that, the woman left them alone together.

Kate turned to Rebeccah. "How are you faring?"

She forced a smile. "As well as can be expected until we have Anne safe."

"We'll find her." Blue eyes pinned her. "Don't lose heart."

"I won't."

The door creaked open and in came a fat little man in a soiled surplice carrying a pile of blank marriage certificates, almost certainly fake, under his arm. Such was his girth, he looked like a black and white cannonball. He beamed at them. "A fine day for a wedding, ain't it?" There was ale on his breath.

He placed the certificates, which carried the royal arms but lacked the official stamp, on the table beside the prayer book, then turned and appraised the two women. "A handsome couple you make too." Rebeccah didn't dare look at Kate.

The parson's gaze turned calculating. "Has the tavern keeper told you my charges?"

"Yes," said Kate.

"Good." He rubbed his hands together. "Now, will you be wanting just the basic ceremony or the certificates and a register entry too?"

"Neither. For we are here not to marry but to gain information."

"What?" His smile disappeared. "Do you mean you have got me here under false pret—"

Kate flipped a silver coin and caught it, earning the parson's undivided attention. "You can still earn yourself a shilling."

He licked his lips and considered. "Make it a shilling and sixpence."

"Agreed." The highwaywoman pulled out the additional coin. "In the last twenty-four hours have you married a couple by the name of Anne Dutton and Titus—" She paused and glanced at her companion.

"Ward," supplied Rebeccah.

The parson's gaze turned inward and Rebeccah held her breath. "Don't think so," he said at last, dashing her hopes.

Kate jingled the coins. "'Think' isn't good enough, sir. Don't you record all the particulars in your pocket book?"

The little man hesitated then nodded.

"Hand it over."

His cheeks flushed. "Hanged if I will! It's private."

Kate chuckled. "I won't tell anyone if you've insulted them. My word on it."

"Why should I take *your* word if you won't take mine?" he grumbled.

Kate pretended to consider, then pulled out another sixpence. "Is this a good enough reason?"

There was a pause, then he grunted. From somewhere he produced a ragged pocket book and handed it to Kate. She passed it at once to Rebeccah, and while Kate gave the roly-poly parson his two shillings, a trembling Rebeccah opened the pocketbook.

The light was poor so she moved a few steps closer to the dirty window. The pages were foxed, the handwriting crabbed and in places almost illegible, made more so by bad spelling and ink blots. Each entry noted the details of the couple getting married, and included personal remarks, such as "NB The woman was bigg with chyld, and they wanted the certifycate antidated." She glanced up and saw both Kate and the cannonball watching her.

"The most recent entries," reminded Kate.

"Sorry." Rebeccah riffled through the flimsy pages until she found the entries for yesterday and today. Anne's name was nowhere to be found, and none of the jotted descriptions matched her or Titus. With a sigh she closed the pocket book.

"Nothing?" asked Kate.

She shook her head.

"Ah well." The highwaywoman took back the book and handed it to the parson. "Our thanks, sir."

He sniffed, tucked the pocket book and certificates under one arm, and sauntered out, presumably to quaff more ale. After a moment, Kate and Rebeccah followed him.

"What about the wedding feast?" called someone as they made their way back through the smoky bar, which was busy even though it was still early.

"Ay." The blowsy landlady gave them a hopeful smile. "Our bride cakes are a bargain at sixpence."

Kate shook her head and strode on. Rebeccah hurried after her, catching her at the street door. Together they emerged into the open, the stink of the Fleet Ditch making Rebeccah want to gag.

"What shall we do now?"

Kate took her elbow and urged her towards the first of the streets adjoining the Farringdon Road. "Thirty-nine to go," she muttered.

"Pardon?" Rebeccah blinked up at her.

"There are about forty marriage houses in all," explained the highwaywoman, with a look of apology. "Come, my dear. We have no time to lose."

✄

Rebeccah's feet hurt. In the last hour they must have covered miles, tramping up and down the streets and stinking alleyways that surrounded the Fleet Prison, entering each tavern and brandy-shop that doubled as a marriage house. The Red Hand and Mitre, the Swan, the Lamb, the Horse-shoe and Magpie, the Bishop Blaise, the Two Sawyers, the Fighting Cocks, the Bull and Garter, the King's Head . . . her own head was spinning with their names, and if she never saw the inside of another marriage house it would be too soon. But what choice did she have? They had still found no trace of her sister.

"Don't give up hope yet," counselled Kate. "That we have not found Anne could be a good sign. For your footman will have woken sober this morning and may have had a change of heart. Even now, she could be safe at home."

Rebeccah pursed her lips. "Do you think so?"

The highwaywoman hesitated, then sighed. "No. Titus could also feel he has gone too far to retreat."

"Alas, knowing him, that sounds all too likely. But thank you for trying to raise my spirits." Her back ached from all the walking but a rest was out of the question until they found her sister. "So. Where shall we try next?"

Kate resettled her tricorne, took stock of her surroundings, then pointed. "There."

At the end of the alleyway was the most unprepossessing marriage house yet. The windows were so grimy they could barely see through them, and the sign of the joined hands had faded until it was barely visible. Rebeccah squared her shoulders and marched towards it. Kate's longer legs easily overtook her, and she opened the door with a flourish and ushered Rebeccah inside.

"Can't go in there," growled the bearded man behind the bar, as Kate headed towards the back room. "Parson's busy." She ignored him and pressed on, Rebeccah hard on her heels. "Are ye deaf?" He came out from behind his bar, hands bunched.

Kate stopped and turned. "No. I heard you." Her tone was measured, but there was something dangerous in the blue gaze that made the landlord stop, uncertain, and Rebeccah draw in a sharp breath.

"Tom," called the landlord, his frowning gaze fixed on Kate. "Sam."

At his summons, two unsavoury characters looked up from their play-ing cards, then lumbered to their feet. One produced a club and began to smack it rhythmically against his palm.

Kate rested her hand on her sword hilt and arched a provocative eyebrow. The morning's frustrations had worn away the last of the highwaywoman's patience, realized Rebeccah with a jolt, and she was spoiling for a fight.

"Please, there's no need for violence." She stepped forward, hands raised palm outward. "We just need to ask the parson something and then we'll be on our way."

Thwack, thwack went the club, while the landlord regarded Rebeccah with puzzlement. A well-bred young gentlewoman must be quite a rarity in a rough establishment like this. "'At's as may be, Madam," he said. "But I don't like yer friend's manners. 'E needs teaching a lesson."

"Are you volunteering?" asked Kate with a sneer.

"Oh, stop it!" A cross Rebeccah backhanded the tall woman in the belly, eliciting a surprised grunt. She turned back to the landlord. "You'd be wise not to cross h . . .him. Don't you recognize him?" She jerked a thumb at Kate.

"Now ye come to mention it, there *is* something familiar." The man scratched his beard. "'Anged if I can put me finger on it, though."

"Imagine a mask," said Rebeccah helpfully, "and those blue eyes peering through the eye slits at you."

The landlord's eyebrows shot up and he took a nervous step back. "'S wounds, but 'e's the spitting image of Blue-Eyed Nick!"

The two bouncers looked at one another, then at Kate. They seemed less confident than they had.

"His reputation as a crack shot is well deserved," added Rebeccah, for good measure.

The landlord bit his lip. "A word with the parson's all ye want?" Rebeccah nodded and glanced at Kate who after a pregnant pause nodded too. "And ye'll pay for breakages?"

"Ay," growled Kate, and to Rebeccah's relief she let her hand drop from the sword hilt.

"Very well." The landlord retreated behind his bar. "Let 'em through, lads." Tom and Sam exchanged a glance, shrugged, then went back to their cards.

Rebeccah smiled warmly. "Thank you." The landlord gave her a grudging nod.

After a moment, she and Kate resumed their progress towards the back room. Kate turned the handle and opened the door.

There were five people in the make-shift chapel—a lean as a whippet parson in a black coat and hat, an over-rouged harlot in a red gown and a chap-handed washerwoman in a mantua that had seen better days (presumably the witnesses), a wide-eyed Titus Ward, and a young gentlewoman wearing velvet slippers.

"Anne!"

At Rebeccah's glad cry, her sister turned, and would have fallen had the footman beside her not steadied her. "Beccah!" Her voice was slurred, her movements uncoordinated.

"She's been drugged," said Kate. "Look at her pupils."

Anger surged through Rebeccah and she rushed forward. Titus cursed, hooked an arm round Anne, and pulled her in front of him like a shield.

"You're too late. She's my wife." He glanced at Rebeccah's sister and grinned. "Aren't you, my love?"

Lord save us! Rebeccah halted, feeling as though she had been hit in the stomach.

"I'll make her your widow if you don't let her go," threatened Kate, pulling out her pistol. A loud *thud* was the open Book of Common Prayer falling from the startled parson's fingers.

"The Devil you will!" From somewhere Titus produced a wicked looking knife and pressed it to Anne's throat. Her eyes were glazed and she remained statue still.

Better paralyzed terror, thought Rebeccah, *than an attempt to free herself that would surely put her life at risk.*

"Release Anne I said." Kate cocked and aimed her pistol at the only bit of Titus now visible—the top of his head.

"No!" Rebeccah stretched an arm towards the highwaywoman. "You could hurt her."

"Don't you trust me?"

There was hurt in those blue eyes, and Rebeccah remembered the words she had spoken so blithely a few moments ago: "a crack shot." *Did I mean that?* A memory surfaced, of a masked rider galloping across the heath, and a pistol shot tearing apart the night and saving her from harm. Wordlessly, she let her arm drop. Kate nodded then turned her attention back to Titus.

"For a start, why should we take Titus's word for it?" Kate glanced at the trembling parson. "Have you pronounced them man and wife?" He opened and closed his mouth like a fish. "Speak up, man."

"N . . . not yet." His reply was almost drowned by Titus's shout of "Liar!" He frowned at the footman, then continued rather prissily, "The gentleman had made *his* vows, 'tis true, but the lady had yet to make hers."

"Ah. Not wed then." Kate gave a satisfied nod. "A close run thing, though, and no thanks to you." Her voice dripped contempt. "Could you not see that the bride was being forced against her will?"

The indignant parson drew himself up to his full height. "She seemed amenable. I thought—"

The tension proved too much for the harlot hired to witness the marriage. She shrieked, lifted her scarlet skirts, and dashed out the open chapel door; after a moment's hesitation, the washerwoman rushed after her.

"Christ's wounds!" yelled Titus. "Come back, the pair of you. I paid—"

Kate lunged past Rebeccah and yanked the distracted footman's knife hand away from Anne's throat. "Take her." She tore Anne from his grasp and shoved her towards Rebeccah.

"Oof!" The collision almost sent both sisters flying.

Preoccupied with steadying a shrieking Anne—the sudden wrench had penetrated her drug-induced stupor—Rebeccah was only peripherally aware of what was going on. She heard a sickening crunch, then what sounded like something heavy crumpling to the floor.

By the time Anne was calm again and Rebeccah was able to take in her surroundings, Kate was standing over a supine Titus, his nose oddly flattened, his chin, cravat, and waistcoat drenched with blood. The knuckles of Kate's right glove were also bloody.

"Is he—?"

"Dead to the world, maybe, but he'll live." Kate flexed her fingers then tucked her unfired pistol back in the waistband of her breeches.

Rebeccah couldn't think what else to say so contented herself with, "Oh."

"Where am I?" slurred Anne. "Is Titus here? I seem to remember . . ." Her brows knit, but after a moment her eyes lost their focus and dreaminess returned.

"There, there, my sweet." As Rebeccah chafed her sister's hands she felt the presence of a wedding ring. It was cheap and nasty, and she eased it off and flung it at the footman—it bounced off his waistcoat and skittered into a corner of the chapel with a *clink*. "You're safe now." She turned a concerned glance on Kate. "What drug can he have used?"

"Poppy juice, I expect. It'll wear off." Kate addressed the parson again. "Give me your pocket book. There must be no record of this."

"What?" He gaped at her.

"You heard me." She held out her hand and tapped a booted foot.

Reluctantly, he produced the slim volume. Kate flipped through it, found what she wanted, and tore out a page.

"You can't—"

"I just did." As the parson subsided, muttering, she put the folded page in her waistcoat pocket then handed back his book. "Anything else?" He gaped at her. "Signatures, certificates . . ." He shook his head. "If I find out later that you're lying . . ." Her glare made him flinch.

"That's everything, cross my heart."

"Good."

"I don't feel well." Anne's murmur reclaimed Rebeccah's attention. Her sister's complexion had gone a greenish-white, she saw with some alarm.

"Faith!"

Somehow Kate was on the other side of Anne, draping her arm over her shoulder and helping Rebeccah to support her to a corner, where she was violently sick.

"That's pleasant," said the parson.

Kate ignored him and said over Anne's bowed head, "She'll feel the better for it."

"Will she?" asked Rebeccah.

Stumbling footsteps and the parson's exclamation made them turn. Kate was the first to glance to where Titus no longer lay and put two and two together. She cursed and began to free herself from Anne.

"Leave him." Rebeccah was glad to see the back of the footman.

"But—"

"He has too much of a head start, and besides we must get Anne home and into Mary's care."

The tall woman hesitated, clearly torn between wanting to chase the footman and to help Rebeccah with her sister. In the end, Rebeccah's needs won. "Very well." Kate took a firmer grip on Anne's arm and between them they got her to the door. The Parson didn't offer to help.

Glances and muttered asides followed their progress through the bar towards the tavern exit. Tom and Sam glanced at their bearded employer for instructions. The landlord blinked at the two unevenly matched figures supporting a swooning woman between them, shook his head, and went back to mopping his counter top.

Rebeccah was glad she had Kate to help her—Anne was heavier than she looked, and on her own, Rebeccah would have been struggling. She tightened her grasp on her sister's waist and noted with relief that Anne's colour had improved. Kate must have been right about the vomiting.

"They say that's Blue-Eyed Nick," stage-whispered a bulbous-nosed drinker, looking away when Kate's keen blue gaze raked him.

"Lud!" exclaimed his companion, a woman whose numerous patches drew attention to her pock-marked cheeks rather than the reverse. "She's wearing slippers!"

Anne squirmed in Rebeccah's grip. "Do I know you?" Rebeccah was about to answer when she realized that her sister's unfocussed gaze was fixed on the highwaywoman. But Kate merely grunted, and to Rebeccah's relief after a moment Anne lost interest in her and began to sing—a lullaby that had been their father's favourite.

"Hush, dear," said Rebeccah. "Quietly now." Anne's smile was groggy but she obediently muted her singing to a hum.

"Too much gin, if you ask me," called a card player.

"No one did." Kate glared at him, and he turned hastily back to his cards.

They emerged outside into the ever present stench of the Fleet Ditch.

"Ugh!" said Anne, and Rebeccah couldn't help but agree with her.

"Which way?" Rebeccah's sense of direction was weak at the best of times.

Kate pointed, and the two women took a firmer grip on the invalid and set off along the pavement, attracting raised eyebrows as they went. After a while, Anne was able to support some of her own weight, which made the going easier.

Rebeccah began to recognize her surroundings. *Let Robert be there with the carriage*, she prayed, as they turned onto the Farringdon Road. But there was no sign of the coach and four. A church bell chiming twelve o'clock surprised her—enough had happened to her today for it to seem like late afternoon.

"If he doesn't come soon," said Kate, "we should find some small beer for your sister. She needs to drink something."

"Small beer," repeated Anne, before resuming her humming.

"What about coffee?" asked Rebeccah. "They say it makes one more alert."

"Even better," agreed the highwaywoman. "There's a coffee house just around the corner."

"Coffee," said Anne.

Before Rebeccah could reply, the clip-clopping of hooves brought her to a halt. She shaded her eyes against the sunshine. The Dutton coach and four was heading towards them, with Robert at the reins.

"Thank God!" She exchanged a relieved smile with Kate.

The carriage pulled up beside them, and Robert climbed down. Before he could help, Kate had got the carriage door open and handed Rebeccah up.

"I'll pass your sister up," she said, as Rebeccah took her seat, then turned arms outstretched. "Ready?" A powerful hand boosted Anne's rump.

"Whoops!"

Once more, the sisters fought to keep their balance. It took them a moment to untangle themselves, straighten their dresses, and settle themselves more comfortably, and by then, Kate had closed the carriage door behind her and was taking the seat opposite.

Rebeccah took a moment to luxuriate in the fact she was sitting down at last, then rapped her knuckles on the carriage roof. "Home, Robert."

"At once, Madam." The coach lurched into motion.

"I know you, do I not?" Anne was staring at the highwaywoman again.

"Of course you do, dear." Rebeccah threw Kate an anxious glance. "It's a good friend of ours."

Anne grabbed Rebeccah's hand. "Look!" Her voice was urgent.

Rebeccah followed the direction of her sister's gaze and saw that Kate's coat had come open, revealing the pistol tucked in her breeches. Kate closed her coat at once, but it was too late.

"It's that highwayman," continued Anne, her voice a quaver. "What was his name? Blue-Eyed something?" She was looking at Kate like a rabbit at a stoat.

The grip on Rebeccah's hand was almost painful. "Don't be frightened," she said. "He's helping us. Remember? He rescued you from Titus."

At the footman's name, Anne's gaze turned inwards. At least she was no longer staring at Kate. "Titus said I am to marry him." She frowned. "But that cannot be right, can it, Beccah?" She gave her sister a pleading glance. "For I'm to marry Mr. Ingrum, am I not?"

"Indeed you are." At least Rebeccah hoped so.

"Oh, my head aches." Anne rubbed her temple. "Why does it ache so?"

"Because you have been ill." Kate's intervention drew a startled glance from Rebeccah. "But you will be better shortly. We are taking you home and Mary will soon be on hand to take good care of you."

"Mary?" The mention of the plump maid who had nursed the Duttons through numerous illnesses seemed to calm her, and Rebeccah turned a grateful glance on Kate.

Anne's eyelids fluttered closed. Soon after, soft snores filled the carriage. Rebeccah exchanged a relieved smile with Kate and relaxed back in her seat. In the peace and quiet, she had time at last to consider the worrying subject of her sister's maidenhead. Would Frederick Ingrum still marry Anne if Titus was found to have violated her? She looked up, and found Kate watching her.

"Her fiancé will undoubtedly still marry her," said the highwaywoman, somehow divining her thoughts and keeping her voice low so as not to wake Anne, "for her fortune is intact even if she is not."

The logic of her reply struck Rebeccah. "And that her fortune is intact is thanks entirely to you."

"And to you," countered Kate, with a smile. "She is fortunate to have such a quick-witted sister."

Rebeccah pinked at the compliment. "I would feel more content," she continued, "if I could be certain that she will not forever bear the scars of this . . . ordeal." Kate nodded her understanding. "To think of my sister helpless and alone with that despicable . . ." She trailed off, unable to put her outrage and disgust into words.

"If Titus *did* force himself on your sister," said Kate, "it will have been while she was under the influence of the poppy juice. She will have little memory of it and hopefully no lasting distress."

"I hope for her sake you are right."

The coach began to slow, and Rebeccah looked out the window and recognized her surroundings. "We're almost there."

Kate didn't reply, and Rebeccah remembered with a jolt of distress that the house in St. James's was not Kate's home and her departure was imminent. The urge to express her admiration and gratitude before it was too late overwhelmed her, and careful not to disturb her sister, she reached forward and pressed Kate's hand.

"Thank you from the bottom of my heart."

The eyes that met hers were gentle. "I need no thanks, Rebeccah. I owed you my life, remember?"

"Oh, if we are keeping score, I owed you mine before that."

"Well." Kate shrugged and smiled.

"Don't 'well' me, Kate. You are the . . . the truest friend I have ever known." The light in the carriage was dim, but Rebeccah would have sworn that the other woman was blushing. "You always come to my aid in my hour of need," she continued. "The Duttons are in your debt and if there is ever anything we can—Oh pish!"

For the coach had given a lurch and stopped, waking Anne and putting an end to any more conversation of an intimate nature.

Anne yawned and stretched and looked about her. "Are we home, Beccah?"

Rebeccah exchanged a rueful glance with Kate. "Yes."

Then the handle turned and the carriage door opened, and the coachman was looking up at them and holding out his hand.

♔

"My dears!" Mrs. Dutton rushed across the hall towards Rebeccah and her sister, arms outstretched. "You are both safe. As the hours passed without news I had begun to fear the worst. I was never so relieved to see you in all my life!"

She engulfed Anne in a hug, then held her at arm's length. What she saw made her frown.

"We think it is poppy juice." Rebeccah beckoned to Mary, who had appeared from downstairs to see what all the commotion was.

"Poppy juice!" Her mother pressed a hand to her throat. "By all that's . . . The ruffian!"

With a glance for permission to Rebeccah, who nodded, Mary took Anne's hand, talked soothingly to her, and led her away. They started up the stairs to the bedchambers, and Anne's own maid, Nancy, hurried to help. As Rebeccah watched the three women ascend, it came home to her that her sister was safe. The tension in her neck and shoulders that had been with her since the discovery last night of Anne's absence eased, and a wave of giddiness swept over her.

"Breathe slowly and steadily," came Kate's voice in her ear, and a firm hand took her elbow. Rebeccah did as she was bid, and her racing heart slowed. Her vision cleared.

"Thank you."

Kate smiled, released her hold, and took a step back.

Mrs. Dutton's attention had been all for Anne. Now it switched to Kate, and her eyes widened at the sight of Blue-Eyed Nick without his mask and kerchief standing bold as brass in her hall. She licked her lips, but to Rebeccah's relief didn't burst into hysterics, and when she found her voice, sounded almost calm.

"Will told me you had succeeded in finding the highwayman while I slept." Though she addressed the remark to her daughter, it was Kate she kept in her sights.

For all the world as though she is some dangerous beast who might attack at any minute, thought an amused Rebeccah.

"Why did you not wake me?"

"You had been up all night with worry, Mama," chided Rebeccah. "I thought it best to let you rest."

"Well, it is true I was quite worn down by your sister's disappearance," conceded Mrs. Dutton, "so I will forgive you this once." To Rebeccah's astonishment, she made Kate an elaborate curtsey. "If my daughter has not already made it clear (and I hope I have taught her better manners) we are in your debt, sir. Please let me express my profound gratitude."

Kate tipped her hat and said gruffly, "Think nothing of it, Madam."

"Indeed I'll do no such thing," said Mrs. Dutton. She paused, then added, "Would you care to partake of some refreshment with us? A dish of tea, perhaps?" If Rebeccah had been sitting on a stool, the shock of this polite invitation would have toppled her off it.

Kate's lips twitched. "That is kind," she said. "But . . . another time, perhaps? For I have stayed too long and must take my leave of you."

For the past few minutes she had looked increasingly restless, and now the reason for it dawned on Rebeccah—Kate felt too exposed and vulnerable here. And who could blame her? Hadn't the eldest daughter of this household, the very one she had just rescued from an unwanted marriage, in fact, hired a thieftaker to go after her? The unfairness of it made Rebeccah wince inwardly.

"As you wish," said her mother, looking both disappointed and relieved. "Another time, then."

Silence fell and everyone looked at everyone else. "Er . . . The whereabouts of my horse?" prompted Kate.

Will cleared his throat. "If I may be of assistance?" Mrs. Dutton nodded her permission, and the footman stepped forward. "Clover is stabled in the Mews." He glanced at Rebeccah then back at Kate. "Shall I fetch my spare wig and livery?"

Rebeccah's mother looked mystified. "Your wig and livery?"

Before Rebeccah could enlighten her about the makeshift disguise they had used previously, a loud hammering at the front door pre-empted her.

"Open up in the name of the Law," came a man's muffled shout, between the blows. "We know Blue-Eyed Nick's in there. Surrender the highwayman or it will go the worse for everyone."

Rebeccah turned an appalled glance towards Kate, who bit off a curse and dashed for the stairs leading down to the basement.

"Faith! What are we to do, Beccah?" Mrs. Dutton had gone pale.

Rebeccah stared at her. "How can you possibly ask that after what has happened, Mama? You must not let them in!"

"But if we do not . . . Oh, if only your father were here!" She composed herself and considered her daughter's suggestion. "But you are right, my dear. It would be poor thanks indeed." She turned to the butler. "On no account, George, are you to give them admittance."

He bowed his head. "Very good, Madam."

Rebeccah threw her mother a grateful glance, then hurried after Kate, but no sooner had she started down the narrow steps than she saw Kate hurrying back up.

"They've come in the back way." Her expression was grim.

"Oh!" Rebeccah pressed herself against the wall to allow Kate past. The highwaywoman headed for the stairs to the rest of the house, taking the steps two at a time with long, booted legs. With a glance at her mother and a helpless shrug, Rebeccah lifted her skirts and followed, finding Kate on the first landing, examining her surroundings.

"What do you intend?" panted Rebeccah, as Kate resumed her ascent and she struggled to keep up.

"If I can escape across the roof to one of the neighbouring houses . . ."

"Is that not dangerous?"

Amused blue eyes turned to regard her. "More dangerous than falling into Josselin's clutches?"

"I see what you mean."

Shouts from below indicated the intruders were swarming into the hall. Her mother's voice rose in protest, and Rebeccah's heart swelled with love for her parent. The hammering at the front door stopped.

They must have let their colleagues in.

"I am sorry to involve your family in this." Kate stopped at the next landing, spotted the door to Rebeccah's bedchamber, and headed for it. Inside, she crossed to the window and peered down at the square. "Devil take it!" Her shoulders sagged.

"What is it?" Rebeccah hurried to the other woman's side and gazed down. The last time they had both stood here looking down seemed an age ago. The square was crawling with unsavoury looking men clutching staves and clubs—Josselin's bully boys. Residents from some of the other houses had gathered too, curious to see what was going on.

"See those fellows there?" Kate pointed a gloved finger. Rebeccah saw but was none the wiser. "They're guarding the front and back of the houses adjacent. Even if I make it across the rooftops, it will do me no good."

Rebeccah looked at her. "What are you saying?"

"That this time Josselin has got me. Fair and square."

"But you have your pistol. Can you not shoot your way out?"

"And risk some innocent getting caught in the crossfire?" Kate shook her head.

A suddenly shaky Rebeccah crossed to her bed and sat on the edge of it. "This cannot be happening!" She rubbed her eyes with the heel of one hand and pursued a thought that had been nagging at her. "How did Josselin know you were here?"

"Titus." The bed sagged as Kate sat next to her. "He must have deduced I would bring your sister back here, and run straight to the thieftaker."

"And I told you to let him go." Rebeccah stared at her in horror. "This is my fault."

The blue eyes were gentle. "No, my dear. I should have hit him harder."

"But if I hadn't asked you to help me find Anne—"

"Then your sister would be in dire straits indeed. I am glad you came to me, Rebeccah. Glad that I was caught in the act of being a Good Samaritan rather than a thief."

The resignation in her tone struck Rebeccah like a blow. "You talk as if it is all over," she accused. "As if he has already caught you."

Kate arched an eyebrow. "He has as good as."

"No." Rebeccah surged to her feet. "Use me as your shield, Kate, the way Titus used my sister. Threaten to shoot me if they do not allow you free passage."

"And risk your life?" The other woman shook her head. "Never. Besides." She gave a wry smile. "No one could possibly believe I would harm you. But I thank you for your generous offer, Rebeccah. Indeed I do."

Rebeccah stared at Kate in growing despair. "If you will not use me, then one of the servants, perhaps. I'm sure Will—"

The highwaywoman stood up. "Stop this, Rebeccah." She rested her hands on Rebeccah's shoulders and gave her a gentle shake. "Think! Do you suppose Josselin cares whether anyone in this household gets hurt? All that matters to him is the reward he'll get for catching me."

"But—"

"Your wish to save me warms my heart, but you must face it, my dear. He has me boxed."

"No!" Rebeccah threw herself at Kate, pressing her face into her shoulder and beginning to sob. After a moment, Kate's arms came round her and held her close.

"There, there," soothed Kate, her breath warm against Rebeccah's ear. "It was always on the cards that it would end this way. At heart I knew it, and so must you have. But I am glad it did not come before I had made your acquaintance. Very glad."

Kate's shirt and coat were now quite damp. Rebeccah pulled back and looked up at the other woman, her vision blurry. "There must be something we can do."

"Ask for a free pardon from the Queen herself perhaps?" joked Kate. She wiped away Rebeccah's tears with a finger. "Tsk! Your pretty eyes are quite red with weeping."

For several minutes the sound of men's voices and booted feet clumping up the stairs had been growing louder, now came sounds of movement outside the room as they plucked up their courage. The two women exchanged a glance.

"They must have got past Mama," murmured Rebeccah.

"Ay." Kate pulled out her pistol and handed it to Rebeccah. Then she took off her baldric and sword. "Take these, so there can be no misunderstanding."

They were heavier than she expected and she almost dropped them. After a moment, she discarded them on the bed.

"Kate!" she whispered, barely able to get the words out round the lump in her throat. "Please don't do this."

"Hush. Be brave now. It's almost over." Kate took another step away from her. "You can come in now, gentlemen," she called. "I am unarmed and willing to surrender."

A man peered round the doorway, his face ruddy, his wig askew. His gaze skipped over Rebeccah and settled on the tall figure of the highwaywoman. Kate held her hands clear of her body so it was obvious that she was unarmed.

"Looks all right," said the ruddy-faced man to someone out of sight. "Come on." And with a rush, the room filled with his companions who pushed Rebeccah aside and surrounded Kate in a circle that kept them just out of arm's reach.

On the surface Kate appeared calm, almost somnolent, but Rebeccah could see the wariness as she eyed the rank-smelling thugs surrounding her, some smacking clubs into meaty palms. Should they choose to beat her to a pulp, there would be little she could do.

"Do not hurt him, he is unarmed," blurted Rebeccah. "His weapons are over there." She pointed to the bed.

"You mean her, don't you?" came a deep voice. "We'll not hurt her more than she deserves." A man she hadn't seen before entered the bed-chamber.

Elegant clothing couldn't disguise the brute beneath. Something about the new arrival's solidity, the pugnacious set of his jaw and broad shoulders perhaps, put Rebeccah in mind of a bull terrier.

"Josselin." Kate's eyes sparked with hatred. But her obvious dislike seemed only to amuse the thieftaker.

Something clinked, and Rebeccah saw that Josselin was holding a pair of shackles. He handed them to one of his men. "Put those on her."

The man took them and edged forward, clearly reluctant to leave the protection of his fellows. His eyes were fixed on Kate's face, and she arched an eyebrow at him, then smiled mockingly and held out her hands. He grunted, checking as though for a trap, then slipped the shackles over her wrists and began to fasten them.

Seeing the highwaywoman accepting her fate so meekly sent a pang through Rebeccah. *If it weren't for me . . .*

Once Kate was safely shackled, the tension in the room eased perceptibly.

"Told you Blue-Eyed Nick's reputation was overrated," said Josselin, looking at his men with an air of triumph. "Let's get her to Newgate, where she belongs. Bring her."

He turned and strode towards the door, then paused and looked back at Rebeccah. "Shall I tell your sister the good news, Madam, or will you?"

For a moment she didn't know what he was talking about. Then it clicked. *Anne hired him to capture Kate. He has completed his task.*

She strove for dignity. "My sister is indisposed at present. I will tell her."

"As you wish." He nodded and disappeared from the room.

"Come on, you. Get moving," said someone.

"Oof!"

It was Kate's voice, and Rebeccah turned and saw a club had thumped into Kate's kidneys, forcing her forward. "There's no need for that!"

The owner of the club sneered at Rebeccah, but he didn't use it again. Kate smiled her thanks as she let herself be escorted from the bedchamber. Frozen by misery and helplessness, Rebeccah stood on the landing, watching them descend, then she followed.

Her mother and the servants were waiting in the hallway, white-faced but unharmed. A mute Mrs. Dutton held out a hand to her daughter, and Rebeccah hurried to her side and clasped it. Together they followed the prisoner and her escort outside. A cheer went up from the watchers when they emerged into the square, where a cart now waited, its horse looking bored.

"They've caught Blue-Eyed Nick," yelled someone, and the news spread rapidly through the knots of onlookers gathered there.

Kate halted by the cart and glanced back to those waiting on the front step. Rebeccah raised a hand. Kate nodded, her gaze understanding.

Josselin drew one of his men to one side and spoke to him. The man nodded then turned and strode towards Kate, grinning and smacking his club into his palm. Kate said something sharp and tried to back away from him, but the cart blocked her path. The man raised his club and brought it down.

"No!" screamed Rebeccah, as Kate crumpled under the vicious blow to her head. Only her mother's grip prevented her from running to Kate's side.

"You cannot help him now, Beccah," said Mrs. Dutton, her voice sharp. "Come away. Your sister needs you."

She watched Josselin's men throw the limp highwaywoman into the cart, as though she were a sack of potatoes, then turned on her mother. "Why should I care what happens to Anne?" She was trembling with fury. "After what she's done to Kate?"

"Kate?" Her mother looked at sea. Then she gave Rebeccah a little shake. "Tsk, Beccah. You are upset, so I will make allowances for your unkindness to your sister. I said only that we cannot help your friend *now*. If we put our heads together it should not be beyond us to find some way to help later. Now come inside. The neighbours are staring."

Later.

Still trembling, Rebeccah allowed herself to be ushered indoors.

Chapter 18

The day was overcast, but after the gloom of Newgate the light was still dazzling. Kate halted to let her eyes adjust. A stave *thwacked* against her back.

"Move along, Milledge," ordered Simpkins. "Haven't got all day."

"Should have let me out of these leg irons then."

Kate shuffled forward, taking an appreciative breath of fresh air as she did so, before noticing that most of those present in the Session House had nosegays pressed to their noses. The perception of fresh air was relative, it seemed. Or perhaps it was just that the prisoners stank. She grimaced down at the stained shirt and breeches she had been wearing since she was caught three days ago.

As she took her seat on one of the prisoners' benches, she glanced round the covered outdoor court. The Old Bailey had been half-empty yesterday, at her arraignment, when she had heard the charges against her and with tongue firmly in cheek pleaded "not guilty." Today it was full. But trial proceedings always attracted a larger audience, especially when highwaymen were involved.

"All rise for the Queen's Justice," cried a court official, and everyone got raggedly to their feet as a corpulent man in a full wig and black robes arrived and took his seat.

"That's Judge Turnley," muttered John Figg, who was sitting two along from Kate. "He don't like snafflers." The coin-clipper glanced at her. "'Specially the female variety."

"Quiet!" Simpkins shot Figg an annoyed glance.

Kate shrugged and, when everyone else sat, resumed her seat. The charges against her were so serious that it would make little difference who the judge was.

Turnley began to speak. While he droned self-importantly on about the solemn duties and responsibilities of citizens in general and jurors in particular, Kate let her gaze drift round the Session House, over the twelve jurymen, yawning and picking their noses, the correspondent of the Post Man, whose pencil was at present motionless, and the gloating figure of Samuel Josselin. She curled her lip at the thieftaker, whose smile broadened.

The spectator's gallery was packed. She scanned the crowded rows, stopping with a jerk. *Rebeccah!*

The young gentlewoman was sitting in the second row, next to her mother, her fair head bowed. There was no sign of the young man who had escorted her in St. James's Park. *What kind of a suitor is he, not to lend her his support in such circumstances?* As if she could sense Kate's regard, Rebeccah raised her head and their gazes locked. Green eyes widened and Kate wondered if Rebeccah's heart was pounding as hard as hers, and if her own lips had curved into a smile.

She felt honoured and humbled that Rebeccah had come to see the trial. A felon like Kate did not deserve such consideration. But whether the young woman's presence in the Session House this morning was a good thing or a bad was debatable. The charges of highway robbery laid against Kate could surely come as no surprise to Rebeccah, but one other charge would: murder. Josselin had done his homework, Devil take him!

Afraid it might tarnish your image as her knight in shining armour? taunted an inner voice. *That she will see you as you really are?*

I'm not that person any more. She must know that, mustn't she?

Must she? How well do you two really *know each other?* Kate studied her clasped hands. *It doesn't matter which version of you killed him anyway*, continued her taunter. *They're* both *going to hang.*

She shifted on the hard bench and the woman sitting next to her grumbled.

Anyway, wouldn't it be better for Rebeccah if she despised you? She wouldn't have to grieve for you, then. You're just being selfish.

The truth of that stung. But perhaps Rebeccah would find comfort for her grief in the arms of her suitor . . .

Movement brought her back to her surroundings. Rebeccah had cupped a palm to the top of her head, and was frowning in query. Kate mirrored the action, fingering the egg-sized lump. The swelling was reduced but it was still a little tender; thankfully the blinding headaches had gone. She removed her hand and gave a reassuring smile. Rebeccah's frown eased.

"Bedded 'er yet?"

The low voice drew Kate's attention to the woman sitting next to her. "What?"

"'Er." Deb Wordwand nodded at Rebeccah.

"Mind your own business."

There had been little else to do in the Hold except gossip. Word that Blue-Eyed Nick preferred women had spread quickly and been met with indifference, disgust, or, as in Deb's case, prurience.

Deb chuckled. "That means you ain't." She scratched her broken nose. "They say you never regret the things you 'ave done, only those you ain't."

"I don't give a fart what they say."

"Quiet!" hissed the turnkey.

At least I'm only facing hanging, thought Kate. Until Deb's drunken husband took to beating her black and blue, she had been quite pretty. In the end she'd had enough of his abuse. But stabbing him to death would probably get her burned at the stake, though at least these days the executioner throttled you first with a cord.

The Queen's Justice wound up his preamble, adjusted his wig, and said, "Call the first prisoner, please."

An usher glanced at a slip of paper, cleared his throat, and shouted, "The court calls Judith Ferren to the dock."

At the turnkey's urging, a middle-aged woman in a shabby brown dress rose from the prisoners' bench, shuffled over to the dock, and stood there, head bowed.

Kate already knew the charges against most of her fellow prisoners and listened with one ear while keeping her eyes on Rebeccah.

The court heard that the accused specialized in the "question lay." Dressed as a milliner, she would call on persons of quality on the pretext of having brought "something for the lady of the house"—gloves and fans were the usual bait for Judith's trap. Then while the maid went to fetch her mistress, she robbed the unwatched parlour and made her getaway. Her final haul, from a house in Soho Square, had been plate worth £50.

It was a straightforward case. The witnesses were educated, reliable, and to the point, and the jury came to its verdict quickly: Guilty. Judith Ferren's shoulders sagged, and the turnkey had to help her back to the bench. Sentence would be passed on her tomorrow, when the Queen's Justice would pronounce his judgment on them all in ascending order of severity.

One by one the prisoners rose and took their places in the dock, heard the indictments against them and the testimony of witnesses both for and against, and if inclined, argued in their own defence. The jury deliberated quickly, sometimes taking mere minutes to reach a decision, then their foreman rose to give their verdict, his words sometimes drawing groans from the spectators, sometimes jeers and catcalls. Throughout, the correspondent of the Post Man licked his pencil stub and scribbled, his eyes brightening at every juicy titbit.

Walter Ashwell was found not guilty of embezzling—since it was obvious to everyone that he had, he must have bribed the jury. The rest of the prisoners weren't so fortunate. James Leaver was found "Guilty" of attempted sodomy; if he was pilloried in Cheapside, he could expect near fatal injuries. Also guilty was John Figg; Phebe Woolley—the T branded on her cheek meant she could expect to hang this time; wart-afflicted Isaac Minshul, who was a surprisingly big man for a burglar; foul-mouthed footpad Jemmy Powell; blacksmith Dick Barnes, who had accidentally killed his young apprentice; and sixteen-year-old Ned Lando, whose theft of three shillings would see him flogged at the cart's tail. As expected, Deb Wordwand was found guilty of petty treason.

Then it was Kate's turn.

"I call Catherine Milledge," called the usher, "otherwise known as Blue-Eyed Nick to the dock."

Here we go.

A buzz went round the Session House at the highwayman's name and the correspondent of the Post Man straightened in his seat, pencil poised. Kate stood up and shuffled her way over to the dock, leg-irons clanking. Aware that every eye was on her, including a pair of fine green eyes in the spectator's gallery, she squared her shoulders and held her head high.

"Before I read the list of indictments against the accused," said the corpulent Queen's Justice, his expression grim, "let me state that, while the more ignorant among us may hold the view that highwaymen are romantic and dashing figures, *I* do not. They are no better than the other thieves that infest our cities and highways. Such ruffians are not 'gentlemen of the road' but leeches on society and deserving only of our deepest contempt. Like vermin, they must be exterminated."

His gaze swept round the court before returning to Kate. "As for this particular highwayman, Blue-Eyed Nick," his lip curled, "why, the accused is not even a man, but a woman disguised as one! What kind of an example does this set impressionable womenfolk?" Kate returned his glare with one of her own.

"According to records, the accused escaped justice once before," continued Turnley, addressing the jury. "She must not escape a second time." The foreman nodded, and the correspondent's pencil scribbled.

"The indictments against you, Catherine Milledge," the judge turned back to Kate, "are many and serious. Twelve counts of highway robbery— more still could be laid at your door, I'm certain—and one of cold-blooded murder." The spectators gasped, and Kate fought an overwhelming urge to look at Rebeccah. Had her expression changed to one of horror and disgust?

"Call the first witness."

A succession of those whose coaches she had robbed, and a few she hadn't, took the witness stand—the Duttons had sent no one to testify against her, she saw with relief. For identification purposes, Kate was handed an eye mask and kerchief and told to put them on. Muttering, she did so. In each case, identification was almost instantaneous.

"Yes, that is the person who robbed me of my diamond-and-amber necklace," agreed the final witness, an old woman in a black-and-gold mantua, pointing at Kate. "I'd recognize those eyes anywhere."

The fat judge nodded. "Thank you. You may step down." As the woman left the stand, the spectators took the opportunity to mutter, cough, and fidget.

"Now to the final charge laid against the accused: that on the night of October 18th, in the year of our Lord 1694, she did murder Mr. Philip Wildey." The Queen's Justice glanced at the usher. "Call the witness, if you please."

The usher checked his list of names. "Call Mary Dan," he yelled. Moments passed then a middle-aged woman on crutches emerged from the crowd.

Kate had not seen the whore since that night, twelve years ago, and time had not been kind. Mary Dan had been quite a beauty; now her ravaged face and crippled gait indicated, to Kate at least, that she was suffering from syphilis. Mary's cheap dress reinforced the impression that she had fallen on hard times.

"In your own words, Mistress Dan," said Turnley, "what was your relationship to Philip Wildey."

"We were to be married, your honour."

The baldness of that lie made Kate blink. Wildey liked nothing more than a good fuck, as his many flashy women would testify—nothing could have been further from his mind than marriage. But maybe Mary had truly believed she would be the exception. Kate shifted her weight and folded her arms.

"Then your loss was great indeed," said Turnley. "Allow me to convey my sympathies . . . Now, can you remember what happened on the night of his murder?"

This should be interesting, thought Kate. For, to her certain knowledge, Mary had not been present when she killed Wildey.

"Alas, your honour, my memory of that night is clear and will always remain so," said Mary. "Would that it were otherwise. For I saw that . . . that animal," she shot Kate a hate-filled glance, "torture him then kill him stone dead."

Has Josselin paid the whore to perjure herself?

"Mistress Dan." The Queen's justice pursed his lips. "Consider your response to my next question carefully. Could it have been self-defence? Was Mr. Wildey trying to kill the accused at the time?"

"No, your honour. Philip's hands were bound and he was unable to defend himself. Yet still she tortured him and shot him through the heart."

A ripple of disapproval spread round the Session House. Kate ignored it. Mary's facts were essentially correct. *I knew I should have buried the body.*

"And you saw it, you say?" Turnley's eyes bored into the witness. "You saw the accused murder Philip Wildey?"

Mary Dan held his gaze and lied through her teeth. "With my own eyes, your honour. I swear it on my life."

Flickering candlelight cast shadows on the bedchamber curtains. Kate grimaced. From the thrusting, bobbing shapes, her quarry was already hard at it.

It had taken the seventeen-year-old Kate months to trace Philip Wildey's whereabouts, months during which nightmares of Newgate brought her awake, gasping, on far too many nights and the desire to get even made her guts churn. The churning intensified when she learned that she was far from the first to fall prey to Wildey's smooth-tongued charm, to accept his loan of a horse and brace of pistols and be lured into a trap. Because of him eight young highwaymen—that she knew of; there were probably more—had been taken by dragoons and met their deaths on Tyburn Tree. And Kate had nearly been the ninth.

She had finally succeeded in tracking him down though. These days

Wildey went nowhere without his bodyguard—perhaps he sensed that he had made one too many enemies. But on Tuesday nights, he liked to spend between ten and eleven of the clock at Mary Dan's cottage. While Wildey was fucking his pretty whore, his moustachioed, over-muscled thug of a bodyguard, who carried his two pistols permanently cocked, had to wait on the front porch. It was the perfect opportunity and Kate intended to take full advantage of it.

Gusts of wind were tearing leaves from branches and threatening to whip off Kate's hat. It had begun to rain too. She settled her hat more firmly. Far from putting her off, the stormy Autumn weather suited her mood. Tonight she would pay Wildey back. And not a moment too soon.

She pulled a knife from her coat pocket and snicked open the catch of Mary's bedchamber window, which fortunately was on the ground floor. As she eased open the sash, the sound of pants, grunts, and a rhythmic creaking became audible.

"You're so large," came a woman's voice, husky with simulated passion. "I've never had a man as large as you."

Kate rolled her eyes—how could any cully believe such ridiculous flattery?—and eased herself over the windowsill, placing her booted feet with care so that the couple writhing on the bed remained unaware of her presence. The creaks grew faster.

"Oh, oh, you're such a stud!"

"Get on with it," cried Wildey. "I'm almost there."

Kate took a deep breath. It's now or never. *Two quick steps carried her past the discarded hat, wig, and coat on the floor, then she leaned over, grabbed her victim's ear, and yanked back his head. Pressing her blade against his throat cut off his startled protest and made him freeze.*

"Why have you st—" Mary opened her eyes, saw the menacing masked figure, and gasped.

"Scream and I'll slit his throat," growled Kate. "And what a mess that will make of your fine silk sheets." The whore blinked up at her then closed her mouth.

Kate moved back a step, forcing Wildey to disentangle himself from Mary and come with her. His breeches were round his ankles and he almost tripped. Kate steadied him, then glanced down. Not everything about him was stiff with fear.

"Pull up your breeches. I have no wish to look at that *all night." His face flushed but he did as he was told. "Now put your hands behind your back."*

She tied his wrists with a short piece of rope from her coat pocket, holding her knife between her teeth as she did so. Then she stuffed a kerchief in Wildey's mouth and took a moment to admire the half-naked whore's attributes.

"Your turn." She pulled out another length of rope, and an indignant Mary was soon bound and gagged.

Kate turned back to Wildey. "Move." She gestured with the knife towards the open sash window. He didn't move, but a thump to his kidneys soon spurred him on his way and he cracked his head on the window frame as he climbed through. The rain was coming down in torrents now, and thunder rumbled overhead.

Taking care to keep him out of the drenched bodyguard's line of sight, she pushed her dazed prisoner towards the stand of trees where she had tethered her horse. Wildey twisted to glare at her, just as lightning streaked across the sky. Perhaps this was the first time he had got a good look at her. Whatever the reason, his eyes widened.

"Yes, it's me." The kerchief hid her savage grin.

He tripped and fell quite heavily. Fortunately, the ground was too soft to do him much damage. Kate dragged her now muddy captive to his feet and urged him on.

The horse shied at the approaching figures, but a few words from Kate soon calmed it. She bound Wildey's ankles and heaved him over the horse's withers, face down. It swished its tail in annoyance.

"Sorry, boy." She paused to get her breath back. "'Tis just for a little while." She rubbed the horse's nose. "Then we'll get you warm and dry, and some oats inside you. How does that sound?" Ears that had been laid flat back relaxed, and a nicker showed she was forgiven.

"Mph . . . fmph." Wildey squirmed in discomfort but Kate ignored him, untied the reins, and mounted up.

Thunder and lightning provided a fitting accompaniment to the pounding of hooves as she rode. The lateness of the hour and the rough weather meant the road was deserted. Wildey grunted every time Kate's knees jabbed into him or the bony withers threatened to drive the breath from his lungs.

It was only a couple of miles to the clearing. She reined in, dismounted, and pulled Wildey from the horse without ceremony. He hit the ground with a thump and a muffled cry, then rolled over onto his back, blinking rain from his eyes.

Kate tramped over to the two storm lanterns she had left there earlier, pulled out her flint, and spent a moment lighting them. She straightened and turned to face her prisoner, uncovering her face so he could be in no doubt who she was. "This is where it ends."

Flickering light now illuminated the clearing. Wildey's face went ashen when he saw the halter draped over a stout branch of the oak tree and the tree stump she had placed directly under it. She pulled the sodden kerchief from his mouth.

"You can't!" were his first words.

"Watch me."

He licked his lips. "We were friends once, Kate. And we can be again. Spare me and you can have anything you want. Name it and it's yours."

She pretended to consider. "The lives of Dick Trebeck, Isaac Kerrils, John Grierson," she counted the names off on her fingers, "Walter Lilley, Jim Barker, Ben Comyngs, Ed Lance, and Tate Nolan."

He gaped at her in dismay. "Who?"

"The highwaymen you betrayed . . . Oh, but you can't give me their lives, can you? So much for promises." She grabbed him under the armpits and dragged him across the clearing.

"I can get you a free pardon, Kate. I'm a man of some influence. I can—" He squawked as the noose settled round his neck.

"Save your breath." She tightened the loop of hempen rope. "It's time to make your peace with God."

Kate didn't bother hooding him, the way they did at Tyburn—it was more to spare the spectators' feelings than the criminal's, and she was determined not to flinch from the consequences of what she was about to do. She sliced through the bonds around his ankles, then reached for the free end of the halter. Then she paused, suddenly doubtful. It had been one thing planning this moment, but now that it was actually here . . .

Once I do this there is no going back. *She glanced at her victim; he was whimpering and the whites of his eyes were huge.* But have I not already come too far to go back? For if I let him go now, he won't rest until he sees me hang. *She sighed.* So be it. *She spat on her palms, grabbed the rope, and began to haul.*

With a cry, Wildey scrambled up onto the stump, trying to keep the noose from tightening round his neck. When he was fully stretched on tiptoe, Kate tied the free end of the halter securely round the tree trunk.

"For the love of God, spare me!" he choked out. "Have mercy."

Kate remembered the hell that was Newgate and imagined the fear of the eight terrified young highwaymen who had died at Tyburn. Wildey had not been merciful to them.

He must have read his fate in her face, for his shoulders sagged and he closed his eyes tightly and began to pray.

She waited until he had finished, then said, "May God have mercy on your soul," and kicked away the tree stump.

The noose cut Wildey's shriek short as he toppled. His eyes bulged and rolled up in his head, and his feet began to kick. There were no hangers-on to speed his passage to the next world, no one present except his nemesis. For a moment longer Kate let him strangle, then she pulled the loaded pistol from her coat pocket, cocked it, aimed, and fired.

The streaks of lightning and crashes of thunder had been growing fainter and more infrequent as the storm moved away to the north, and for the first time that night, the wind dropped. A numb Kate listened to the pattering of rain on the leaves and the creak of the rope. For a while she simply stood watching the halter and its macabre burden swinging gently to and fro, then she staggered to the side of the clearing, grabbed a branch and leaned over, and was violently sick.

"And you saw the accused shoot him dead?" pressed Turnley, his gaze intent.

"Ay, your honour." Mary Dan shifted on her crutches and glanced at Kate, her gaze vindictive. "Cold blooded it was. The woman's a fiend incarnate."

"Thank you." The Queen's Justice turned to Kate. "You have heard this witness. Do you have anything to say in your defence?"

"Other than that she is lying? No, your honour." A murmur of disappointment rippled round the Session House. They had expected Blue-Eyed Nick to give them more of a show. *Too bad.*

People thought a highwayman's life was all glamour and excitement. It had its moments, true—there were plenty of bored young women as eager to be bedded as robbed, and Kate had seen her share of rubies and pearls—but there was also as much fear and exhaustion as there was exhilaration. How many would envy the long nights spent in the cold and wet waiting for a coach that never arrived, the violent squabbles and brawls when partners fell out, the peril that came not just from the Law but from an unscrupulous rival?

Once, the danger had made her feel alive, but lately . . . well, just lately, all the running and hiding had begun to pall. Perhaps she was simply getting too old. They said few highwayman lived past thirty, and it would be Kate's thirtieth birthday in a few months. For a moment she wondered what her life might have been like had she completed her apprenticeship as a seamstress, then she dismissed it with a mental shrug. The point was moot, and anyway, she wouldn't have met Rebeccah.

While the judge dismissed the witness, summed up the case against Kate, and directed the jury to consider its verdict, Kate stared into space, remembering the precious days she had spent in St. James's Square recovering from her bullet wound under Rebeccah's tender care. Then the motion of the jury foreman standing up and clearing his throat drew her back to her surroundings. She squared her shoulders and waited.

"Have you reached a verdict?" enquired Judge Turnley.

"We have, Milud."

"Let the court hear it then, and speak up."

"We find the accused, Catherine Milledge, otherwise known as Blue-Eyed Nick, guilty on all counts."

A mix of groans and cheers went up, and the correspondent of the Post Man finished his scribbling, rose, and dashed from the court.

"An admirable verdict. You and your fellow jurors have acquitted yourselves honourably." The foreman gave a complacent nod and sat down.

Turnley glanced at the prisoner's bench, saw that all had been tried, and gave a satisfied grunt. "Tomorrow I will pronounce sentence. In the meantime," he brought down his gavel with a *crack*, "remove the prisoners from my court."

♌

Kate blocked out the hell that was Newgate's Condemned Hold by daydreaming. One of her favourites was to imagine herself out riding, the wind in her hair, sun warm on her back, and Clover's hooves drumming across the turf.

The sentencing two days ago had been perfunctory, its outcome entirely predictable—she was to hang. She had shuffled back from the Old Bailey to the accompaniment of shrieks, agonized groans, and the stink of burning flesh as the brazier at the side of the Session House was dragged out and the branding got under way. The Keeper had informed Kate that, as was usual, the Court Recorder would send a report of all capital sentences, including Kate's, for review by Queen Anne and her cabinet. But it was but a formality. Kate knew she had not the remotest hope of obtaining a pardon, even a conditional one. The next hanging fair was on Monday, and she could expect to be an unwilling participant.

In a way she was glad her time left was so short. She had merely to get through three more days without going mad from the stench and horror of her surroundings. And how better to do that than by thinking about riding, or Rebeccah's smiling face.

The young woman hadn't been in the public gallery during the sentencing, nor had she been to visit Kate since. And who could blame her after hearing of Wildey's murder?

I hope she has washed her hands of me, thought Kate, even as she hoped no such thing.

A door banged open. Curses and catcalls followed the progress of one of the turnkeys across the hold towards her. Kate squinted at him through the gloom.

"On your feet, Milledge." Simpkins kicked the sole of her ill-fitting shoe (her own boots had been taken from her when they put on the leg-irons).

She stood, fetters clinking. "What now?"

"Follow me and you'll find out, will ye not?"

Every eye in the place turned to watch the two of them. "She won't let you fuck her, Simpkins," yelled someone. "She plays the Game of Flats." Coarse laughter met that remark. But the turnkey ignored it, and so did Kate.

Outside, she waited while he locked the door behind them with a key from the huge bunch jangling at his belt. Then he turned and pointed down the corridor. She arched an eyebrow, but no explanation was forthcoming, so she began shuffling in that direction.

They had walked only a few paces when he said, "Stop."

She found herself standing outside one of the private condemned cells. "I can't afford this!"

"Just as well it's already paid for, then." He selected another key from the bunch, inserted it, and opened the door with a screech.

The cell was dirty, and cramped, its only furniture a chipped chamber pot, a rickety table on which lay a large padlock, and a chair. But what drew her eye was the small barred window, through which came welcome light and air. Cells with windows cost even more.

"Get in."

She hesitated. If this was some kind of cruel trick, if Josselin had paid Simpkins to dangle the prospect of a private cell in front of her then withdraw it . . . "Who paid?"

"I said get in." Simpkins shoved her and she stumbled into the cell, then turned and gave him a baleful look. He pointed to the chair, and after a moment she sat. A staple was sunk into the floor at her feet, she saw then, and the next minute he was bending down and padlocking her ankle fetters to it.

"My instructions are to make sure you don't escape again," he explained, finishing and straightening with a groan.

Kate gave the fetters a tug, aggravating ankles already rubbed raw. The staple was as solid as a rock.

The turnkey folded his arms and observed her for a moment then chuckled. "I've got good news and bad news, Milledge. Which do you want first?" She shrugged. "The bad news is, we received the Dead Warrant this morning, and your name is on it."

No Queen's pardon then. Hardly a surprise. "And the good news?"

"This cell is yours until you go to get your neck stretched." He walked towards the door.

"But who paid for it, Simpkins?" He grinned and began to close the door. "Who the Devil paid for it?" The key turned with a screech.

"You should see your face." His laughter was muffled by the thickness of the door.

Kate ground her teeth. "Hellfire and damnation, Simpkins!" she shouted. "What harm can it do to tell me?"

The silence lasted so long that she thought he had gone. Then she heard, "A Mistress Dutton paid for your cell, Milledge. I hope you are suitably grateful."

Her heart leapt. "Rebeccah Dutton?"

There was a brief pause. "It says 'Anne' here."

She blinked. "Are you sure?" But this time there was no reply, and she knew the turnkey had gone.

Chapter 19

"Turnkey Wryneck will escort you to see the prisoner, Mistress Dutton."
The Keeper gestured at the bewhiskered little man with the bunch of keys
at his belt who had just entered his office.

"Thank you," said Rebeccah.

"No, Madam, thank you." The Keeper grinned, jingled the money she
had given him, then slumped back into his chair. He selected a legal-looking
document from the untidy pile on his desk and began to read. Rebeccah
glanced at the turnkey, who folded his arms and scowled.

"You'll get your share later, Wryneck," said the Keeper, without looking
up. The turnkey grunted, unfolded his arms, and beckoned to Rebeccah.
After a moment, she followed him, hurrying to keep up.

Wryneck turned left outside the Keeper's Office, heading away from the
entry gate and into the candle-lit bowels of Newgate. Cockroaches scuttled
across the floor, and without breaking his stride, the turnkey crushed one
under his heel. The soft crunch made Rebeccah wince, and she lifted her
skirts a few inches and tried not to step on anything that moved.

They descended a flight of stairs, then set off along a corridor. Progress
was slow. Every few yards, it seemed, yet another locked door or gate
barred their way, and Rebeccah had to wait while Wryneck unlocked it
then again while he relocked it behind them. The reek of unwashed
bodies and piss intensified the deeper into the prison they went, and breathing through her mouth became preferable. It was harder, though, to block
out the noises coming from behind the locked doors on either side, the
shouting and cursing, the high keening sobs.

"You ain't Milledge's first visitor this morning," said Wryneck, glancing
back at her.

"Oh?"

"Highwaymen are always popular."

They descended yet another stairs and turned right. In the distance she could hear someone laughing—the unnerving, high pitched laughter of the insane.

"The Ordinary was with her for an hour," continued Wryneck. "Getting her life story for one of his pamphlets. Then half an hour ago there was a woman. Crying, she was, even before she went in." He glanced at Rebeccah again.

She kept her expression neutral. "Indeed."

Disappointed at her lack of reaction, the turnkey faced forward once more.

They turned left at the next junction, then right. By now Rebeccah was hopelessly lost.

Coming towards them along the corridor were two figures. In the gloom it was impossible to make out much more than that one was a man, the other a woman. But as the latter drew nearer and passed a guttering candle, Rebeccah caught a glimpse of red hair. There was something very familiar about—

With a cry the woman launched herself at her. "It's all your fault," railed Kate's landlady, hands flailing. "Everything was fine before she met you." She caught hold of Rebeccah's hair and pain stabbed through Rebeccah's scalp.

"Let go of me!" She tried to prise open the vice-like grip.

"Oi, stop that!" Wryneck's attempt to help earned him an elbow in the eye for his pains. "Give me a hand, Simpkins," he yelled at the turnkey who had been accompanying Alice Cole.

Simpkins helped his smaller colleague pull the red-haired woman off Rebeccah, but not before he had received a kick in the shins. By now, faces were pressed to the grilles all along the corridor. Rebeccah tried to ignore the muffled shouts of encouragement, hoots, and obscene suggestions coming thick and fast from the excited inmates and retain her dignity. She reordered her hair as best she could and smoothed her dress.

Alice meanwhile was continuing to struggle in the turnkeys' grip. Only Simpkins' slap and threat to lock her in a cell brought her to her senses. She subsided, panting and looking baleful.

"Get that baggage out of here before I do something rash," growled Wryneck, rubbing his bruised eye.

Simpkins gripped Alice—none too gently from her exclamation—and limped off down the corridor with her. One by one the faces behind the grilles vanished.

"Women!" Ignoring Rebeccah's indignant glance, Wryneck reached for the keys at his belt. "Milledge's cell is just at the end of this corridor." He strode towards it; Rebeccah followed. Her cheek stung and she touched a fingertip to it; Alice must have scratched her.

The door they stopped at was indistinguishable from any other. The turnkey selected a key and inserted it in the lock. It turned stiffly and with a nerve-grating screech.

"Visitor for you, Milledge," he called, pushing open the heavy door. "And this one ain't like that last one. She's a lady, so just you behave yourself." He stood back and motioned to Rebeccah.

"Thank you." She took out a shilling and gave it to him. "For your assistance."

Wryneck flipped the coin, then pocketed it. "My pleasure, Madam. You have half an hour. I'll be out here if you should need me. Just shout."

She took a deep breath and stepped inside.

The door swung closed behind her, the lock screeching again, but Rebeccah barely noticed it. Her attention was on the seated figure and the wide blue eyes fixed on her.

"Rebeccah!" A pleased smile curved Kate's mouth and with a metallic *chink* she rose to her feet. Only then did Rebeccah realize that the shackles around Kate's ankles were stapled to the floor.

"Good morrow, Kate."

She took in her surroundings at a glance. The cell was smaller than she had expected, and dirtier, and the draught from the barred window couldn't mask the unpleasant smell coming from the uncovered chamber pot. Lord knows what the Condemned Hold must be like if this was an improvement.

She turned back to a much more pleasant sight. There were shadows beneath Kate's eyes, and she was grimy and unkempt, but apart from that she looked well enough.

"You must thank your sister for the great kindness she has done me," said Kate. "This cell is a godsend."

"Anne will be very glad to hear it. When our lawyer mentioned the possibility of such a thing, she insisted on doing it at once."

"Lawyer?"

"We have been busy these past few days," said Rebeccah a little ruefully.

"Busy" didn't come close to describing it. Her time had been spent on visits to lawyers and consultations with friends and relatives (Caro and her husband had been particularly helpful with their advice), all trying to find a way out of Kate's current predicament. As well, she had had to help nurse a still emotionally fragile Anne (she had at first been plagued by nightmares) and apprise Anne's fiancé of just enough about what had happened to make him sympathetic yet not enough to scare him off. She had had to also help her mother find and hire a replacement for Titus.

"Ah." Kate nodded. "How is Anne, by the way? Recovering from her recent ordeal?"

"She is well, thank you. Improving by the day. She's quieter than she was, and chastened. Still somewhat shaken, I think—she has yet to leave the house for any length of time. But we are all very grateful for her escape. And Mr. Ingrum is being surprisingly considerate."

"I am glad."

Rebeccah felt in the pocket of her skirts and found what she wanted. Her maid had thought she was mad to bring it, but Rebeccah had insisted. "Have you any use for this, Kate?" She held out the nail. "I seem to remember that once before an item such as this helped you to escape."

Kate took it and started to laugh. "Thank you, my dear. But alas," she pointed at the sturdy padlock and staple, "this time I fear they are beyond its scope."

Rebeccah sighed. "Ah well. It was worth a try." She looked around the cell once more. "Are we to stand for my entire visit?"

Kate grimaced. "I'm afraid there is only the one chair." She pulled it out from behind her with a scraping of wood on stone. "Here. You take it."

Rebeccah was about to do so when a much better solution presented itself. "Keep it. I shall sit on your lap."

The highwaywoman blinked at her then arched an eyebrow. "Nothing would give me greater pleasure." She smiled. "But I cannot remember the last time I changed my clothes or had access to a bath. At close quarters I fear I smell . . . less than fragrant."

"Nevertheless. Is it not the most practical solution to our problem?"

With an acquiescent tilt of the head, Kate retrieved the chair and sat down. Then she patted her lap and waited for Rebeccah to make herself comfortable in it. After an awkward moment she did so, smoothing her skirts over her behind before lowering herself rather gingerly.

Kate's hand came up to clasp Rebeccah's waist, making her breathing catch. "Don't want you sliding off," she murmured

Silence fell as each woman adjusted to this new intimacy, Rebeccah acutely aware of the pale blue eyes regarding her from mere inches away.

The "less than fragrant" odour Kate had mentioned wasn't as bad as she had made out, and anyway it paled into insignificance under the barrage of other sensations. The current of attraction that had flowed between them since their very first meeting was as strong as ever.

"Are you comfortable?" asked Kate at last.

"Indeed I am." A belated thought occurred to Rebeccah. "Am I crushing you?"

"You are as light as thistledown."

"We both know I am not, but thank you for the compliment."

Kate smiled, then stroked Rebeccah's cheek with a forefinger. "What happened?"

Her touch made the pit of Rebeccah's stomach flutter, and it was a moment before she registered the question. "Um . . ." She had no idea what Kate was referring to.

"You have a nasty scratch. And then there is your hair." Kate tucked a stray lock behind Rebeccah's ear. "Your maid does not usually let you out of the house in so dishevelled a condition."

"Ah." Rebeccah bit her lip. Should she tell Kate about Alice Cole's strange behaviour?

"Come now. Let there be no evasions between us."

Rebeccah sighed. "It was your landlady. I passed her in the corridor outside and . . ."

Dark eyebrows shot up. "Alice attacked you?"

Rebeccah nodded. "She seems to think your being in here is my fault." She frowned. "For a landlady, her behaviour is a little . . . extreme."

"You did not deserve such treatment at her hands. It is I she should be angry at." Kate looked away. "I treated her badly, Rebeccah."

"Do you owe her rent? If so, tell me the sum and I will—"

"It's not that." Ashamed blue eyes met hers. "We were more than land-lady and tenant. Alice loved me, and even though I did not return her feelings I . . . I took advantage."

Certain things that had puzzled Rebeccah now dropped into place. Her thoughtful silence brought a grimace from the other woman.

"I suppose now you despise me." Kate sounded resigned. "But then, what is one more crime when I have already been found guilty of so many?"

Rebeccah was about to answer when a muffled shout interrupted them.

"Twenty minutes, Madam," came Wryneck's voice through the cell door.

The two women glanced at one another, then both spoke at once. "Kate, I came to tell you not to give up—" "This is no place for a gentlewoman alone. Why did not your maid accompany you, or your suitor?"

Rebeccah's train of thought was completely derailed. "My suitor?"

"The young man I saw you walking with the other day, in St. James's Park."

"Oh! You saw me? But that was my best friend Caro's husband."

Kate blinked. "And what were you doing out walking alone with your best friend's husband?"

"She was indisposed. He was there with her full knowledge and permission. He is to look for a husband for me."

Kate's expression was hard to decipher.

"And a hard job he will have of it too. For he rates my chances of success as slim at best."

"Does he think no man would want you for his wife?"

Kate's indignation amused and touched Rebeccah. "No. He fears that it is I who would decline them," she said. "For I am too choosy by half."

The other woman cocked her head. "Are you?"

"Oh yes." Rebeccah held Kate's gaze. "For I have insisted that my future husband must bear an uncanny resemblance, in every respect, to a notorious highwayman known as Blue-Eyed Nick." She paused. "Perhaps you have heard of him?"

Blue eyes filled with astonishment. Then Kate chuckled, and her other hand came up and clasped Rebeccah round the waist. "The name is vaguely familiar," she murmured, and Rebeccah found herself suddenly fascinated by Kate's lips which had moved tantalizingly closer.

She was in a noisome cell at Newgate, sitting on the lap of a convicted felon, a woman no less, who, if things didn't work out as Rebeccah hoped, was going to hang in two days' time. And she had never felt so at home or so alive in all her life.

"I often think of that kiss," murmured Kate.

Rebeccah didn't need to ask to which kiss she was referring. Her cheeks grew warm at the memory. "As do I."

Kate's face drew closer still, and Rebeccah could feel the warmth of her breath on her cheek. Then soft lips were pressing against hers. After a frozen moment, Rebeccah returned the pressure, which turned into a sensual nibbling that brought that fluttering to the pit of her stomach again.

How shocking! she thought. *I am kissing another woman. What's more,*

I am enjoying it very much. But the realization caused her no distress, and she couldn't seem to bring herself to stop the pleasurable activity. Indeed if Wryneck's muffled shout of "Ten minutes" hadn't reminded her that time was running out she might be there still.

She pulled away. "I didn't come here to be kissed."

The highwaywoman went very still. "Didn't you?" Her hands dropped from Rebeccah's waist.

"Though if I had known how pleasurable it is I certainly would have." Kate's smile returned and so did both hands. Rebeccah resisted the urge to resume where they had left off. "Kate, as I said before, I came to tell you not to give up hope."

The other woman sighed. "Then your journey was in vain, my dear. For the Dead Warrant came this morning, and my name is on it."

"I know. News of it reached us at home. But Mama and I have been discussing the matter with friends and lawyers, and there is one avenue left: a petition of mercy to the Queen."

"She has already declined to pardon me once," objected Kate. "What makes you think you can change her mind?"

Rebeccah interlaced their fingers. "Because it will be presented to her by her closest friend."

Blue eyes widened. "The Duchess of Marlborough?"

"The very same. Do you not remember I told you that she and Mama are second cousins?" Kate's gaze turned inwards then she nodded. "As children they were very close. If Mama asks Aunt Sarah to help her with Queen Anne, she likely will . . . This month the Duchess is residing at Windsor with the Queen. At this very moment, a carriage is waiting outside; Mama and I are to travel there directly I leave here."

"That is kind indeed of you and your family, Rebeccah, to risk jeopardizing relations between your family and the Duchess on my behalf."

"It is the least we can do, after the many services you have rendered us."

Kate chuckled. "Such as robbing you of your valuables."

Rebeccah frowned. "Do not make light of your actions. If you had not been on hand to save my sister from Titus's clutches . . . Not to mention saving my life."

"You forget you have saved my life once already. You must not be unduly distressed if you are unable to save it a second time."

"How can you say that?"

Kate shrugged. "I am a cold-blooded murderer and the time to pay for my crime has come." She became thoughtful

"What are you thinking?"

"That I was certain once you knew what I did to Philip Wildey I would not see you again." She smiled a little uncertainly and bounced Rebeccah on her knee. "Yet here you are."

"At first I did not know what to think, it is true. I feared I had misjudged you. So I asked Mary to find out all the facts of the matter." Her maid's contacts were sometimes unsavoury but frequently useful, Rebeccah had found. "What you did was indeed shocking, Kate. But it was also understandable." She regarded the other woman with compassion. "You were seventeen, and the man you trusted had betrayed you. Because of him the dragoons beat you near to death. And if you had not escaped from Newgate, you would have been transported or hanged." Kate blinked at her. "In some circles, folk still feel that Wildey got what he deserved."

"Not respectable circles, I'll wager."

Rebeccah smiled. "Perhaps not," she conceded.

"Five minutes," yelled Wryneck.

"Maybe it is selfishness on my part," continued Rebeccah, "but I am glad that it was Wildey who died and not you." The earnest sentiment earned her hands a warm squeeze. "Given the right circumstances, do we not all have the potential to be felons?"

Kate's smile was sceptical. "I do not think you could do anything unlawful."

"Then you'd be wrong. For only a few days ago I tried to bribe a Queen's Justice." Rebeccah sighed. "For all the good it did."

Kate's eyes widened. "Judge Turnley?"

"The same." The memory of his derisive laughter was still raw. "Had it been anyone but a female highwayman," *and one who loves women,* "I think he might have taken it too. You might now even be facing transportation rather than the noose."

"Then I am glad he did *not* accept," said Kate. "For transportation would have taken me away from you as effectively as hanging."

Rebeccah blinked then pressed a kiss on Kate's cheek. When she pulled back, Kate was regarding her gravely.

"Will you do something for me?"

"Name it."

"If your petition of mercy should fail in spite of your aunt's entreaties, and no pardon is forthcoming—"

"Don't say that!"

"My sweet, you must not get your hopes—"

Rebeccah silenced her by pressing two fingers to Kate's mouth. "I mean it, Kate."

Kate sighed and waited for Rebeccah to remove her fingers. "Very well. I have sold a version of my life story, such as it is, to the Ordinary. My share of the proceeds from the pamphlets he sells should be enough to pay for my coffin and any debts incurred during my stay here—"

Rebeccah stared at her, aghast. "Your coffin!"

"—with a little left over," continued Kate, doggedly. "I have dependants. There is a woman named Jane Allen who cares for my mother. And Eliza Wagstaff—her boy is my brother Ned's son. Lord knows it will be little enough to keep them off the street but . . ." She trailed off, eyes pleading.

Rebeccah pressed Kate's hand. "Write down their addresses and I will make sure the money reaches them," she managed round the lump in her throat. "And if they should have further need of anything, I will see to it that they get it."

"God bless you!" Kate raised their clasped hands and kissed Rebeccah's fingers. "I will rest easier knowing that."

"But it will not come to that," insisted Rebeccah. "You will be here to take care of them yourself."

The screeching of the lock made both women glance at the door. Kate kissed Rebeccah quickly on the mouth, then stood, tipping the startled younger woman off her comfortable perch. By the time the door had swung fully open Rebeccah was standing at a respectable distance from Kate, and looking, if not as well groomed and dignified as she would have liked, then at least nonchalant.

"Time's up," said Wryneck, giving both women a sharp glance before beckoning to Rebeccah.

She nodded and walked towards him. At the door she halted and looked back.

"I will see you soon," she said. "Do not give up hope yet, I beg of you."

Kate smiled gamely. "I'll try."

ℳ

The door slammed shut and the carriage lurched into motion before Rebeccah was ready. She regained her balance, then with Mary's help began to straighten her dress and smooth her hair.

"I take it you saw him . . . I mean her," said Mrs. Dutton, over the clatter of hooves on cobblestones.

"Yes, Mama. The Keeper allowed me the full half hour. Ow! You're stabbing me, Mary."

"Beg pardon, Madam." The plump maid readjusted the hairpin, then, from somewhere about her person, produced a pot of face powder and dabbed some carefully over Rebeccah's scratch.

"Is she well?" continued Mrs. Dutton.

Rebeccah grimaced. "The term is relative. Kate is as well as anyone can be in Newgate."

Mrs. Dutton gave Rebeccah's knee a pat through her skirts. "Well you have nothing to reproach yourself for, my dear. For you have done as much as you are able for your friend, indeed more than most."

Rebeccah gave her mother a sharp glance, but saw that the remark was innocent. It had upset Mrs. Dutton to learn that her youngest daughter had nursed an injured felon under her roof without her knowledge, but in the light of subsequent events her hurt had proved fleeting. It was probably just as well, though, that she was unaware of the true nature and depth of her daughter's feelings for that self same felon.

The carriage's three occupants were flung first one way then another as it swung to the left, then right, before straightening. Once they were out of London the route would be more straightforward but progress would be slower. It was only twenty-four miles to Windsor, but the terrible state of the roads meant it might well be nightfall by the time they reached their destination. By then she would no doubt be aching and headachy from the clatter and constant jolting, and envying her frail sister's reluctant but in the circumstances prudent decision to remain in London.

"I sent a messenger ahead," said Mrs. Dutton, "to warn your Aunt Sarah we are coming." Sarah, Duchess of Marlborough wasn't Rebeccah's real aunt, of course, but it was easier to call her that than find a suitable appellation for a mother's second cousin.

"What if she is busy entertaining other guests, Mama?"

"Then we will have to put up at an Inn close by until she can find a moment to see us. We shall cross that bridge when we come to it, Beccah, but I doubt it will be a problem. For the Great Lodge is in all likelihood spacious enough that she can spare us a chamber or two even if she is entertaining."

"Do you really think she will help us?"

Her mother smiled. "I don't see why not. And with her assistance . . . well, you know how the Queen dotes on her."

Indeed Rebeccah did. It was common knowledge that Queen Anne was besotted with the charismatic Sarah Churchill, though it was also rumoured she had cooled a little towards her of late. The Duchess was but the latest in a long line of female favourites, and for a moment Rebeccah wondered if the monarch might be like her and Kate. Then she remembered the Queen's amiable consort, Prince George, and the brood of children (none of whom had survived) that had resulted from their marriage, and dismissed it as idle fancy.

Mary produced her sewing bag, pulled out a square of white silk destined to become a pocket *mouchoir*, and began to sew. She caught the direction of Rebeccah's gaze. "I have brought the cards with me, Madam. If you would rather play . . ."

"Thank you, Mary. Perhaps later. For now I am content to admire the view."

Rebeccah settled back in her seat and gazed out the window. They had reached the outskirts of London at last and open fields and woods stretched on all sides. But she was soon insensible to the beauty of the passing landscape. Her gaze was turned inwards to those moments when she had sat on Kate's lap, the other woman's hands around her waist, returning her kiss. And if either Mary or her mother noticed her enigmatic smile and were curious as to its cause, they had the good sense to keep it to themselves.

🖎

"Are your rooms to your liking?" The Duchess of Marlborough gestured to the serving woman that she should pour the tea and offer biscuits.

"Indeed they are, your ladyship. Aren't they, Beccah?" Rebeccah nodded and took a high-backed seat next to her mother at the tea table. "We are greatly in your debt. I regret having to impose on your hospitality at such short notice, but—"

"'Your ladyship'?" The Duchess's eyebrows rose. "We have always been Sarah and Elizabeth to one another, have we not?"

Mrs. Dutton visibly relaxed. "That is kind of you, Sarah. Thank you." With a smile, she accepted a porcelain dish of tea.

There was a brief pause, during which Rebeccah listened to the logs shifting in the fireplace and the caged nightingales trilling in one corner of the spacious drawing room, then her aunt said, "I was sorry to hear about Mr. Dutton's death last year."

"It hit us all very hard," agreed Rebeccah's mother with a sigh. "We miss him terribly, don't we, Beccah?" Rebeccah nodded. "But we are slowly growing accustomed to his absence. And how is your own husband? The War must be keeping him from home more than you would wish."

"Indeed it is."

In Rebeccah's opinion, the famous Duke's absence was more than made up for by his many portraits throughout the Great Lodge, so she tuned out the reply and bit into a ratafia biscuit. She had hoped for something more substantial, but this would have to do until supper.

Discreetly, she eyed the Duchess, of whom she had only the most vague memories. Sarah must be in her late forties now, but Rebeccah would never have guessed it from her appearance. Her unblemished face had no need of patches, and her reddish-yellow hair was as lush as ever—probably due to the daily wash in honey-water she gave it, according to Rebeccah's mother.

Sensing her scrutiny, Sarah turned to regard Rebeccah. "But enough of my news. How old are you now, Rebeccah?"

"Three-and-twenty, Aunt."

"Indeed! You were only a tiny thing when I last saw you. It was that visit to us at Syon House, was it not?" She looked at Mrs. Dutton who nodded. "A mere scrap of a girl you were, then, your petticoats in tatters, dirt on your cheeks—*so* unlike your sister. Ran your poor maid ragged." Rebeccah's cheeks grew warm. "You took a fancy to the patch of garden we called The Wilderness, I remember. You were always to be found there, up one tree or another."

Rebeccah blinked as a long forgotten memory of gnarled trees surfaced. They had seemed to spear the sky and, for whatever reason—the challenge of the ascent, or the view from the top (sometimes she would daydream that the sky was the sea and a dashing pirate captain, who, come to think of it, looked remarkably like Kate, was coming to carry her off)—she found climbing them irresistible.

"One night you refused to come down. Said you were going to sleep up in the crow's-nest, whatever that was. In the end your poor father himself had to climb up and fetch you down." Aunt Sarah chuckled. "And look at you now! Every inch the elegant young lady." She cocked her head and assessed Rebeccah. "A little on the short side, mayhap, but you have a good figure, fine eyes, and a passably pretty face."

Passably pretty! Rebeccah wondered whether to be pleased or insulted. Her aunt turned back to her mother. "I'll warrant young men flock round her like bees round honey." Since nothing could be further from the truth, Mrs. Dutton wisely kept silent.

The Duchess sipped her tea. "And how is your oldest girl? Anne has not come with you, I gather. She is not ill, I trust?"

"She has been a little unwell of late, but she is fast recovering. Other matters keep her in London. She is engaged to be married soon and there are preparations to be made."

"Indeed?" Sarah clapped her hands together in delight. "High time too! My four girls were all married in their teens and have thrived on it." She looked complacent, as well she might considering the advantageous matches she had contrived: two of her daughters were now Countesses, the others Duchesses. "Do I know the groom?"

"I doubt it. His name is Frederick Ingrum."

For a while the conversation continued in this vein, the two cousins catching up on family news and gossip, and then at last, etiquette and politeness satisfied, the conversation turned to the matter at hand.

"Now, about this errand that has brought you so precipitously to Windsor, Elizabeth," said the Duchess. "Your note said only that it concerns Rebeccah and requires my help." She pursed her lips. "Do you require me to find her a match perhaps?"

"Um, no," said Mrs. Dutton. "It is a horse of quite a different colour."

"Indeed?" Aunt Sarah looked intrigued. "Pray enlighten me."

"We are here to ask you to use your influence with the Queen. We desire you to ask pardon for an . . . acquaintance of ours." Mrs. Dutton gestured to Rebeccah, who extracted the petition of mercy from the pocket of her skirts and held it out.

"An acquaintance," repeated Sarah. "How very mysterious." She took the folded document and opened it, her eyes widening as she read the contents. "Good Lord!" she murmured. Then a little later, "A highway-woman!" When next she looked up, it was with open astonishment and not a little distaste. "Why should a respectable family like the Duttons concern themselves with a creature like this?"

Rebeccah bridled at the remark, but had the good sense not to say anything.

"I take it, from your fierce expression," continued the Duchess, fortunately not taking offence, "that there is more to this than meets the eye, Rebeccah. If I am to help you, my dear, you must tell me *everything.*"

So with a nervous glance at her mother and a deep breath, Rebeccah did so, not only detailing the many occasions on which Kate had come to the Duttons' aid but also other good deeds, in particular the purchase of freedom for several debtors in the Fleet (a cause she knew was dear to the Duchess's heart, as Sarah's own father had been a bankrupt). And if in the process she omitted the strong attraction she felt for Kate, who could blame her?

"Well I never!" said the Duchess, when Rebeccah had wound down and the only sound in the drawing room was the crackling of the fire and the nightingales' sweet song. "If I hadn't heard it from your own lips, I would have thought it a play. Thank heavens your sister is recovered from her ordeal! That fellow—Titus, was it?—deserves to be flogged." She shuddered. "If such a thing had happened to one of my daughters . . ."

She retrieved the petition of mercy from her lap and read it once more, her expression thoughtful. "This is just the sort of tale that would touch the Queen." Her expression became wry, self-deprecating. "Passionate friendships between women have always appealed to her." Then she sighed. "But alas, this is bad timing indeed! If only you had come to me yesterday."

Rebeccah's heart sank.

"Why, what is the matter?" asked her mother.

"We had a falling out this morning and the Queen is still irked with me . . . Oh don't look at me like that, Elizabeth. It is not my fault. Indeed I put up with her for as long as I could. But sometimes she is most tedious." Aunt Sarah's expression soured. "All she can talk about is her wardrobe, her lapdogs, and her husband's asthma. It's enough to try the patience of a saint."

She caught the direction of Rebeccah's nervous glance. "Oh, you need have no fear that our words will reach the Queen's ears, Rebeccah. We may speak freely in front of Betty. She's been with me since I was a girl, haven't you, my dear?" The silent serving woman smiled and nodded. "But you see my dilemma? With the Queen in her current temper, if I were to plead your friend's cause it would do only harm." The Duchess pursed her lips. "We must wait a few days. By then the Queen will in all likelihood have forgiven me and—"

"But Kate is to hang on Monday!" blurted Rebeccah, before subsiding with a blush.

The Duchess blinked at her and exchanged a glance with Mrs. Dutton. "Then there is only one thing for it." She grimaced and got to her feet.

There was a little mahogany writing table and chair to one side of the drawing room, and Aunt Sarah made herself comfortable there, selected a fresh sheet of paper, dipped a quill in the ink well, and began to write. Her handwriting was large and flamboyant, and Rebeccah could make out the letter's appellation if she squinted: "My dear Mrs. Morley."

How strange! The logs shifted, the pen scratched, and the nightingales warbled. Rebeccah's gaze drifted around the drawing room, resting on the blue and white porcelain ornaments on the chimney piece for a moment before coming back to the Duchess.

With a flourish, Aunt Sarah signed "Your devoted friend, Mrs. Freeman" (the Queen and her favourite must have pet names for one another), sprinkled sand on the wet ink and tapped it off, creased the letter into sharp folds, and addressed it.

"There . . . Betty." The serving woman came forward. "Ask one of the footmen to take this to the Castle as a matter of urgency."

Betty accepted the letter, curtseyed, and hurried out.

With a swish of her skirts, the Duchess rose and came back to join Rebeccah and her mother at the tea table. There was still some tea in the pot, so she poured herself a fresh dish. "I have eaten humble pie," she announced melodramatically. "Something that always disagrees with me. I hope you are grateful."

Mrs. Dutton opened her mouth but Rebeccah beat her to it. "Oh, we are indeed, Aunt. Thank you, thank you."

"This is but the first step, my dear," cautioned the Duchess, but she was smiling. "For we must wait to see if the Queen is willing to forgive me at once or if I must be made to suffer a while longer."

☐

A profligate number of candles illuminated the faces of the Duchess and her guests, who were sitting round the supper table.

There was still no reply from the Queen, much to Rebeccah's dismay. She had sated her hunger on slices of venison—game was plentiful in Windsor Great Park—followed by some cheese and fruit, and was now sipping a cup of sack-posset that her aunt's butler had prepared, hoping the hot mixture of eggs, wine, and spices would soothe her jangling nerves.

The murmur of conversation stopped as the door opened and a footman entered carrying a silver salver on which lay a letter. The Duchess took the letter, opened it, held a candle close so she could read its contents, and scowled.

"It seems I am not to be forgiven just yet."

Rebeccah's heart thudded. What exactly had Aunt Sarah *said* to the Queen to cause her to turn on her favourite? It was inconvenient, to say the least. Time was ticking, and with it were going Kate's chances. The thought of the shackled highwaywoman depending on Rebeccah alone to save her from the gallows was daunting, and she couldn't hide her downcast mood.

"Don't lose heart yet, my dear," said the Duchess. "I shall just have to cram down another mouthful of humble pie." She glanced at the ornate clock on the chimney piece. "With luck the Queen will relent tomorrow. There is still time for you to save your friend."

With that she signalled to Betty to bring pen, paper, and ink, and right there and then on the white linen table cloth, she dashed off another flamboyant missive to "Mrs. Morley."

෴

Rebeccah shifted on the hard pew, trying to get comfortable. She hadn't felt like attending church this morning, but her mother thought it better to keep occupied than wait aimlessly at the Lodge. The Duchess had told them that on Sundays the Queen breakfasted and then attended a private service in the Castle Chapel, so there would probably be no reply to her letter until after that at least.

Mrs. Dutton had sent for the carriage and ordered it to take herself, Rebeccah, and Mary to the little church in Windsor. Aunt Sarah didn't join them. She might not be on speaking terms with the Queen, but as a courtier of some importance (not only was she Duchess of Marlborough, she was Groom of the Stole, Mistress of the Robes, Keeper of the Privy Purse, and Ranger of Windsor Great Park) she was still expected to attend the private service.

The sermon was dull and unoriginal, so Rebeccah tuned out the parson's nasal drone and let her thoughts wander. If the little man in the pulpit could have read her mind he'd have been scandalized. She began by savouring that kiss with Kate, then progressed to wondering what *exactly* it was that two women did together in private. The kiss seemed to have unlocked sensual feelings of which she had previously been unaware, and though still slightly shocked to learn about this side of herself, Rebeccah was rapidly coming to terms with it. Inevitably, though, the tenor of her thoughts gradually darkened, and once more the question nearest to her returned—whether the highwaywoman could survive the savage sentence due to be carried out tomorrow morning.

Suppose the Queen is so upset with Aunt Sarah she doesn't forgive her in time. Suppose she does forgive her, but she declines to grant the petition anyway. Suppose . . . suppose . . . Bless me! I told Kate not to give up hope, but just suppose . . .

The gruesome image of Kate strangling on Tyburn Tree was too horrific for Rebeccah to contemplate without feeling agitated and sick so she forced it away and surfaced to hear Mary on her left and her mother on her right saying, "Amen."

"Amen." She rose to her feet with the rest of the congregation, and if she did not actually sing the words to the next hymn, she mouthed them creditably enough. It was a relief when at last the service was over, and she and her companions were free to board their carriage and drive back through the Park.

They were almost at the Lodge when they saw Aunt Sarah striding back from the Castle in what appeared to be high spirits. Rebeccah and her mother exchanged a puzzled look, then Mrs. Dutton banged on the roof and ordered the driver to stop. She and Rebeccah alighted, leaving Mary to travel on alone.

"Good morning, my dears." The Duchess greeted them with a smile then closed her eyes and tilted her cheeks towards the sunshine. "Isn't it a lovely day?"

"Is it?" wondered Mrs. Dutton.

"Indeed it is, Elizabeth. For the Queen snubbed me."

Rebeccah's mother's eyebrows rose. "And this fact *pleases* you?"

"Oh yes. For now she has had the satisfaction of humiliating me in public, she will be able to behave magnanimously towards me in private."

Rebeccah blinked at this convoluted logic but said nothing. The Queen and Aunt Sarah must by now be more than familiar with each other's quirks. And sure enough, the Duchess had judged the situation correctly, for they had been back at the Lodge barely half an hour before a panting footman arrived from the castle, bearing a message from the Queen.

The Duchess broke the royal seal and read the contents. Then she chuckled and looked up. "We are to attend the Queen at once."

"We?" Mrs. Dutton paled.

"Alas, not you, Elizabeth. Rebeccah and I."

Rebeccah gaped at her aunt. "The Queen wants to see *me*?" The last word came out as a squeak.

"Indeed," said the Duchess. "So you'd better get that plain-faced maid of yours to help you look respectable, my dear, and be quick about it. We leave in ten minutes."

☙

Rebeccah's heart was in her mouth as she climbed the turret stairs to the royal boudoir—Queen Anne favoured a room above the Norman gateway of Windsor Castle. It was just as well Rebeccah was wearing gloves, or her damp palms would have smeared the ink on the petition of mercy. *Courage*, she reminded herself. *You are doing this for Kate.*

"What shall I say to her?" she asked the Duchess who was one step ahead of her.

Aunt Sarah turned. "Lord, child! You're as white as a sheet." She chuckled. "She is not a monster. Just speak when you are spoken to. Answer her questions, but do not babble." She halted at a door, smoothed her skirts over her hips, then rapped the door sharply. It swung open to reveal a maid. She was obviously expecting them, for she curtseyed and stood back.

The room they entered was polygonal with lots of windows, but its light and airy feel was spoiled by the clutter of furniture. A tiny chestnut-coloured dog scurried towards the two women. Rebeccah flinched but it merely sniffed the toe of the Duchess's shoe with a wet nose, yapped a greeting, then raced back to its mistress, scrambling up into her ample lap.

Rebeccah had seen paintings of the Queen but none conveyed how poxed was her face, or how obese she had become. *Must be due to her gout, poor thing.* At her elbow stood a small table, on which lay all the condiments for Bohea tea.

"Mrs. Freeman." Queen Anne stroked the dog with fat fingers.

"Your Majesty." The Duchess curtseyed, and after a frozen moment, Rebeccah copied her.

"And is this your niece?"

"Yes, Your Majesty."

The Queen fed a ratafia biscuit to her pet. "Come forward, child."

Rebeccah did so on shaky legs. She tried to stand straight under the regal gaze, which, she saw now, was more of a squint.

"You have something for me?" prompted the Queen.

Rebeccah remembered the piece of paper in her hand. "Y . . . yes, Your Majesty."

The maid appeared at her elbow. Rebeccah gave her the petition of mercy, which she in turn transferred with a curtsey to the royal hand.

Queen Anne unfolded the crumpled petition, smoothed it, and read its contents. There was no sound in the turret room except for the contented grunts of the lapdog, and Rebeccah wondered if anyone else could hear the pounding of her heart and roaring in her ears.

"A highwaywoman?" The stout monarch looked up, astonished. "You wish me to pardon a convicted thief and murderess? What an *extraordinary* request!"

Is it my imagination or is the room swaying? wondered Rebeccah.

"Speak, child. Oh my! Is she going to . . . A chair for your niece, Mrs. Freeman. Quickly!"

Something hard pressed into the back of Rebeccah's knees and she crumpled gratefully onto it and tried to catch her breath.

"Rebeccah." Someone was chafing her hands. A blur resolved itself into Aunt Sarah's concerned face. "Are you well, my dear? You almost swooned."

"Give her some tea," came the Queen's voice, and Rebeccah remembered where she was. "That always makes *me* feel better."

How mortifying! She turned to see the seated Queen regarding her and her aunt with interest. "I'm so sorry, Your Majesty."

A royal hand waved dismissively, and the maid pressed a dish of tea into Rebeccah's hands and urged her to drink it, so she did, tasting the unmistakable tang of orange brandy. A welcome, warm tingle began to spread through her limbs.

"There." The Queen looked smug. "What did I tell you, Mrs. Freeman? Her colour is coming back." She waited, stroking her dog, until Rebeccah had handed the empty cup back, then said, "And now you are recovered, tell me the story of you and this highwaywoman. For Mrs. Freeman here has promised me an entertaining tale."

Rebeccah glanced at the Duchess, who smiled and gave her an encouraging nod. "Of course, Your Majesty." She took a deep breath and clasped her hands together and for the second time in as many days began. "The first time I met Blue-Eyed Nick we were returning in our carriage from Chatham . . ."

"Such a tale!" said the Queen, eyes bright, when Rebeccah finally drew to a close. The story of two women bent on saving each other's lives had indeed piqued her interest and she had listened intently, only asking the occasional question. "Your devotion and loyalty to your friend does you credit, Mistress Dutton. If only all women could be as fortunate as we are."

She threw the Duchess a fond glance, her tiff with her favourite evidently forgotten. "But in all good conscience I cannot grant Mistress Milledge a free pardon." Rebeccah's breathing hitched. "A *conditional* pardon is a possibility, however." She breathed freely once more.

"If I were to free your highwaywoman," continued Queen Anne, combing the lapdog's chestnut coat with her fingers, "would she give up her criminal ways? For I *will* not have my lawful citizens being threatened and robbed as they go about their business."

"Yes, Your Majesty," said Rebeccah instantly.

The Queen leaned forward and fixed her with her disconcerting squint. "Your quickness of response does you credit. But your word alone is not enough, I fear. Would the Dutton family be prepared to provide surety for her good behaviour?"

Rebeccah blinked. "I have no authority to speak for my sister or my mother," she said, "but for myself, I am prepared to stand surety for Kate . . . I mean Mistress Milledge." She blushed at the slip, but the Queen only smiled.

"And if a condition of her release were to be that she take up employment with your family?"

For a moment Rebeccah was at a loss. Did Queen Anne mean to humble Kate by making her a servant? She couldn't imagine the highwaywoman being happy in such a mundane job, but since for now just keeping Kate alive was her aim she said, "That would be agreeable, Your Majesty."

Satisfied, the Queen sat back. "Good," she said. "You are prepared to provide more than mere words in support of your friend. That deserves to be rewarded." She signalled to her maid and whispered something in her ear. The woman curtseyed and scurried out, returning minutes later with a beanpole of a man, so well dressed he bordered on the foppish. The dog rushed over to him, gave an agitated bark, and retreated to the safety of its mistress's lap.

The new arrival looked down his long nose at Rebeccah and the Duchess, then bowed to the Queen. "Your Majesty?"

"Mr. Wyatt, I have a task for you." Queen Anne handed the well-travelled piece of paper to the maid who handed it to the tall man. "I am minded to grant this petition of mercy. Issue a pardon for Catherine Milledge at once." The lapdog snuffled at a royal palm for biscuit crumbs.

"Conditional upon her consenting to work for the Dutton family of St. James's Square."

No mention of any surety, Rebeccah noticed with relief. Perhaps that had been merely a test.

"At once, Your Majesty. Will that be all?" The Queen nodded, and Wyatt bowed and backed towards the door. But before he got there, the Duchess crossed quickly to the Queen's side, stooped, and whispered something in her ear. She looked perturbed.

"Mr. Wyatt, wait." He paused and looked expectantly at her. "How long will it take for the pardon to reach Newgate?"

"Um." His gaze turned inwards. "The paperwork must be correctly prepared, Your Majesty. But all being well it should arrive by Tuesday morning." He seemed pleased with this answer and was obviously taken aback when the Queen didn't share his view. Rebeccah too was stunned— if her quick-thinking aunt hadn't intervened, the pardon would have arrived too late.

"Too slow, Mr. Wyatt," said the Queen with a frown. "Too slow by half! For I am given to understand that Mistress Milledge is due to hang tomorrow." Absently she stroked her pet. "You will prepare the pardon yourself, sir, and deliver it in good time with your own hands. Mistress Dutton and her mother will be travelling back to London tonight or on the morrow. They will not mind you joining them, I'm sure."

Wyatt looked as if he had swallowed something bitter, but he said evenly enough, "As you wish, Your Majesty." And with an extravagant bow, he backed out of the room, pulling the door closed behind him.

"Oh thank you, Your Majesty," cried Rebeccah. "Thank you with all my heart."

The Queen smiled at her then yawned, a hand rising too late to cover her mouth. "Bless me! But all this excitement has left me feeling quite fatigued." She glanced at the Duchess. "Mrs. Freeman, you will stay and keep me company awhile. I'm sure your niece can find her own way back to the Lodge—it is not far, after all, and the walk back will do her good." She gestured to the maid. "Show Mistress Dutton out."

And with that, Rebeccah found herself dismissed.

Chapter 20

A buzz went round the prison chapel as Kate came through the door, brushing past the turnkey acting as ticket-taker.

"Over there," said Simpkins. "Between Minshul and Powell."

She followed the direction of his pointing finger to the dock. The pews inside the black-painted enclosure were reserved for those prisoners condemned to die, and several coffins had been stacked in there with them, to bring home the fact of their imminent mortality.

As if that is necessary, thought Kate with an inward grimace. She knew the drill. This service would be all about fire and brimstone. Not only would the Ordinary preach his "condemned sermon," those in the dock would be required to hear prayers for their souls and join in the responses to their own burial service.

Shackles clinking, she shuffled forward, aware of the faces staring down at her from the crowded public galleries upstairs on either side, and the excited whispers of "Blue-Eyed Nick." The prisoners sitting in the body of the chapel were not so restrained. Catcalls, jokes, and obscenities followed her all the way to her seat.

"Having a private cell didn't exempt you from this, then," said Isaac Minshul, his warty face breaking into a smile as she squeezed in next to him.

"I'm just glad to be able to stretch my legs."

"Got you stapled to the floor, have they?"

"Ay."

"Whoresons!" said Jemmy Powell, who was sitting on the other side of her. "And what a farce this is." He pushed lank brown hair out of his eyes. "Trying to save our souls when they should be saving our lives."

"This service isn't about our souls, Jemmy," said Kate. "'Tis about giving those in the galleries their monies' worth."

"They should look to their own souls if this is the kind of entertainment they choose of a Sunday," remarked Minshul.

A rustle of movement drew Kate's attention to the front, where the Reverend Francis Rewse, Ordinary of Newgate, now stood in the chapel's simple pulpit. He looked much smarter than when he had questioned Kate so closely about her life story for his pamphlet; he was wearing his best wig, cassock, and surplice.

"We are gathered here tonight," he began, peering at his congregation over the top of his half-spectacles, "to pray for the souls of these poor benighted sinners." He gestured at those in the Dock.

"Bollocks, you whoreson!" shouted Powell, and a turnkey leaned over and cuffed him on the ear.

The Ordinary didn't seem in the least put out by Powell's trenchant criticism. He bared his teeth in a benign smile and continued, "'I am the resurrection and the life, saith the Lord: he that believeth in me, though he were dead, yet shall he live . . .'"

While he wittered on, Kate scanned the chapel, her gaze resting on the rickety little table that served as an altar, before travelling to the commandments painted on the wall above it which had faded so much they were barely legible.

"Let us turn to Psalm 39," announced the Ordinary. Kate sighed and reached for the Book of Common Prayer that had been so thoughtfully provided.

As the service proceeded, with no hymns to relieve the unremitting gloom, many of the prisoners grew restless and bored. But their every heckle was greeted with a poke in the ribs from a turnkey's stave or a clip round the ear. Then it was time for the Ordinary's address.

"'And they shall go away into everlasting punishment; but the righteous into life eternal,'" intoned Reverend Rewse. "Matthew 25 verse 46." He paused then repeated with lip smacking relish, "Everlasting punishment."

Kate sighed and turned her thoughts inwards. If Rebeccah's mission had been successful, she would surely have heard from her by now. She had known it was but a fool's errand. Her last hours on Earth would have passed far more pleasantly, and, on the evidence of that kiss, far more pleasurably if Rebeccah had stayed with her instead of haring off to Windsor. And a large bribe to the turnkeys might have made that possible. Still, it was touching that the young woman would go to such lengths to save her.

That Alice had attacked Rebeccah in the corridor outside her cell and scratched her pretty cheek had come as an unwelcome shock. Kate grimaced. *She should have scratched my face not sweet Rebeccah's.*

Alice's visit had been a strained one, to say the least. That she had come at all after their argument was a surprise. Kate had wanted to make things easier on Alice, who had obviously been crying . . . and in the process salve her on conscience, she supposed. Alice should not shed a single tear for her, she'd urged, for she was not worth it. And then she'd begged forgiveness and sincerely hoped that in time Alice could grant it. But it seemed that, from the widowed landlady's subsequent assault, Alice would far rather blame Rebeccah for the deterioration in their relationship than admit that Kate had never really loved her in the first place.

An elbow nudged her back to the here and now and she saw that Powell was rummaging inside his shirt. A sarcastic remark died on her lips when he produced a louse and placed it on the open prayer book in front of him. As it scurried across the page, Powell grinned.

"A shilling says it reaches the bottom of the page before—Ow!"

A turnkey had reached over the edge of the Dock and slammed closed the prayer book, sending the louse to an early grave. Then he whacked Powell round the head with it.

"Forsake your evil ways and repent before it is too late," thundered the Ordinary.

Kate sighed and willed the interminable service to its conclusion.

Chapter 21

"You will wear out your Aunt's carpet with your pacing, Beccah," chided Mrs. Dutton.

"I'm sorry, Mama. But where *is* he?" Rebeccah halted and peered out of the drawing room window, as she had done every other minute for the past half-hour. "He should have been here ages ago."

The horses had been hitched and the Dutton carriage, with Robert in its driving seat trying not to nod off, was waiting outside the front entrance of the Great Lodge.

"Mr. Wyatt will come soon," soothed the Duchess of Marlborough from her easy chair by the fire, where she was sipping a dish of chocolate, "or the Queen will know the reason why."

"He had better," muttered Rebeccah.

It had not been light long, and mist still hung low over Windsor Great Park's rolling acres, but if they were to make it to Newgate before noon, they needed to get under way early. Wyatt knew that. He had promised to be here with Kate's signed and sealed pardon at five o'clock on the dot. It was now five-thirty.

It had been still dark when Mary helped Rebeccah and her mother dress, then they had gone down to breakfast with the Duchess, who, as she was dining only with close relatives and all of them female, had chosen to remain *deshabille* in a loose nightgown but had lost none of her charisma or dignity in the process. Aunt Sarah was unaccustomed to being up at this ungodly hour (as she told them several times) and her constant yawning threatened to become contagious. Rebeccah was dry mouthed with anxiety, and had to use her dish of tea to wash down the cold meat and slices of bread and butter.

"There he is!" cried Mary.

Rebeccah followed the maid's pointing finger and saw a rider on a brown horse galloping towards the Lodge. As he drew closer, she saw that the man in the saddle was an unusually dishevelled-looking Wyatt. He must have overslept.

Thank God he has come!

The Queen's official reined in next to the carriage, dismounted, handed the reins to a footman who had appeared to lead the beast away, then looked round uncertainly. Robert leaned down from his perch and said something. Wyatt nodded his understanding then opened one of the carriage doors and climbed aboard.

"Come, Beccah." Mrs. Dutton swept towards the drawing room exit. Rebeccah hurried after her with Mary in tow. At the door, all three turned and curtseyed to the Duchess, who had remained seated by the fire and was stifling another yawn.

"Thank you with all my heart, Sarah," said Rebeccah's mother. "We are obliged indeed for the hospitality and assistance you have rendered. Maybe one day we can return the favour."

The Duchess waved a dismissive hand. "Think nothing of it, Elizabeth," she called. "Only too happy to help. Just send me word how it all turns out, Rebeccah, will you, dear?"

"With pleasure."

Chapter 22

"Sorry." Wryneck looked rueful. "The Keeper says the shackles come off in the Press Yard and not before."

Kate grimaced. "In that case," she separated the breeches and hose from the clothes he had purchased on her behalf, and held them out. "See if you can find another use for these."

The turnkey accepted them with a nod of thanks—they were neatly mended and freshly laundered and should fetch him a shilling or two. Then he cocked his head and grinned. "Keeper didn't say anything about this, though." He reached for the keys at his belt, stooped, and unlocked the padlock connecting her leg irons to the staple in the floor.

"Much obliged," she told him, meaning it.

He grunted then glanced at the basin of water, soap, towel, comb, tiny looking glass, clay pipe and pouch of tobacco she had also requested he bring, and paid dearly for the privilege. "I'll leave you to it then."

After he had locked the cell door behind him, Kate set about stripping and washing off the worst of the grime. What she wouldn't give for a soak in the local bathhouse's hot pool, but she would have to content herself with the cold water from the basin.

She shook out the clothes, which came from Godfrey Gimbart's secondhand clothes shop in Long Lane, and examined them. It was a tradition of Newgate that the condemned should look their best when they went to the gallows. Lord Ferrers had worn his white satin wedding suit, so it was said. Kate's outfit wasn't in the same league, but it would do. Shame about the breeches, stained as they were with splashes of tallow and something unidentifiable that she had sat in while in the Condemned Hold; still, the knee-length coat would hide the worst.

She donned the shirt and buttoned it, enjoying the feel of clean fabric against her skin, then eased on the blue brocade waistcoat and fawn coat.

Her cravat she tied in a simple Steinkerk, knotting it then tucking the ends through the top buttonhole of her coat.

The tenor bell of St. Sepulchre-without-Newgate tolled mournfully as she combed her hair and tied it at the nape of her neck. Kate was heartily sick of the sound of bells. As if the condemned prisoners' last night weren't made restless enough with nightmares of Tyburn, at midnight St. Sepulchre's bellman had paced up and down outside the condemned cells, ringing his hand bell and chanting:

"All you that in the condemned hold do lie, Prepare you, for tomorrow you will die."

When he had reached the end of the verse, he started to repeat it. Kate stuck her fingers in her ears.

After he had gone, she rolled awkwardly onto her knees—the leg irons and staple made everything awkward—and prayed . . . not for her soul, as the bellman had been urging, or even for a pardon (for if it were coming, it would surely have done so by now), but that she might meet her end bravely and, God willing, see Rebeccah one last time.

Kate picked up the looking glass and checked her appearance as best she could. Her outfit looked incomplete without a tricorne and a baldric, and she missed the weight of a sword against her hip, but it would do. She brushed a speck of lint from her sleeve, then shuffled over to her chair.

For a long moment she sat, listening to the muffled tolling of the bell and the sounds of the prison going on all about her, then she took the scrap of paper and stub of pencil Wryneck had provided, and set to work on her speech.

Chapter 23

They had just crossed over the Thames near Staines when the carriage slowed and a few moments later came to a dead stop.

What now? Rebeccah glanced at her mother in dismay. She opened the door and leaned out. The coachman had jumped down and was stooping beside the lead horse, examining its fetlock. "What is it, Robert?"

He straightened and looked back at her. "This horse has gone lame, Mistress Rebeccah."

Stifling a very unladylike curse, she relayed the information to the other passengers, then hopped down, and went to join him. "Can he continue as far as London?"

"No, Madam. We must have a replacement."

Rebeccah's mother had come to join them and was in time to hear his unwelcome verdict. She gave their surroundings a dubious glance. "But will we be able to find a replacement here, Robert?"

Rebeccah shared her mother's doubts. They had stopped in the middle of a village that comprised precisely four small houses and a seedy-looking tavern called the Cock Inn.

"No, Madam," agreed Robert. "But Egham isn't far. And if I remember correctly from the journey down, there is a coaching inn there that will have horses for hire. If you and the others care to wait in the coach, I will lead poor Conker to the Red Lion, arrange to have him cared for, then set about hiring us a replacement."

"If Egham is the nearest place to hire a horse, then Egham it must be," said Mrs. Dutton with a heavy sigh. "Do as you suggested, Robert. Get them to send me the bill and don't worry about the cost—for we must have a replacement, and that's that."

"And please hurry," added Rebeccah. "For every minute we delay . . ."

She trailed off, thinking of Kate and her approaching appointment with the hangman.

He gave her a nod and said quietly, "You may rely on me, Mistress Rebeccah. I know what's at stake."

"Thank you, Robert."

While he unhitched Conker, Rebeccah's mother took her by the arm and led her back to the carriage.

"What's happening?" Wyatt peered down his nose at the two women from the open door. "Can your driver not even take a stone out of a hoof?"

Rebeccah frowned up at him. Her mother was more diplomatic. "Alas, Mr. Wyatt, if it were only that straightforward. The horse is badly lamed and we must find a replacement. While our coachman is gone to get a fresh horse, we can wait in the carriage . . . or repair to that hostelry." She pointed.

Wyatt stared at the ramshackle Cock Inn with open dismay, and a wicked impulse overtook Rebeccah.

"Since we are bound to be cooped up in this contraption for the rest of the day, Mama," she said, indicating the carriage, "perhaps it would be as well to avail ourselves of the tavern's facilities while we can."

Her mother nodded. "Good idea, Beccah."

"Very well." Wyatt climbed down, followed by Mary, who gave her mistress a suspicious glance. "Perhaps the inn won't be as bad as it looks." He sniffed.

Rebeccah kept her face straight with difficulty. She seriously doubted it.

Chapter 24

It was almost noon when they came for her.

Kate had long ago finished her speech. She filled the remaining hours smoking a last pipe of her favourite tobacco, singing "The Female Frollick" (which earned enthusiastic applause from the inmate in an adjoining cell), stretching the cramp from her legs, or peering out the barred window.

If she leaned over far enough she could just catch a glimpse of sky—it promised to be a fine day for it. A fine day for riding too. She sighed. At least Clover would be in good hands with the Duttons.

As the morning dragged on, Kate felt more and more unreal. She kept thinking that at any moment she would wake to find that the last few weeks had been a nightmare. Alice would be lying next to her, the shells from their oyster supper stacked on the plate on the bedside table. But if it were just a nightmare, then Rebeccah would be but a dream, which would be a mixed blessing indeed.

The cell door creaked open. "It's time," said Wryneck, beckoning.

Heart thumping, Kate stood. As they walked along the maze of corridors and up and down stairs, at a painfully slowly pace due to her leg irons, prisoners pressed their noses to the grilles and yelled obscenities or good wishes. Kate acknowledged a shout of "God Speed, Nick," with a smile and a nod and kept on going, pausing only when Wryneck had to unlock and then relock the numerous gates that barred their progress.

The journey seemed endless, but at last the turnkey led her, stooping, through a low door out into the open air. She glanced up at the sky for a long moment before turning to scan the Press Yard, a long narrow yard with high spiked walls. Two open, horse-drawn carts were waiting there, with prisoners sitting in the back. The dung from their horses added to the general stench.

Kate curled her lip at the onlookers, faces flushed with excitement, eyes avid, who had paid to join the turnkeys and prisoners. The Ordinary was also there, making a nuisance of himself as usual, praying loudly and giving counsel, whether wanted or not. A man in a black mask stood a little way apart from the others. He raked Kate from head to foot with calculating eyes.

Assessing how much my clothes will fetch, I'll wager.

"Oi, you there. Come here." A blacksmith with bulging biceps beckoned to Kate. She shuffled over, and as instructed put a foot on his wooden anvil. Deftly, he hammered the rivets from her leg iron.

"Other foot."

The hammer came down again and Kate's fetters clattered to the flag-stones. Before she could stoop to rub the raw welts, the turnkey assigned as Yeoman of the Halter came over. He tied one cord round her wrists then slipped another through her elbows and pulled it tight, pinioning her. Finally, he looped a halter round her neck and curled its free end round her body.

Thus bound, her movements were restricted and she had to be helped up into one of the carts. Isaac Minshul made room for her on a coffin. She grimaced and sat between him and Jemmy Powell. Both felons were look-ing unusually clean and dapper.

"Not wearing skirts?" asked Powell, grinning.

Kate gave him a mock glare. "As you would say, Jemmy . . . Bollocks!" Minshul chuckled.

The cart rocked and she saw that the Reverend Rewse was scrambling up into their cart, while the hangman was to travel with the other. On balance, she decided, as the Ordinary launched into a Psalm and urged the three prisoners to join in for the sake of their immortal souls, her cart had drawn the short straw.

A turnkey unbolted the barred gate, which swung open with a screech that set Kate's teeth on edge, and the drivers urged their horses forward. As the carts emerged from the Press Yard into the street, the roar from the waiting crowd made Kate blink. An escort of peace officers, constables, and javelin men fell in around them, the City Marshal and the Under-Sheriff took their places at the head of the procession, then they were off.

The cart rumbled over cobblestones, jolting every bone in Kate's body, but she barely noticed it for a loud rhythmic chant of "Blue-Eyed Nick, Blue-Eyed Nick" that had started up. Better acclaim than a rain of rotten cabbages, she decided, nodding and smiling at the sea of faces surrounding her, none of whom she recognized.

"They're lively," said Minshul.

"Ay," said Kate.

The Ordinary finished his Psalm and started on another.

The procession had barely got going before, at St. Sepulchre's entrance, it halted to allow the sexton to ring his hand bell twelve times. (*More poxy bells!*) Then he began his address.

"All good people," he intoned, "pray heartily unto God for these poor sinners, who are now going to their death . . ." Kate tuned him out until the final "Christ have mercy on you." There were only so many exhortations to repent she could take.

He presented each prisoner with a nosegay of flowers (Kate tucked hers in a buttonhole) and a cup of wine. There would be much more to drink along the route—she could arrive at Tyburn roaring drunk if she wished—but she decided she'd rather keep her wits about her, drank only half her cup, and gave the rest to an appreciative Powell.

With a cheer from the crowd, the procession resumed its progress, the carts turning a sharp left at the bottom of Snow Hill and crossing the foul sewer that was the Fleet Ditch. Kate remembered the last time she had walked these streets with Rebeccah, searching for her sister, and sighed. Then they were climbing towards High Holborn, the smell receding with every yard, and she sucked in a welcome breath of fresh air.

The journey to Tyburn was a long one, the roaring of the crowd a constant, almost physical, battering. It was made slower by frequent stops at taverns. At the first stop, the Bowl Inn in St. Giles, Kate accepted a beer from someone anxious to say they had drunk with Blue-Eyed Nick. She made the customary joke, "I'll buy you a pint on the way back," took a mouthful and left the rest. Then it was back into the cart and on to the next tavern.

The crowds along the route were getting thicker by the minute. People leaned out of windows and thronged rooftops. At last Kate began to see faces she knew. There was Tom the stableboy, his expression doleful. And Henry Flude the little fencing cully, straightening his wig and nodding as their eyes met. John Elborrow was standing with several of his regulars, trying to comfort the Rose and Crown's buxom barmaid, Nan. He doffed his tricorne to Kate, and she had a sudden hankering for a last taste of his wife's pies. Inexorably the cart moved on.

Chapter 25

"Look at the crowds!" Rebeccah stared out the window in dismay. "We're never going to get there in time."

Delay had dogged them all the way from Windsor. They had hitched up the replacement horse only to find that the team was now unbalanced. The carriage had almost run off the road twice, before Robert pulled up and set about moving a different horse into lead position. Unhitching and rehitching the team consumed valuable time, and there was no guarantee that things would be any better. Fortunately, Robert knew his horseflesh, and when they set off once more it soon became clear that the horses were pulling smoothly again. The passengers' relief was short lived though, for a few miles later, and perhaps because of the strain they had been put under, the traces parted and they had to halt for half an hour while they were repaired.

Rebeccah had long ago given up all hope of reaching Newgate in time and, with Wyatt's reluctant approval, had told Robert to head straight for Tyburn. She had forgotten how clogged the streets would be though. And now the carriage had ground to a halt.

"We must force our way through," said an irritated Wyatt. "For it's the Queen's business we're about and none shall stand in our way." He opened the door, leaned out, and yelled, "Driver, use your horsewhip to clear the way if you have to."

Rebeccah exchanged an appalled glance with her mother and hoped Robert would have more sense. If the mob were to turn against them things could get nasty, and the presence of the horses should surely be enough to make people stand clear.

She willed the carriage forward. After a moment, it lurched into motion, but its progress was now at a mere snail's pace. She blocked out the noise of the crowd and the relentless tolling of the bells. *Wait for me, Kate. I'm coming.*

Chapter 26

When they left the Mason's Arms in Seymour Place, the last tavern on the route, Jemmy Powell was so drunk he had to be carried back to the cart.

The gallows loomed at the end of the road, and as the procession drew closer, Kate's guts tightened. Especially when she saw the wide cart standing empty beneath one of the three huge beams, waiting to ferry its unwilling passengers to the other side.

Will it hurt? she wondered, as the halter around her neck seemed to grow heavier. *Will there be any hangers-on willing to do for me what I helped Moll do for John Stephenson?*

The hanging procession halted at last, and was met by a resounding cheer. The constables, peace officers, and javelin men hurriedly formed a new configuration around the prisoners. They gripped their staves and javelins with white knuckles, and looked about nervously as though expecting the crowd to rush them at any minute. Rescues of prisoners had been known, but Kate knew better than to pin her hopes on one. The crowd might say how much they loved a charming rogue, but they loved a good hanging better.

She searched the faces of the onlookers, especially those at the front with the best view, since they were probably the prisoners' relatives. She was relieved to see no sign of her addled mother. If Jane Allen was the woman Kate hoped she was, she had kept Martha ignorant of her daughter's fate. The two women were probably at this very moment sitting in Jane's comfortable kitchen, trying not to pinch Beau the lurcher's tail beneath the runners of their contentedly rocking chairs. At least she hoped so.

Samuel Josselin was there though, arms folded, eyes triumphant. So was a tall young man in a black cassock who seemed oddly familiar. Wasn't he the clergyman she had bested in a swordfight? *Berry something*

. . . *Berrigan, that was his name.* He caught her gaze and nodded. A flash of red hair drew her attention further along the row. *Ah, Alice. Have you not yet had your fill of me?* The landlady looked haggard with weeping. Would she be willing to help speed Kate's passing from this world to the next? Kate doubted she was capable of such a thing.

There was no sign of the Dutton family. She pursed her lips, uncertain whether to feel chagrin or relief then opted for the latter. They had done enough for her. That Rebeccah had even *attempted* to obtain a pardon meant everything. Let the young woman's last memory of Kate be a pleasant one.

"Down we get," cried the Ordinary, leaping down, then turning to grin up at those still in the cart.

"Bollocks!" slurred the inebriated Powell.

The Under-Sheriff's officers hurried over to help the prisoners down. One urged Kate towards the gallows. She felt off-balance without the leg irons, and for the first time her courage failed her, and she faltered.

"Keep moving," ordered the officer. Kate tried to slow her racing heart. "I said—"

"I heard you." Teeth gritted, hands balled into damp fists, she resumed her awkward progress.

The noise of the crowd swelled and ebbed as Kate and the others, eight in all, took their places on the wide cart. The only other female to hang today was Phebe Woolley; the skinny young woman looked even more pale and pinched than usual and was panting with fright.

"Breathe slowly," Kate advised her, but the other woman was too deep in her panic to hear her. As for the men, some were befuddled by drink and others were either cursing or cracking black jokes. Isaac Minshul still seemed relatively sober. He caught Kate's gaze and gave her a rueful shrug.

A flurry of movement proved to be the constables and peace officers parting to allow through the prisoners' relatives. Kate tried not to feel alone and unloved as they swarmed round every prisoner except her, hugging, kissing, and crying—even Powell had a sister with the same lank brown hair. It was a relief when at last they were escorted back to their places among the crowd.

That part of the proceedings over, things moved swiftly on to the next.

The hangman climbed up to join the prisoners. At his appearance, the crowd let out a great roar, which frightened the horse. The cart lurched and bucked under Kate's feet until the animal could be calmed down. The man in the black mask began working his way along the row of prisoners, tying the free end of each halter around the massive beam above.

"Those of you who have farewell speeches to give, give them now," said the Ordinary, also joining them. "Go to God with a clean breast. Confess your sins and admit your guilt."

"Bollocks!" slurred Jemmy Powell, swaying until someone steadied him.

While some might wish to prolong their stay on earth by speechifying, Kate just wished this ordeal were over and done with. So her speech was short and to the point, with none of the expressions of false humility or religiosity that she was sure the Reverend Rewse would have liked.

"My name is Blue-Eyed Nick," she shouted, as onlookers hushed one another so they could hear, "and I have lived a short life but a merry one. I've taken the cards Fate dealt me and played the best game I could. That in the process I hurt those who didn't deserve it pains me, and I am heartily sorry for it. But as for hurting those who deserved it . . . To the Devil with them!" The unrepentant tone drew a cheer from the crowd and a black look from the Ordinary.

Isaac Minshul was next to speak, the sobbing of his wife almost bringing the big man himself to tears. Then came the swaying Jemmy Powell, whose obscene suggestions about what the Ordinary could do with himself left his sister blushing and the onlookers howling with laughter. Terror had stolen Phebe Woolley's voice so she did not speak. The remaining prisoners' speeches were longwinded, slurred, and inaudible, and by the time they drew to a close, the crowd was visibly restless, anxious to get on with the main event. There also seemed to be some kind of disturbance going on at the back, though Kate couldn't make out its cause—a drunken dispute probably.

The hangman reappeared with some white sacks, asking each prisoner whether they wished to be hooded. Kate had no desire to witness Josselin's enjoyment of her final moments, so she accepted, and as the hood dropped over her head, the crowd disappeared from view.

Whatever its cause, the disturbance seemed to be spreading. The shouts and curses were more widespread and growing louder.

"Make way," came a man's shout, as horses whinnied and people screamed insults.

"The Lord giveth and the Lord taketh away," droned Reverend Rewse from close by. "Blessed be the name of the Lord."

"Make way, I said," shouted the man again. "We have a message for the

City Marshal. Let us through." The clatter of shod hooves and ironbound wheels on cobblestones drew nearer.

"Get back, you whoresons!" screeched a fishwife. "You're blocking my view."

"We are on the Queen's business," came the man's shout again, this time a little closer. "Make way there, I say. Make way."

"The Queen?" muttered someone. "Did he mention the Queen?"

"Lord, let me know mine end," continued the pious drone of the Ordinary.

"What's going on?" That was Minshul's voice, coming from beside Kate.

If she gave voice to her slender hopes, would they vanish like morning mist? "Hanged if I know."

"Is it a reprieve?" called someone. And at the question, the crowd exploded into noise. "Reprieve, reprieve, reprieve," they chanted, their joy obvious. Then, "Who for, who for, who for?"

"Now for the Lord's Prayer," said the Ordinary. "Say it with me, 'Our Father, who art in heaven—'"

The clip-clop of hooves and clatter of wheels stopped abruptly and Kate's keen hearing picked up the sound of a carriage door opening.

"My name is Wyatt," shouted a man, "and I have here an order for the City Marshal."

"'Hallowed be Thy name—'"

"Can't it wait until after the hanging?" came a testy voice, presumably belonging to the Marshal.

"No it cannot, for if it does a pardoned woman will hang." (Kate's heart skipped a beat.) "Don't stand there like a fool, fellow. This is the Queen's business. Read this document at once."

"'Thy kingdom come—'"

The cart sagged beneath her feet, and Kate struggled to keep her balance.

"'Thy will be . . .' Young woman." The Ordinary sounded scandalized. "What do you think you're doing? Get away from those prisoners at once!"

A familiar, enticing fragrance met Kate's nostrils and she blinked as she tried to identify it. *But it can't be!* "Rebeccah?"

For a moment she feared she was dreaming, then a hand clasped hers in wordless reply. Which was just as well, since at this latest development the noise from the crowd had grown deafening and Kate could hardly hear herself think.

"I won't tell you again, Madam," screeched Reverend Rewse. "Get away from her! Constables!"

"Leave Mistress Dutton alone, sir," bellowed Wyatt. "I asked her to point out the prisoner. If that is Catherine Milledge, then she is the one to be pardoned. Come on, man!" He must be addressing the Marshal. "Free her at once or you'll answer to the Queen."

The touch of Rebeccah's hand disappeared, then something deliciously warm and curvaceous eased behind Kate. Fingers plucked at her hood.

"What are you doing, Madam?" cried the Ordinary.

"It is as Mr. Wyatt said," came the Marshal's voice again, no longer testy but resigned. "Release her at once. It is the Queen's orders that Catherine Milledge be granted a conditional pardon. She is to be transferred into the custody of Mistress Rebeccah Dutton. I presume that is you, Madam?"

"Yes, sir," came Rebeccah's voice.

"They are pardoning Blue-Eyed Nick," cried the mob in growing delight.

"The Queen is pardoning the highwaywoman?" "Are you sure?" "They've pardoned the snaffler?" "Blue-Eyed Nick's neck is safe!" "Gawd Bless our good Queen Anne."

The hood was whisked from Kate's head and she blinked the dazzle away. Next came the halter. She twisted round and gazed at Rebeccah in astonishment.

Rebeccah smiled at her. "Told you I would come," she mouthed.

"Cut her loose." The Marshal brandished an important-looking document bearing the royal seal.

The Under-Sheriff's officer who had escorted Kate to the gallows climbed up and sliced the ropes binding her wrists and elbows with a knife. She half jumped, half fell out of the cart, then turned and assisted Rebeccah down.

Kate was about to head for the coach Rebeccah had pointed out when she realized that Josselin was standing just a few yards from her. Rage replaced his look of stunned disbelief, and his face suffused with blood until he looked quite apoplectic. A fit of hilarity overtook her and she felt the urge to thumb her nose at him. Then the urge died, for she had just caught sight of Alice—the widowed landlady's face was a mask of confusion and heartbreak.

For a moment, Kate could not fathom it. Alice should be pleased she was alive, shouldn't she? Then it dawned on her. The red-haired landlady had just seen her hated rival save Kate from the gallows and now they were about to leave together. As far as Alice was concerned, she had lost Kate just as surely as if death had taken her. Kate couldn't help but feel pity for her.

"Come on! This way." Rebeccah shoved Kate towards the waiting coach and four.

"Have they saved you, Kate'?" It was Minshul's muffled shout, and Kate glanced back to the cart where the big man still stood, blinded by his hood.

"Ay," she called. "I am to live another day."

"You always did have the Devil's luck!" But there was no rancour in his tone. And beside him Jemmy Powell, who had opted to go hoodless, swayed and grinned and mouthed something that might have been "Bollocks!"

Kate raised a hand in farewell. "God Speed, my friends."

"Hurry," said the younger woman. "For I do not wish to witness what they are about to do here."

Then they had reached the carriage, and Kate was hauling herself inside, blinking when she found herself face to face with Rebeccah's mother and Mary. Rebeccah piled in after her and pulled the door closed.

"But what about Mr. Wyatt?" asked Mrs. Dutton. "Are we not to wait for him?

"He will have to make his own way back to Windsor in any case." Rebeccah rapped her knuckles on the ceiling and yelled, "Home, Robert."

The coach's lurch pinned Kate to her seat, as it began its slow progress back the way it had come. It had gone barely thirty yards when a great sigh seemed to go through the surrounding mob, followed seconds later by a rousing cheer.

Minshul and the others must have embarked on their journey to the next life, thought Kate, chilled by just how close she had come to accompanying them. She exchanged a wordless glance with Rebeccah. And when a small hand slipped itself into hers, she held on tight, as though her life depended upon it.

⌀

Mary knelt beside Kate's bare feet and dunked a clean rag in the basin.

When they had arrived back at the house in St. James's Square, Rebeccah had sailed past her smiling sister with a brief, "We are very well as you can see, Anne. I will talk to you later," and started up the stairs.

Barely stopping in the hall to hand her wrap and gloves to a waiting Nancy, and declaring loudly that as Kate was assigned to her custody *she* would take care of her herself ("And besides, Mama will no doubt wish to change out of her travel-stained clothes and regale Anne with the details of our trip to Windsor."), Rebeccah had taken no time in urging both Kate and Mary up the stairs to her bedchamber.

There, the young gentlewoman gasped when the full extent of the sores on Kate's ankles was revealed, and gasped again at the condition of her knee breeches. Ignoring Kate's joke that they would have been far worse had she kept her appointment with the noose, Rebeccah had summoned Will and instructed him to fetch a spare pair of his own breeches—he need not worry, she would recompense him handsomely.

When the footman returned, she bundled the garment into Kate's arms, shoved her into the little dressing room she had last occupied under very different circumstances, and told her to change. Kate did so willingly. A neatly darned bullet hole marred one thigh, but Will's breeches were still a distinct improvement on those she had arrived in. Once Kate was more fragrantly attired, Rebeccah asked Mary to take a look at Kate's ankles.

"That was closer than I would have liked," said Rebeccah, now she had time to draw breath.

Kate threw her an amused glance. "It was closer than I would have liked too."

Rebeccah grimaced. "I did not intend you to go through such an ordeal. If things had gone to plan we should have arrived in good time. But . . ." She raised her hands and let them drop.

"Nevertheless," said Kate, smiling warmly, "you arrived in the nick of time, and I am forever in your debt." The younger woman's cheeks pinked at the sentiment.

"This may sting," warned Mary, wringing out the excess water and dabbing at the welts on the highwaywoman's ankles.

That was something of an understatement. A hiss escaped Kate's gritted teeth, and Rebeccah hurriedly sat beside her on the bed and took her hand.

"I was going to ask you to pinch me, to see if I was still dreaming," managed Kate, "but Mary's attentions have convinced me that I am wide awake."

The maid threw her an apologetic glance, dunked the rag once more, then resumed her dabbing. "A moment more. Then I have a salve that will help."

"Ow!" But it was Rebeccah who had exclaimed aloud not Kate.

"Sorry." Kate released Rebeccah's hand at once.

She flexed her fingers. "You have a grip like a vice." Then she smiled and took Kate's hand in hers once more.

Mary looked from one woman to the other and lifted an eyebrow. Kate arched her own eyebrow in response. The corner of the maid's mouth twitched, and she resumed her dabbing. "Nearly done . . . There." She reached for a pot of foul-smelling paste and began to apply it to the sores. Almost at once, the pain began to ease.

Kate exhaled with relief. "You're an angel, Mary."

"A saint's more like it," muttered the maid, earning a good-natured "Tsk!" from her young mistress. "There. All done."

She put the lid on the pot of salve then rose and started tidying her things away. Kate sat quietly, content just to hold Rebeccah's hand and adjust to the realization that she had a future once more.

"Shall I have these . . . *things* laundered, Madam?" Mary was pointing at the stained breeches lying on a chair.

"Please do. Then that will be all for now . . . Look to your own needs, Mary, for you must be as weary after the journey as the rest of us."

"Thank you, Madam." The maid curtseyed and exited, carrying the breeches at arm's length in a way that made Kate chuckle rather than take offence.

"She's a character," she said.

Rebeccah nodded. "Irreplaceable. And she knows it too, unfortunately."

Silence fell. Now the shadow of Tyburn that had loomed over her for so long had been lifted, Kate felt oddly weightless. Had Rebeccah's thigh not been pressed against hers, her soft hand anchoring her, she felt she could have floated away.

"How are you?" came a soft voice.

Kate turned and smiled at Rebeccah. "I feel . . . strange," she admitted. Then she broached the subject that was bothering her. "I confess, I am also concerned that my now being your servant will affect . . . things between us."

"Kate, you are not my servant!" protested Rebeccah. "The pardon's condition is merely that you must obtain employment with my family, which is not the same thing at all."

"Oh." Kate blinked then said slowly, "Then what job do you have in mind for me? Are you in the market for a highwayman?" She chuckled at Rebeccah's expression. "I didn't think so. Whatever it is, my dear, I hope it can hold my interest. For the last thing I would want after all the trouble you have taken on my behalf is to be tempted back into my bad old ways."

Rebeccah cocked her head and looked at her. "Will you miss being Blue-Eyed Nick?"

"In truth?" Kate rubbed her neck where the halter had chafed it. "No. For of late it had begun to pall. And also my profits had dropped alarmingly." She grinned. "For I was more interested in the kisses of a pretty young woman with green eyes than I was in her valuables." She lifted Rebeccah's unresisting chin and kissed her on the lips. "I still am." She pulled Rebeccah onto her lap and kissed her again, more deeply. For a moment, both women lost themselves in the pleasant activity, then pulled back, looked at one another, and smiled.

"So what job would you *like* to do?" asked Rebeccah, still looking flushed and sounding breathless.

"Ah. That is the difficulty. For I fear those skills I have are of little usefulness."

"I cannot believe that."

Kate thought for a moment and began to list them on her fingers. "I can sing," she said.

Rebeccah gave a delighted smile. "Really? I cannot wait to hear you."

"And sew . . . but I am not the girl I was at thirteen—mantua-maker would no longer suit me, alas. And I kiss tolerably well, or so I have been told." She gave the younger woman a sly glance.

"Indeed, I can attest to that." Rebecca became thoughtful. "But you do yourself an injustice if you believe those are your *only* skills." Kate looked a query. "I'm serious. The journey back from Windsor was fraught, but it gave me time aplenty to consider possibilities. Tell me, Kate. As Blue-Eyed Nick, did you not outride, outshoot, and outfence the best of them?"

A memory of swords clashing in the moonlight, and of the Earl of Avebury flinging Kate's winnings at her surfaced. "Ay," she said, without false modesty.

Rebeccah's face lit up. "Well then, I believe I have come upon the very thing. Mr. Ingrum hasn't yet got his hands on the money Papa left Anne, so before he does I will persuade her to put a portion of it towards the Dutton Fencing Academy. You will be its master."

Kate blinked at her. "A fencing academy?" Rebeccah nodded. "With a woman as its master?" Rebeccah nodded again. "It has never been done before."

"Until now."

"But such an establishment would be considered outrageous," objected Kate. "Especially once it got around that its master was not only female but had once been a notorious highwaywoman."

Green eyes twinkled. "And it would get around—we would make certain of it." Kate snorted. "For Blue-Eyed Nick would be an irresistible attraction, Kate. Potential students would flock to the school, just to satisfy their curiosity, and once they had seen you fight they would be clamouring to sign up. Word would spread. Being taught to fence by you would soon acquire a *cachet*."

Kate gave her a doubtful look. "I'm not *that* good!"

"Practice makes perfect. Come now. It's just the thing. For you and for the Duttons, for we would all profit from its success."

"Assuming it *is* a success."

Rebeccah let her smile speak for itself.

Kate settled the other woman more firmly on her lap while she mulled over the idea. The more she thought about a fencing academy, the more it appealed to her. "We would need to hire at least one other master," she said at last, "but I know just the man. His name is Berrigan. He's a clergyman, and I sense he has grown tired of his current employer."

"A clergyman and an ex-highwayman." Rebeccah clapped her hands together. "Better and better."

"And if we are going to be novel, I could take women as pupils as well as men."

"Only the plain ones," warned Rebeccah, "for I would not want any to catch your eye."

Kate laughed. "That would be unnecessary, for I have eyes only for you." The look that brought her was one she was beginning to recognize. It meant "Kiss me." So she did, thoroughly.

"That's settled then," said Rebeccah when they parted at last. She gave a satisfied sigh, though whether its cause was the kiss or Kate's agreement about their new business venture, Kate was unclear.

They sat in contemplative silence, Kate stroking the back of Rebeccah's hand with her thumb and thinking about the surprising future that had suddenly opened up in front of her. Then something else occurred to her.

"There is another matter that must be addressed, my dear. But you have already done so much for me . . ."

Rebeccah looked at her. "What is it?"

"Where am I to live? For I cannot go back to Alice's, that much is certain."

"Not if you want to escape with your hair still attached," agreed Rebeccah. She thought for a moment. "I will have to ask Mama, but I see no difficulty. There's a spare room in the attic—that will surely serve for now. And once the fencing academy is up and running, it would make sense for you to have rooms there."

"Thank you."

Rebeccah's brow creased. "If it proves as successful as I think it will, you will be spending all your time there, Kate. Perhaps I should find some reason to be there often too." Her brow cleared. "With Mr. Edgeworth's help—he's Papa's clerk," she explained, "perhaps I could learn to handle the academy's administrative side. For I cannot imagine it would involve anything beyond my capabilities. Then you and I would have the perfect excuse to be in one another's company throughout the day."

"That sounds a tempting prospect," agreed Kate. But what about the nights?

Rebeccah was not like Alice, though. She was still green in the ways of love, and a respectable gentlewoman besides. Kate could not ask her to share the pleasures of her bed without the promise of more. And indeed, she realized, wondering when exactly it had happened, the prospect of settling down with this young gentlewoman for the rest of her life had become not only irresistible but necessary to her sense of wellbeing.

She felt her way carefully. "Would not your family mind you being involved with the academy and with me? For surely they have plans to marry you off to some gentleman and breed more Duttons."

"Anne will be married to Ingrum soon, with no time to concern herself with my affairs. As for Mama . . ." Rebeccah shrugged. "I suspect she is already half resigned to my becoming an old maid. And after Windsor, she must suspect that I feel for you what Queen Anne feels for Aunt Sarah—she will not forbid me your friendship."

"What I feel for you is more than friendship!" protested Kate.

"Indeed I hope so. But it might be more circumspect to leave Mama her illusions."

Kate squeezed Rebeccah's waist. "You continue to surprise me, my dear." She considered her next words. "One of the daydreams that has kept me going of late has been of you and me."

"Yes? What are we doing?"

"Aside from the obvious?" Rebeccah's cheeks pinked prettily and Kate chuckled. "Living together. In a little cottage with a garden."

"We have set up home together?"

Kate nodded. "It was but an idle daydream," she said. "But now . . ." She trailed off.

"But now?"

Get on with it, fool. "It has crossed my mind," said Kate, pretending diffidence, "that we might indeed set up house together. But of course, if you are averse to the idea . . ." She held her breath.

"Indeed I am not," said the younger woman at once. Then she frowned. "But would it not be considered scandalous?"

Kate resumed breathing. "We could keep separate rooms for appearances' sake. But when our visitors are gone, and the curtains are drawn, we would be snug together in one bed." She tried to gauge the other woman's reaction.

"I confess," said Rebeccah, looking at her through lowered eyelashes, "that I am becoming more and more curious as to what goes on between two women in private."

"Are you, my dear?" Kate laughed. "I will be only too glad to enlighten you. You have but to say the word."

Rebeccah's brows drew together. "But what about the servants?"

"In our cottage?"

She nodded.

"That should pose no great difficulty. For Mary could come with us. And she already knows about us and does not disapprove, if I do not miss my guess."

"Her speaking glances are very eloquent," agreed Rebeccah, with a laugh. "Ooh!" Her smile grew wider. "Set up house together. Oh, Kate, I like the sound of that."

Her reaction was everything Kate had hoped for. "We could find a place not far from my mother's perhaps."

"Your mother! Faith, but I hope she likes me, Kate—" Rebeccah caught sight of the clock on the chimneypiece and stopped abruptly. "Oh no! We must go down and join the others for we have stayed too long. Look at the time."

"Must we?" Kate bounced Rebeccah on her knee.

"Yes. Or they will send a servant to fetch us for supper." With a flattering show of reluctance, she untangled herself from Kate and stood up.

"Pox on it!" Kate grabbed for her once more.

"Ah ah!" Rebeccah danced out of reach. "We have much to discuss with Mama and Anne. And the sooner we get started persuading them to fund our dreams, the sooner they will become a reality."

Kate groaned but gave in to the inevitable. "You have convinced me. After all I can always ravish you tomorrow." Ignoring Rebeccah's amused exclamation, she rose creakily to her feet and crossed to where the young woman stood waiting for her by the bedchamber door. "Blue-Eyed Nick stands unmasked before you." She gave a jaunty bow. "Command me."

Rebeccah caressed Kate's cheek. "Then come with me, my bold highwayman," she said, green eyes sparkling, "for I have need of you to rescue me one last time."

"From whom?" asked a puzzled Kate.

"Why, from my own family, of course."

Kate chuckled and reached for the door handle. "Lead on."

Epilogue

Chapter 27

A knock at her door made Rebeccah look up. "Come in."

It opened to reveal the servant she and Kate had hired two weeks ago and who was thankfully proving both efficient and reliable. From behind Walter's lanky frame came fierce shouts, effort-filled grunts, and the sound of blades clashing.

"I have brought the cards from the printer, Madam." A brown paper parcel, tied up with string, was tucked beneath the young man's arm.

"Thank you, Walter. Bring it here, will you?" She made room on her desk, moving to one side the scrap of paper with her calculations on it, the heavy accounts ledger, and the quill and ink well. "Did you have any difficulty?"

He shook his head. "The price was as expected." He placed the parcel in front of her and pulled a crumpled piece of paper from his coat pocket. "Here is the bill of receipt."

She glanced at it and set it to one side for later. "Thank you, Walter. That will be all."

"Very good, Madam." He bowed and went out, closing the door behind him and muffling the sounds of combat once more.

She broke the seal and untied the knotted string. *I hope they have made a good job of it.* The brown paper rustled as, holding her breath, she peeled it back to reveal four neat stacks of trade cards. She picked one up and examined it, then gave a relieved sigh. *No spelling mistake, thank heavens. And it looks quite handsome.*

The card replicated the advertisement they had put in both the *Gazette* and the *Daily Courant*. Beneath a silhouette of two swordsmen in action, rapiers clashing, was printed:

DUTTON FENCING ACADEMY
Soho Square, LONDON

No need for an arduous Journey to the Continent. Our
salle d'armes provides expert fencing Tuition in the
English and French Style.
Equitation Tuition also available on request at reasonable
Rates. Please enquire.
NB Both Gentlemen and Ladies welcome.

She would have liked to add that one of the two fencing masters was the notorious former highwayman Blue-Eyed Nick but had run out of space.

The idea for the cards, to be distributed first to London's many coffee-houses, had been Kate's, but the design was Rebeccah's. She hoped it was striking enough to catch the eye and bring in custom. Not that they were doing badly for such a recent enterprise. Already, five gentlemen had signed up for fencing tuition, one the firebrand son of the Earl of Carlisle, who lived in the mansion two doors down. And the exhibition bout Kate and Berrigan were staging in two weeks' time at the bear garden in Hockley-in-the-Hole—a wretched locality, but Kate assured her that, as long as they took care to avoid Mondays and Thursdays, when the bulls and bears were baited, it was *the* place to hold combats of this kind—would raise their profile even more.

No women as yet though. I will have to devise some more . . . feminine means of bringing our establishment to their attention.

Setting that problem aside for later discussion with Kate, Rebeccah retrieved the scrap of paper and rechecked her estimates. It wasn't strictly Academy business, but it did have a bearing on her future. She totalled up the column of figures twice and sat back.

Drumming her fingers on the table, she considered the matter of pride—her own and Kate's. Though the money Rebeccah's father had left her meant she could afford the lease of a small house, she suspected Kate would not countenance it. She would expect to assume the entire burden herself, even though she now earned far less than she had as a highway-man.

Fortunately, if Rebeccah's figures were accurate, the rent should be well within Kate's compass. Rebeccah smiled as a further thought occurred to her. Since Kate's wage from the fencing academy was coming from Dutton coffers anyway, they could *both* be said to be paying the rent. In which case, she could let Kate have her way with a clear conscience.

Someone rapped at the door. "Come in." She was expecting Walter again, or the mouse-like little chambermaid, Judith, whose duty it was to keep the Academy's rooms clean and tidy, but the opening door revealed two visitors.

Rebeccah blinked at the imposing woman standing behind her mother then stood up with a loud scraping of chair legs. "Good morrow, Aunt. This is unexpected."

She frowned at her mother, who replied composedly, "Do not give me that look, Beccah. I could not warn you, as I did not myself know your Aunt Sarah would be in town."

"A pleasant surprise, I trust?" The Duchess of Marlborough didn't wait for an answer. With a swish of her fashionable skirts, she came more fully into the little counting house, making it feel even more cramped than usual.

"As your mother indicated, I am newly come up to town, but I got wind of your enterprise and must come at once to satisfy my curiosity." She studied Rebeccah. "You're looking well, my dear. I am glad to see more colour in your cheeks than last time we met."

Rebeccah blushed. "Thank you, Aunt. I am well indeed."

"And I understand your sister has recovered well from her ordeal too?"

"Indeed she has, thank heavens."

The Duchess's gaze took in the untidy desk and Rebeccah's ink-stained fingers. She touched a gloved forefinger to the ledger then examined her smudged fingertip. "If you don't mind my saying so, my dear, keeping accounts seems a strange occupation for a young woman of your breeding."

"I do more than mere clerking, Aunt," said Rebeccah, trying not to sound indignant. "To me falls the running of this establishment."

"Goodness!" Sarah frowned. "Could not you have hired someone? Your father's man of business. What was his name?" She glanced at Rebeccah's mother.

"Mr. Edgeworth," supplied Mrs. Dutton. "But he cannot possibly run the Academy in addition to our original business, Sarah. Since dear John passed away, Edgeworth has been fully occupied—for goods will not ship *themselves* from the Indies, you know."

Sarah arched an eyebrow at her cousin but said nothing.

"However Mr. Edgeworth has been kind enough to give Rebeccah a few hours' tutoring," continued Rebeccah's mother. "And has opined she is an apt pupil." She gave Rebeccah an approving smile.

"I know my times table," agreed Rebeccah, "and keeping accounts is not such an arduous matter as some might think. Indeed, it is quite within my capabilities, and I thought it might be amusing, not to mention economical, to handle the academy's affairs myself. For I earn no wages and we would not be able to hire a reputable clerk on such terms." She smiled to show she was being humorous.

"I see." Sarah looked doubtful for a moment longer, then her face smoothed. "Well, if it affords you amusement, my dear, then of course, you must do as you see fit."

She turned and walked back towards the door. "From the sound of it, your *salles d'armes* is busy this morning."

She waited for Rebeccah and her mother to join her. "Will you introduce me to your fencing masters? For I understand one is the highwaywoman whose pardon you went to such extraordinary lengths to obtain." She threw Rebeccah a wry glance. "For I must confess, my dear, that the remarkable account you gave me at Windsor, concerning her endeavours on your family's behalf, lodged itself in my mind and I have been curious to meet her."

Rebeccah hoped she wasn't blushing. "With pleasure, Aunt." She glanced at the clock on her desk. "The current lesson should be drawing to a close. Follow me."

∅

Outside the counting house, Rebeccah turned right and followed the sounds of clashing steel, thudding feet, and shouted instructions. She covered the few steps to the fencing salon quickly. Just inside its arched entrance, she paused and waited for her companions to join her.

"Impressive," murmured Sarah, her gaze lifting at once to the lofty ceiling with its huge chandeliers, before travelling down the tall windows, whose heavy curtains were drawn back to admit every scrap of weak October daylight.

The salon occupied almost the entire first floor of the building. That two classes could be taught in it simultaneously was one of the reasons they had rented it, the other the conveniently located stables in Hog Lane to the rear. At one end of it, soles scuffed and squeaked on the floorboards as Kate parried the swords of three men at once with insolent ease. At the other, a tall young man in a black cassock was correcting his two students' stances.

Kate's gaze flicked to the new arrivals, and she shouted to her opponents to put up their swords before dropping her own point. She leaned her rapier against a chair, wiped her palms and face on a linen cloth, and strode towards Rebeccah. Berrigan also hurried to join them.

"My mother you already know." Rebeccah addressed both of them after they halted. "But may I present Sarah, Duchess of Marlborough?" The eyes of the eavesdropping students widened at the name of Queen Anne's favourite and they murmured amongst themselves.

Rebeccah turned to the waiting Duchess. "Our two fencing masters: Mistress Catherine Milledge—formerly known as Blue-Eyed Nick—and the Reverend Thomas Berrigan."

"Honoured to make your acquaintance, Your Ladyship," murmured Berrigan, bowing. Kate also sketched a bow.

But in her male attire a curtsey would have looked very odd, thought Rebeccah.

The Duchess's keen grey eyes raked Kate from head to foot. "So this is your notorious highwayman, niece." At that "your" Rebeccah was sure her cheeks must have gone pink.

"These days I am but a respectable fencing master, Your Ladyship," said Kate smoothly, "fortunate to have been given a second chance by a family as well regarded as the Duttons." She smiled at Mrs. Dutton then at Rebeccah before regarding the Duchess once more, her eyes seeming very blue in the Autumnal light. "I understand, Your Ladyship, that the fact I did not swing from Tyburn Tree is due to your good offices on my behalf." She bowed again, more deeply. "I am in your debt."

Was it her imagination, or was the Duchess blushing? Rebeccah hid a smile. A susceptibility to Kate's charms must run in the family.

"Well, well." Sarah gave a dismissive wave. "You may with ease redeem it, Madam, by ensuring that my niece's fencing academy is the best in London."

"I had already intended to make it so," murmured Kate.

"You are very tall for a woman," continued the Duchess. "And why are you *still* dressed like a man?"

To Rebeccah's relief, Kate was amused rather than offended. "I find skirts a hindrance when fencing, your ladyship."

At that, all eyes tracked to Berrigan's cassock. His lips twitched but he kept his countenance. "Indeed they can trip the unwary, Your Ladyship," he concurred. "For it was catching my heel in the hem that cost me a previous bout with Mistress Milledge . . . not to mention twenty guineas."

Sarah arched an eyebrow at him. "But are you not a man of the cloth?"

He nodded. "Former chaplain to the Earl of Avebury."

An expression of distaste crossed her face. "That old roué," she murmured. "No wonder you sought a change in occupation."

"I am still chaplain, Your Ladyship, but to a local family. They require my presence in the afternoons solely, which leaves my mornings free to give instruction here."

"Some might find that arrangement strange, sir."

"I find it . . . congenial." He cocked his head and smiled at her, as though inviting further comment.

Sarah gave him a thoughtful look then nodded approval. With a last assessing glance at Kate—a relieved Rebeccah sensed that Kate had passed muster—she turned her attention to the watching students. "But I see we have interrupted your lesson. Pray, do not stop on our account." Evidently Aunt Sarah desired to see some swordplay.

An idea struck Rebeccah. "Perhaps they could give us a preview of the exhibition they are planning to give a fortnight hence." She looked a query at Kate, who arched an eyebrow at Berrigan. He nodded.

"An exhibition of fencing?" The Duchess brightened. "Just the thing."

"Walter." Rebeccah beckoned to the servant who had been hovering nearby. "Fetch chairs for the Duchess and Mrs. Dutton, please."

"At once, Madam." He hurried away.

Moments later, Sarah and Elizabeth were making themselves comfortable on high-backed cane chairs, and Kate and Berrigan had fetched their respective rapiers and were preparing to fight.

The bout was fast and furious, its participants' intent not to skewer their opponent but to display their skills to good effect. And skills they had aplenty, though very different. It was the first time Rebeccah had seen Kate fight the chaplain in earnest and she found it fascinating. Kate's style was more down to earth, even brutal at times, while Berrigan's was elegant and full of graceful flourishes. But then, the former highwaywoman had learned her swordplay at her brothers' hands, while Berrigan had received his training at the *Académie d'Armes de Paris*. Even so, the two were evenly matched and their styles complemented one another, and when after twenty minutes of intense fighting they came to a panting halt, the students were clapping and crying "Bravo!" and the Duchess's eyes were bright, her cheeks pink with excitement.

"They are considerable swordsmen," she told Rebeccah, who felt a warm glow on Kate's behalf.

"Thank you, Aunt."

"Now I must go, for I have stayed longer than I meant to." Sarah rose then glanced at Rebeccah's still seated mother. "Do you mean to stay longer, Elizabeth, or will you come with me?"

Mrs. Dutton rose at once. "I will come, for I have much still to attend to concerning my oldest daughter's wedding."

The Duchess gave her a nod and turned back to Rebeccah. "Will you send a servant to fetch our chairmen, my dear?"

"At once, Aunt."

Chapter 28

Kate was kneeling, making up the fire in her grate, when the door to her garret room creaked open and a fair head peeked round it.

"Mary told me you were back," said Rebeccah. "Mama and Anne think I am tired and have come to bed early."

Rebeccah's family could not fathom why she would want to spend her evenings with Kate when she had already spent all day in her company. *And if they knew how things really stand between us, I would be shown the door.*

"May I come in?" continued Rebeccah.

Kate rested the fire irons on the firedog and got to her feet, taking care to stand where the sloping ceiling would not dash out her brains. "You know very well that you may."

Rebeccah grinned, closed the door behind her, and flung herself at Kate, who wrapped her arms round her. They stood for a moment, holding one another, then Kate noticed the smudges beneath Rebeccah's eyes.

"Was your evening very tedious, my love?"

"Very." Rebeccah pressed her face into Kate's shoulder, muffling her voice. "I think you had a better time of it. Did you go riding as planned?"

Kate nodded. "Clover was fractious with me for neglecting her at first. Although your stable boy exercises her well, she still prefers my company." She pursed her lips. "I think she misses our midnight jaunts more than I do. But I took her out to Blackheath and gave her her head for an hour and all was soon forgiven."

"Horses are more forgiving than humans."

Kate laughed. "Not always. And then I went to visit my mother."

"How does she fare?" Rebeccah had met Kate's addled mother briefly and spoken kindly to her, and Martha, for her part, had seemed to like the young gentlewoman, much to Kate's relief.

"Well enough, thank you. She did not remember me as her daughter, of course, but we whiled away the hours pleasantly enough. We played shove-ha'penny at the Rose and Crown and dined on oyster pies."

"Your evening was indeed less tedious than mine." Rebeccah raised her head. "For we had the pleasure of the company of Mr. Ingrum's parents. And a more grasping pair it would be hard to find. I thought their son was bad enough, but . . ." She rolled her eyes. "Poor Anne, to have such people for her In Laws!"

Kate chuckled.

"But perhaps I am too harsh on Frederick." Rebeccah became thoughtful. "For unless I miss my guess, he is developing a real affection for my sister."

"That's a blessing," said Kate, surprised.

Rebeccah nodded. "Especially after that wretched business with Titus."

"Ay." Kate imagined how differently things might have turned out for Rebeccah's spoiled sister—though to be fair, Anne was far less obnoxious these days—had they not rescued her in time.

"As if that were not tedious enough," continued Rebeccah, "we discussed yet more arrangements for the wedding." She sighed. "Thank heavens there is but one week remaining, for I can bear no more discussions on the matter."

"If only your sister had settled for a Fleet wedding," said Kate, amused. "The happy couple would have been spliced in ten minutes flat, then drinks and bride cakes all round."

Rebeccah shuddered. "Do not remind me!" Then her mood lightened, and she threw Kate a playful look. "But our discussions were not only about the bride . . . The consensus is that you must wear women's attire."

"Me?" Kate's heart sank. "Who says I am going to your sister's wedding? The last time I attended church was at Newgate, and listening to my own funeral sermon quite put me off."

Rebeccah waved her objection aside. "In that case, a wedding is just the thing. You are to sit in the family pew next to me and Mama."

From the decidedness of her reply, Kate knew better than to argue. *A funeral. A wedding.* "What next?" she wondered aloud. "A baptism? Is Anne with child already? I did not think Ingrum had it in him. Or Anne in her, come to that."

"Kate!" Rebeccah let out a gurgle of laughter. "Do not be indelicate."

Kate gave the slender waist a squeeze. "Surely the question is whether your sister has been indelicate."

"To return to the subject of the wedding," said Rebeccah, ignoring her teasing. "Of course you are going. It is through Anne's good offices that we have the Academy. The least you can do is attend her nuptials and wish her joy."

Kate sighed. "Oh very well."

"As to your dress, its colour must not clash with the bride's. And Anne's gown is to be of blue silk, her garters blue and white."

"As if I care a farthing about your sister's garters," growled Kate. "A pox on all marriages!"

Rebeccah gave Kate a fond look. "You do not mean that."

"No?"

"No. Why, only the other day you were wondering whether we should have a Fleet marriage. For you said it is not unheard of for a parson in one of those marriage houses to wed couples of the same gender, do you not remember?"

"Of course I do." Kate had not been in earnest, but now . . . She studied Rebeccah's face. "If it would convince you of the seriousness of my intentions . . ."

Rebeccah's cheeks flushed prettily, and she pressed a finger to Kate's lips. "Hush," she said. "I am already convinced."

"Are you?" Kate bit the finger gently, then kissed Rebeccah, receiving a flatteringly ardent response, which threatened to escalate into something more.

A pleasantly surprised Kate realized, rather groggily, that Rebeccah had forgotten her rule against taking their relationship to its natural conclusion while under her mother's roof. Kate was sorely tempted to take advantage of the lapse, for her bed was conveniently to hand, but after a moment, when matters could have gone either way, her conscience got the better of her and she broke off the kiss with a sigh.

Rebeccah's eyes were glazed, her colour heightened, and her breathing ragged. She blinked and came back to herself with a start, then licked her lips and said huskily, "Thank you for your restraint, Kate. For a moment, I forgot myself." She gave Kate's hand an apologetic squeeze. "When we have our own chamber, things will be different. I promise."

They had better. Kate returned the squeeze.

"On that subject," continued Rebeccah, smoothing her dress and putting a little distance between them, "I have been doing my sums, and you are correct. We should be able to afford the rent on a little house somewhere."

"Good." Kate put her hands safely behind her back—Rebeccah's curves were just too tempting.

Rebeccah glanced a query at her. "I take it you saw Jane Allen tonight, and that there is no news?"

"No. But she is continuing her vigil and will send word when she hears of a suitable tenancy." Rebeccah's disappointment was obvious. "I am confident that something will soon turn up," said Kate. "For in Alice Cole's boarding house, tenants came and went with very great frequency."

As though pulled by an invisible magnet, the two had drawn closer to one another once more. Rebeccah hesitated then reached for Kate, and Kate resisted the lure for all of two seconds before enfolding her in her arms.

"Look at us," she murmured into a conveniently placed ear. "We can't keep our hands off each other."

For reply, Rebeccah simply hugged her tighter.

The coals in the grate were burning fiercely now, and the draughty garret had become quite snug. The bed beckoned. What Kate wouldn't give to wake up in it tomorrow morning with Rebeccah snuggled tightly against her. She opened her mouth to suggest Rebeccah stay the night, but Rebeccah beat her to it.

She brushed her fingers against Kate's cheek and said softly, "I should go."

Kate sighed, took the fingers and pressed them to her mouth. "As you wish, my dear." Reluctantly she released her.

At the door, Rebeccah paused and looked back. "When we have our own chamber," she repeated.

Kate nodded. "I'm counting on it."

Chapter 29

"Where is your mother, Beccah?" Caroline Stanhope's voice was good humoured. "Surely she is not going to be late for her own daughter's wedding?"

Rebeccah twisted in her pew and saw that her best friend and her husband were sitting directly behind her. She returned their smiles. "She will be here presently, Caro. Anne needed Mama's assistance with something at the last minute and Kate went with her."

She gave a mental wince as Kate's name slipped out and in response Caroline leaned forward, her expression eager.

"Do you not find it uncomfortable, Beccah," asked her friend in a low voice, "to be so often thrown into Mistress Milledge's company, after the gross way she misled you? For I remember well the fond way you used to speak of Blue-Eyed Nick." She glanced at her husband. "Don't you, Thomas?"

He shot Rebeccah a look of apology. "This is neither the time nor the place to discuss your friend's confidences, my dear."

Her husband's reproof, though a mild one, surprised Caroline. She flushed and sat back, then proceeded to bite her lip and fiddle with her gloves. After a moment, Thomas reached over and took her hand between his, and gradually her high colour returned to normal.

Rebeccah made a note to have a heart to heart with Caro later. She would not confide that her feelings for the dashing highwayman, despite the revelation of his true sex, remained unchanged. For Caro fancied herself of a liberal persuasion, but Rebeccah knew she was easily scandalized. But she wished to retain her friendship, and was determined to reconcile Caro to the presence of Kate in her life, especially as they were to set up house together.

From the twinkle in Thomas's eyes, he had guessed how the land lay;

yet his manner towards Rebeccah remained cordial and he had not forbidden her his wife's acquaintance. Fortunately, he was not the type to tittle-tattle. He would quietly drop the search he had undertaken to find Rebeccah a suitable husband, and that would be the end of it.

"Thank you," she mouthed. He smiled and nodded, and she turned to face the front once more.

Mrs. Dutton appeared at the far end of the church, and close behind her came Kate in a blue gown that matched her eyes to perfection. The two hurried along the aisle towards Rebeccah's pew and with a rustling of skirts made themselves comfortable. No sooner had they done so than the bride entered on her uncle's arm, for Uncle Andrew had travelled up from Chatham with the purpose of giving his niece away. Then in came the clergyman, and the service got underway.

⌘

"I shall be glad when this day is over," Rebeccah confided to Kate. They had transferred to the Bond Street townhouse that would be Anne's future home, and very smart it was too, what Rebeccah had seen of it. "For I ate too much at the wedding feast and these new shoes have pinched me since I put them on."

"Not much longer," said Kate, whose height enabled her to see over the heads of the other women (the men were in another room with the groom). "Here is your sister."

A loud "Huzzah" went up and the crowd surged forward. Rebeccah caught a glimpse of Anne, hands raised in mock alarm but making no real attempt to resist those seeking to prepare her for her marriage bed. The gap closed again.

"Remove her clothes," instructed someone, "but leave the garters. Pull them lower, though, for the men will want to remove those themselves and pin them to their hats."

Willing hands set to work and voices rang out at intervals giving advice, some useful.

"Do not keep any of the pins. For they bring bad luck." "We will need those stockings for the men to fling. Put them to one side." "Where is her nightgown? Bring the nightgown." "All must have favours. Share out her bride lace and knots."

Anne's gloves and scarves, ribbons and bows were handed from person to person. Kate frowned at the red bow that had appeared in her hand, gave it to Rebeccah, and stood on tiptoe once more.

"She is in her nightgown," Kate reported. "They are brushing her hair. She is smiling and looks quite gay."

Rebeccah pocketed the bow and nodded her thanks. Evidently Anne was revelling in being the centre of attention and looking forward to her first night with Ingrum, which was a relief. The sisters had not discussed to what extent Anne's drunken footman had forced his attentions on her, but it had clearly done her no lasting harm.

"Now comes the hard part," shouted her sister's childhood friend, Anne Lock. "One, two, three. Whoops!" She had evidently taken more wine than she was used to.

"I hope they don't drop her," murmured Rebeccah, as her sister was lifted so high even she could see her above the heads.

"That foot is loose—someone take hold. More support under her back, if you please. There. We have her safe. Huzzah!"

Slowly and slightly unsteadily, the procession began to move towards the open door.

"To the bridal chamber," yelled someone.

"Have you given her the book yet?" called out someone else. "For she will have need of it tonight."

"What book?" called out Anne.

"Why, *Aristotle's Masterpiece* of course," came the answer. "Every married woman's friend."

A roar of laughter went up, for everyone there had heard of the best selling sex manual. A blushing Rebeccah glanced at Kate, who grinned back, unperturbed.

In great high spirits, the bride's attendants moved out into the passage taking their precious burden with them. Kate and Rebeccah followed.

ॐ

"Bless me, what a day!" said Rebeccah's mother, allowing the maid who had replaced Nancy—Anne had been allowed to take the skinny maid with her to her new abode—to relieve her of her wrap and gloves. "Will you take some brandy, Andrew?" Her brother-in-law, who was relinquishing his hat, smiled and nodded.

"George," she continued to the waiting butler. "We'll have brandy in the drawing room, if you please." She glanced to where Rebeccah and

Kate were handing over their outer garments to Mary. "You too, my dears. For without your help I do not think I would have got through this day unscathed."

"With pleasure, Mama," called Rebeccah.

"I would prefer beer," murmured Kate.

"Then have some," said Rebeccah. "I intend to take sherry." She beckoned the butler over and said in a low voice, "George, will you bring me some sherry, and some strong beer for Mistress Milledge?"

He smiled. "Of course, Madam."

Kate nodded her thanks.

When the plump maid had bobbed a curtsey and hurried away with their outer garments, Rebeccah started up the stairs. Kate followed close behind her.

A fire was burning in the drawing room fireplace, and Rebeccah paused to warm her hands at it before crossing to an easy chair. It was a relief to sit comfortably at last, after the hard pews and carriage seats. She eased her feet out of her shoes and gave her toes a blissful wiggle—surreptitiously, she had thought, until she saw Kate's amused expression.

The drawing room door opened and George entered bearing a silver tray. He served the mistress of the house first, then moved on to Rebeccah's Uncle. Andrew Dutton had taken possession of Anne's chair by the fire, which had once been Papa's. Indeed he looked disconcertingly like his dead brother, though a good deal fatter.

"Sit down," Rebeccah whispered to Kate, who was still standing. Kate took the easy chair closest to hers and accepted her beer from the butler with a nod.

Uncle Andrew exchanged a glance with his sister-in-law and stood up. "Are all glasses charged?"

They nodded.

"Then I propose a toast." He raised his glass. "To the bride and groom. May Fortune smile on them."

"And may they find great happiness," added Rebeccah.

They drank.

"And to Mistress Dutton," he continued, glancing at Elizabeth, "for allowing me the great privilege of giving away my dear brother's daughter on such an auspicious and important day." At the mention of Rebeccah's much missed father a shadow fell over the room.

"First my husband, and now my eldest daughter," murmured Rebeccah's mother. Tiredness tended to bring out her maudlin side, and it had certainly been a long day. "I shall miss Anne."

"I am sure we shall see as much of her as we ever did, Mama," said Rebeccah briskly. "For Frederick has his own carriage, as he never stops telling us, and it is not far from here to Bond Street."

Mrs. Dutton sighed. "Perhaps you are right." She forced a smile, which became genuine as her gaze rested on Rebeccah. "At least I still have you to keep me company, my dear. For I don't know what I should do if *both* my daughters were to desert me." She laughed and took another sip of her brandy.

Rebeccah couldn't help but throw a perturbed glance at Kate, who gave her an arched eyebrow in return.

Chapter 30

It had rained during the morning and Hockley-in-the-Hole was living up to its name as Kate picked her way through the mud and puddles that covered the narrow, rutted street. The breeze was in the wrong direction, funnelling the stench from the nearby Fleet Ditch between the crumbling houses on either side towards her. She switched to breathing through her mouth.

Already spectators were gathering for the bull-baiting due to start in half an hour, and she used her elbows to make progress, stopping to hand out the cheaply printed bills she had tucked under her arm. Behind her, Walter was doing the same. And though many bills were instantly balled up and ground underfoot, a few went in pockets, which was all she could ask for.

The bill was identical to the advertisement she had placed in today's *Postboy*, though that was aimed at more respectable readers:

> At the Bear Garden, Hockley-in-the-Hole, to begin at two o'clock precisely tomorrow, Tuesday, a Trial of Skill is to be performed, between two Profound Masters of the Noble Science of Self-defence, both currently in the Employ of the Dutton Fencing Academy.
>
> I, Catherine Milledge, also once known as Blue-Eyed Nick, the highwaywoman lately pardoned by the Queen, do invite you, the Reverend Thomas Berrigan, to meet and exercise at the usual weapons.
>
> I, Thomas Berrigan, once chaplain to the Earl of Avebury, will not fail to meet this brave and bold inviter at the time and place appointed, desiring sharp swords and, from her, no favour. No person to be upon the stage but the seconds.
>
> Vivat Regina.

"Profound masters" was laying it on a bit thick, but Kate had researched advertisements for similar combats and used the language expected.

She busied herself handing out more of the bills, not discriminating between high born or low, male or female, old or young, hale or crippled, gin hawkers or their inebriated customers, soldiers or their trulls, for whores were as likely to send clients the academy's way as anyone else. Breaking the fingers of any cutpurse foolish enough to target her came so automatically she was barely conscious of doing it. She was aware, however, of the sloshing sounds following in her wake, and the accompaniment of mutterings and curses.

She glanced back at the academy's servant and grinned. "Aren't you glad I asked you instead of Berrigan to assist me, Walter?" The chaplain had not been able to evade his religious duties this afternoon having begged off tomorrow for the exhibition.

Her question distracted the young man, and his foot squished down in a pile of horse droppings. He bit off a curse, and Kate let out a bark of laughter as, face the picture of disgust, he scraped his shoe clean.

"I am glad to be of service, Madam," he assured her, unconvincingly.

His reply made a one-legged, old soldier on crutches turn and scrutinize Kate more closely, raise his grizzled eyebrows, and curse in disbelief under his breath, for she was wearing male attire. It made things much simpler; a dress in this mire would have been a nightmare. She was glad that she had managed to convince Rebeccah not to come. The young gentlewoman had given in with ill grace, but even on a dry day Hockley-in-the-Hole was not the most salubrious of places.

The yelping and yapping of dogs had been getting louder and now the sound of the crowd changed. She turned and saw people further along the street parting to allow through the animals to be baited today.

First came a bull, its rolling eyes and reluctant gait revealing unease verging on panic; then came a young bear, confused and howling, led by a rope at a distance thought safe from those lashing, lethal claws. Finally came the dogs, at least thirty of them, some mastiffs, some of no particular breed, all yapping and slavering, lunging and straining at their leashes, with an evil gleam in their eyes.

Kate grimaced as the procession drew abreast of her, and stood back to allow it past. The animals were bound for the Bear Garden at the end of the street, which tomorrow would host her exhibition but today was to bear witness to more bloody sights.

It seems poor sport to tether a bull or a bear and set on it maddened dogs with jaws like vices.

She checked the number of bills remaining and found she had only two left. "Let us call it a day and go home, Walter." She turned to the servant and slapped him on the shoulder. "What say you?"

He gave her an enthusiastic nod.

℘

The garret door creaked open and Rebeccah slipped through, giving a quick glance behind her before closing the door softly.

She hurried into Kate's embrace murmuring, "One of these days my mother will discover us."

Kate was guiltily aware that a part of her hoped it would be soon. At least it would force the issue to a conclusion. Being so close to Rebeccah all the time yet not being able to bed her was straining her self-control.

"How has she been today? Still melancholy about your sister?" Mrs. Dutton had visited her daughter last week and returned concerned she was lonely.

"I fear so. She misses Anne's presence about the house, and so of course is convinced that Anne must miss us that much more." Rebeccah bit her lip and looked up. "I had not anticipated this, Kate. How can I possibly desert Mama at such a time? With both her daughters gone, she will be all alone."

Not quite, thought Kate, *for there are still the servants.* But prudence kept her from speaking that thought out loud. She said instead, "I see."

"Do you?" Rebeccah studied her then disentangled herself from Kate's arms. "You think I grow cool towards our plan to set up house together, but I assure you," she said, her tone growing heated, "it is very far from the case."

"Indeed I think nothing of the sort, Rebeccah," said Kate mildly. "You are a kind and considerate daughter, concerned for her widowed mother's welfare. Why should I think otherwise?" Kate had been in the same situation with her own mother, worse in fact, for her mother's wits had been addled. Then she had stumbled upon a treasure: Jane Allen.

"Forgive me." A chastened Rebeccah took her place in Kate's arms once more.

Thinking of Jane had given Kate an idea. "Would your mother countenance a companion?"

Rebeccah blinked at her and became thoughtful. "Like Jane Allen, you mean?"

"Not *quite* like Jane. For she is my mother's nursemaid as well as companion. Your mother would require far less attention."

Rebeccah smiled. "I do not think Mama would countenance a lurcher like Jane's."

"Beau is not to everyone's taste," agreed Kate with a straight face.

Rebeccah sighed. "It is an excellent idea, Kate, but I am not very confident of its success. For Mama prefers her family about her. But there can be no harm in suggesting it, can there?"

"Make it seem like her own notion," advised Kate.

Rebeccah's eyebrows rose. "You are artful!"

Kate shrugged. "Is it artful to try every avenue in pursuit of something you desire?"

Rebeccah's manner became arch. "Do you desire something, Kate?"

Kate smiled and didn't answer.

Rebeccah stood on tiptoe and wrapped her arms around Kate's neck. "This, perhaps?"

She kissed Kate thoroughly, igniting a fire in her guts, then broke it off—far too soon for Kate's liking. Kate took a calming breath and clamped down on her need to ravish the young woman there and then.

While Rebeccah pretended to explore Kate's garret—what little there was of it could be discovered in seconds—Kate flung herself down on the bed, laced her hands behind her head, and let her gaze dwell pleasantly on the curves filling out Rebeccah's dress.

"How did things go at Hockley today?"

She came back to her surroundings with a start and became aware that Rebeccah was looking at her. Blinking, she replayed the question. "Oh. The advertisement ran as expected." She picked up the copy of the *Postboy* from the stool beside the bed, opened it to the right page with a rustle, and pointed to the advertisement in question.

Rebeccah crossed over to her and peered down at it.

"And Walter and I succeeded in distributing all but a few of the bills," added Kate refolding the newspaper and throwing it carelessly aside.

"Splendid," said Rebeccah. "Do you think many will come?"

"I am hopeful. If nothing else, it has spread the Dutton Fencing Academy's name abroad."

Rebeccah nodded. "I meant to ask you. Who will be your seconds?"

"Walter, of course." Kate chuckled. "I think he will find the task much more to his taste than was today's. And your footman, Will. Your mother has agreed to lend him to me for a few hours."

"What do either of them know about swordsmanship?" asked Rebeccah, confused.

"This is not a hostile bout, love. They need only to know the sharp end of a sword from its hilt. They are there to hold our coats, mop our brows, bandage our cuts, keep the stage clear of anything that might impede us . . . and of course gather up any coins thrown."

"Cuts!" Rebeccah's eyes widened in alarm. "You may tell Berrigan that if he harms you I shall never forgive him."

Kate grinned. "He already knows and is quaking in his boots."

"I'm in earnest, Kate."

She reached out and grasped Rebeccah's hand. "I know." She raised it to her lips. "But your concern, though it warms me, is misplaced. For any cuts we take will be slight at best as both Berrigan and I will be using the flats of our blades and pulling our strokes. It is only an exhibition of skill, after all."

"You are certain?"

"Trust me." Kate patted the mattress next to her and after a moment Rebeccah sat down.

"If you have lied I shall be furious," she warned.

"As is your right." Kate draped an arm around her. "And as is *my* right, if I am wounded, I shall require you to kiss it better."

Chapter 31

"We shall have to keep our wits about us," said Kate, giving the platform a dubious glance. It was as high as her chin and had no railing.

"Ay," said Berrigan. "For if one of us were to slip and fall . . ."

"It would be an embarrassing, not to mention bruising, experience," completed Kate. "Unless a spectator were to break our fall, of course."

The chaplain grinned and indicated the noisy rabble in the front seats. "And they would break our heads for our impertinence. Either way, we'd end up sore."

Some spectators were clearly drunk, others belligerent. Some were squabbling and hitting each other, trying to place bets or get better seats. A few were trying to scale the scaffolding that supported the gallery, their efforts to climb into the more expensive seats met with catcalls and unsavoury missiles from the gallants ensconced there. Kate was relieved Rebeccah had not come to watch, though she had taken some convincing and given in with bad grace, saying rather sulkily that she would visit her sister instead.

"They will settle down when the bout starts," she said, more in hope than expectation. "Walter, what o'clock is it?"

The servant, who had been looking about him with a faintly horrified air, pulled out the pocket watch she had given him for safe keeping. "Five minutes to the hour, Madam."

She arched an eyebrow at Berrigan. "Shall we?"

He nodded.

She handed Walter her tricorne and pulled her baldric over her head so she could remove her coat. It was a cool day for only a shirt, breeches, and boots, but she would soon work up a sweat. Once the servant had relieved her of the coat, she unsheathed her rapier and handed him the baldric. "Thank you, Walter."

Berrigan, meanwhile, had handed their other second, Will the footman, his hat, and was reverently undoing the catches of the rectangular wooden case he had cradled protectively all the way from Soho Square. Cushioned inside it, in an elaborately tooled scabbard, was his swept-hilt rapier, made of the finest Toledo steel, and every time Kate saw the magnificent weapon she felt a pang of envy.

She sighed, raised her own more mundane rapier, and made a few practice passes with it, then threw it onto the platform and leaped up nimbly after it.

The crowd noticed her at once and catcalls and shouts greeted her. "That's Blue-Eyed Nick!" "Women with swords? What next? Bears in sedan chairs?"

Berrigan's cassock hampered him, and it was only with Walter and Will's help that he succeeded in clambering up onto the platform.

Amazed cries met his appearance. "A frigging priest?" "Why is *he* in skirts rather than her?" "Clergymen can't fight worth a damn! Give me my money back."

"Ignore them," said Kate.

"I have every intention of doing so," said Berrigan.

"What o'clock is it?" she called down.

"Two exactly," answered Walter.

She nodded her thanks and turned to face Berrigan. "Ready?"

"Ready."

Their expressions solemn, standing side by side, they bowed to each section of the crowd in turn, raising a hand in acknowledgment of the more polite and encouraging exhortations. When they had finished, Berrigan turned to face Kate, raised his rapier in a salute, and assumed the on guard position. She did the same.

As they held one another's gazes and began to circle, searching for an opening, the crowd noise faded to a less distracting level.

Kate's lips curled into a reflexive snarl. An answering and very unchristian gleam appeared in the chaplain's eye. Mentally she licked her lips at the prospect of a good scrap. She adjusted her stance until she was poised over the balls of her feet and beckoned.

Come on, Berrigan. Let's put on a show.

As he lunged towards her, the crowd roared their approval.

🙎

An old woman in a sedan chair gave Kate a horrified glance as her bearers hurried past.

I must look a sight.

She dabbed her kerchief to her eyebrow and examined it. The bleeding had stopped, thank heavens. The cut looked far worse than it was or than her bloody shirt, visible beneath her open coat, would indicate. "Hang me!" she muttered. "When Rebeccah sees this she's going to draw and quarter me."

"As long as she doesn't draw and quarter *me*," said Berrigan, clutching his precious sword case more tightly.

He looked every bit as disreputable as she did. He had a pronounced limp, and his left eye had almost swollen shut. The hem of his cassock had come unstitched and threatened to trip him at every other step.

Kate grinned at him and shifted her baldric into a more comfortable position. "It was the edge of a flung coin that clipped me, not your blade."

"Make sure she knows that."

"Worry more about that God fearing family of yours. What will they think when their chaplain appears tomorrow in your condition?"

Berrigan's wince was expressive, and not solely due to his injuries.

"They'll think that I deliberately pitched you off the stage," she continued.

"In a way you did. For it was your blood I slipped in." His laughter was infectious and she joined in.

"We certainly made an impression," she said ruefully. "Whether it will result in more custom for the Academy . . ." She waved a hand, indicating doubt.

"At least we had displayed our skills for a good half hour." He rubbed his hip. A spectator had broken his fall, sparing him worse injury. Unfortunately, that selfsame spectator had taken exception to being used in such a fashion, hence Berrigan's black eye. "And if it is any consolation, the sparks in the upper gallery seemed to enjoy it. In fact it was their coin that brought our bout to its untimely close."

Kate produced the culprit from her coat pocket and flourished it. "A guinea too," she said. "No one can say they are cheapskates." She shoved it back in her pocket.

The turn off to Soho Square lay just up ahead. She slowed and glanced back to where Will and Walter were walking, heads together in animated conversation. They had become fast friends over the course of the afternoon.

No doubt exchanging juicy titbits about their respective employers.

She waited for them to catch up, then addressed the Dutton family's footman. "We are almost back to the Academy, Will. Thank you for your services this afternoon. You may return to St. James's Square with a clear conscience and my thanks."

He bowed, smiled a farewell at each of them, and hurried away.

Chapter 32

The footman led Rebeccah upstairs, opened the door, bowed, and waited for her to enter. She went through into what was obviously the drawing room and spied her sister sitting at the spinet by the window. Anne smiled and waved, and Rebeccah was about to return her greeting when something brown-and-white made a dash for her.

She flinched as the spaniel bitch, for such it was, seized her right shoe and began to worry it. Its low growl unnerved her until she saw the furiously wagging tail.

"Stop it, Queenie." Anne surged to her feet and hurried towards her. "Stop that, you silly dog." She reached for the spaniel's collar. "Leave my sister alone."

Faced with giving up its new chew toy or being throttled, the spaniel let go.

Anne gave it a little shake before releasing the collar. "Bad dog."

Queenie didn't look in the remotest bit chastened, and her tail wagged as she gazed up at her mistress. Anne sighed, rolled her eyes, and pointed to the basket that lay close to the hearth. Queenie hesitated, and Rebeccah braced herself for a resumption of the attack, but the spaniel trotted meekly back to her basket and resumed chewing what had once been one of Anne's slippers.

"My apologies, Beccah," said Anne, her cheeks an embarrassed pink. "We only got her last week and she is not yet fully trained. Has she done much damage?"

Rebeccah examined her shoe. "It is a little the worse for wear," she admitted.

"I will buy you a new pair."

"There is no nee—"

"I will not hear otherwise, Beccah."

Rebeccah blinked at her sister's fierce tone then acquiesced. "That is kind. Thank you."

"Think nothing of it. Queenie was Frederick's idea—company for me while he is away—so he cannot carp at any expenses caused by her transgressions."

Anne led Rebeccah to an easy chair in front of the fire then, as Rebeccah sat, rang for a servant. While her sister gave orders, Rebeccah glared at Queenie before turning her attention to her surroundings. Everything about Anne's Bond Street house was up-to-the-minute. There was even wallpaper.

The servant departed and Anne took another easy chair. "I have sent for tea," she said.

"Thank you. Your house is very grand, Anne."

"It is, isn't it?" Her sister's expression became complacent. "Frederick says that a new house must have the very latest in furniture and furnishings."

"Where is he?"

Disgruntlement replaced the complacency. "He is very little here at present. For Mr. Edgeworth is teaching him the business of trading."

It was a moment before Rebeccah understood her reference. "He is to take an active part in Dutton's?"

"Yes." Anne grimaced and for a moment Rebeccah wondered if her sister was being disparaging of her husband's business acumen. But Anne continued, "Though it may soon be renamed Ingrum's if Mrs. Ingrum has any say in the matter."

"But *you* are Mrs. Ingrum," said Rebeccah, confused.

"I suppose I am." Anne laughed. "I must confess, though I have been practicing signing my married name, I am still unused to the sound of it. But in this case, Beccah, I was referring to Frederick's mother."

Rebeccah frowned. "But why would she risk losing the goodwill that has accrued to the Dutton name? It took Papa years to build his company's reputation and she would dispense with it at a stroke?"

"I do not suppose that has occurred to her," said Anne. "But do not worry. For Frederick is conscious of its value, and he will not change it." She pursed her lips. "At least on that matter he is willing to stand up to his mother."

Rebeccah was about to ask her what she meant by that when the door opened and a maid brought in their tea. Conversation became of a necessity inconsequential while the servant poured the tea into expensive china.

Anne's wistful demeanour as she enquired about the health of everyone at St. James's Square made Rebeccah wonder if her mother hadn't been right about her sister missing them. Which would be strange, for she and Anne were kin, true, but different temperaments and attitudes meant they had never really liked one another.

The maid curtseyed and departed.

Rebeccah sipped her tea and frowned at Queenie, who was lapping water from a dish. She couldn't help contrasting the spaniel unfavourably with Jane Allen's amiable lurcher. "What did you mean about Frederick not being able to stand up to his mother, Anne?" she asked.

"Is it not obvious? She has decided opinions. Even about things that should not concern her. And she is not backward in expressing them. She thinks, for example, that I should have children sooner rather than later, for I am not getting any younger. The impertinence! And that I should have two of each at least. I dread to think what state my figure will be in after that."

Rebeccah winced. "Does Frederick agree?"

Anne shook her head. "He was an only child and says it never did him any harm."

Rebeccah laughed.

"But it is worse than that," continued Anne. "Mrs. Ingrum was used to managing Frederick's household as well as her own and sees no reason why his marriage should change that." Spots of angry colour burned in both cheeks. "*I* am mistress of this house, Beccah, but when she is here, which she is most mornings, she thinks nothing of giving me unlooked for advice, or of countermanding my orders. It makes me look foolish in front of the servants. Undermines my authority."

"And Frederick does nothing to stop her?"

"No. Oh, in private, he agrees she is wrong to carry on this way. He says she means well, and after all, why should she *not* pass on her experience and advice if it will be of use? But . . ." Anne sighed and shook her head.

"What about Mr. Ingrum?" asked Rebeccah. "Can he not see that his wife is exceeding her authority?"

Anne gave a hollow laugh. "Frederick's father is never home, Beccah. He spends his time in coffee-houses, and who can blame him when *she* is waiting there for him? Not that her meddling isn't in part his fault. For if he kept her amused and content and *occupied*, she would not feel the need to meddle in my affairs." She sighed and said plaintively, "I already have one mother, Beccah. I do not feel the need of another."

"If Mama were to live with you, Frederick's mother would not dare to interfere," joked Rebeccah. "For the post of provider of maternal advice would be already filled."

Anne stared at her as though dumbstruck.

"I did not mean it seriously."

"I know you did not but . . ."

Rebeccah watched a range of emotions flash across her sister's expressive face.

"Even if Frederick *would* countenance such a proposition," said Anne at last, sounding disappointed, "I doubt if Mama would agree. For she has lived in St. James's Square since her marriage, and will surely be loath to leave it. Then there is your future to consider, Beccah."

Rebeccah's heart raced and her mind whirled. Was this the chance she and Kate had been waiting for? "I do not think Mama would mind leaving that house as much as you think," she said slowly. "For you must have noticed that the memories of Papa it holds can make her very melancholy."

Anne nodded. "I have."

"And there is an argument to be made in favour of combining two households. For it would save expenditure, and surely neither Mama nor Frederick could find fault with that."

"But what about you, Beccah? If she were to let go the house in St. James's Square, where would you live?"

Rebeccah took a deep breath and let it out. "With Kate."

Anne's eyebrows shot up. "*Kate?*" She smiled as if Rebeccah had made a joke, then the smiled faded and she frowned. "You are in earnest?"

"I am," said Rebeccah composedly.

"But . . . a former felon, Beccah!" At the sharpness of her tone, Queenie raised her head and whined.

"Queen Anne herself saw fit to pardon her," protested Rebeccah.

"Even so—"

"I would trust Kate with my life. In fact she has already saved my life once, Anne. Not to mention our family's honour."

Anne flushed. "You are referring to *my* honour, I collect!"

Rebeccah let silence speak for her. Her hand shook as she raised her dish of tea to her lips, but gradually it steadied and her pulse slowed.

"Well, well," said Anne, after a long pause during which they both concentrated on their tea, "perhaps you are right. I spoke only out of concern for your welfare, Beccah. If I have offended you, forgive me."

Surprised and pleased, Rebeccah acknowledged her sister's capitulation with a smile and a slight inclination of the head.

At length Anne resumed, "But where would you live, Beccah? For Kate occupies one of our garrets, does she not?"

"Not there, of course." Rebeccah shrugged. "But the location is immaterial. We would rent somewhere suitable." She studied Anne. "It would be no hardship, I assure you. Kate and I are . . . comfortable with one another."

"I had noticed," admitted Anne. "And, I confess, found it somewhat surprising, given the differences in your backgrounds and temperaments."

"Perhaps that is why."

Anne bit her lip. "But what of your plans for a husband, Beccah? For children?"

Rebeccah held her sister's gaze. "In truth it has been some years since I had such plans. I do not think I am the marrying kind."

Anne blinked at her.

"When Caroline Stanhope asked her husband to find me a suitable match from amongst his acquaintance," continued Rebeccah, choosing her words carefully, "it proved impossible. It was his considered opinion that no man can ever meet my expectations."

"But surely that is true of all women," objected Anne. "Yet in the end we settle for less." She gave Rebeccah a self-deprecating smile.

"Perhaps we do. But I for one am unwilling to do so," said Rebeccah. "But neither do I wish to be always under my mother's roof."

Anne studied her. "You are a strange creature, Beccah. I have never really understood you."

"No," agreed Rebeccah. She smiled. "But I believe Kate does."

"In any case," said Anne, putting down her empty tea dish, "it is early days, and this plan of ours may come to nothing."

"Indeed," said Rebeccah, but that "ours" lifted her spirits.

"After all," continued Anne, "Mama may throw up her hands in horror at the very idea of coming to live with me and Frederick. And so may Frederick!" She smiled and sat back in her chair. "Speaking of Kate, where is she this afternoon? At the Academy?"

Rebeccah glanced at the clock. "She and Berrigan have been giving a fencing exhibition in Hockley-in-the-Hole. It should be concluded by now."

Anne's eyes widened. "Hockley-in-the Hole? Faith, Beccah! Is that not where they hold the bear baiting?"

"The very place."

✍

Rebeccah paced as much as the garret would allow, glancing frequently towards the bed, where a seated Kate was letting Mary examine her eyebrow.

Kate didn't seem concerned enough about what had happened for Rebeccah's liking. Indeed she seemed to find it amusing. Rebeccah resisted an unladylike urge to curse.

"The bleeding has stopped." The plump maid peered at Kate's brow. "If you had come to me sooner it might have been better, Madam. I have a salve for cuts such as this."

Kate expression became suitably penitent, but Rebeccah doubted she was sincere.

"As it is, it might leave a scar," continued Mary sternly. Then she relented. "But if so, it will only be a small one, barely noticeable."

"So I am to keep my good looks?" Kate grinned. "Thank you, Mary."

"Yes, thank you, Mary." Rebeccah stopped her pacing and fixed Kate with a frown. Kate's smiled vanished at once. "That will be all."

"Very good, Madam." Mary packed away her medical supplies, curtseyed, and departed.

"Do not be cross with me, Rebeccah," said Kate, the moment Mary had closed the door behind her.

Rebeccah put her hands on her hips. "It could have *blinded* you!"

Kate stood up and came over to her. "Do not dwell on what *might* have happened, my love." She pulled Rebeccah into her arms. Rebeccah put up only token resistance before acquiescing. "I am safe and here with you."

"It could have *blinded* you," repeated Rebeccah against her shoulder, but her heart wasn't in it.

"Save your sympathy for Berrigan. The fall shook him and for the next few days he will be limping like an old man."

"Is that supposed to make me feel better?"

"No, but this is." Her fingers lifted Rebeccah's chin, then she kissed her.

As Kate's mouth explored hers, Rebeccah lost herself in the sensation, her body almost melting with delight. *If kissing Kate is so pleasurable, how will it feel when we—?*

Strong arms swept her up, and the world shifted and lurched, and when it had steadied again, Kate was sitting on her bed with Rebeccah cradled in her lap. Rebeccah moulded herself to Kate's body, and Kate's arms wrapped her in a tight embrace. She basked in the feeling of warmth and protection and realized that she did indeed feel much better.

"How did things go at your sister's this afternoon?" asked Kate, after a while.

A change of subject? Very well. "Well, thank you. Anne now has a companion: a spaniel."

"A spaniel." Kate's tone made it obvious she thought little of the breed.

"Named Queenie," added Rebeccah. "She tried to relieve me of my shoe."

Puzzled blue eyes regarded her. "Anne did?"

"No, Queenie. Frederick gave her the dog, to keep her from being lonely."

Kate snorted. "They are newlyweds! He would have done better to stay with her himself."

"My thought exactly," said Rebeccah. "But he is intent on making his mark and at present is immersing himself in Papa's business. For on his marriage, Anne's property became his, you know."

"At least when I robbed coaches," murmured Kate, "the theft was above board." She studied Rebeccah. "So your sister is lonely as your mother suspected?"

A shiver of anticipation ran through Rebeccah as she considered how to broach her news. "And yet, not as lonely as she would wish, Kate. For Frederick's mother is to be found at Bond Street more often than Anne likes."

Kate scratched her nose. "With mothers-in-law, that is often how the land lies."

"Not for much longer, perhaps. For there may be a solution to Anne's loneliness that will prove satisfactory to both her and Mama . . . and us. And in the process put Mrs. Ingrum's nose out of joint." She let loose the smile she had been suppressing and opened her mouth to continue. Kate beat her to it.

"Your sister wants to combine her household with that of your mother?"

"Trust you to steal my thunder." Rebeccah pretended to pout.

"Forgive me." Kate studied her, blue eyes suddenly intent. "But . . . Am I correct?"

Rebeccah nodded, and Kate smiled.

"And you believe your mother will agree?"

"There is every chance."

Kate let out a shout of delight. "And if she does, you will be free to set up house with me."

Rebeccah laughed and rested a hand against Kate's belly. "Now, all we have to do is *find* a place!"

A knock at the door interrupted them. Rebeccah stood up, smoothed her skirts, and put a respectable distance between them.

"Enter," she called.

Mary's head appeared round the door, followed by the rest of her. She was clutching a letter. "I beg your pardon, Madam," she said, "but George has just told me a message came for Mistress Milledge while she was out. It has been sitting in the drawing room and no one thought to bring it up. I thought you would not wish to wait until tomorrow to have it."

Kate got up and stepped towards her, hand outstretched. "Thank you, Mary. You thought right."

Mary gave her the letter, curtseyed, and made herself scarce.

"Who is it from?" Rebeccah wandered over to join Kate, who was studying the handwriting with a frown.

"'Tis Jane Allen's hand."

Rebeccah's heart began to race. "Has something happened—?"

Kate tore open the letter and read the contents swiftly. Her frown gave way to a pleased smile and she turned to Rebeccah, eyes dancing.

"Martha is well. This concerns the tenancy we asked Jane to keep her eyes open for."

Rebeccah's breath caught. "You mean . . ."

Kate nodded. "The lease has fallen vacant on a small house three doors down from hers. It has five chambers and a small patch of ground that might serve Mary for an herb garden."

"How many bedchambers?"

"Two large, one small."

Rebeccah let out a sigh of relief. *Enough for us to keep up appearances.* "And when may we view it?"

"We have an appointment for tomorrow morning."

"So soon?"

Kate nodded and became thoughtful. "Mary must accompany us, of course. For if she is to be our maid, her opinion must be taken into account."

Rebeccah's heart was pounding with excitement. "Can this really be happening? It sounds too good to be true."

"It may be infested with rats," agreed Kate, but she was smiling, "and the roof may leak. But I doubt it. For Jane Allen is sensible. She will have inspected the place and decided it will suit." She arched an eyebrow. "The more pertinent question is, will it suit Mary?"

"It will if she knows what's good for her," muttered Rebeccah.

Chapter 33

A rumble of cartwheels made Kate peer out the window. A horse-drawn cart piled high with tables and chairs, mirrors and bookcases, candlesticks, curtains, and who knew what else that Rebeccah had selected had pulled up in the street outside. Several of their new neighbours were standing in their doorways, gaping at it.

"Your furniture has arrived," she called, sucking a skinned knuckle. They had taken delivery of the beds earlier and she had only finished assembling them half an hour ago.

"*Our* furniture," came Rebeccah's voice from upstairs, where she was putting the finishing touches to the bed hangings. "Coming."

Mary appeared in the kitchen doorway. From the bunch of horsetail clutched in one hand, she had been polishing the pewter. "Do you need me, Madam?"

Kate considered. "You may assist Rebeccah in directing us."

The maid nodded, set aside the rushes, and wiped her hands on her apron.

Rebeccah appeared at the top of the stairs, beaming. "Isn't this exciting?" She lifted her skirts and started carefully down the steep steps.

"'Tis not as if the furniture is new," said Kate, but she was smiling.

It had been Mrs. Dutton's idea to furnish their house, which they had leased unfurnished, with items from St. James's Square. For, as she said, she would have no need of them in Bond Street, where Anne had excitedly insisted on buying everything new for her mother's chamber.

Rebeccah could have had more of her family's belongings if she had wished, but they had not the room for it. So with Kate's help, she had settled on necessities and a few items of sentimental value, such as her father's favourite barometer and globe. Rebeccah had been quite happy about having to choose; Kate suspected her sister would not have been so sanguine.

"We are lucky the weather is fine." Rebeccah peered out the front door to where Will and Henry, Titus's replacement, had jumped down from the cart and started unloading.

"Can you remember where you want everything?" asked Kate.

Rebeccah looked at her in surprise. "Of course. For I made a note of it." She pulled from her pocket a diagram she had sketched. As Kate was rapidly learning, Rebeccah had a talent for organization. "See." She handed the piece of paper to Mary, who squinted at it, frowned, then turned it the right way up.

Kate pressed Rebeccah's hand. "Then if you are ready for the fray, my dear, I will fire the starting pistol." She went outside to help the two servants.

✑

The positioning of everything to Rebeccah and Mary's mutual satisfaction lasted a couple of hours and left Kate with a stubbed toe, a ripped pair of knee breeches, and an aching back. A bed for her and Rebeccah, a pot to piss in, and an easy chair strong enough to bear their combined weight, situated in front of a roaring fire, were all that Kate required, so she kept out of their sometimes heated discussions. But she had to admit, the results of their deliberations were worth it.

Her chamber now sported curtains, a clothes chest, a chair, a tripod-legged table on which sat a bowl and a very expensive bar of Castile soap, a mirror, and of course the bed, which was large enough for two.

For appearances' sake, the chest had only Kate's clothes in it, but Rebeccah was to share the room with her, as the dressing case with its set of ivory combs and brushes indicated. She felt a tingle of anticipation at the prospect of the coming night.

Sucking a stinging knuckle—a different knuckle from earlier; manoeuvring furniture up tight stairs was hard on the hands—she turned her attention to the street, where Will and Henry were driving away the empty cart at a much brisker pace than they had arrived. From downstairs came the sound of the kettle boiling. She would have welcomed something a little stronger but Rebeccah had asked Mary for tea. An urge to sing overtook her and she gave into it, though softly.

Movement from the corner of her eyes was followed by an arm

slipping round her waist. "You have a wonderful voice, Kate," said Rebeccah. "What is that song?"

"'Tis called 'The Female Frollick.'" She draped her arm round Rebeccah's shoulders. "I have you to myself at last."

The younger woman leaned against her. "And I you."

"Now we may relax."

But even as she spoke, a coach and four was rumbling along the street towards them, and as it drew closer Kate realized she recognized both carriage and driver. She arched an eyebrow at Rebeccah. "Is that . . . ?"

"Mama," finished Rebeccah with a sigh.

Robert reined his team to a halt, vaulted down, and opened the door for the carriage's elegantly dressed occupant. Seconds later came a rap at the front door, and they heard Mary going to answer it.

"We had better go down," said Kate reluctantly.

Mrs. Dutton was standing in their parlour cum drawing room when Kate and Rebeccah arrived. Her smile encompassed both of them.

"I trust your move is proceeding well, my dears?" She finished handing her hat and gloves to Mary.

"Thankfully, yes, Mama." Rebeccah gave her mother a kiss on the cheek. "Though it was touch and go at times, for our stairs are narrower than those at St. James's Square. We were just about to take some tea." She glanced at the maid. "Mary? Would you?"

Mary curtseyed and disappeared into the adjoining kitchen. Kate took it upon herself to make up the fire with more coals from the scuttle. Rebeccah threw her a grateful look and turned back to her mother.

"Mama." She gestured to one of the armchairs. "Please, make yourself comfortable."

Mrs. Dutton smiled and did so. "I won't stay long, Beccah. I just wanted to make sure things were proceeding as planned. For if they are not, you can always spend tonight at St. James's Square, for I am not due to vacate the house until Wednesday."

"Thank you, Mama, that was thoughtful. But indeed, we are already quite settled, as you can see."

Mrs. Dutton scanned the little room assessingly, before continuing. "I am glad to hear it, Beccah. Though of course I shall miss your company." She sighed. "But change comes to all of us, and we must make the best of it, must we not?"

"Indeed," said Rebeccah. "Let us try to think of it as a new chapter."

Her mother smiled and nodded.

Mary returned bearing a tea tray. She placed it on the table, set out the crockery, and began to pour.

"And Mary." The maid looked up at her name. "Dear Mary," continued Mrs. Dutton. "I shall miss you too, you know. For you have been with our family so long, I have come to think of you almost as a member of it."

Mary's expression was a blend of gratitude and disbelief, Kate saw with amusement. "Thank you, Madam. That's kind, I'm sure. I shall miss St. James's Square, but I am flattered Mistress Rebeccah wants me with her." She threw Rebeccah a fond glance. "For I have been with her since she was a babe. And besides," she added, scrupulously honest as always, "the duties promise to be more varied here."

"Indeed. On that subject." Mrs. Dutton sounded concerned. "Is Mary to do *all* the work, Beccah?"

"If you mean by that, is she to be our only servant, the answer is yes, Mama. But her duties will not be arduous. For the house comprises but five rooms, and Kate and I will be busy at the Academy during the week."

"As for our meals," added Kate helpfully, "there are taverns and cook-shops aplenty, Mrs. Dutton."

That made Rebeccah frown. "I hope you are not intending us to eat our dinner *often* in such places, Kate. For with Mary's help, I wish to put into practice my lessons from Mrs. Priest's boarding school. After all, cooking can not be so difficult, can it?" She glanced at the maid.

"I'm sure I couldn't say, Madam," said Mary with commendable restraint.

"Oh pish!" said Rebeccah, seeing her mother's astonishment and Kate's amusement. "Do not give me those looks." Her own lips curved into a reluctant grin. "I can attempt it at least, can I not?"

Kate laughed out loud and nodded.

♌

Candles flickered in their holders, a fire crackled in the hearth, and on the little table next to Kate lay dirty supper plates and the clay pipe she had smoked earlier.

My own drawing room. My own fire. And my lover in my lap. What more could I ask for? She gave a contented sigh, stroked Rebeccah's hair, then let her hand drop and dangle by her side.

"I think I ate too much." Rebeccah shifted a little in her lap. "Am I too heavy for you?"

"You are as light as thistledown." A memory of the private condemned cell at Newgate, when in spite of a shackled Kate's less-than-fragrant odour, Rebeccah had also sat in her lap, surfaced, and she couldn't help but marvel at the remarkable change in her fortunes since that day.

"Hardly that," murmured Rebeccah with a smile. But she made no move to get up and take the other chair. "Do you think Mary is spending the evening with Robert?" They had given the maid the night off, for if Rebeccah required help undressing later, Kate would provide it.

Kate adjusted her arm around Rebeccah's waist and considered the gleam in Mary's eyes when she had hurried away. "Undoubtedly," she said. "Have you seen the way they look at one another?"

"How long has it been going on, do you think?"

Kate shrugged.

Rebeccah twisted round to look at her. "If she wishes to bring him back to her chamber, should we allow it?"

Kate arched an eyebrow. "Would you deny them that?"

After a moment's thought, Rebeccah shook her head. "So long as it makes Mary happy and does not inconvenience us overmuch." She faced the fire once more. "I wonder if Mama is aware of their relationship."

"I doubt it. She is unaware of our feelings for one another."

"She knows we are friends," corrected Rebeccah.

"More than that, I hope," said Kate. Which reminded her . . .

"Though she has never said, I believe she thinks we are like the Queen and Aunt Sarah," added Rebeccah, then she let out an indignant squeak, for Kate had leaned sideways and was fishing in the pocket of her breeches. "What are you doing?"

"Aha!" Kate straightened up and Rebeccah resettled herself in her lap then blinked at the object Kate was now holding out to her between her finger and thumb.

It was a gold wedding band. Kate had taken the measurements from the garnet signet ring that Rebeccah always wore and that had once belonged to Rebeccah's father. The band had been expensive, but not as much as it might have been, for Kate still had useful contacts from her days as a highwayman.

"Is that—?" asked Rebeccah faintly.

"It is." Kate reached for Rebeccah's hand and slid the ring onto her ring finger. To her relief, it fit perfectly. "For better or for worse," said Kate solemnly. "Until death do us part."

Words failed Rebeccah, and for a moment she could do little except gape alternately at the ring and its giver. Then she grabbed Kate's face between her hands and kissed her enthusiastically and, to Kate's gratification, expertly.

The candles had burned down a good inch and Rebeccah's clothes were rumpled and in disarray, though her stays had thwarted Kate's attempts to pay proper homage to her breasts, when Kate became aware of their surroundings once more. Her mouth was dry and she felt an urgent need to take Rebeccah to bed *right now.*

"Shall we go upstairs?" Her voice cracked.

"In a moment." Rebeccah's emotions were visible in her eyes. "Thank you for this, my love." Gold glinted in the firelight as she held out her hand the better to admire the ring. "With all my heart."

"It is but the outward sign of my feelings," said Kate, who would far rather demonstrate than talk about her emotions, but who also sensed that Rebeccah needed to hear this.

"It is beautiful." A thought struck Rebeccah and her face creased with distress. "But I shall be unable to wear it in company. For it is sure to elicit too many questions."

"Wear it when we are alone together." Kate eased Rebeccah off her lap and stood up.

Rebeccah searched her face. "That will content you?"

"It will," said Kate firmly.

Rebeccah's frown smoothed and she began to straighten her clothing. Kate wondered why she was bothering, for her intention was to strip Rebeccah of it in the next few minutes.

"Will you come to bed?" she asked again.

The roughness of her voice made Rebeccah look hard at her. Seeing Kate's outstretched hand and impatient expression, her lips curved into a knowing smile. "With pleasure."

♌

The sound of church bells roused Kate from a dream in which she was riding across the heath, the wind in her hair, a song on her lips, and Rebeccah in the saddle behind her, arms clasped tight around Kate's belly. For a moment she wondered where she was, then the soft, even breathing and warm press of curves against her arm reminded her.

She turned to study her sleeping companion. Rebeccah's face was open and relaxed. Kate pinched herself to make sure she was awake and smiled. *No fever dream, this!*

For a while she simply gazed at Rebeccah, remembering last night's activities and the soft exclamations of surprised pleasure, and resisting, just barely, the urge to take Rebeccah in her arms again. Outside, the church bells continued to summon worshippers to prayer. Kate intended to worship at quite a different altar when her lover awoke.

The need to make water made itself felt. Careful not to disturb Rebeccah, Kate eased herself out of bed. The fire had almost gone out, and the bedchamber was chilly, so she used the chamber pot as quickly and as quietly as she could, then draped the cloth over it and shoved it back under the bed.

As she snuggled back under the warm bedclothes, Rebeccah's breathing caught and then resumed. Kate turned just in time to see awareness returning. The tip of a pink tongue emerged, licked dry, slightly bruised lips, and vanished whence it came. Pale eyelashes fluttered open and green eyes gazed rather blurrily at Kate then struggled to focus. She waited, slightly anxious, and was relieved when gladness filled Rebeccah's gaze.

"Good morrow, Kate." Rebeccah's voice was husky.

"Morrow, my love." Kate leaned over and kissed her on the cheek, then pulled back. "Are you well?" She brushed the soft cheek with her finger.

Rebeccah's gaze turned inwards. "I am a little . . . tender . . . up here," she indicated the breasts that had so enthralled Kate last night and were now hidden beneath her shift. "And, um, down there." She whispered the last two words, then blushed.

"To be expected," Kate reassured her. "It will ease."

Rebeccah regarded her from under lowered lashes. Then she rested a hand on her arm and murmured in her ear. "But I am not so sore that I would not welcome a repeat of . . . you know." Her blush deepened. "Indeed, I would very much like you to . . . That is, if you are willing."

Kate laughed and kissed her again, on the lips this time. "Of course," she murmured against Rebeccah's mouth. "For where you are concerned it is no hardship." And she set about proving it.

A knock at the door forced her to break off her attentions—fortunately they had not gone very far.

"Mary?" wondered Rebeccah a little breathlessly.

"Who else? Come in," called Kate.

Rebeccah let out a squeak of dismay, pulled down her shift, and tried to hide behind Kate as the door opened and the maid entered, carrying a ewer from which emerged wisps of steam. Mary's lips twitched when she saw the two women in bed together, but she said only, "Good morrow, Mistress Milledge, Mistress Dutton."

She placed the ewer beside the bowl on the tripod-legged table and drew back the curtains. From the look of it, it was another fine day, though cold. She turned and, with a pained glance but without comment, began to retrieve items of Rebeccah's clothing from the floor.

"We were in a hurry," explained Kate, ignoring Rebeccah's intake of breath.

"Garments last longer if they are cared for," chided Mary, shaking out a stocking and draping it over her arm.

Kate donned a penitent expression. "I beg your pardon."

Mary nodded as if that ended the matter, and placed the clothes, now neatly folded, on the clothes chest. "Shall I make up the fire?"

"If you would be so kind." Kate was acutely aware that a red-faced Rebeccah was peeking over her shoulder.

Mary crossed at once to the grate, knelt, reached for the fire irons, and added more coals to the embers.

"Otherwise," continued Kate to Mary's back, "we shall not require your assistance until much later. For we can make shift to get our own breakfast, and Mistress Dutton will not be attending church."

"Kate!" exclaimed Rebeccah in her ear. "If I do not go, Mama will wonder where I am."

"Let her wonder."

"But—"

"Hush," whispered Kate, reaching back and giving Rebeccah's hand an encouraging squeeze. "Would you rather go to church or stay here in bed with me?"

Rebeccah opened her mouth then shut it again. Kate took her silence for assent.

"Very good, Madam," said Mary from the fireplace.

When the maid was satisfied with the fire's progress, she replaced the fire irons, got creakily to her feet, and turned and looked at the two of them. How Mary was keeping her countenance Kate couldn't imagine. Perhaps she was saving her reaction for later when she regaled Robert with tales of what she had seen and heard.

"May I say what a handsome wedding band that is, Mistress Dutton," said the maid.

The hand resting on Kate's shoulder whipped back out of sight then, a second later, gingerly returned.

"Thank you, Mary," said Rebeccah hoarsely.

Kate could contain her grin no longer. She winked, and the maid's eyes twinkled in response. "That will be all for now, thank you, Mary. Mistress Dutton will ring for you if she needs you."

Rebeccah cleared her throat. "Yes," she said awkwardly. "I will."

Mary curtseyed and made her way towards the door. It was only as it was closing behind her that Kate at last caught the sound of a low chuckle.

She twisted round to face Rebeccah, who was regarding her with an expression part exasperation, part mortification, and part affection.

"Does nothing embarrass you, Kate?"

"No," said Kate, smiling. "And soon you will be more easy about us too. Why, in time you may even be able to make water in front of me!"

Rebeccah blushed and demurred. Outside the church bells had stopped ringing and it was blissfully silent.

"In the meantime," said Kate, "Mary had made our chamber warm and tidy once more. And we have the morning to ourselves." She cocked her head. "Who would have thought that a random encounter on Shooter's Hill could lead to this?" She gestured at the bed and the two of them in it.

"Who indeed?" asked Rebeccah. Her gaze turned inwards. "You were very forward that day, Kate. You asked me to hand you my valuables. Starting with 'that pretty trinket around your even prettier neck.'"

Kate tried to remember the details, but all that came to mind was a pair of fine green eyes regarding her and her cocked pistol with a mixture of shock, apprehension, and grudging fascination. "Did I?" she murmured.

"Indeed you did," said Rebeccah. "For that meeting is fixed in my memory and always will be."

Kate laughed then sobered as a revelation struck her. "And you have obliged me by giving me something far more precious."

Rebeccah's lips trembled, then tears filled her eyes and spilled down her cheeks. Her chest began to heave. A perplexed Kate gathered the suddenly sobbing young woman into her arms.

"Hush, my love," she murmured. "Do not cry. There, there. 'Tis all right. Hush now."

But Rebeccah's sobs continued, and Kate contented herself with rocking her and stroking her hair. Time passed, and eventually, the only sounds in the bedchamber were the crackle of flames from the fireplace, and the occasional sniff, and, on one occasion, a hiccup, from Rebeccah.

"Did I say something to upset you?" asked Kate at last.

Rebeccah lifted her head. Her eyes were red-rimmed, her face blotchy, but to Kate's eyes she had never looked so lovely. "*Upset* me? Far from it." She gave Kate a rather sheepish smile. "Forgive me, Kate, for alarming you. In truth, I have never been so happy in all my life."

"Oh." A relieved Kate chuckled. "In that case." Tenderly, she wiped the tear stains from Rebeccah's face with the sleeve of her shift. "I know something that will make you even happier." She gave Rebeccah her best seductive look. "I forget quite where we had got to when Mary interrupted us. Can you remember, my dear?" She arched a knowing eyebrow, smiled, and waited.

It took but a moment for Rebeccah to understand, then her eyes filled with desire and she licked her lips. "I remember very well," she said. Then, blushing shyly at her own daring, she whispered, "Shall I show you?"

"I insist on it," said Kate.

ABOUT THE AUTHOR

Barbara Davies was born in Birmingham, England. A graduate of York University, she spent more years than she cares to remember working in IT, first in Surrey then in Gloucestershire.

She published her first short story in 1994. Since then, her fiction has appeared in various genre magazines, ezines, and anthologies, including *Marion Zimmer Bradley's Fantasy Magazine, Khimairal Ink, The Lorelei Signal, Byzarium, Neo Opsis, Andromeda Spaceways Inflight Magazine*, and *Bash Down the Door and Slice Open the Badguy*.

Bedazzled Ink previously published Barbara's western novel, *Christie and the Hellcat*, and a collection of her specfic short stories: *Into the Yellow and other Stories*.

Barbara now lives in Gloucestershire, where she reviews Fantasy fiction for *Starburst*. Her website is: www.barbaradavies.co.uk

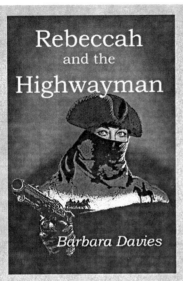
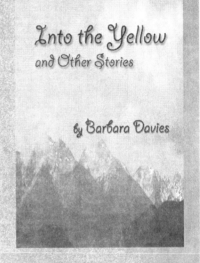

Printed in the United States
213742BV00001B/39/P